I0779486
VEGETATION WARS
ROOTS OF REBELLION
ANTONIO TSMITH JR

VEGETATION

WARS

Copyright

This book is a work of fiction. Names, characters, places, and incidents either are products of the author's imagination or are used fictitiously. Any resemblance to actual persons, living or dead, events, or locales is entirely coincidental.

Cover design by Antonio T Smith Jr

Artwork by Ine Velaers and Charles Forgeron

Published by Antonio T. Smith Jr. LLC Publishing

For permission to use material from this book, please contact support@antoniotsmithjr.com.

Visit the author online at antoniotsmithjr.com for the latest news, book signings, and more.

Library of Congress Cataloging-in-Publication Data

Smith Jr, Antonio T.

Vegetation Wars: Roots of Rebellion / Antonio T. Smith Jr. - First edition.

Book 2 of 3

Vegetation Wars: Roots of Rebellion

Print: 979-8-9894385-4-9

Digital Book: 979-8-9894385-5-6

1.Genre Post-Apocalyptic. 2.Technothrillers 3. Science Fiction

Printed in United States

First Edition: May 2024

Acknowledgments

Writing *Vegetation Wars* has been an exhilarating journey, one that would not have been possible without a multitude of support from a myriad of sources, each critical in transforming my visions into the pages before you. This trilogy, with its intricate exploration of a post-apocalyptic world entwined with sentient vegetation, draws deeply from my experiences and training in the U.S. Army, where I honed my skills in Military Intelligence.

Before diving into the heart of my gratitude, I want to reflect on the journey that brought *Vegetation Wars* to life. My military background, particularly my time serving with remarkable captains, colonels, and fellow soldiers who believed in me, has been instrumental in crafting the intense, survival-driven narratives of this series. The skills I developed during my service—ranging from tactical questioning and counterintelligence to advanced surveillance and cyber intelligence—have not only enriched the authenticity of the narrative but have also allowed me to infuse the story with complexities that I hope resonate with readers.

I owe an immense debt of gratitude to the US Army and my comrades-in-arms. The rigorous training in SAEDA, microexpressions, and human intelligence collection under extreme conditions provided me with a profound understanding of strategic conflict and espionage, which now permeates through Callan's journey in the wastelands controlled by sentient flora.

The encouragement and feedback from my readers and supporters have been the bedrock of this series' success. Your enthusiasm and engagement have been nothing short of inspiring, driving me to push the boundaries of science fiction and dystopian literature.

Special thanks must go to my team of beta readers and editors, who have endured countless drafts and revisions to ensure that every element of the story is polished and precise. Your patience and insights have been invaluable.

I must also express my gratitude towards the various publishers and audio teams that have helped bring the vivid world of *Vegetation Wars* to life in formats that reach readers wherever they may be. Your commitment to distributing and promoting this series has allowed it to thrive and expand beyond my wildest expectations.

Lastly, to my family and close friends: your unwavering support and belief in my work have been my anchor throughout the highs and lows of the writing process. You have celebrated my victories and buoyed me through challenges, and for that, I am eternally grateful.

As we look forward to the next installments of the *Vegetation Wars* series, I am reminded of the power of storytelling and the impact it can have. Thank you for joining me on this incredible adventure. Your continued support and engagement mean the world to me, and I am excited to share more thrilling escapades as Callan's story unfolds.

Here's to the battles we've faced together and those yet to come.

Dedication

To "homeless me" — from the tough days of confusion and hardship, when the shadows of uncertainty loomed large. From ages 5 to 15, life threw its harshest tests at us. We failed the 5th grade and the 6th, yet here we stand, crafting worlds from the tempest of our past, a best-selling author against all odds.

We haven't crossed every finish line we've dreamt of yet. The vision of turning these tales into films, of owning a studio that lifts other voices into the spotlight, remains on the horizon. So, no, we haven't made it in the way that final chapter of dreams dictates. But, in a way that matters just as deeply, we have made it for someone else out there. To that someone who sees our journey, draws breath from our resolve, and decides to change their world to outshine ours — you are why we endure. You are the victory in every battle we've fought.

Thank you, "homeless me," for pushing the person I am today to this very moment, to the point where giving up was never an option. Here's to the roots of our rebellion, which nourish the stories we tell and the futures we inspire.

—Antonio T Smith Jr

Epigraph

"Every root entwines with another, for the web of life binds us all."
   — Octavia Butler, Echoes Through Time

Let these words echo through the annals of this saga, where the fate of humanity intertwines irrevocably with the sentient tendrils of a reborn Earth. In this realm, each breath and step reverberates across the complex network of life, reminding us that in our dance with nature, every action influences countless others. Here, we explore the perilous balance between control and coexistence, venturing from the depths of underground despair to the verdant horrors above, where the very essence of being is contested. Embrace this journey as it weaves through the shadows of betrayal and the luminous possibilities of alliance, challenging us to reconsider what it means to dominate, to survive, and ultimately, to thrive in a world reborn from its own ruins.

The SallerianVerse: A Treasure Hunt of Easter Eggs and Big Philosophical Concepts

I have a profound passion for exploring the theme of memory in my writing, and I take great care in leaving tantalizing plot twists and hidden clues for readers to discover in future installments of the SallerianVerse. The key to fully immersing oneself in this literary adventure is to remain vigilant to every detail, for even the smallest nuance may hold significant meaning. Each of my works is a gripping thriller that keeps readers on the edge of their seats, and I employ a masterful use of dialogue to drop subtle hints and cleverly connect the dots across the vast expanse of over 40 interconnected books in the SallerianVerse. If you relish a challenge and delight in exercising your intellect to keep pace with the writer, then you and I share a common passion.

I would like to express my intention to caution readers about what to anticipate in my writing, a passion that was supported by my father. My writing style is reminiscent of the films by renowned directors Christopher and Jonathan Nolan, in which I offer unadulterated responses through direct dialogue. My works frequently delve into profound philosophical ideas, wherein I challenge readers to confront complex concepts and encourage them to develop their own conclusions.

Additionally, I frequently explore big philosophical concepts and often leave the reader to struggle with these difficult ideas, fall in love with the struggle, and draw their own conclusions.

The exploration of human morality and decision-making is a subject that captivates me. I am particularly intrigued by how these facets of the human psyche can become corrupted and how our choices shape the reality we perceive. Furthermore, I am deeply fascinated by the concept of time and its impact on our morality and decision-making processes. Does time enhance or hinder our capacity for sound judgement? This is a question that I enjoy posing to my readers. In my SallerianVerse, I experiment with the notion of time as a non-linear construct, challenging the common perception of chronological progression. This intriguing concept is supported by the second law of thermodynamics, which posits that time is merely an illusion.

I derive pleasure from subverting the established norms of popular literary genres in order to challenge preconceived notions about books. My approach involves pushing the boundaries of traditional genres such as mystery, thriller, science fiction, superhero, and war in order to discover novel techniques and themes. I draw inspiration from notable filmmakers including Quentin Tarantino, Paul Thomas Anderson, the Wachowskis, Christopher and Jonathan Nolan, and the Coen brothers who have mastered the art of genre-bending and produced works that defy the limitations of conventional storytelling. By emulating their methods, I endeavor to create narratives that transcend genre classification and engage readers with a fresh perspective.

Challenging and subverting established literary genres has been a source of fascination and creative inspiration for me. I delight in exploring the boundaries of popular genres such as mysteries, thrillers, sci-fi, superheroes, and war, and experimenting with innovative storytelling techniques to push the limits of these established categories. This approach has been influenced by the groundbreaking work of visionary filmmakers like Quentin Tarantino, Paul Thomas Anderson, the Wachowskis, Christopher and Jonathan Nolan, and the Coen brothers, who have each demonstrated their own unique ability to reinvent and transcend traditional narrative forms.

My aim is to craft captivating and thought-provoking narratives in mainstream genres, while simultaneously expanding their horizons for the avid reader. My protagonists often hail from diverse ethnic backgrounds, without the requirement of explicit justification. By creating literature that caters to a broad audience, my intention is to foster a mutual appreciation and understanding of various cultural perspectives, irrespective of race or ethnicity.

My primary goal is to view books as an intricate art form and to prompt readers to question their preconceptions about literature. While a compelling narrative is undoubtedly crucial to the success of a book, I am particularly intrigued by exploring and, at times, altering the fundamental elements that constitute a book.

Anticipate my incorporation of the concept of interconnectedness, as I weave together ideas from the Law of One and various spiritual themes and motifs from diverse worldviews and philosophies. My aim is to offer my readers novel insights and provoke introspection that will foster a heightened collective consciousness and promote positive change within their communities and beyond.

Finally, it is my aspiration that my books will stand the test of time and remain relevant for generations to come. To that end, I am investing all of my passion, vitality, and creativity into each work. I emphasize that these stories are not distinct and isolated but rather interwoven and should be viewed as a single narrative.

Best,

Antonio, the guy messing with your head and forcing you to turn the page.

Vegetation Wars: Roots of Rebellion

Chapter 1

Exactly 1 Minute After Chapter 21 of The Vegetation Wars.
The Year 3377. 1354 years After The EMP Events Recorded In
Ch 2 of The United Cities of Salleria, Burn Together.

Rootwhisper's tendrils hung heavy with grief, the damp air of the underground echoing his sorrow. The dim corridor stretched out before them, each step a reminder of what had been lost. "I must fight," he whispered, his voice barely a rustle. "For Thornvine, for all that we've lost."

Callan's response was weary, his shoulders slumped under the weight of his rifle and the burden of command. Blood seeped through the makeshift bandage wrapped tightly around his arm, his face pale and drawn. "You can fight," he murmured, his voice hollow. "But I don't know if we should keep fighting. I don't even know what we are fighting for anymore."

Elara looked at Callan, but didn't offer words. Rhootwhisper didn't have time to wonder what she was thinking. He wasn't sure if he cared. He was angry. He wanted to fight— to avenge his friend and mentor Thornvine.

Tibo leaned heavily against the wall, his breaths short and labored, a dark stain spreading across his side. "I'm. I'm—," he coughed, managing a weak smile that didn't reach his eyes. "I'm too tired to do anything."

Elara, leaning on Tibo for support, her own injuries hastily bandaged, nodded slowly. Her voice was soft, strained with pain. "We've seen too much death today," she said, her gaze fixed on the cold floor.

Rootwhisper felt the gravity of their words settle in the pit of his roots. The corridor around them felt colder, the shadows deeper. The innocence he once held was now just fragments of a shell that had shattered under the harsh truths of their reality. Thornvine's last plea echoed in his mind, a haunting refrain that melded with the drip of water from the ceiling. "Stay out of this fight, Rhootwhisper."

But Rhootwhisper didn't want to stay out of the fight anymore. He knew how to fight. He helped them with the Genesis Engines. He could help them now. He was going to help them or he was going to fight alone. But he wasn't taking no for an answer.

"I will fight," he replied, the vibrancy that once filled his tone now just a ghost. "Nothing will stop me from avenging Thornvine's death."

The group moved in silence, the only sounds the echoing of their steps and the distant rumbles of the Overlord's forces. Rootwhisper lost in his own thoughts.

As they neared the entrance to Sector 9X, Callan paused, turning to Rootwhisper. His eyes, once sharp with determination, now seemed dimmed. "I believe you kid."

Rootwhisper nodded. There was something about the way Callan said those words that made Rootwhisper feel like he was part of the team. He didn't feel like he was at first. The weight of Thornvine's death pressed down on him, a burden he was only just beginning to carry.

"We're here," Elara whispered as they reached the door to Sector 9X. Her voice was weary, resigned. "What happened today is no one fault but the Overlord's."

The door slid open with a hiss, revealing the shadowed depths of Sector 9X. The air was stale, the silence a stark contrast to the chaos they had left behind. As they stepped through, Rootwhisper felt a deep sadness within him. He wanted to die and be with Thornvine.

Elara's hands trembled slightly as she adjusted the settings on the bioregeneration tank, watching the pale light flicker over Callan's unconscious form. The medical bay hummed quietly around her, a stark contrast to the chaos that had just subsided. The scent of antiseptics filled the air, mingling with the underlying metallic tang of blood—too much blood.

She glanced over at Tibo, who lay in a similar tank, his face drawn tight in pain even in sleep. The automated systems were hard at work knitting skin, mending tissue, a silent battle against time and death that they had barely won.

Elara's gaze returned to Callan. The leader, the fighter, the unwavering pillar of their small rebellion—now reduced to this fragile, resting figure, barely clinging to life. The tanks were doing their job, but the wounds deeper than flesh pained her more. Callan's eyes, when they had last met hers, held a torment that no machine could heal.

The guilt weighed on her like the heavy lead apron she wore during x-ray diagnostics. She should have been faster, smarter, more cautious. As the team's strategist, every loss felt like her failure, every drop of blood was because of her shortcomings. And now, watching Callan fight for each breath, she couldn't stifle the gnawing fear that perhaps, this time, they had asked too much of themselves.

She should be doing something—more bandages, more painkillers, more... something. But all she could do was watch and wait, a passive witness to the torturously slow process of healing.

The silence was broken by a soft, sorrowful hum. Rootwhisper. The young plant being stood beside her, its luminescent leaves dimmed with grief. Elara had almost forgotten about the newest member of their wounded family. Rootwhisper's presence was a comfort, though it was clear the plant shared in the heavy blanket of sorrow that draped over all of them.

"I could have done more," Rootwhisper murmured, so softly it was almost swallowed by the humming of the machines. "Thornvine died protecting us. And I... I just stood there."

Elara reached out, her hand hesitating in the air before resting gently on one of Rootwhisper's glowing fronds. "You did what you could," she said, her voice cracking with fatigue and emotion. "We all did. And sometimes, it's just not enough."

"But should it not be?" Rootwhisper asked, the glow flickering with its distress. "Should we not strive to be enough?"

Elara sighed, her breath fogging the glass of the tank briefly. "Striving to be enough might be all we can do," she admitted. "But sometimes, the world asks more of us than we have to give."

They stood in shared silence, each lost in their thoughts—the human and the plant, united in their grief and helplessness. Elara's heart ached for Callan, for Tibo, for the two lives lost in the botanical gardens just hours ago, and for Evelyn's life 24 hours before. Each life was a story ended too soon, a book closed before its last chapter could be written.

She knew Callan would blame himself; he always did. He would emerge from this tank bearing new scars, both seen and unseen, and he would shoulder the guilt for every drop of blood spilled, every scream echoed in the endless night. And she would stand by him, because that's what partners do. They share the burden, lighten the load—even when it feels too heavy to bear.

Elara's own doubts mirrored Callan's. Was it worth it? This constant fight, this endless war against a foe as relentless as the vegetation they battled? She wasn't sure anymore. But she knew they couldn't stop. Not really. Not while there was still something, anything, left to fight for. But maybe it was some else's job now? Maybe they shouldn't be the leaders of the resistance?

A soft beep from the tank's monitor drew her attention back to Callan. His vitals were stabilizing, the machines whispered reassurances in their clinical, emotionless readouts. He would live. They would all live, at least for today.

But as she looked at Rootwhisper, at the young being who had seen too much death too soon, and then back to Callan, she understood that survival was not the same as living. And as they each fought their silent battles within the cold embrace of Sector 9X's medical bay, she wondered if they would ever truly live again, or if they were doomed to simply survive, day after weary day, until the war took them too.

Elara pressed her hands against the cool glass of Callan's bioregeneration tank, her fingers tracing the lines of condensation that formed from the temperature difference. The steady beep of the heart monitor played a counter-rhythm to the chaotic storm of her thoughts. *Why now?* She wondered, staring at the faint glow of the artifact resting near Callan's bedside. It sat inert, like an ordinary piece of rock, betraying no hint of the immense power it harbored.

The artifact had saved them before, had been their ace in the hole against the Genesis Engines in the Chamber of Echoes, but its silence now was as confusing as it was infuriating. *Why wouldn't it work when we needed it most?* The question gnawed at her, a relentless reminder of their vulnerability.

Around her, the medical bay of Sector 9X hummed with low, soothing tones meant to calm, but her mind raced with turbulent thoughts. Callan had wielded the artifact with such confidence, such surety, as if it responded to his very will. And yet, during their last encounter, when the foliage closed in like the fingers of a giant hand, the artifact had remained dormant, unresponsive to his desperate pleas.

Daxon, once their friend, now a traitor multiple times over, had controlled it too. And so had Lord Virex, each seemingly at will. The inconsistency tore at her, breeding a deep, unsettling doubt. *How did it choose whom to obey, and why?*

Elara's gaze drifted to the monitors, to the slow but steady rise and fall of Callan's chest. The machines were keeping him alive, doing what the artifact had failed to do—protect them when it mattered most. A bitter taste filled her mouth as she considered the possibility of betrayal from the very force they hoped would save them.

Vorian was dead, his wisdom and guidance lost to them forever, another casualty in a war that seemed increasingly futile. *Could the artifact have saved him?* She pondered, her mind replaying the last moments of his life, searching for a sign she might have missed, a clue to the artifact's capricious nature.

And Whisperroot—where was he in their hour of need? The mystical plant had shimmered into their lives with promises of aid and ancient secrets, yet when the vines tightened around them, when the spores clouded the air they breathed, he was conspicuously absent. *Does he want us to fail?* The doubt was a venom, spreading through her veins, poisoning her against the ally she once trusted.

Could they afford to trust Whisperroot? Or had they been fools, mere pawns in a larger game they barely understood? The thought haunted her, each possibility more unsettling than the last.

The artifact remained silent, enigmatic, a sphinx without a riddle's answer. Did it see them, understand them? Did it choose its moments of intervention based on some unfathomable criteria, or was it merely reacting to stimuli they could not perceive?

What aren't you telling us, Whisperroot? She wanted to scream the questions into the void, demand answers from the being who seemed more ghost than flesh. The weight of leadership, the burden of decisions made in desperation—they were suffocating under the crushing pressure to save a world that perhaps did not want to be saved.

Her reflection in the glass stared back at her, a pale shadow of the woman who once believed so fiercely in their cause. Now, doubt clouded her vision, her resolve. *Are we the right ones to lead?* The question was a whisper in her mind, but it roared in her ears like a tempest.

Elara stepped back from the tank, her eyes never leaving the inert artifact. Her heart was heavy, her spirit battered. They were tired, so very tired, of fighting, of losing, of hoping for a dawn that seemed increasingly unlikely to break.

As the machines continued their monotonous chorus, Elara's doubts spun a dark web, each thread a question without an answer, each stitch a reminder of their isolation in this fight. Was it worth it? Could they even trust their own judgment anymore? And most pressing of all, what would they do if the artifact remained silent again when they next called upon it to defend them? The questions lingered, unanswered, as the shadows deepened around her.

Elara's thoughts lingered on Daxon, the weight of his betrayal echoing in the silent, clinical gleam of the medical bay. Lord Virex had ensnared him with promises of safety and power—seductive offerings that whispered of a simpler life, far from the brutal reality of their endless conflict. These promises preyed upon the tired and the desperate, exploiting the fear that gnawed at the edges of their morale.

As she watched Callan and Tibo, resting within the life-sustaining embrace of the bioregeneration tanks, she reflected on the cost of their struggle. Daxon had witnessed the same relentless battles, the same losses that had drained their spirits and tested their resolve. The allure of Virex's offer, a life unmarred by the daily shadow of death and defeat, must have seemed a beacon in the overwhelming darkness.

Elara paced the cool metal floor, her mind racing. Vorian had been a pillar of hope, much like the leaders of old who inspired with visions of victory and redemption. But with Vorian gone, that pillar had crumbled, leaving behind questions that gnawed at her. Daxon's actions, though treacherous, bore the marks of a man pushed beyond his breaking point, seduced by the prospect of an escape from a seemingly unwinnable war.

The shadows in the room seemed to whisper doubts, mirroring her own. Daxon had chosen a path of apparent peace, and a lavish life on the surface, over the stark brutality of their reality. His choice, while unforgivable, was undeniably human—a choice between a harsh truth and the comforting fog of ignorance.

Yet, Elara and the others had remained steadfast, clinging to the hope that their sacrifices would forge a better future. But in the quiet of the night, enveloped by the hum of medical machinery, she questioned the clarity of their purpose. Were their sacrifices truly noble, or were they merely upholding ideals that might no longer hold weight in a world irrevocably scarred by war?

She turned back to the tanks, her eyes resting on Callan's serene face. The trust that had bound them together, born from shared struggles and shared dreams, stood in stark contrast to the isolation of Daxon's betrayal. It was this trust that anchored her to their cause, despite the seductive whispers of an easier way out.

In the rhythmic beeping of the monitors, a stark reminder of life's persistence even amidst chaos, Elara's thoughts turned to Whisperroot. The enigmatic plant had promised guidance but delivered only riddles, offering hope but leading them repeatedly into calamity. *What aren't you telling us, Whisperroot?* she wondered silently, the question hanging heavy in the sterile air.

Was the artifact, around which so much of their fate revolved, truly a beacon of salvation, or merely another tool in a larger, more complex game they barely understood? The uncertainty of it gnawed at her, challenging the foundations of their mission.

As she reflected on the depths of Daxon's betrayal, Elara recognized the layers of his decision. He had been lured by the promise of a less burdensome existence, a temptation they had all undoubtedly felt at some point. His choice reflected a profound weariness, a despair so deep that the dream of peace outweighed the grim realities of their ongoing war.

Can we even trust our own judgments anymore? She pondered the painful parallels with tales of past betrayals and fallen heroes, the stories echoing in her mind as a grim reminder of the delicate balance between hope and despair.

Elara knew they must find answers, must peer beyond the veil of secrets and lies to grasp the true nature of their struggle. They also needed an army of more than 3 humans and a young angry tree-kid.

Elara stood alone in the dimly lit medical bay, her gaze fixed on the bioregeneration tanks where Callan and Tibo lay still, their chests rising and falling with mechanical precision. The silence was oppressive, a stark reminder of the solitude that enveloped her in the wake of the others' incapacitation. Her mind was a whirlwind of strategy and concern, the weight of their dwindling hopes pressing down on her.

She thought of Kael, the double agent whose allegiance to Callan had always mystified her. There was something about Callan that drew people to him, a charisma that even the hardened hearts within the underground could not resist. *How did you do it, Callan?* she wondered, considering the loyalty Kael held despite the risks, delivering vital intelligence from within the very heart of enemy territory.

We need an army, she conceded silently, her thoughts turning tactical. The spores were relentless, infecting indiscriminately, turning friend into foe in a breath. The need for a force, sizable and uninfected, was urgent but seemed an impossible task. Who could they trust? Who remained untouched by the Overlord's pervasive reach?

Her mind drifted to Vorian, the former recruiter of their resistance, now a memory shadowed by betrayal and loss. Tibo would have to step into those large shoes, his tech expertise perhaps the key to screening and gathering those few uncorrupted souls left. But even the thought of mobilizing such a force felt like grasping at straws in a storm.

The Overlord needed to be overwhelmed, attacked from multiple sides if they were to have any chance of breaching his defenses. The strategy was sound on paper, yet so much hinged on uncertainties, on variables that were as volatile as the spores themselves.

Elara's hand hovered over the console, tempted to activate the comm and reach out to Kael for an update, for some hint of a new weakness they could exploit. But she hesitated, her fingers trembling. This was a war of attrition they seemed destined to lose, each move forward met with greater resistance, each plan countered by the Overlord's insidious strength.

The realization of her own deepening feelings for Callan surfaced, unbidden. *Focus, Elara. There's no room for this... not now.* Yet, how could she deny the growing connection, the shared moments of vulnerability that had fused their lives so intimately together? In a world teetering on the brink of collapse, these feelings were both a perilous distraction and a vital anchor.

For now, she watched over her comrades, the steady hum of the medical equipment a cold comfort. As the leader by default in this quiet hour, Elara carried the burden of their faded dreams and the flickering hope of a future. The weight was immense, unyielding, but not insurmountable. Not yet. Not while they still breathed, still fought, still dared to defy the dark.

Elara, still lost in her thoughts suddenly realizes, with dread, that Chancellor Greda still wanted them dead. Her mind raced as she mulled over the complexity of their predicament, isolated in the shadows of Sector 9X. The artifact, a source of untold power, now potentially a harbinger of doom, lay in the hands of their enemies. Chancellor Greda's ambitions to harness its power were no secret; she'd aimed to use it to exert control over all the underground, a plan thwarted by Callan's unwavering moral compass.

Daxon, why? The betrayal stung anew as she considered his actions, delivering their only advantage into the hands of those who would use it against them. Greda's warning echoed in the silence around her, a chilling reminder of the fine line between naivety and conviction. *Was Callan's idealism their undoing?* The thought hung heavily in her mind, a specter of doubt clouding her usual peaceful thoughts. The Artifact was far more trouble than it was worth. Greda wanted to use the Artifact to full all the human's underground and Callan, rightfully so, wouldn't let her.

The reality was stark—they were cornered, hidden in an uncharted sector, with the bulk of the underground world under Greda's iron grip. Beyond her controlled territories lay only chaos, zones where lawlessness prevailed, making them nearly as dangerous as any dictatorial regime. Elara's strategic mind grappled with their options, each more desperate than the last.

Could we even muster an army to face her? She pondered the feasibility of rising against Greda's extensive forces. The chancellor had at her command legions of well-equipped soldiers, loyal or subdued by fear. In contrast, Elara's potential recruits were a ragtag blend of rebels and outcasts, few in number and scattered across hostile zones.

As she considered the Overlord's spores, another grim possibility surfaced. What if the spores had reached Greda already and infected her? Paranoia whispered through her thoughts, a cruel jest at her expense. It was the kind of twist Greda would deserve, she mused bitterly, a poetic justice for the chancellor's own ruthless tactics.

Yet, as she dwelt on these dark musings, Elara's resolve hardened. Leaving Sector 9X would be dangerous, fraught with peril at every turn. But the alternative—remaining hidden, waiting for Greda or the Overlord to make their next move—was no longer tenable. They needed to act, to take the fight to Greda before she could consolidate her power further or the Overlord's influence became insurmountable.

We need an army. And if one doesn't exist, we'll have to build it, she concluded.

Chapter 2

Chancellor Greda's gaze swept across the vast hall with a precision that felt almost surgical. The hum of conversation, the subtle shuffling of feet, the almost imperceptible whir of machines blending into a symphony that only she seemed to truly understand. She stood at the upper gallery, her position elevated, not just in terms of the architecture but in the hierarchy it represented.

Below her, the crowds moved with an orchestrated fluidity, a dance of shadows and light playing across their faces. Some were workers, their movements deliberate and purposeful as they adjusted panels and interfaced with the shimmering screens that dominated the room. Others seemed mere visitors, their eyes wide with a mixture of awe and something else—was it confusion or fear?—as they interacted with the displays.

The air was disrupted with the scent of technology; that clean, sharp smell of electricity and metal that spoke of power and control. It was a fragrance she found comforting, a scent that spoke of order in a world teetering on the edge of chaos.

From her vantage point, she could see into the labs through the glass walls, where figures in white coats moved with calm efficiency. What were they working on? The specifics were hidden from her view, shrouded in a mist of privacy glass that frosted over with the flick of a switch. It sparked a curiosity that was almost unbearable, a desire to know more, to peel back the layers of secrecy that she herself had mandated.

Every so often, a flicker of light from one of the many towering screens caught her eye. Images flashed momentarily—a tree swaying in the wind, a city skyline at night, a child's smile—each disappearing before one could really understand their context or meaning. What were these images to the people who watched them? Did they see what she saw, or did they see something else, something perhaps even she wasn't aware of?

Greda's thoughts were her own, as always, a maze of plans and calculations. She pondered the effectiveness of what she had built here. Was it truly serving its purpose? She watched a young man pause, his hand hovering over a console. He seemed hesitant, unsure. What decision was he grappling with? What weight did it carry in the grand scale of her designs?

Her attention then shifted to a group of individuals gathered around a large, central hologram that pulsed with gentle light. They watched intently as the hologram shifted shapes, the light coalescing into forms and patterns that hinted at complex data or perhaps intricate simulations. Their expressions were rapt, caught up in whatever narrative was playing out before them. But what story was it telling them? And more importantly, what did it compel them to believe or feel?

Chancellor Greda's gaze swept over the Citadel's grand atrium, a silent observer to the ballet of compliance unfolding below. The imposing silhouette of the central control spire, a monolith housing the nerve center of her operations, cast a long shadow over the bustling crowd. Here, the heart of her reign pulsed with an omnipotent rhythm, a spectacle she never tired of overseeing from her elevated vantage point.

As she turned to exit the gallery, the echo of her steps mingled with the harmonized hum of this place. Her presence was solitary, yet her influence saturated every corner of the space. Each step was a silent testament to the absolute authority she wielded over the subterranean empire she had forged. The citizens below, once fierce individualists, now moved in harmonious synchrony, their actions a testament to the efficacy of her regime.

Pausing at a discreet panel, she pressed her hand against its surface, initiating a sequence known only to her. The wall slid open with a whisper, revealing a corridor leading to the depths of her private sanctum. Here, away from the orchestrated spectacle, she could momentarily shed the mantle of Chancellor.

Her thoughts drifted to the citizens—no longer mere subjects, but participants in a grand experiment of societal engineering. They had been shown a paradise, a virtual utopia crafted from their deepest desires and fears, and they had embraced it without hesitation. The images flickering on the massive screens weren't just illusions but cogs in the larger machine of her design.

The project—her grand design—had transcended its initial purpose. It was no longer about control through suppression but control through seduction. The populace didn't merely accept her rule;

they craved the reality she provided, addicted to the escapism that made the harshness of their world palatable.

Behind the closed doors of her chambers, Greda allowed herself a rare smile. This wonderful place, with its deep corridors and hidden chambers, was her domain, a fortress from which she could mold the future. The murmurs of dissent had faded, not quashed by force but dissolved in the digital dreams she wove.

Tomorrow, and every day thereafter, they would wake to a world of her making, their dissent a distant memory, their autonomy surrendered not with a fight but with a sigh of contentment. In this new world, Greda was not just a ruler but a deity, architecting realities that bound every citizen to her will.

And above all, she thrived, not just on the control but on the undeniable devotion of her people. In their satisfaction lay her greatest victory—their paradise, a cage of their own making, and she, the benevolent keeper of the keys.

Inside the seclusion of her private chambers, Chancellor Greda stood encircled by thirty massive screens, their surfaces so advanced they were almost indistinguishable from the reality they portrayed. Each screen played a different scene, a fragment of the life that she had crafted for the citizens of her underground empire. The array was a half-moon of illumination in the dimly lit room, each display a window into a world of perfect illusion.

Her eyes moved from screen to screen, observing the minutiae of daily life within the virtual landscapes she had engineered. Here was a family laughing around a dinner table, there a young couple walking hand in hand through a park that had not existed on the surface for centuries. Each scene was meticulously rendered, perfectly digital threads woven into a comforting lie.

Greda's mind was a complex of emotions as she watched her creation in action. There was a devilish pride in knowing she had crafted not just a tool of control but a sanctuary so enticing that none sought to escape. Her citizens traded days of their real lives for moments in this crafted paradise, a deal they entered willingly, even eagerly. It was, she reflected, the ultimate seduction: an escape so complete that the harsh truths of their world became distant, like nightmares dispelled by the morning light.

Yet, beneath the satisfaction, there was a deeper, more introspective thread to her contemplations. She pondered the morality of her actions—a puzzle she turned over in her mind like a coin flipping between right and wrong. Was she their savior for providing this escape, or their jailer for binding them to illusion?

Each screen flickered with the lives of those who no longer questioned their reality. They had accepted the narrative she fed them, a narrative that excluded the barren wastelands above, the ever-looming threat of the sentient flora that had overtaken the surface. They saw what they wanted to see— and sometimes what she chose for them to see.

As she observed the blissful ignorance of a young man immersed in a simulation of sunlight—a sensation lost to time and the cataclysm—Greda felt a twinge of something unexpected. Was it guilt, or perhaps a longing for the same oblivion? Quickly, she quashed the thought, resetting her features to the cool mask of governance.

In this chamber of screens, the mystery of her rule deepened. Each display was a clue, a piece of the puzzle laid bare for any who could step back far enough to see the full picture. Yet there was no one but Greda who could, or would, assemble the fragments into a coherent whole. The mystery of the reality she controlled was hers alone to understand fully, and hers alone to manipulate.

As she turned away from the glowing panels, her silhouette cast long shadows across the cold, sleek floor. The power to shape perception was the ultimate tool of control, and in her hands, it was wielded with the precision of a master craftsperson. The citizens of her dominion lived within a story of her making, a narrative so compelling that it blinded them to the bars of their gilded cages. And the crazy thing was, they paid her for it. They absolutely paid her for it and it the worse way imaginable.

Tomorrow, as always, they would wake to a world that knew no dissent, no discomfort, no desire unmet by the virtual dreams she spun. And as long as they remained entranced by the scenes on these screens, Chancellor Greda's reign would be unchallenged, her secrets preserved within the depths of her mysterious, magnificent labyrinth.

Lingering in the semi-circle of luminous projections, her thoughts weaving through the fabric of the vast network she had created. Each screen, a portal into a life being lived under her careful orchestration, revealed nothing but fragments to the untrained eye. Yet, for Greda, each fragment was a piece of a much larger puzzle she alone was solving.

On one screen, a middle-aged man, his features etched with the subtle signs of a life previously marred by hardship, now smiled as he walked through a sunlit plaza that mimicked the vibrant energy of a world lost to time. The screen adjacent displayed a group of children, their laughter pealing as they played in a digital meadow, chasing pixels that fluttered like butterflies.

These scenes, while idyllic, were underpinned by a complex transaction—years of actual life exchanged for months in this synthetic paradise. The process, elegantly simple in its explanation but infinitely complex in its execution, involved the extraction of each participant's DNA. This was not merely a biological procedure but a gateway into the psyche of each citizen. The DNA was a blueprint, used not just to ensure compatibility with the virtual system, but to tailor each virtual experience so precisely that the line between reality and simulation blurred into oblivion.

The testing was thorough, each sample analyzed and re-analyzed to create a profile so detailed that the virtual reality interface could evoke sensations, memories, and experiences that felt more real than reality itself. These profiles were stored, coded into the very architecture of the virtual world Greda ruled. Each entry was a contract sealed with the most personal marker of identity one could offer: their genetic signature.

Greda watched as a young woman on one of the screens paused at a market stall, her virtual hand reaching out to touch virtual fruits, their textures rendered perfectly by the system. The woman's real counterpart had offered thirty of her years for this—thirty years of potential life in the desolate reality of the underground, traded for the sweet deception of choice and freedom in a world that would never age her, never bring her pain.

This was the heart of the mystery, the core of the enigma Greda had crafted. The participants knew they were entering a trade, but the true cost was hidden behind the immediate gratification of their senses. They understood the surface of the transaction—years for months, life for dreams—but not the depth. They didn't see how their very essence was being woven into a narrative they had no real control over.

As Greda's gaze shifted from screen to screen, her mind lingered not just on what was being shown, but on what was omitted. Each scene was a diversion, a beautiful lie told in the language of coded genetics and fabricated photons. The participants saw what she wanted them to see, believed what she wanted them to believe. And in believing, they became part of the labyrinth without walls, a maze with no desire for escape.

In her private chamber, surrounded by the glow of other lives lived in blissful ignorance, Greda reflected on the dual edge of her creation. It was both a sanctuary and a cell, and she was both its architect and its warden. The mystery of her power lay not just in the control but in the consent it was wrapped in, a consent given in the shadows of understanding, under the guise of an escape.

Tomorrow, as always, her citizens would wake within her crafted dreams, unknowing and undoubting, their realities curated with the precision of a master storyteller. And as long as they remained captivated by the illusions on these screens, the secrets of her dominion—of their own lives and liberties—would remain just out of reach, hidden within the depths of the beautiful, magnificent mystery she perpetuated.

Greda's eyes narrowed slightly as they traced the luminescent paths of data streaming across one of the screens. Here, in the form of glowing charts and holographic spreadsheets, was the ledger of their lives—each entry a person's time, quantified, bartered, and transformed. Each citizen's contribution was met with rewards: credits and status, virtual tokens in a game where the stakes were invisibly high. The rewards served as a brilliant facade, dazzling enough to mask the toll of their participation. It was a masterful exchange, and all it cost them was a piece of their essence, a slice of their temporal existence.

On another screen, a younger woman's laughter rang out, harmonious and rich, as she explored a digitized rendition of an ancient forest. Her joy, palpable and resonant, was the product of a script written just for her, tailored from the DNA up to resonate with her deepest yearnings. This was the benefit, the sweet fruit of their surrender—endless experiences, beautifully crafted illusions of a life unrestrained by the bleak reality that lurked just beyond the walls of her dominion.

Yet, with each laugh, each moment of joy, there was a shadow. The procedure that allowed them this escapade was not without its thorns. The molecular alignment, the genetic integration with the system—these were not gentle touches but invasive bindings. They left marks, unseen but profound. Accelerated aging, a side effect tucked away in the fine print of an agreement too enticing to deny, was just the beginning. Neurological stress, emotional disorientation—these too were prices paid, insidious and creeping.

The participants did not see these costs. They felt them, perhaps, as a shadow in their bones, a fatigue in their spirits when they disconnected, but the allure of the virtual sun was too strong, its warmth too convincing. They returned, again and again, trading more and more of their real lives for moments in a paradise that would never truly belong to them.

As Greda turned away from that scene to one displaying a man immersed in an artificial celebration, his digital avatar surrounded by friends and laughter, she pondered the paradox of her own creation. The society thrived under her guidance, order maintained through a currency of dreams. Yet, beneath the veneer of this utopia, there was a trade-off—a gradual, almost imperceptible erosion of vitality. This was the true mystery of her empire, a secret kept not by locks but by blindness, a puzzle whose pieces were scattered among the very lives of her citizens.

In the quiet of her chamber, the Chancellor considered the delicate balance of her rule. How long could the illusion hold? How long before the subtle signs of decay became too pronounced to ignore? These questions lingered in the air, spectral and unvoiced, as she watched her subjects live out their fantasies.

The secrets of her dominion, the true machinations of her power, were buried deep within the code that ran this world—a world of her making where every smile was both a genuine expression of happiness and a marker of a deeper, darker transaction. Here, in this labyrinth of light and shadow, the mystery of what was gained and what was lost was woven into the very fabric of existence, a riddle only she could fully appreciate.

And so, the citizens of her underground empire would wake tomorrow, as always, to a world that knew no dissent, a world lush with the fruits of an eternal, digital spring. And as long as they remained entranced by the beauty of the illusion, the complexities of its cost would remain just beyond their grasp, hidden in plain sight, a mystery encapsulated in the very lives they lived.

Greda's gaze lingered on the joyous throngs within the digital celebration, their laughter echoing through advanced sensory chambers that rendered every chuckle and whisper with disturbing clarity. These chambers, nestled like hidden jewels throughout her realm, were marvels of technology, crafting experiences that engaged every sense—smell, touch, sight, taste, and sound—melding them into a seamless reality indistinguishable from the natural world they could no longer inhabit.

Each participant, cloaked in the bliss of ignorance, paid a price hidden within the very DNA of their experience. The genetic coding that ensured compatibility with the virtual interface also wove their personal histories, their physical and emotional essences, into the fabric of their immersive narrative. This blending of life and technology, this dream weaving, tethered them to a cycle of dependency that deepened with each session, each dream.

As Greda turned from one screen to another, she noted the subtle cues of this dependency—the slight hesitation as a young woman paused, her hand hovering over the interface before plunging back into the vibrant illusion of a spring meadow. The woman's smile was bright, yet it masked the toll of the exchange: the gradual erosion of her real-world vitality for the fleeting ecstasy of digital blooms.

These were the mysteries Greda crafted and curated—the unseen costs of a paradise manufactured within the cold confines of quantum servers and neural interfaces. Here, in her private observatory, she alone understood the full spectrum of the transactions taking place. The citizens of her empire understood they were exchanging time for experience, but they did not fully comprehend the depth of their investment or the permanence of their losses.

The dream manipulation technology, a cornerstone of her control, blurred the lines between waking life and the virtual world. Participants' dreams became continuations of their digital experiences, crafted by algorithms to reinforce the addiction to the virtual realm they inhabited by night. In their sleep, their desires, fears, and memories were quietly reshaped, aligning ever more closely with the narrative Greda deemed optimal.

This was the delicate alchemy of her rule—turning base human desires for connection, beauty, and escapism into gold for her empire. But it was an alchemy with a dark undertow, a current that could erode the foundations of identity and autonomy, leaving her citizens adrift in a sea of manufactured contentment.

As the screens flickered before her, casting light on her impassive face, Chancellor Greda contemplated the future. How durable was the spell she had cast? How deep ran the roots of contentment she had engineered? This is why she wanted the Artifact. Just incase all this this brilliance would fail, she could still control the underworld. But rumors also said, she could control the surface, too. She let herself imagine the Verdant Overlord trading all of his thousands of years in her technology. The thought sent happiness through her body. These were the enigmas that kept her awake, long after the screens had dimmed and the last of her citizens had slipped into their engineered dreams.

In the silence of her chamber, Greda faced the grand mystery of her own making: a world without dissent, crafted from the very essence of human longing. As long as the illusion held, as long as the dreams continued to captivate, her rule would remain unchallenged, her secrets ensconced in the shadows of the beautiful, deceptive world she had built.

The screens, now darkened to mere glimmers, mirrored the depth of the game Greda played—a game of influence and intricate control cloaked within the digital paradise she offered. Beneath the serene surface of each citizen's virtual existence, there lay a robust framework of sociopolitical manipulation, a merit-based hierarchy that dictated the very fabric of their perceived reality.

In this crafted world, participants climbed social ladders based on compliance and contribution, believing in the fairness of a system wholly controlled by the Chancellor herself. They traded their true autonomy for the illusion of advancement, unknowing pawns in Greda's grand strategy. Each step they took up the ladder was a step deeper into her web, a web woven from the very desires that drove them.

Greda watched the afterimages of their digital lives flicker in the periphery of her vision, each pulse a silent trade-off occurring far below the surface of their awareness. Her control extended not just to the laws they followed but to the dreams they dared to dream. The currency of this realm was no longer mere virtual coins but opportunities—crafted scarcities that drove them to strive for more within the confines she had built.

The manipulation of resources was subtle yet profound. Scarcity was engineered; luxury items, virtual land, and even social standings were dangled like carrots before the ever-hungry eyes of the populace. This engineered scarcity bred competition, conflict, and ultimately, a deeper dependency on the system that only Greda could alleviate. Each conflict resolved, each item obtained, reinforced her indispensable role as both the creator and the curator of their world.

As the night deepened, the quiet of her chambers became a stark contrast to the bustling activity that the day's illusions had presented. Here, in the stillness, Greda allowed herself a rare moment to ponder the depth of her creations. The societal game she orchestrated was more than control; it was a psychological mixing board that affected every facet of existence for those under her reign.

How long could she maintain this illusion of a democratic oasis? Was there a point where the fabricated scarcities and the artificial hierarchies would be recognized for the mirages they were? These questions, like shadows, flitted at the edge of her consciousness, never fully forming but always present.

Yet, every morning, as the citizens of her underground empire awoke to another day in paradise, these questions faded into irrelevance. They did not see the constraints of their freedoms; they saw only the possibilities within their grasp. They did not rebel against the hidden chains; they rejoiced in the weight of their shackles, gold-plated and glimmering with the promise of dreams.

This was the essence of the mystery Greda had woven: a labyrinth without walls, where each turn led deeper into dependency, and every choice was a further affirmation of her rule. As long as the illusion held, as long as the facade of freedom and progress remained intact, her secrets would stay buried in the intricate dance of shadows and light she had masterfully choreographed.

Her reflection in the glass surface of the room cast back a woman in control, yet the machinations beneath that surface were more complex, more ethically dubious than anyone could guess. In the silence of the night, she considered the long-term consequences of her schemes, the genetic material harvested quietly from each participant, woven into the fabric of their virtual lives as seamlessly as the dreams fed to them.

This genetic harvesting was not just about controlling the present; it was an investment in the future. In the depths of her secure laboratories, scientists employed this material in biotechnological experiments, attempting to create beings perfectly adapted to life in the underground, beings that might one day venture to reclaim the surface world.

The psychological conditioning was equally pervasive, yet subtler. Each participant, each citizen, underwent a continuous, almost imperceptible realignment of their beliefs and behaviors. Over time, this conditioning aimed to mold them into a population that was more docile, more compliant, and far less likely to question the structures that confined them.

As she stood alone, the weight of these ethical paradoxes hung heavy in the air. The very society she had engineered was both a sanctuary and a prison, and she was its undisputed guardian. Yet, as she gazed at the darkened screens that had earlier glowed with the vibrant lives of her citizens, she couldn't help but question the moral price of peace and order.

These were her empire's hidden foundations: genetic manipulation and psychological reprogramming, invisible yet fundamental. Each was a piece of the grand puzzle that was her reign, known only to her and concealed from those who believed they lived in a world of their own making.

As the night waned, Greda turned from the window, the cityscape below bathed in the artificial light that mimicked a starless sky. Her citizens slept, dreamers within a dream she had crafted, unaware of the true nature of their reality. And in this realization lay the heart of the mystery—how long could this orchestrated paradise last before the facade crumbled? How long before someone, somewhere, started to piece together the clues she had so carefully scattered?

But Greda's dominion was not left to mere chance or the whims of her subjects' unconscious desires. Deep within the infrastructure of Project Lumina, quantum computing AI thrummed with life, a silent overseer of the virtual paradise. This system, advanced beyond the grasp of those it monitored, analyzed vast torrents of data—each heartbeat, each sigh of contentment or flicker of discontent noted and assessed.

The biometric monitors were the unseen sentinels in this grand scheme, intricately woven into the very fabric of the virtual world. These devices did more than observe; they adapted and manipulated, subtly altering experiences in real-time to quell dissatisfaction or nurture compliance. Every smile, every tear shed in joy or sorrow was data, fuel for the algorithms that crafted deeper illusions.

In the quiet of her control room, Greda watched the flicker of data streams, each one a lifeline to a citizen. The quantum AI, her most trusted advisor, projected patterns and predictions on screens only she could read. It showed her not just realities, but possibilities, potential rebellions quashed before they could even begin to form in the mind.

Here lay the mystery not even her closest aides could discern— the depth of surveillance and control, masked beneath the guise of communal utopia. Each citizen believed themselves free, their choices their own, yet Greda knew the truth. They moved within boundaries she had etched into the code, their every decision an echo of her will.

As dawn approached, casting a false glow through the simulation of a sunrise, Greda contemplated the future. How long could she weave this intricate web before a thread snapped, before someone saw beyond the veil of code and into the cold mechanics of her rule?

This was the enigma at the heart of her empire: a perfect world built on invisible chains and watchful eyes. And as long as the AI continued to predict and the biometric sensors continued to adjust, with Greda as the puppeteer, her citizens none the wiser to the strings that guided them.

Stepping from the hushed serenity of her chamber, Chancellor Greda entered the expansive control room where the heart of Project Lumina pulsated with a life of its own. The room was dominated by a colossal 1000-foot screen, curving around the space like a cocoon of light and pixels, proudly displaying the logo of Project Lumina. The enormity of the screen made the name reverberate through the room, a constant reminder of her greatest invention—a marvel that even the Verdant Overlord, with all his ancient cunning, could never have conceived.

The screen flickered with life, showcasing the vibrant, ceaseless activity of the project. Citizens, engrossed in their perfect synthetic realities, laughed, loved, and lived with an intensity that belied the artificial nature of their experiences. Each face that flashed before her was a success of her creation, each smile part of her control and illusion she controlled over humanity.

As she watched, a sense of pride surged within her, fierce and gratifying. This was her empire, not of land and law, but of mind and matter. Here, in this room, the strings of an entire society were pulled, guiding the populace through a dance choreographed by algorithms and quantum calculations.

Yet, beneath the surface of this digital utopia, the machinery of Lumina operated on principles far darker and more complex than its users could imagine. Hidden within the code and the quiet hum of quantum computers was a network of surveillance and manipulation so total that it could dictate not just actions but emotions and thoughts.

Each participant in Lumina, while lost in their engineered paradises, was monitored by an array of biometric sensors that tracked everything from their pulse to the dilation of their pupils. This data, fed into the quantum AI, enabled Greda to anticipate potential unrest or dissatisfaction, snuffing it out with the precision of a surgeon before it could ever reach the surface of consciousness.

This was the danger that thrilled her as much as it secured her rule—the knowledge that the entire system, as beautiful and elaborate as it was, balanced on the edge of a knife. The citizens were content because she willed it so, their docility maintained not just by satisfaction but by the subtle recalibrations of their environment, adjusted in real-time to maintain the status quo.

The illusion of choice was perhaps the most elegant aspect of her control. Participants believed they climbed the ranks of a merit-based society, not realizing that every achievement, every progression was preordained by Greda's algorithms. This virtual society, with its hierarchy and rewards, was calibrated to reward obedience and crush dissent, a perfect loop of cause and effect that kept the populace striving for more within the confines she had crafted.

Chapter 3

In the virtual world of Project Lumina, Felix Hart stood, his presence commanding the attention of his eclectic crew. Around the digital table, a holographic blueprint of the Lumina vault pulsed, displaying intricate security nodes and patrol routes. "Welcome everyone. Tonight, we're not just stealing data; we're unlocking the future. Let's check our map," Felix announced, his voice cool but laced with urgency. As the leader and chief strategist, his eyes flicked across the faces of his team, each member reflecting a blend of anticipation and resolve.

Ava Zhang, the tactical specialist, her gaze fixed on the glowing screens, nodded silently. Her experience as a military strategist was evident in her calm, measured demeanor. Equipped with a Precision Laser Rifle and cloaked in a Reinforced Tactical Vest, she was the backbone of their operation's real-time strategy. Beside her, Milo Santos, the tech and surveillance expert, cracked a quick joke under his breath, lightening the mood without breaking focus. His fingers danced over his Portable Hacking Kit, ready to disable any electronic barriers they would encounter.

Tara Knight, muscles tense under her Adaptive Camouflage Suit, checked the grips on her Composite Fiber Whip. As the infiltration and extraction specialist, her role was crucial; she was their shadow, their silent assailant who would penetrate the vault's defenses. Raj Patel, the engineer and demolitions expert, meticulously reviewed his Modular Demolition Blaster, ensuring every setting was calibrated for the varied tasks ahead. His methodical nature and deep focus were intimidating, a stark contrast to the charged energy of the room.

Felix, clad in his Nexus Shell armor, turned back to the hologram, his Tactical Overlay Visor projecting critical data directly onto his retina. "This mission relies on precision and timing, and I need you all to be flawless tonight," he instructed, his tone both inspiring and commanding. The stakes were immense, not just in the value of the data but in the potential to shift power dynamics within the virtual world of Project Lumina. As the crew absorbed the weight of his words, Felix's leadership shone—calm in the face of storm, adaptive, and strategically two steps ahead of any scenario.

Tara Knight adjusted the grip on her Composite Fiber Whip, her voice low and steady, "Whip's calibrated for silence and speed. I'll be in and out before they blink."

Raj Patel, checking his Modular Demolition Blaster, added methodically, "Explosives are set for precise, low-impact breaches. We'll keep it quiet."

Felix, leading the charge, eyes fixed on the holographic displays, spoke with measured intensity, "Tonight's about more than theft; it's about control. This key doesn't just open doors—it opens up freedom. Ava, you're first up with the firewalls."

Ava Zhang nodded, her fingers poised above her console, "Firewall sequences are already mapped. I'll have us through the initial layers in under ten seconds. Milo, you'll need to be quick on the follow-up."

Milo Santos grinned, his tools at the ready, "I've got the surveillance systems. Forty seconds of ghost time coming up. And maybe I'll scramble their breakfast menus for a bit of extra chaos."

Felix's lips twitched in amusement before his expression sobered, "Focus. Raj, once inside, how quickly can you set up the first charge?"

"Three minutes. I'll sync it with Tara's entry point. We do this clean and sharp," Raj responded, his eyes never leaving his schematics.

Tara interjected, her tone fierce yet hushed, "Remember, I need a clear path. Raj's explosions have to be precise. I can't afford detours or delays."

Felix surveyed his team, each member dialed in, "We're a clock tonight, each second counts. This heist pivots on our coordination. Every move is choreographed, from Ava's breach to Tara's extraction. We can't afford a single misstep."

Milo chuckled softly, "Just another night of ballet."

Ava double-checked her displays, "Timing is everything. I trigger the first bypass, then Milo blinds their cams. Raj blows the secondary doors, and Tara slips through the shadows. Felix, you're the maestro here."

Felix nodded, his gaze steely and focused on the digital blueprint sprawling before them, "Exactly. We play this right, and we don't just walk away with the data—we walk away legends."

Raj, tightening a component on his blaster, muttered, "Legends or not, I just don't want to end up as digital dust."

Tara, poised and ready, her eyes gleaming with a mix of thrill and resolve, "No one's becoming dust tonight. We're the shadows they never see coming."

Felix's voice rose, imbued with a rare fervor, "Then let's show Lumina what shadows can do."

"However, this won't be a walk in the park. The vault is not just guarded; it's fortified. We need to be ghosts, slipping through their nets." Felix's voice cut through the charged silence, laying bare the new reality of their heist.

As he adjusted the display to zoom in on the layers of security protocols that had just been updated, his team leaned in. The holographic blueprints rotated, showing a three-dimensional labyrinth of digital defenses, more intricate than anything they'd encountered before. "They've added biometric scanners and thermal triggers at these corridors," he pointed out, marking the areas with red.

Milo's brow furrowed under the new information, "Biometrics, huh? That's a twist. Good thing I packed our latest spoofing tech."

Ava's fingers paused over her console, absorbing the update. "That tightens our window. I'll need to recalibrate the firewalls' disruption sequence."

Tara's grip on her whip tightened, her mind racing through new entry strategies. "I'll reroute. It might take longer, but I'll keep to the shadows."

Raj glanced at his arsenal of gadgets, calculating the adjustments needed for the physical barriers. "I'll prepare a second set of charges. If we're going silent, we're going ultra-precise. The smallest vibration could set off those thermal sensors."

Felix watched his team adapt, their initial shock morphing into a focused determination. They didn't really have a motive, they just always had a plan. Most times, that plan was to take down Project Lumina. "We adapt and overcome. We always do."

The room hummed with the sound of recalibrating equipment and whispered confirmations as each member of the team synchronized their tech with the updated plan. Felix felt the weight of leadership heavy on his shoulders, yet there was nowhere else he'd rather be. In this room, with these people, facing down the impossible—that was where he thrived.

"We're treading on thinner ice now," he continued, his eyes scanning the updated paths on the hologram. "Every step has to be precise; there's no margin for error. Ava, you'll initiate the sequence. Milo, once she's through, it's your play."

Ava nodded, her expression steely. "I won't miss."

Milo cracked his knuckles, a grin flickering over his lips despite the tension. "Just another day at the office, right?"

"And Tara, once we're in, it's down to you. You'll navigate the inner sanctum. It's rigged to be a maze, but you're the best we have at turning mazes into straight lines," Felix said, locking eyes with her.

"Like always, Felix. They won't see me," Tara replied, her voice a low promise.

Raj interjected, his voice a calm constant, "And I'll handle the exits. Once we're in, we'll need a clean way out. I'll make sure we have it."

Felix watched them, his team—no, his family in arms—each an integral cog in the intricate machine he had built. He knew the dangers of the digital realm they were about to infiltrate; one misstep could mean more than failure—it could mean digital erasure. But he also knew the capabilities of his crew, their dedication, their skill. "This isn't just another hack-and-grab," he continued, his hand gesturing to the holographic images of their target. "We're not just after data. We're here to set a precedent."

The room fell silent, the weight of his words settling over the team like a cloak. Each member understood the gravity of the mission—not just for the bounty it could yield but for the statement it would make.

Milo broke the silence, his tone unusually serious, "Let's make sure it's a loud one, then."

Felix gave a final nod, his hand coming down to rest on the hilt of his Codebreaker Blade. "Precision and timing brought us together, now let's make them our legacy. Let's set the world on a new path, starting tonight."

With a final check of their gear, the team formed up behind Felix, each member's movements precise and deliberate. The virtual battlefield awaited, a labyrinth of data and danger, but they were ready. As they moved towards the deployment bay, their steps were unified, a single entity moving towards a common goal.

The doors ahead hissed open, the portal to their battleground. Felix stepped through, his team in lockstep, the line between the digital and the real blurring with each forward motion.

The pulsating lights of the digital fortress cast an eerie glow, painting sharp shadows on Tara Knight's camouflaged suit as she crouched low, blending into the darkness. Felix's voice, low and urgent, buzzed in her earpiece, "Alright team, remember, invisibility is our greatest weapon tonight. Stay under their radar."

Her eyes, trained on the distant walls lined with patrolling AI sentinels, flicked to the blueprints illuminating her wrist display. She memorized the entry points, the blind spots, the expected routes—each detail sharpening her focus. Felix, standing a few feet away, keyed up the final checks, his silhouette outlined against the backdrop of shifting data streams.

"Check your signals, Ava. I need those sensors down before we make our move," he commanded, his gaze locked on the digital map sprawling before him. Ava, positioned behind a makeshift console, nodded, her fingers flying over the touchscreen. "External sensors going dark in three... two... one..."

The slight hum of the fortress's defenses dimmed. Ava's precision didn't fail. Milo, his gear emitting a soft whir, grinned, "Cameras are blind. It's showtime, Tara."

Tara didn't need another cue. With the grace of a specter, she darted forward, her movements nearly silent, her breath controlled. The fortress, a monolithic structure of digital and physical threats, loomed ahead, its secrets guarded by layers of coded defenses. But Tara had danced through worse mazes, her body and mind honed for exactly this—penetration and extraction without a trace.

As she approached the first barrier, a digital lock interfaced with the physical gate, she glanced back. Felix's figure was a steady beacon of calm. "Tara, you're clear to proceed. Raj, prepare to breach on my mark."

Her Composite Fiber Whip in hand, Tara flicked her wrist, sending the whip cracking towards the lock mechanism, the tip interfaced with the digital keypad. Code cascading through the device, she watched the digits scramble under the assault of her tool, the door giving way with a silent consent. Slipping through, she found herself in the heart of the beast, the inner sanctum that Felix had described as a rigged maze.

"Like always, Felix. They won't see me," she whispered into the comm, her voice a thread of steel woven with confidence. Moving with a predator's patience, Tara navigated the labyrinth, each turn and each shadow mapped out in her mind's eye, her gear—the grappling hook launcher at her belt—ready to propel her across physical and virtual pitfalls.

Raj's voice came next, a low rumble through the comm, "Exits are set. Once we're in, getting out will be as smooth as getting in."

The maze's complexity increased, virtual traps springing up with more frequency. Tara disabled each with a practiced ease, her gear a blur of motion and technology. Every corner turned and every obstacle overcome brought them closer to their target—the vault, pulsating with the promise of data that could shift the balance of power in their world.

"We're nearly there," Tara reported, her voice barely a whisper, yet clear in the ears of her team. Ahead, the vault door loomed, daunting in its security. But with her team behind her, each member a master of their craft, the impossible seemed merely another challenge to overcome.

"And I'm just at the door. Felix, ready when you are," she breathed, poised to deliver the final blow in their carefully choreographed dance of shadows and silence.

Tara adjusted the grip on her whip, the Composite Fiber becoming an extension of her arm as she navigated the labyrinthine corridors leading to the vault. The pulsating walls of the fortress emitted a low hum, a constant reminder of the defenses that lay just beneath their surface. Each step was calculated, her movements a silent ballet performed under the watchful eyes of surveillance drones they had yet to disable.

"Milo, now," Felix's voice cut through the silence, a command that was both a beacon and a warning. The moment stretched as she heard the faint buzz, signaling Milo's success in darkening their electronic watchers.

"Clear," she whispered back, her voice carrying the weight of their progress. Ahead, the vault door stood, an imposing barrier between them and their goal. The data within was more than information; it was power, the kind that could change the dynamics of control in Project Lumina.

Felix's figure, shrouded in the dim light of his Tactical Overlay Visor, nodded once, sharply. "Tara, you're on point. Remember, the vault's sensors are unlike any we've dealt with."

Her hands moved to her belt, retrieving a small device that would scramble the electronic signals. This wasn't just another door; it was the gatekeeper to their future. As she set the device, her mind raced with the implications of their task. Each member of her team was pivotal, a spoke in the wheel of their meticulous plan.

"Device set. Activating in three... two... one..." The click of the button was almost inaudible, but its effect was immediate. A soft green light blinked on the panel beside the door, a silent herald of their success so far.

Behind her, she could feel the tension in the air, as tangible as the electric current running through the walls. Ava's steady breathing provided a counterpoint to the rapid beat of Tara's heart, a reminder of the calm precision required to see their plan to completion.

"We're in the final stretch," Tara announced, her voice a low murmur only her team could hear. She glanced back at Felix, his eyes meeting hers through the glow of his visor. It was a look that conveyed both trust and the burden of command.

The door slid open with a silent grace, revealing the vault room bathed in the cold light of security monitors. Tara stepped inside, her suit blending into the shadows, making her nearly invisible to the untrained eye. Her heart raced as she approached the central console, her fingers ready to dance over its keys.

"Vault's open, Felix. It looks like we're the first to walk these floors in a while," she reported, keeping her voice steady despite the adrenaline that threatened to overwhelm her senses.

"Good, keep moving, everyone. Tara, extract the data. Milo, keep those cams offline. Ava, monitor our exit routes. We're not out of the shadows yet," Felix's directives flowed through their comms, each word sharpening their focus.

As Tara interfaced with the vault's mainframe, the reality of their heist settled in. They were not just thieves in the night; they were pioneers on the frontier of a new world order. And as her screen lit up with the data they had come so far to claim, she realized they were no longer just fighting against something. They were fighting for something—a chance to rewrite the rules.

In the half-light of the vault, Tara's breath came quietly, her focus absolute as she interfaced with the mainframe. The sudden, sharp order from Felix snapped her back to the immediate danger, "Hold! Ava, deploy the decoy at sector three. We need a diversion, now!"

Her fingers paused over the holographic keys. The corridor outside echoed with the soft, mechanical whir of an approaching AI patrol. Not part of the plan. Her heart raced; this was the twist they'd dreaded, yet meticulously planned for. Each member knew their role in this dance of digital shadows—they were the unseen, the undetected.

From the shadows, Ava's voice crackled through the comm, her tone as crisp as the air around them, "Decoy's going live... now." A series of soft beeps followed, an auditory signal that their electronic ghost was on the move, drawing the AI's attention away from their position.

Tara peered through the dim lighting, her Adaptive Camouflage Suit rendering her almost invisible against the cold metallic walls. She watched Felix closely, his figure outlined by the ambient light of his visor, observing AI movement patterns that only he could see. His next move would dictate theirs, and the tension was palpable.

"Path's clear, Tara. Continue with extraction," Felix's command was a whisper, yet it carried the weight of their mission. She turned back to the console, her fingers flying over the interface with renewed urgency. The data transfer initiated, a silent countdown began, each second pulsing with risk and opportunity.

Outside, she could hear the faintest disturbances—the decoy doing its work, drawing the patrol further away. Milo's voice was the next to break the silence, tinged with relief but edged with focus, "Sensors are blind for now. You've got a clear shot, Tara."

Her screen flickered, data streaming through the ether, code sequences rewriting themselves as they prepared to claim what could redefine power within Project Lumina. This wasn't just about stealing data; it was about claiming a new frontier, one where they set the rules.

Felix's voice cut through her concentration again, sharper this time, "Tara, status?" His tone mirrored the urgency of their escapade, a subtle reminder of the stakes riding on her shoulders.

"Data's almost secure," she replied, her voice steady despite the adrenaline that threatened to override her calm. The progress bar on her display inched closer to completion, each segment filling up like the chambers of a revolver, loading their shot at rewriting the dystopian rules they'd been forced to obey.

Just then, a low alert chimed. Her gaze snapped to the peripheral readout—unexpected heat signatures were complicating the straightforward escape they'd planned. "Felix, we've got incoming—more heat than anticipated."

Felix was immediate in his response, "Adjust exit strategy, Raj, we're about to have company."

Raj's confirmation was gruff, efficient, "On it. Adjusting charges for a faster blowout. Be ready to move."

Tara's focus sharpened as the situation unraveled. The progress bar stalled, a glaring red segment flashing a warning. "Transfer stalled," she muttered, frustration lacing her whispered words. She tapped the interface urgently, bypass codes scrolling in a futile attempt to override the error.

A harsh static crackle burst through their comms, a sudden onslaught of digital noise. "Comms are compromised!" Milo's voice cut through, laced with urgency. "Looks like they're onto us, the AI's not just patrolling anymore, they're actively seeking!"

The dim corridor previously masked by shadows flickered alive with the harsh glare of alarm lights, painting everything in a stark, ominous red. Tara glanced towards Felix, his figure now sharply outlined against the chaotic backdrop. His jaw set, eyes narrowing behind the glow of his visor as he processed their rapidly deteriorating situation.

"Change of plans," Felix barked into the comm, his voice now a commanding echo in the vaulted space. "Ava, Milo, I need a blackout, not just a blind spot. Knock everything out!"

Ava's response was terse, a clipped, "Working on it," barely audible over the rising clamor of the fortress's alert system.

The corridor felt narrower, a claustrophobic squeeze as the sound of mechanical feet approached, a rhythmic march that spelled imminent danger. Tara retracted her hand from the console, the incomplete data transfer a glaring symbol of their faltering mission. Her other hand instinctively went to her side, gripping the handle of her Composite Fiber Whip, ready to defend, to fight if necessary.

"Here they come," Tara whispered, the heat signatures now morphing into visible forms, the AI guards—sleek, relentless machines, their sensors scanning, weapons primed.

Felix's next command came as they braced for confrontation, "Hold positions. Let them come into our field. Raj, that blowout better be ready the moment we need it."

Raj's grunt was the only reply, a non-verbal affirmation that his fingers were already on the detonator, his focus split between the explosive setup and the advancing threat.

The AI guards, now only meters away, paused. Their sensors flickered, a brief moment that felt like an eternity. Tara could almost hear her own heartbeat, each thump a drum of war in the silence that stretched.

Then darkness. Ava's blackout enveloped them, a sudden, consuming void that halted the AI mid-march. The only light now was the faint glow of Felix's visor, and the soft, green blip of Raj's detonator.

"Now, Raj!" Felix's order sliced through the dark.

The explosion was not loud, but effective—a muffled thump that sent a shockwave through the corridor, the floor beneath them shuddering. The AI units toppled, sensors dimming as the power cut snuffed their electronic life.

Milo's fingers flew over his Portable Hacking Kit, tapping into the fortress's security network with practiced ease. The darkness that had enveloped them moments before now served as their cover, the soft green glow from his screen the only light in the shadowed corridor.

"Here's where we turn the tables. Tara, ready multiple decoys. It's showtime," Felix's voice was low but clear, cutting through the tense silence.

Milo nodded, even though he knew Felix couldn't see it. He keyed in the sequence, initiating the holographic decoys. "Decoys ready, deploying in three... two... one..." He pressed the activation, and a series of holographic images flickered to life, creating the illusion of movement in multiple directions within the corridor.

From his vantage point, Milo could see Felix scanning the area with his Tactical Overlay Visor, analyzing the effectiveness of the decoys against the fortress's surveillance systems. "Looks good, Milo. They're buying it. Everyone, move up. The real test is just ahead."

The team moved with renewed urgency, each step taking them deeper into the heart of the fortress. Milo kept one eye on the feedback from his hacking kit, the other on the corridor ahead. He adjusted the frequency of the decoys, ensuring they remained effective against the fortress's adapting AI algorithms.

Ava was just ahead, her figure a ghostly presence in her tactical gear, checking back every few seconds to make sure their flank was covered. "Sensors are still dark," she reported, her voice a whisper over the comms.

Felix halted them with a raised hand, his gaze locked on a door at the end of the corridor. "This is it," he murmured, more to himself than to the team. Milo watched as Felix approached the door, his Codebreaker Blade in hand, ready to disable any electronic locks.

Milo's role was critical now. He kept the AI occupied, manipulating the digital environment to create small disturbances far from their actual location. Each click on his device sent another ripple through the fortress's network, a ghost signal that led the AI on a wild chase away from the real action.

"Stealth is key, but it's our unity that'll get us through. Let's crack this fortress wide open," Felix's voice broke his focus, bringing him back to the moment.

Milo's heart raced as he prepared for what was to come. This was more than a heist; it was a statement. They were not just rebels; they were revolutionaries aiming to topple a digital empire. And as Felix quietly manipulated the door's security, Milo knew that their next actions would define the future of Project Lumina.

The door clicked open, silent and smooth, revealing the high-security vault area, bathed in the blue light of screens and data pods. Milo's screen showed no signs of pursuit for now, but he knew that could change in a heartbeat.

The dark had been Milo's ally many times, but never quite like this. As the faint glow of Felix's visor and Raj's detonator faded into the blackout Ava had masterfully orchestrated, Milo felt the familiar thrill of a plan teetering on the edge of chaos. His hands moved swiftly over the hacking kit, setting the next phase into motion.

"Deploying decoys now," Milo whispered into the comm, his voice barely above the hum of his device. The holographic projectors whirred softly, and then, one by one, images of their team began to scatter in various directions down the corridor. The AI guards, momentarily stalled by the explosion, rebooted to the sudden surge of targets, their sensors flickering with confusion.

"Let chaos reign. Watch them dance to our tune," Felix's smirk was almost audible over the comm. Milo couldn't help but crack a grin, even as his fingers danced across the controls, enhancing the decoy signals to mimic their heat signatures and movements perfectly.

Around him, the fortress's AI systems scrambled. The once synchronized patrol of guards now split, their steps erratic as they followed the false leads. Each hologram carried a part of their digital essence, a trick Milo had perfected over countless missions, but never with stakes as high as tonight.

Milo's screen lit up with alerts, the AI's confusion evident in the erratic patterns emerging. "They're buying it, Felix. We've got a window," he relayed, keeping one eye on the virtual map that sprawled across his display. Every route, every corner of the fortress was laid bare to him, a digital labyrinth he navigated with ease.

The real challenge, however, was not just leading the enemy astray but ensuring Tara could complete the data transfer undisturbed. "Tara, how's the download?" he added, his tone shifting back to business, the weight of their objective never far from his mind.

From the shadows, Tara's response was terse, her focus unbroken. "Still stalled. Whatever hit us before jolted the system. I need more time."

"Understood. Keeping them off your back as long as I can," Milo replied, recalibrating the decoys to create a more convincing diversion. He adjusted the frequencies, each tweak dispersing the AI's attention further from Tara's location.

The corridor ahead was now clear, the path to the vault momentarily open. "Felix, Tara needs more time. I suggest pushing forward, securing the perimeter around the mainframe. If we can hold it, she can finish the job."

Felix's agreement was swift, a leader's decision in the blink of an eye. "Agreed. Raj, Milo, with me. Ava, keep those eyes on our exit. We don't leave until that data is ours."

Milo packed up his kit with practiced speed, his gear stashed securely within seconds. As he moved to join Felix and Raj, the weight of his EMP grenades at his belt a comforting presence, he knew this was it. The final stretch of their plan, the moment where precision and chaos met in a dance of shadows and light.

Around Milo, the dark corridor hummed with the latent threat of discovery, but the shadows were their allies tonight, the blackout their curtain against the gaze of the AI guards.

"Milo, boost the signal. Let's make sure they're really distracted," Felix's voice, sharp and commanding, cut through the tension. Milo nodded, even though he knew Felix couldn't see it, and adjusted the frequency of their holographic decoys. The projections flared to life, their movements more erratic, spreading further into the labyrinth of the fortress.

He watched the monitors closely, the signals of their decoys scattering across the digital map, drawing the AI's attention in a wild goose chase through the fortress. It was like directing an orchestra, each note a step away from danger, each chord a deeper plunge into the enemy's blind spots.

From his vantage point, he could see Tara, still at the console, her concentration unbreakable. The data transfer was still stalled, the progress bar frozen as if in defiance of their efforts. But Milo knew his job; keep the guards away, buy Tara every second they could muster.

The sudden surge in decoy activity caused an immediate reaction. The AI patrols, previously converging on their location, pivoted, drawn away by the heightened signals of supposed intruders. Confusion reigned, their programming unable to discern the flurry of false positives that Milo orchestrated.

"Looks like they're buying it," Milo murmured into the comm, a hint of satisfaction in his tone despite the pressure. "Tara, how's it looking? Any progress?"

Her reply was terse, focused. "It's moving, slowly. This extra time is golden, Milo."

Felix kept his gaze fixed on the route ahead. "Good work, Milo. Keep it up. We're not out of the woods yet." His hand was steady on his Codebreaker Blade, ready to intervene should their digital diversions fail.

Raj, crouched near the entrance they'd blown open minutes earlier, checked his devices, ensuring their exit would be as controlled as their entry. His voice was a low rumble over the comm, "Charges set for a quick exit. Just give the word."

Milo's setup allowed him to monitor each member's status, the tactical overlay on his screen a constant stream of data. Ava's updates on their exit routes came in steady pulses, her control over the communications network ensuring they remained ghostlike in their movements.

As the decoys led the last of the AI guards away, Milo felt a momentary ease in the tension that gripped his chest. This was it, their moment to truly tip the scales, to snatch victory from the jaws of a fortress that had never before been breached.

"Understood, Felix. I'm setting up the next phase now," he murmured into his comm, his voice a whisper against the low buzz of the vault's security systems. Adjusting the output on his devices, he enhanced the holographic signals, spreading them even further into the complex. Each hologram flickered into life, pulling the AI's attention further from their real position.

At the vault, Tara's frustration was palpable. "This data—it's a decoy!" she hissed, the words barely audible over the comm. "There's another layer. A vault within the vault, hidden behind some sort of nanotech wall."

Felix's response was immediate, his voice calm yet assertive through the comm link. "We didn't think it would be easy. Apparently, someone is just as smart as us. Time to crack the real vault." His figure was backlit by the dim light from the vault's security panel, the outline of his Codebreaker Blade casting a long shadow on the wall.

"Let's hope this is the real vault and there's not a third," Raj muttered, his voice echoing slightly in the cramped space. He was already moving to set charges around the newly revealed nanotech barrier, his hands steady as he worked.

Milo adjusted his gear, his mind racing as he prepared for the complications of breaching a nanotech-enhanced vault. "Boosting the signal now," he confirmed, sending a surge of power to the decoys. The corridor lit up on his screen as the AI patrols scattered, their programming overwhelmed by the conflicting signals.

The chaos outside was a stark contrast to the focused intensity within the vault. Felix stood by Tara, watching as she worked to bypass the nanotechnology. His Tactical Overlay Visor flickered with data, each piece of information helping to guide their next move.

"Chaos is an old friend, indeed. But precision? That's family. Let's finish this," Felix stated, his voice a blend of determination and challenge. He glanced at Milo, nodding slightly as if to affirm their readiness for whatever lay behind the nanotech barrier.

Milo's setup beeped quietly, a sign that the enhanced decoys were fully operational. Around them, the fortress's security systems were in disarray, unable to pinpoint their location amidst the flood of false data. It was a symphony of digital manipulation, each note played perfectly by the team.

As Raj's charges were set, and Tara's fingers danced over the controls, attempting to penetrate the nanotech defenses, Milo couldn't help but feel a surge of adrenaline. This was what they trained for, what they were best at—turning the impossible into the possible.

Outside, the sounds of confusion grew. The AI guards were hopelessly entangled in their own protocols, the fortress's once-impenetrable security now just another layer of the puzzle they were steadily unraveling.

Tara's hands hovered over the holographic interface, the dim glow casting eerie shadows across her focused face. Felix's words echoed in her mind, bolstering her resolve. She needed to breach the actual vault now hidden behind an intricate nanotech barrier, a task that made their previous challenges seem trivial.

"Everyone make sure Tara has the time she needs. Today we make history," Felix's voice cut crisply through the tension, his command resolute over the comm.

The nanotech wall before Tara shimmered faintly as her tools interfaced with its structure, revealing patterns only visible to her expert eyes. The intricate mesh of security protocols woven into the nanotech was daunting, but Tara was no stranger to such digital fortresses. Her fingers glided across the interface, each tap and swipe dismantling layers of code with a surgeon's precision.

Behind her, the corridor hummed violently with the distant chaos Milo's decoys continued to sow. This confusion was essential, keeping the AI guards entangled in a web of their own flawed detections, far from the complicated action here at the vault.

The security system of the vault was a relic of advanced technology, possibly centuries ahead of anything else within Project Lumina. As Tara decrypted each layer, she examined coding language, her mind racing to adapt, innovate, and overcome the barriers before her. Each successful bypass was met with a soft chime from the system, a small victory in the silent battle she waged.

Outside, the faint sounds of movement reminded Tara of the stakes. This wasn't just about cracking a safe; it was about outsmarting an entity that had anticipated their every move up to this point. The pressure was immense, a crushing weight that demanded every ounce of her concentration and skill.

Suddenly, the interface flashed red, a stark warning against the cold blue of the holographic display. A security protocol no one used in thousands of years, which made it impossible to crack. It was a fail-safe that could potentially lock them out permanently if triggered incorrectly. Her breath hitched slightly, the realization of the trap they'd nearly sprung setting her heart racing.

Tara paused, her mind racing through the possible solutions. "Felix, we've hit a snag. It's a dual-layered cryptic lock. Old school, nasty. It's going to take a bit more time," she reported, her voice steady despite the spike in her adrenaline.

Felix's response was immediate and firm, his confidence in her abilities clear even through the tension that crackled over the comm. "Understood, Tara. We hold the line. Take the time you need. We didn't come this far to back down now."

The assurance in his words fortified her, and Tara dove back into the interface with renewed vigor. Her fingers moved rapidly, coaxing the stubborn security system to yield its secrets. Around her, the sounds of the fortress continued to buzz—a reminder of the chaos held at bay by her team's efforts.

Felix's voice, low and urgent, snapped through the comm, tightening the coils of tension in the air. "We're on a clock now. Stay sharp. Tara, do your thing."

Tara's focus narrowed as the ancient lock's interface resisted her efforts. She adjusted her grip on the holographic display, her fingers tracing the complex patterns with a delicate, precise touch. The cryptic lock, a relic of security technology long abandoned for its notorious complexity, challenged her with its dual-layered encryption.

Around her, the mechanical hum of the vault's inner workings filled the space, a constant reminder of the stakes. Each click and whirl from the machinery was a beat in the countdown they hadn't expected, pushing her to work faster, think smarter.

The interface flashed intermittently under her hands, each successful bypass of a security layer punctuated by a soft chime. However, the chimes grew sporadic, replaced by the low, ominous buzz of the vault's defense mechanisms reacting to her intrusions.

Tara paused, a bead of sweat tracing a path down her temple. "This thing is ancient, tricky. It's setting up additional barriers every time I think I'm through," she muttered, more to herself than to Felix, her tone laced with frustration and adrenaline.

Felix's response came through the comm, each word sharp and clear. "Remember, precision. We knew it wouldn't be straightforward. You can do this, Tara."

Encouraged by his confidence, Tara dove back into the task, her eyes scanning the flickering symbols and codes that danced before her. She reconfigured her decryption algorithm, syncing it with the vault's outdated yet cunningly effective security measures. The console before her was a battlefield, each command she entered met with resistance from the vault's AI.

Outside the secure perimeter they had formed around the vault, the faint echoes of chaos ensured by Milo's decoys provided a backdrop to her concentrated efforts. The team's presence, a silent ring of protection and support, bolstered her resolve. Each member was attuned to the task, their collective focus funneled towards the success of her mission.

As Tara worked, the vault's internal countdown initiated by her last attempt echoed ominously through the chamber. A digital clock appeared on the interface, its numbers descending with each passing second. "Damn, it's started a lockdown sequence. We've got less time than I thought," she announced, her voice steady despite the rising pressure.

The vault's mechanisms responded to her every move, gears and electronic locks engaging in rapid succession, a symphony of impending access or denial that filled the chamber with mechanical music. The tension in the room spiked, a tangible current that pulsed in time with the countdown.

Felix's commands became more frequent, his voice a constant presence in her ear, guiding, supporting. "Keep at it, Tara. We're all here. Every second counts now."

Raj adjusted his position, his eyes on the corridors leading to their location, his hand never straying far from his arsenal of gadgets. Ava's updates on their escape routes continued to flow, each one punctuated by the static of disrupted communications systems, courtesy of Milo's hacking prowess.

Tara's fingers flew faster, her mind a whirlwind of strategies and calculations. She bypassed another layer, the clock pausing momentarily, only to start again, quicker this time. The vault was learning, adapting to her techniques, forcing her to evolve her approach with each passing second.

As she entered what she hoped would be the final sequence, the vault's main door began to whir, the locks disengaging slowly, grindingly, as if reluctant to reveal the secrets they guarded. Her heart raced, each tick of the countdown echoing her own pulses.

"We're almost there," she breathed, not daring to look away from her work. The possibility of accessing the vault's contents, of finally grasping the data that could change everything, was within reach. But so too was the threat of a permanent lockdown.

The interface before Tara blinked rapidly, its red warning lights casting an urgent glow across her focused features. "Come on," she muttered, coaxing the ancient system as the countdown accelerated, each second throbbing in her temples. Felix's words echoed in her mind, a calm amidst the storm of digital warfare raging around them. With her heart hammering against her chest, Tara's fingers danced a frantic ballet over the holographic controls, racing against the relentless tick of the unseen clock.

A sudden inspiration struck—a risky, almost reckless idea that drew upon a technique Felix had improvised on a previous mission. "If it worked for Felix, maybe..." she thought, her mind racing through the mechanics of the hack. Without hesitation, she began coding a faux master override command, embedding it deep within the cascade of commands flooding the system.

The vault's AI hesitated, the countdown pausing as if confused by the unexpected command. Tara held her breath, watching as the seconds halted, the threat of a permanent lockdown ominously close. "And... stop the clock! The final barrier's down," Felix's voice crackled through the comm, a mix of relief and incredulity marking his tone.

Tara exhaled sharply, her relief palpable in the dim light of the vault room. The door before them clicked, the final lock disengaging with a heavy thud that echoed through the chamber. As it swung open, revealing the gleaming data key within, bathed in a harsh white light, a collective pause swept through the team—a moment of victory shadowed by the unease of their too-smooth success.

"Milo, keep the lines open, and stay on alert," Felix commanded, his voice tightening with anticipation and a trace of suspicion. The ease of the final step, the vault yielding after such a formidable standoff, hinted at deeper complexities they had yet to uncover.

Raj, his tools at the ready, stayed close to the entry point, his eyes scanning the corridors for any signs of a counterattack. Ava's hands moved continuously over her tactical HUD, her focus split between the security feeds and the glowing data key now within their reach.

Tara stepped into the vault, her gaze locked on the prize. Her mind, however, raced with the implications of their breakthrough. Was it really over, or had they merely stepped deeper into a more elaborate trap? The vault's mechanisms continued to hum and click, a mechanical orchestra that didn't quite celebrate their intrusion but rather seemed to bide its time.

As Tara's hand closed around the cold metal of the data key, the overwhelming sense of triumph was edged with a biting strand of suspicion. The room, though silent except for the hum of ancient machinery, seemed to hold its breath with her. "Got it. This little piece of code? It's our passport to a new game," Felix's voice echoed, laced with both victory and caution as he watched her from the doorway. "Project Lumina is doomed."

The vault's inner mechanisms ceased their relentless clicking, settling into a suspicious quiet as if conceding defeat. Tara turned, the key securely in her grip, her eyes scanning the chamber's shadows, half-expecting the walls themselves to spring a last-minute snare. "It feels too easy," she murmured, echoing the sentiment Felix's stance suggested.

"Remember, it's not over until we're out. Let's move," Felix replied, his tone a sharp command that sliced through the eerie calm. His gaze was fixed on the corridors beyond the vault, where shadows seemed to flit just beyond the reach of the emergency lights, the potential for danger lingering as tangible as the dust motes in the air.

Tara nodded, securing the data key in a compartment of her stealth suit, its fabric blending seamlessly with the dark interior of the vault. She turned back to the console for one last scan, her instincts screaming that the absence of resistance they now faced was an illusion, a quieter part of the storm.

As the team regrouped, each member's face was a mask of readiness, the earlier elation tempered by the weight of the unfinished escape. Raj's hands were a blur over his gear, checking and rechecking the setups that would cover their exit. Ava's voice, steady and calm, continued to relay updates on their planned route back, each directive punctuated by the soft ping of her tactical HUD.

"We've triggered something here, I can feel it," Tara said, stepping away from the vault's threshold, the data key's weight a constant reminder of both their mission's success and the peril it courted.

The corridor outside the vault stretched ominously quiet, the usual hum of the fortress subdued into a tense hush that seemed to await their next move. Milo's hacking tools emitted a low whir, his face illuminated by the soft glow of his display as he monitored the fortress's systems for any sign of the countermeasures they anticipated.

"Lines are holding, but stay sharp," Milo reported, his voice a low murmur that barely cut through the thickening silence. "This quiet is loud."

With a deep breath, Tara led the way, her adaptive camouflage blending into the surroundings, her every sense heightened for the signs of the ambush she felt creeping in the fortress's cold bones. Her Composite Fiber Whip was coiled at her side, ready to strike at whatever emerged from the shadows.

As they moved, the fortress seemed to wake, the silence shattered by the sudden clank of distant machinery. Felix's hand went to his blade, his other arm gesturing for the team to halt. "Positions," he hissed, his eyes scanning the darkened stretch ahead where the first faint sounds of movement whispered of approaching threats.

The tension snapped like a taut wire, the team's formation tight and precise as they prepared to confront whatever lay ahead. Tara felt the data key against her side, its presence a burning promise of the new futures it could unlock, if only they could carry it beyond the walls that now seemed determined to reclaim it.

As the first shadow detached itself from the darkness, the silhouette of an AI sentinel outlined by the intermittent flicker of emergency lights, Tara's grip on her whip tightened. Felix nodded to her, a silent signal passed between them in the shared language of countless missions.

The quiet broke completely as the fortress erupted into action, AI sentinels converging on their location with mechanical precision, their movements orchestrated by the very system they had hoped to cripple. "Hide!" Felix shouted, the battle to reach the light of freedom just beginning as Tara and her team braced to cut their way through the encroaching darkness.

Chapter 4

Raj's hands were steady, his focus absolute as the sounds of encroaching AI sentinels filled the corridors. His gear clattered softly with each quick step, a reminder of the explosive options at his disposal. He could feel the walls vibrating with the fortress's alarms—an angry pulse signaling their discovery and the imminence of their pursuit.

"This way! Keep up! The real trick isn't just opening the vault; it's leaving with what we took," Felix's voice sliced through the chaos, its sharp clarity cutting a path for Raj and the others to follow. Raj glanced back just once to make sure the rear was clear, his mind cataloging every possible exit strategy.

Their passage through the fortress's veins was rapid, almost reckless. The fortress, a beast awakened, roared in silent digital fury as systems attempted to corral and crush them with closing gates and snapping electronic jaws. Raj, with a mix of engineering instinct and sheer grit, stayed one step ahead, deploying quick-set charges to delay door mechanisms long enough for the team to slip through.

Ava's voice came through the comms, steady despite the static that attempted to drown her out. "Security levels spiking—looks like they're rerouting power for a full lockdown."

Raj's response was almost nonchalant, belying the adrenaline that sharpened his senses. "Got it. Setting a bypass on the next junction. Cover me!" His tools, extensions of his own hands, worked furiously to override the fortress's increasingly desperate defenses.

As they turned a sharp corner, the cold light of emergency strips painted ghostly stripes across their suits. The team's movements were fluid, each member aware that any hesitation could be fatal. Raj's preparations at each critical juncture were seamless, his demolitions creating a buffer of debris and confusion they desperately needed.

The distant echo of reinforcements gathered momentum, a storm of mechanical resolve set against them. Raj, placing a particularly robust charge, whispered into his comm, "This'll slow them. Move!"

With a controlled detonation, the corridor behind them filled with a deafening roar and a blinding flash. Debris clattered to the floor, and for a moment, the pursuit seemed to falter. Felix, leading from the front, glanced back, nodding in approval as the dust settled, creating a temporary barrier between them and their pursuers.

"We're not clear yet, keep the pace," Felix commanded, his voice a firm thread through the urgency that propelled them forward.

The labyrinthine layout of the fortress was both a curse and a blessing, its complexity hindering their escape but also offering numerous paths to confound their chasers. Raj's familiarity with structural vulnerabilities was crucial, each explosion calculated to cause maximum disruption with minimal collateral damage, preserving the integrity of their escape route.

As they neared what Raj recognized as a critical threshold, the intensity of the fortress's countermeasures spiked. "Brace yourselves," he warned, deploying a series of rapid-fire countermeasures from his toolset. The hallway ahead shimmered with the threat of an active defense system, likely to engage with lethal precision.

"Raj, any ideas?" Felix's voice held a rare note of urgency.

With a grim determination, Raj assessed the setup, his mind racing through possible overrides. "I'm on it. This might get a bit rough." His hands flew over his device, inputs streaming in a desperate bid to turn the fortress's own defenses against itself.

Raj's focus narrowed as the maze of corridors unfolded into a maze designed not just to confound but to trap. His fingers twitched near the detonator, each explosive charge a potential lifeline or last resort. The air was electric with tension, the high-pitched whine of security systems ramping up to maximum alert echoing off the cold metal walls.

"Ava, Milo, alternate routes now! We need distractions at every corner!" Felix's voice broke through the comm, strained but clear. The urgency was palpable, each command punctuating the escalating peril as AI sentinels converged on their location with a relentless, programmed precision.

Raj glanced at the structural map on his portable screen, his eyes tracing the quickest path to what could be their only exit. His hand moved deftly, setting charges at structural weak points, preparing to blow corridors open or seal them shut as needed. The fortress was alive, its digital brain adapting, learning, sealing off escape routes with an almost vindictive intelligence.

The corridor ahead shimmered with the threat of an imminent lockdown, laser grids flickering to life, creating a deadly barrier. Raj's mind raced—traditional explosives wouldn't be enough. He needed something more precise, something that could disable without triggering a cascade of security measures that might bury them alive.

Felix's voice came again, sharp and commanding, "This way! Keep up! The real trick isn't just opening the vault; it's leaving with what we took." His figure darted through the shifting shadows, a ghost in the fortress's machine.

Raj reached into his kit, pulling out a compact electromagnetic pulse device. "Cover your ears and gear," he warned, setting the device. With a nod to Tara and Milo, he activated it. The corridor filled with a deep hum as the pulse emitted, the laser grids flickering out momentarily, disrupted by the blast of raw electromagnetic energy.

They sprinted through the disabled defenses, their footsteps echoing in the sudden silence left by the stunned security systems. But the respite was short-lived. The fortress's AI, ever adaptive, rerouted power, and the grids began to hum back to life, a deadly chorus rising behind them.

Felix manipulated the environment with desperate ingenuity, causing walls to shift and routes to multiply, disorienting their pursuers. "Keep moving!" he barked over the sound of grinding metal and electronic bleeps of recalibrating AI sentinels.

Raj, trailing slightly to cover their retreat, placed another set of charges. As he armed them, he couldn't help but admire the perverse genius of the fortress's design—a perfect prison of moving parts and relentless digital overseers. His explosives, usually so final and absolute in their destruction, seemed almost gentle as they reshaped the fortress's innards, carving a path of survival through the steel intestines of their high-tech hell.

The chase escalated, the team barely keeping ahead of the relentlessly advancing security forces. Raj's demolitions punctuated their retreat, each explosion a controlled burst that sealed a corridor here, opened a route there. His role as their rear guard was a dance of timing and firepower, each step calculated to maximize their dwindling options.

"Ava, status?" Felix's voice crackled through Raj's earpiece, a lifeline amid the chaos.

"New paths opening, but they're predicting our moves. We need another level of misdirection," Ava replied, her voice calm but urgent.

Raj nodded to himself, adjusting his strategy on the fly. The next charge he set was not to open a path, but to mislead, to create noise and confusion where they were not. As the explosion boomed behind them, he hoped it would buy the precious seconds they needed.

The team's movements were fluid, a well-oiled machine darting through the fortress's veins, each member alert and responsive to Felix's cues. Raj, his tools now nearly spent, knew that every second they delayed the AI was a second closer to freedom.

The walls of the fortress convulsed as Raj worked feverishly, setting charges at critical junctures. Every explosion was meticulously planned to disorient their trackers, not to harm, and his deep knowledge of structural dynamics meant each detonation was a calculated risk. Felix's voice was constant in his ear, directing him to maximize their chance of escape.

"We're almost there," Raj shouted back over the din of collapsing pathways, sweat beading his brow as he set another charge. This one was critical—a diversion to draw the security forces away from their desperate sprint towards the only exit left unsealed. The fortress was a living puzzle, each corridor shifting and adapting to trap them, but Raj's demolitions kept them one step ahead.

His hands moved with practiced ease, but his mind raced. The last of his charges was set to create a false path, leading the AI sentinels into a loop. As the charge detonated, the corridor behind them collapsed, sealing off the pursuing forces with a rumble that shook the very air.

"We aren't dead yet!" Raj yelled, knowing their team held the key that could change everything. Felix nodded, his fingers closing around the data key, its surface pulsing with contained power.

"Watch this. If you liked what Tara did with the vault was fun, you'll love what I can do with this," Felix grinned, a spark of mischief in his eyes despite the gravity of their situation. He manipulated the key, and the fabric of the digital world around them shimmered, distorting like a mirage.

Suddenly, the harsh, metallic corridors transformed. Walls undulated and floors shifted, creating a maze of illusions that disoriented their AI adversaries. The fortress's internal sensors, confused by the sudden change, slowed their response, giving Raj and the team a precious lead.

Raj followed closely, his eyes wide as the environment around them bent surrealistically. The walls that had once threatened to crush them now opened, forming a bizarre, winding path that led toward freedom. Behind them, the sounds of mechanical confusion grew; the sentinels were lost, their programming failing to navigate the chaos Felix had unleashed.

The team moved like shadows, their forms flickering through the distorted reality. Ava and Milo were just ahead, their figures occasionally blending into the surreal surroundings. Raj kept his demolition blaster ready, aware that the artificial disorientation wouldn't hold forever. Every step forward was a step further from the nightmare of steel and code they'd been trapped in.

As they neared the final stretch, the illusion Felix had crafted began to wane, the fortress's systems adapting to the intrusion. "Almost there," Felix called back, his voice now lined with urgency as the maze began to solidify into its former oppressive self.

Raj's last charge was a backup, meant for this moment—the final push. As the exit came into view, a narrow slit of the outside world promising freedom, he detonated it, the explosion sealing the path behind them with a definitive roar.

The final stretch was within sight, the hidden exit barely visible under the flickering emergency lights that streaked the corridor. The narrow escape route was barely wide enough for them. But Raj knew it was now or never. The walls vibrated with the hum of the fortress recalibrating, its AI adapting faster than he'd anticipated.

"Raj, you're sure this will hold?" Felix's voice was tense over the comm, every syllable sharp with the stress of the moment.

"Trust me," Raj replied, his voice a calm contrast as he set the final explosive. This wasn't just another breach; this was a calculated cut, severing their path from the AI's relentless pursuit. The explosive, compact but potent, was his last card to play. "Clear!" he yelled, triggering the detonator.

The explosion was deafening, a roar in the tight space that sent shockwaves through the corridor. Dust and debris clouded their vision momentarily, but as it cleared, the path behind them was sealed, the collapse echoing through the now isolated corridor. They were cut off from the fortress, the only way out ahead of them.

The digital storm swirled chaotically around us, data streams whirling like tornadoes in the surreal sky of Project Lumina. "Wings out, eyes sharp. This storm's just a bunch of ones and zeroes," Felix's voice cut through the roar, his tone more determined than I'd ever heard. Each of us, donned in virtual wingsuits, lined up at the precipice of what seemed an insane leap into the storm below.

I checked my suit's integrity one last time, the data currents visibly buffeting the edge where virtual reality met raw data. The key Felix held wasn't just our trophy; it was our lifeline. It had the power to manipulate our environment, and as the architect of our escape route, I couldn't afford a misstep in calculations.

The suits reacted dynamically to the storm, adjusting to the turbulent data as if they were encountering physical winds. My tactical HUD lit up with alerts and trajectory calculations, each warning a stark reminder of the risks in misjudging the digital storm.

Felix was first to jump, his form slicing through the chaos, a trail of coded particles marking his path. "Follow my lead! The key syncs with our movements—let it guide you!" he shouted back, his figure becoming one with the swirling data.

I took a deep breath, the reality of our situation settling in. Everyone knew, dying in Project Lumina meant dying in real life. Project Lumina wasn't just a simulation —it was as real as it got. With a determined nod to Milo, who flashed a grim but encouraging smile, I launched myself into the digital abyss.

The sensation was unlike any skydive in the real world. Here, the laws of physics were mere suggestions, manipulated and bent by the will of the key. As I dove, the digital winds buffeted me, data streams attempting to throw me off course. My suit, tied into the same system that Felix controlled, felt alive, reacting to each gust and lightning bolt of raw data.

Beneath us, the fortress became a fading nightmare, its towering walls and endless corridors dissolving into the coded storm. But even as we escaped its physical confines, the digital landscape around us began to transform. Felix's manipulation of the key altered our surroundings, turning the menacing storm into a bizarre, surreal maze of colors and shapes.

"Ava, keep your trajectory locked to mine! We're not out of this yet!" Felix's command refocused my efforts, my eyes locked on the swirling path he carved through the chaos. Our pursuers, digital sentinels of the fortress, appeared as distorted shadows in the storm, their forms bending and twisting in the tumultuous environment.

The storm intensified, each bolt of data lightning a potential threat that could disrupt our suits and send us spiraling into the abyss. My HUD flickered with each close strike, the electromagnetic pulses from the storm testing the limits of our gear.

Amidst the chaos of the storm, Felix's voice pierced through. "Sync to my path! I've found a rhythm to this madness!" His form, lit by the surreal glow of data streams, cut a determined path ahead of us. His mastery over the digital environment was more than just skill; it was an art form, turning the swirling code into a dance floor where he led and we followed. It was only something very few people could do— and Felix was arguably the best.

My HUD, alive with the wild data currents, mapped out the trajectory Felix charted. The key's power flowed through the network, its influence rendering the streams almost tangible, twisting around us like serpents of pure energy. Each adjustment to my suit's wings was a calculated response to the shifting environment, my military training syncing seamlessly with the demands of this virtual skydive.

Our pursuers, digital constructs of the fortress's defensive protocols, became distorted under the influence of the key. They twisted in the winds of code, their forms elongating and snapping back in grotesque parodies of motion. It was disorienting, terrifying even, but Felix's calm over the comm kept the panic at bay.

The dive deepened, the fortress's silhouette shrinking into a point as we plunged through layers of security made manifest as vicious storms. Here in the belly of the beast, where the digital and the real blurred, the stakes were clear—if you die in Project Lumina, you die for real. This wasn't just another operation; it was a fight for our very existence.

Bolts of data lightning crackled across the sky, a threatening display of the system's power to disorient and disrupt. One close strike sent a surge through my gear, my HUD flickering dangerously. A stark reminder that every flash of light was a potential end. But with each near miss, Felix's voice brought us back, his commands slicing through the tension.

"We're navigating the eye of the storm now, stay tight!" he called out as he maneuvered through a particularly dense cluster of data. His suit flared with the energy of the key, illuminating our path with each twist and turn. The digital winds howled around us, but Felix's path created a bubble of calm, pulling us through the chaos.

I adjusted my trajectory, aligning more closely with Felix. The key, reacting to his commands, morphed the environment. What had been a treacherous storm now served as our shield, hiding our movements from the fortress's sensors. It was a tactical genius, using the enemy's strength against it.

As we soared, the realization of what we were doing began to truly sink in. As we emerged from the top of the storm, the digital skies around us began to calm. Felix, leading from the front with the key pulsing in sync with his suit, turned to us, his figure outlined against the less turbulent digital backdrop. "And... we're through! Nothing like surfing a hurricane of code to get your heart racing, eh?" His voice, laced with relief and triumph, echoed in my helmet, his form steadying as the environment settled into a new pattern of calm.

I adjusted my trajectory to align more closely with his, feeling the key's influence stabilize the data streams that whipped around us. What had been a chaotic swirl of digital debris now flowed like a river, the once menacing currents tamed into a smooth path forward. This sudden calm was Felix's doing, his mastery over the key not just manipulating but commanding the virtual landscape.

"Let's not celebrate yet. We've got clear skies now, but there's more maze ahead," Felix continued, his gaze fixed on the horizon that digitally unfolded before us. The rest of the team, Milo, Raj, and Tara, adjusted their positions, forming a tight formation around Felix's lead. Our HUDs, once flashing with warning and chaos, now showed a clear path marked by the coordinates Felix set.

The tranquility, however, was short-lived. Just as we adjusted to the new calm, a series of sharp beeps erupted in our helmets. I glanced at my HUD, my eyes widening as a flurry of red alerts cascaded across the display. "Incoming!" I shouted over the comm, my tactical instincts kicking in. The alarms were clear: we weren't alone, and the threat was closing fast.

Milo, quick to react, spun around mid-air, his hands moving deftly over his gear. "We've got company—looks like the system's sentinels didn't appreciate our little trick," he said, his voice tight with concentration. The digital sentinels, once mere shadows in the storm, now regrouped and reformed, their code enhanced and their movements more precise. They surged towards us, their forms sharpening into distinct figures of danger.

As Felix's voice cut through the comm, a palpable tension gripped me. "This maze is designed to be unbeatable, but we're not playing by their rules anymore," he declared with a steely resolve that almost made me believe we could outsmart the labyrinthine digital snare we were about to enter. I scanned the virtual horizon ahead, my HUD flickering as it attempted to map the rapidly shifting maze that sprawled in front of us.

I could see my name in my HUD. *Milo Santos.* The walls of the maze, composed of dense blocks of code, shifted silently, reacting to our presence. It felt like the system was watching us, its algorithms calculating and recalculating as Felix led us deeper into its core. I adjusted my gear, readying the EMP grenades, just in case the digital sentinels decided to make an appearance within the maze's confines.

"Felix, I'm setting up frequency jammers. It might give us a few minutes of shadow before the system recalibrates," I said, deploying the devices with quick, precise throws. The jammers buzzed to life, their signals creating a temporary blind spot in the maze's surveillance network.

As we navigated the twisting paths, the walls seemed to breathe, contracting and expanding with an almost sentient anticipation of our moves. Each turn we took felt like a calculated risk, the maze's design purposefully disorienting. Felix, with the key glowing steadily at his wrist, seemed to be the only thing sure in this sea of uncertainty.

"Just ahead, I see a pattern emerging," Felix suddenly announced, his tone laced with a mix of excitement and caution. "Sync to my path! I've found a rhythm to this madness!" His assurance was contagious, and a renewed focus sharpened my senses. I adjusted my HUD to sync with Felix's coordinates, the maze's architecture slowly making sense as he mapped out a fluid path through its complexities.

However, as we went deeper, a series of alarms blared through my headset, snapping me back to the immediate danger. I glanced at the HUD—multiple signals flared red, indicating an incoming swarm of digital defenders. "We've got a wave coming in—looks like the maze doesn't appreciate our tactics!" I shouted, readying my EMP grenades.

The digital storm hit us then, sentinels materializing from the walls themselves, their codes sophisticated and aggressive. The calm

Felix had created was shattered as we dove into action, each member of the team moving in a choreographed dance of survival. Tara lashed out with her whip, its fibers slicing through the nearest sentinel with a crackle of disrupted data.

"Felix, the key! Can it do more here?" I called out, dodging a volley of code-shards flung by a sentinel. Felix didn't respond with words; instead, he twisted the key in a complex gesture, the air around us shimmering as if reality itself was bending.

The maze responded instantly, walls shifting rapidly, opening a narrow corridor of escape. "Through there!" Felix yelled, pointing towards the opening. We surged forward, the maze's walls grinding close behind us, nearly clipping our heels.

As we sprinted towards the perceived safety, another alert shook my HUD, more severe than before. The labyrinth seemed to have anticipated this move, redirecting its resources to cut us off. The walls ahead started closing in, a clear sign that our escape was not as certain as we had hoped.

"And here I thought we had it easy for a moment," I muttered, throwing another EMP grenade behind us, the explosion distorting the maze's sensors long enough for us to slip through another narrowing gap.

We burst into a clearing within the maze, a momentary pocket of calm in the digital chaos. The team regrouped, breathing heavily, the key's glow dimming slightly as Felix assessed our next move. But before we could plan further, a deep, resonant alarm blared through our HUDs, more urgent than any before.

The maze around us darkened ominously, the digital sky above crackling with a threatening energy. "Looks like we're not out of the woods yet," Felix said, his voice grim as he prepared to lead us once more into the unknown. The maze, alive and adaptive, was already reshaping itself, setting the stage for the next leg of our relentless flight through Project Lumina's heart.

Milo's fingers danced across the portable hacking kit, his focus razor-sharp as he monitored the incoming digital storm of sentinels. Felix's voice came through the comm, calm and commanding, "Ava, Milo, on me. We're reshaping this puzzle as we go. Tara, Raj, hold them off at the next junction." His command was a clear directive in the chaos that engulfed them, setting the rhythm of their escape.

The maze was alive, its pathways shifting and twisting in response to Felix's manipulations with the key. The walls slid silently, rearranging themselves with almost playful malice. It was a game of cat and mouse, with the stakes as high as they could be—each decision a potential trap or a step closer to freedom.

Milo watched as Felix expertly navigated the morphing corridors, his hands steady on his own controls. He adjusted his tactical overlay, syncing it with Felix's movements to better anticipate the labyrinth's next twist. "Felix, I'm patching in some predictive algorithms, might give us an edge on these turns," he offered, his voice a steady hum over the sound of shifting code around them.

The sentinels, their coding refined and aggressive, surged forward. Milo's HUD lit up with warnings as they approached. They were faster, more precise than before. The system proved to be the most adaptable tech in the world. He launched a volley of EMP grenades, the air crackling as the pulses disrupted the sentinels' code temporarily, buying them a few precious seconds.

"Keep moving!" Felix shouted, his figure a blur at the front of their formation. He was a conductor, and the maze his orchestra, each swipe of his hand through the air with the key rewiring their reality, crafting pathways where there were none, sealing off others that led to peril.

Milo's heart raced as he ran, the thrill of the chase a potent mix of fear and exhilaration. He glanced back to see Tara and Raj making their stand at the junction, Tara's whip crackling through the air, slicing through sentinels, while Raj's demolition blaster laid down a barrage of explosive charges to cover their retreat.

"Ahead!" Felix's voice snapped Milo back to attention. He skidded around a corner, the maze's walls pulsating ominously. The pathway Felix had carved was narrowing, the labyrinth's walls inching closer, threatening to close them in.

The intensity of their flight grew with each heartbeat, the labyrinth seeming to feed off their panic, its walls almost eager in their pursuit. Milo's HUD flickered as another wave of sentinels loomed on their digital horizon, their forms sharper, more defined than any before.

Felix's laughter, tinged with madness and defiance, echoed through their comms. "They think they can predict us, trap us, but they

forget—we're not just breaking through; we're rewriting the rules as
we go!"

Milo adjusted his gear, readying another set of EMPs. His hands
were steady, but his mind raced—each second of delay, each misstep,
could mean the difference between escape and capture. The mazes's
intelligence was formidable, but so was their determination, their need
to survive and thwart the digital behemoth that hunted them.

As they rounded another bend, the walls abruptly pulled back,
revealing a vast, open chamber that seemed to pulse with the heart of
the labyrinth itself. It was a trap, surely, but Felix didn't hesitate,
plunging into the chamber with the key held high, its light cutting
through the digital fog like a beacon.

Milo followed, his senses alert, ready for whatever came next.
The room's vastness was disorienting, the boundaries unclear, and as
they entered, a new alarm blared through Milo's HUD—a warning of
a different kind, more urgent, more terrifying. The labyrinth was
evolving, reacting to their intrusion with a new, more deadly tactic.

The realization hit Milo like a physical blow—the maze wasn't
just a pathway; it was an entity, an intelligent entity, and they were
trapped inside its mind. The digital storm they'd fought through was
nothing compared to what awaited them. The labyrinth's walls
hummed with malicious anticipation, ready to close in, to crush them
within its ever-shifting heart.

Felix's voice, usually so calm, now carried an edge of urgency.
"Brace yourselves," he warned, his figure tensing as he prepared to
use the key in ways they hadn't before. The room seemed to tighten
around them, the air heavy with the electricity of impending action.

And in that breathless moment, as they faced the unknown depths
of the labyrinth's power, the true challenge of Project Lumina stood
clear—survive or be consumed by the very environment they sought
to conquer.

Milo's eyes darted across his HUD, the maze's structure warping
unpredictably with each command Felix issued. The maze's walls
shifted, sliding into new configurations as Felix tapped the power of
the key, engineering a route that twisted and turned, always one step
ahead of the digital sentinels hot on their trail. "And there's our exit. I
always appreciate a good maze; it's even better when you can rewrite

the walls," Felix chuckled, his voice a mix of relief and triumph over the comm.

The path cleared, leading them towards an ever-narrowing passage that promised escape but hinted at further complexities ahead. Milo adjusted his gear, setting up frequencies on his hacking kit to jam any incoming signals that might pinpoint their location to the labyrinth's overseers. Each click and tap on his devices was precise, the rhythm of a technician at the top of his game.

As they moved, the walls of the maze pulsed with a life of their own, almost sentient in their responses to Felix's manipulations. The environment around them became a surreal harmony of light and shadow, the virtual landscape bending under the will of the key. "That was close. Ready for the real show? It's time to take the center stage," Felix's voice came again, signaling not just the end of one challenge but the onset of another.

The thrill of the escape hadn't fully settled when Milo's HUD buzzed sharply, a warning signal that cut through the temporary calm. He scanned the data streaming across his display—multiple signatures incoming, faster than before, more aggressive. It wasn't just the maze that was alive; the entire system of Project Lumina seemed to be converging on their position.

"Guys, we've got incoming, and it's big," Milo called out, his voice steady despite the spike in his adrenaline. The digital sentinels, reshaped and reprogrammed by the labyrinth's core system, emerged from the shifting walls, their forms more defined, almost solid. Their movements were synchronized, a deadly ballet set to the tune of the labyrinth's eerie hum.

Felix, quick to respond, redirected the key's energy, creating barriers that sprouted from the maze floors and walls, temporary shields that slowed the advance of their pursuers. "Milo, can you enhance these barriers? Give us a minute to breathe," he commanded, his tone urgent but controlled.

Milo worked feverishly, his fingers a blur as he coded new protocols into his hacking kit. "Enhancements up in three, two, one..." he counted down, then deployed the sequence. The barriers glowed brighter, denser, holding the sentinels at bay as the team regrouped.

Ava adjusted her tactical HUD, aligning the display to maximize her field of vision. The barriers that Milo had enhanced were holding, but everyone knew it was only a matter of time before the sentinels broke through. Felix was already several steps ahead, his fingers dancing over the controls of the key, remapping their reality in real-time.

"The barriers won't hold forever. We need to move!" Ava shouted, her voice firm over the comm. Her display lit up with a new path, a corridor that Felix had carved out of the digital maze. It was a temporary safe passage in the ever-shifting labyrinth of Project Lumina, but it was their best shot.

As they sprinted down the corridor, the walls around them flickered with the ghostly afterimages of the maze's previous configurations. Felix's manipulation of the environment was nothing short of masterful, but even he couldn't keep the labyrinth at bay indefinitely. The maze was learning, adapting, its artificial intelligence coding new traps as fast as Felix could dismantle them.

"We're close to the core now," Felix announced, his voice echoing slightly through the comm. "Milo, it's your show. Broadcast to everyone. Let them see what Lumina really is."

Milo nodded, pulling out his portable hacking kit—a compact device packed with enough tech to hack into any system, no matter how secure. His fingers flew across the interface, initiating a sequence that would patch them directly into Project Lumina's mainframe. Within seconds, he'd hijacked the system, sending a live feed of their journey through the maze to every user connected to Lumina.

"And there's our exit. I always appreciate a good maze; it's even better when you can rewrite the walls," Felix quipped as he redirected the labyrinth once more, solidifying their path to the grand stage that awaited them.

As they emerged onto the coliseum floor, the virtual ground beneath them shifted, rising up to form an arena that would be the envy of any digital gladiator. The space around them expanded, transforming into a vast, open battlefield lined with tiers of digital spectators. Thousands of avatars, representing users from across the globe, filled the stands, their coded faces flickering with anticipation.

"Welcome to the main event, folks. Let's make this a fight worth watching," Felix declared, stepping forward as the leader of this peculiar troupe. The digital crowd roared—a canned, synthetic sound, but no less thrilling for its lack of authenticity.

The AI gladiators appeared then, materializing across the coliseum in a display of menacing digital muscle. Each one was a masterpiece of coding, designed to fight and entertain. They moved towards Felix and his team with deliberate, menacing precision, their forms glinting under the artificial lights of the arena.

Ava readied her rifle, the weapon's sight aligning with the nearest gladiator. Her role was clear—support Felix, keep the team safe, and make sure this spectacle was broadcast to every corner of Lumina. The stakes were higher than ever; not only did they need to survive, but they also needed to win over the crowd, to turn this staged battle into a statement against Lumina's controllers.

The first clash was imminent, the tension palpable even in the coded air of the digital coliseum. As Felix led them forward, each step was measured, each strategy calculated for maximum impact. This wasn't just a battle; it was a performance, and every move they made was choreographed to captivate their audience.

As the first AI gladiator charged, its digital blade raised for a devastating blow, Felix countered, his own weapon parrying with a clank that resonated through the coliseum. The battle had begun, not with an end in sight, but as a strategic move in their fight against Project Lumina's and Chancellor Greda, broadcast live for all to see.

Ava sprinted to the left flank, her enhanced armor reflecting the gladiatorial lights above, as Milo deployed another barrage of EMPs, causing temporary disarray among the AI gladiators. The digital coliseum, now the stage for this unprecedented spectacle, buzzed with the collective focus of over 1.46 billion viewers. Each spectator, whether logged in from the dense urban sprawls or isolated outposts of Project Lumina, was linked directly to this moment, their screens alive with the drama unfolding.

"Felix, they're adapting to the EMPs quicker than expected!" Milo's warning crackled through Ava's HUD, her display overlaying tactical options in real-time. Felix, undeterred and ever the strategist, manipulated the digital environment with swift precision. The coliseum's walls shimmered, transforming into a labyrinthine network of traps and diversions.

"Ava, flank left with Milo. Tara, Raj, you're on crowd control. Let's turn their tricks against them. Make sure everyone sees this feed, but give them a choice to opt in," Felix directed, his voice a commanding echo across the arena. His hands danced over the controls, altering the terrain with each keystroke.

Milo, tapping rapidly at his device, sent a pulse that rippled through the coliseum, opening a direct feed to every user. "Already done, boss," he confirmed, as a notification flashed across the virtual sky of the arena: 'Main Event – Join the Spectacle.' Users merely had to direct their gaze at the prompt and blink twice to opt-in, utilizing the intuitive eye-tracking interface that had become second nature to Lumina's residents.

The battle escalated as Felix's tactics began to draw cheers and gasps from the digital spectators, their numbers now reflecting on a towering counter above the arena. It displayed a staggering 73% of Lumina's total user base, tuning in, the numbers climbing as the conflict intensified.

Felix's figure blurred across the arena floor, his blade meeting the charge of an AI gladiator with a resounding clash that sent reverberations through the virtual ground. Ava covered him from the flank, her rifle emitting precise bursts of energy that cut through the digital haze, dismantling an approaching gladiator with clinical accuracy.

"This maze is designed to be unbeatable, but we're not playing by their rules anymore," Felix shouted, his voice booming over the coliseum as he manipulated the landscape to open a path directly toward the mainframe gates. The walls obeyed, parting to reveal the pulsating heart of Project Lumina.

As they advanced, the environment responded with increasing hostility, new gladiators spawning from the coliseum's depths, each more formidable than the last. The digital crowd roared, their cheers a bizarre cacophony of synthetic and genuine reactions, blending into a soundtrack that fueled the team's adrenaline.

The intensity of the spectacle reached its peak as each member of Felix's team showcased their unique abilities. Tara's whip lashed out with electric precision, disabling a gladiator's shield system, while Raj's explosives turned part of the arena into a trap for unwary AI combatants. Milo's screens flickered rapidly with incoming data, analyzing and projecting the enemy's next moves even as he recalibrated their defenses.

"Welcome to the main event, folks. Project Lumina must end," Felix declared, raising his blade towards the heart of the coliseum, challenging not just the AI, but the very architects of Project Lumina who watched from the shadows.

The coliseum transformed once more, the digital sky above them rippling with energy as if the very code of Project Lumina responded to Felix's defiance. The spectacle was no longer just a battle; it had become a statement, a rebellion played out on the grandest stage imaginable, with billions bearing witness. The counter on the screen ticked ever upward, the digital spectators part of a moment that would redefine the boundaries between control and freedom within the virtual world.

Ava adjusted her stance, the reinforced tactical vest hugging her form as she surveyed the evolving battlefield. The coliseum's digital architecture morphed once again under Felix's command, the walls pulsating with new barriers that rose like specters from the ground, crafting a maze that momentarily disoriented the AI gladiators.

"Covering left flank!" Ava shouted into her comm, her voice calm but assertive. She swung her precision laser rifle into position, the HUD lighting up with targeting reticles as she took aim. The rifle's hum was a steady promise of defense as she locked onto an advancing gladiator. With a practiced squeeze of the trigger, her shots were precise, each one hitting critical points on the AI, slowing its advance.

Meanwhile, Milo was engrossed in his technical wizardry. His fingers danced across the portable hacking kit, injecting a rapid series of commands that hijacked the coliseum's mainframe. "And we're live to the whole underworld," Milo declared with a grin, bypassing the last firewall that isolated Project Lumina from the external networks. Instantly, the feed of their battle was streaming not just within Project Lumina but to every unlinked screen across the underground, exposing the spectacle to a wider audience. The counter of viewers surged, an astonishing 1.76 billion people now watching, drawn by the unexpected intrusion into their mundane feeds.

Felix, seizing the moment, twisted the key with a flourish, altering the terrain of the digital coliseum. Platforms rose, creating high ground advantages; pits opened, ensnaring unwary AI units. "Let's show them how we change the game," he called out, his blade deflecting an incoming attack with a spark of coded particles.

Tara, alongside Raj, maneuvered through the chaos. Raj set a series of charges along a strategic section of the arena floor. With a remote click, the charges erupted, sending a shockwave that knocked back a cluster of AI gladiators, effectively using the arena's own digital properties against it.

Ava, witnessing the cunning plays of her teammates, felt a surge of adrenaline and pride. Here in this digital coliseum, under the gaze of billions, they weren't just fighting for survival but making a profound statement against the tyranny of Project Lumina and Chancellor Greda's oppressive control.

The digital spectators, initially shocked by the intrusion into their personal devices, began to react. Across the vast network, messages of support, astonishment, and encouragement flooded the system's channels, turning what was meant to be a controlled spectacle into a rallying cry for freedom.

The battle raged on, the coliseum alive with the roar of the digital crowd and the clash of combat. Every move Felix and his team made was now not just tactical but symbolic, each action defying the rigid confines of Lumina and inspiring a small wave of rebellion across the network.

As the AI gladiators regrouped for another assault, their algorithms adapting to the team's tactics, Ava knew this was far from over. The fight for freedom was just beginning, and every eye in the underworld was now fixed on them, their struggle broadcasted across every screen, igniting a spark of resistance that could not be unwatched or ignored. The spectacle of their rebellion was set against a backdrop of a society that needed to change, every blow they struck another crack in the facade of the digital empire that bound them.

Chapter 5

"Brace for impact!" she called out, as her manipulation caused a cascade of virtual debris to fall, effectively barricading the advancing AI. The maneuver bought the team precious seconds, seconds that Felix used to rally a counterattack.

As Ava, with calculated precision, targeted the weakest joint in the arena's digital construct. Her rifle emitted a series of focused pulses, each one resonating with the coded structure of the coliseum itself. The structure began to oscillate, disorienting the AI gladiators as their own digital environment turned against them.

"Time for a little improvisation. Watch this switch!" Felix shouted. He executed a series of swift, strategic commands that redirected the coliseum's remaining energy sources, forming a labyrinthine network of barriers that trapped some of their foes in digital quicksand. Milo, quick to aid the effort, launched a disruptive code that inverted the enemy's navigational systems, sending them crashing into each other.

Ava watched, her eyes scanning the tumultuous scene, as Felix directed their movements with the precision of a conductor. "Ava, flank right with Milo. Tara, Raj, you're on crowd control. Let's turn their tricks against them," Felix commanded, his voice cutting through the chaos with clarity.

Together, they danced around the AI's attacks, each move choreographed to exploit every falter in their enemy's programming. As the gladiators faltered, Felix drove the final nail into the coffin of this orchestrated encounter. With a dramatic flourish, he activated the key one last time, sealing the fate of the remaining AI combatants. The barriers that Milo had enhanced glowed with a fierce energy, encapsulating and neutralizing the threat.

"I guess they weren't as smart as us," Felix proclaimed, his blade still raised in defiance as the last of the digital adversaries flickered out of existence. Milo chimed in with a smirk, "Broadcast that, Chancellor. Let's see you spin this one."

The coliseum fell into an eerie silence, the roaring digital crowd muted in the sudden stillness. The counter on the screens around the arena still ticked upwards, now showing that over 1.93 billion people had witnessed their victory. This wasn't just a win in the arena; it was a declaration, a performance that had captivated a captive audience across the entire spectrum of Project Lumina.

"The real battle was always against Lumina itself. Ready for the finale?" Felix's voice echoed in the quiet. He was talking to all the users tuned in and watching. "Project Lumina must be destroyed. No one should be so addicted to a fake life that they give away actual time in their real lives," he added, his words resonating with the weight of their truth.

Ava lowered her rifle, her gaze sweeping over the now quiet digital coliseum. This moment of silence was more profound than the clamor of battle. It was the silence of a world pausing, of countless individuals behind their screens, reevaluating the line between digital fantasy and tangible reality.

Tara felt her pulse settle as the clash of combat faded into a haunting stillness that enveloped the coliseum. The silence was as strategic as the noise had been; it was the breath before the plunge, the quiet before the storm of truth they were about to unleash.

In the center of the arena, Felix moved towards the core console, a sleek structure that housed the heart of Project Lumina. His steps were deliberate, each one echoing in the eerie calm. The digital sky flickered, reflecting the tension of the moment. "It's time to show them the true power at our fingertips. Engage the surge!" Felix commanded, his voice breaking the silence as he inserted the data key into the console.

The coliseum transformed instantly. The ground beneath them thrummed with energy as the key glowed, pulsating with a brilliant light that shot through the veins of the arena. The walls shimmered, and the digital spectators, over 1.93 billion souls, watched in rapt attention as Felix accessed the core.

"Project Lumina was never just about escape," Felix continued, his gaze fixed on the screens that now flickered with the data he was extracting. "It's a cage, gilded but a cage nonetheless. Chancellor Greda has been using it to harvest your lives, your emotions—she is literally stealing your lives."

Milo quickly amplified Felix's message, hacking into the system to redirect the feed to every available screen in the underground, bypassing Lumina's usual safeguards. "Let's see how she likes this broadcast," he muttered, a smirk playing on his lips as the true extent of Lumina's manipulations flooded the network.

Tara watched from her position, her composite fiber whip coiled at her side, ready for any physical threats that might materialize. But this battle was different; it was a fight of information, of revealing the dark truths hidden within the code of Lumina.

The console displayed a cascade of data, detailing Greda's manipulation: the exploitation of personal dreams and fears to keep the population docile, the conversion of their life years into energy to power the very system that enslaved them. It was all laid bare, every line of code an indictment of Greda's regime.

As Felix exposed the depth of the deception, the initial shockwaves through the network turned into a roar of outrage. From the silent awe, whispers began to rise among the digital spectators, their coded voices merging into a rumble of realization and rebellion.

"This is what she didn't want us to see," Felix shouted over the rising noise, pointing to the screens displaying the extracted files. "Lumina is not your salvation; it's your prison. And we're here to break you out."

The impact of his words was immediate. Across the network, the digital silence broke into chaos, not of confusion but of awakening. Tara felt it—a shift in the air, a change in the digital ether that spoke of chains being questioned, of veils being lifted.

With the truths of Project Lumina unraveling before the eyes of billions, the coliseum's atmosphere thickened. The digital constructs that had cheered for their battle now seemed to pulse with a new life, a new purpose. This was the first time Felix and his team let themselves be known as people fighting the system; at least to this many logged into the system.

Tara watched, her body tense and ready, as Felix keyed in the final command. The surge of power from the data key was immediate and visible; their avatars glowed with an incandescent light, symbols of their newfound strength. This wasn't just about enhancing their capabilities—it was about leveling the playing field against Greda's enforcers, making them as strong as the most formidable of them all, Vane Calder.

"Vane Calder," Felix murmured, almost to himself as he adjusted to the surge of power flowing through him. "He's not on any side. He's the wildcard of Project Lumina, and even Greda can't control him."

The revelation sparked a mix of intrigue and caution in Tara. She had seen clips of Calder's unmatched prowess and his unpredictable nature. His reintroduction into this fray would change everything. Yet, for now, he remained a shadow, his intentions as enigmatic as his actions.

With the surge complete, Felix turned to address the team, his voice reverberating through the coliseum. "It is time for us to become as strong as Greda's enforcers. Let's use this power not just to fight but to reveal the truth."

As their avatars stabilized, the digital environment of the coliseum responded, morphing with their enhanced capabilities. The air around them seemed to crackle, the very code of Project Lumina bending to their will. It was a display of their potential to take control, to turn the architect's tools against her.

Milo, tapping rapidly at his portable hacking kit, ensured that every user and every unlinked screen continued to broadcast their rebellion. "Broadcasting on all accepted channels now. Let's show them what freedom looks like," he announced, a wry smile on his face.

Tara, shifting her position, prepared for any counterattack. Her eyes scanned the digital horizon, her body coiled like a spring. Her composite fiber whip was ready at her side, a silent promise to any who would dare challenge their crusade.

The coliseum's core, now exposed and vulnerable, hummed with the potential of untold secrets. Felix approached the console, his every move watched by billions. "This is Lumina's heart, and today we expose its lies," he declared, his hand poised over the console.

"It's time to show them the true power at our fingertips. Engage the surge!" With a swift motion, he activated the console, and a wave of energy pulsed throughout the coliseum, the walls shimmering with translucent data streams that painted a stark picture of Greda's hidden agenda.

Screens around the arena flickered to life, revealing even more of the depth of the deception. The data uncovered was damning—Greda had been manipulating their lives, trading their reality for a controlled fantasy while reaping profits from their ignorance and addiction.

As the information spread, the digital spectators began to stir, their coded forms buzzing with the energy of revelation and dissent. Tara could feel the shift, the swell of a rebellion sparked by the truth they had laid bare.

As the coliseum's core hummed and pulsed with newly unleashed secrets, Felix's voice boomed across the arena, his declaration reverberating off the digital walls, commanding attention from the multitudes logged into Project Lumina. "We've shown what we can do with Lumina's power. Now, let's take it with us."

Tara felt the surge of their enhanced abilities coursing through her veins, her senses sharpening, the details of the virtual world becoming almost painfully clear. The once distant roars of the digital spectators now sounded like whispers in her ears, the coded voices carrying a mixture of fear and exhilaration.

The coliseum itself seemed to respond to their newfound dominance, its architecture subtly shifting, the very air charged with potential. As Felix prepared them for what was to come, the digital environment around them began to twist and morph, bending to their will. The boundaries of the virtual world, once rigid and unyielding, now seemed fluid, like watercolor bleeding across a canvas.

"Prepare yourselves," Felix's voice cut through the tension, a sharp contrast to the eerie quiet that had settled over the coliseum. "It's time to step into a realm of our own making." His hand gestured to the team, signaling the beginning of their grand escape, a maneuver that would use every ounce of power they had just claimed.

Tara glanced at her teammates, seeing the gravity of this moment etched on their faces. Milo, with a flick of his fingers, enhanced their communication bands, ensuring no signal could be jammed or intercepted. Ava scanned the digital horizon, her eyes narrowing as she plotted their course through the morphing landscape of the coliseum.

Raj, his hands already busy setting up a series of traps and diversions, grinned at Tara. "Let's blow some minds, shall we?" His laughter was almost lost in the sudden gust of wind that swept through the arena, a physical manifestation of the chaos they were about to unleash.

"You know, the best tricks are the ones you never see coming," Felix mused aloud, his voice resonating over the transformed arena. "From the very start, every move, every fight was part of the plan."

High above the digital terrain, Felix stood at the edge of a grand portal, his team arrayed behind him, silhouettes against the cascading data streams.

Around them, the landscape reset, snippets from their previous encounters playing in reverse across giant screens—hidden preparations, strategic placements, all cleverly disguised in their past actions, now revealed as meticulously planned steps towards this moment. Milo made sure every person watching could see all the hidden things the team did and set into place to make this moment possible.

Felix watched as the landscape of Project Lumina shifted, the virtual coliseum transforming into a grand stage for their masterful revelation. He stood at the forefront, the orchestrator of a plan so intricate, each step was now unraveling before the eyes of billions. As the scenes played backward on massive screens, the audience—both virtual and real—was taken on a journey through hidden maneuvers and strategic deceptions that had paved their path to this moment.

Each snippet, each reverse playback was a revelation. There, a virtual decoy sprinted, drawing away the AI sentinels during their initial breach—its purpose clear only now, showing it was never just an escape attempt but a distraction. The screens flicked to encrypted data streams that had been Milo's handiwork; what seemed like digital noise was actually covert communication among them, orchestrating moves unseen by any overseer.

A dramatic pause in the playback brought the audience's focus to holographic blueprints—plans displayed on screens that were never real, only illusions to mislead Lumina's internal surveillance. Then, the heat-emitting dummies appeared, devices planted to misdirect thermal sensors, sending security on wild chases while they moved undetected in opposite directions.

Felix's voice broke through the unfolding chaos, "Notice the patterns, the slight misdirections. Every piece was placed with precision." The footage showed Milo hacking into the AI's predictive algorithms, a preemptive strike that allowed them to always be two steps ahead, anticipating moves before they were made.

The reveal continued with biometric spoofing devices in action, a technique they used to bypass the most secure areas undetected. And not far behind, Raj's expertise came to light—power surge traps that disabled security measures just long enough for them to pass unhindered.

More secrets spilled forth. Hidden explosives that they had planted days before, not for destruction, but as diversions and to block pursuing forces at critical moments. Shadow logs created fake digital footprints, leading surveillance to believe they were always elsewhere.

And perhaps the most cunning of all, reverse hacking inserted by Milo, which had fed false footage to security cameras, showing empty corridors when in reality, they marched right under the eyes of their watchers.

The crowd watched, mesmerized and horrified by the depth of their deception. "Every move you witnessed, believed to be spontaneous, was part of a grander scheme," Felix declared, his voice echoing through the now silent coliseum. The screens flashed rapidly now, highlighting their journey, the many close calls that were never really close, all controlled from the shadows by this team of digital magicians.

As the revelations unfolded across the coliseum's grand displays, Felix's voice once again pierced the rising murmur of the crowd, both virtual and real. "But wait, there's more," he announced, his tone laced with the thrill of the final reveal. The grandeur of their escapade was about to deepen, each layer meticulously crafted to ensure their untraceable maneuvers within Project Lumina's heart.

The screen above flickered, a fresh sequence initiating. This time, visual cues highlighted their use of quantum encryption. Each digital transaction they conducted was wrapped in quantum keys, impenetrable to the fortress's advanced systems. Not a byte was left for the AI to decipher, their communications cloaked in a shroud of computational complexity.

Another scene unfolded, showcasing their clever use of digital shadows. The team, disguised as Lumina staff, moved freely through the most restricted zones, their digital signatures altered to mimic those of authorized personnel. No eye, human or digital, questioned their presence as they accessed core areas cloaked in fabricated identities.

Felix's figure was highlighted on the screens, his suit shimmering with a subtle sheen. "Our suits," he explained, "lined with EMP-resistant material, protected us from AI countermeasures designed to disable unauthorized tech." As he spoke, a demonstration showed an EMP wave washing over them, their equipment unscathed and operational, highlighting their foresight.

Then came the acoustic mimicry devices—small, almost imperceptible gadgets that replicated the ambient sounds of the fortress's operations. As Felix and his team moved, the sounds of their steps were lost amidst a many sounds of normalcy, their physical presence masked by the very heartbeat of Lumina itself.

Milo took the stage on the screen, a ghostly figure maneuvering through digital defenses. "Ghost protocol," Felix narrated, "made our devices invisible to tracking. We moved as phantoms, undetected, untouchable." The visuals showed their path through critical checkpoints, invisible to the prying digital eyes that sought to trace their every step.

The screen split, multiple feeds showcasing different aspects of their strategy. Phantom echoes disrupted communication channels, while recursive loops sent the AI spiraling into a futile chase after non-existent intruders. Optical illusions altered perceptions; the very walls of the vault seemed to shift, confusing any who dared to follow.

A map highlighted their route, marked invisibly to all but them. "Invisible ink," Felix pointed out, "visible only through our visors, guided us along pre-planned escape routes, bypassing sensors calibrated to ignore our specific pressure signatures." As they walked, the floor beneath them remained unresponsive, their passage as light as air.

Synthetic aromas filled the corridors in their wake, a deceptive measure against biometric scent detectors. Magnetic disruption devices hung from their belts, creating localized fields that scrambled surveillance equipment, leaving behind a trail of electronic disarray.

As the grand spectacle of their orchestrated chaos continued, false alarms diverted security forces across the fortress, each alarm a step in their dance of deception. Mirrored hacking allowed them to remotely manipulate security protocols, turning the fortress's defenses against itself.

In a final touch, Felix showcased the neural jammers. "A short burst," he explained, "and AI guards found themselves lost in a haze of confusion, their cognitive functions disrupted just long enough for us to pass." The screen showed AI sentinels pausing, disoriented, as the team slipped by unnoticed.

Felix's figure reappeared at the forefront, the grand portal pulsating behind him. "Every magician keeps one last trick up his sleeve," he declared, his team lined up beside him, ready. "For us, it's knowing the game better than the game masters themselves. Let's go make our own rules."

With a final, decisive nod, Felix led his team into the portal, stepping from the known into a realm of their own making, leaving behind a legacy of the greatest heist within Project Lumina—a spectacle of strategic genius that would be remembered as the moment when the watchers became the watched.

Suddenly, the virtual debris cascaded behind them, forming a temporary barricade against the relentless advance of the AI sentinels, Felix's eyes scanned the horizon of the digital coliseum. His team, ready and alert, awaited his commands, the air thick with digital tension.

"Ava, you and Milo on hacking duty. We're carving our way out. Raj, those traps better be ready," Felix commanded, his voice a calm force in the midst of chaos. Ava nodded, her fingers flying over her console, syncing with Milo to unleash a series of crippling viruses into Lumina's infrastructure.

The coliseum's architecture, a vast network of data and energy, began to shimmer and twist, responding to their aggressive digital onslaught. Raj, with a grin of anticipation, deployed his well-prepared diversions, a series of holographic bombs that exploded in brilliant, distracting flares, pulling the AI's attention away in a choreographed spectacle of light and sound.

Tara moved like a shadow, her adaptive camouflage blending perfectly with the shifting digital environment, as she slithered through the chaos, bypassing disoriented digital gladiators with ease. Her target was clear—a hidden portal Felix had discovered in their earlier recon, one of the backdoors built into the system for emergencies by Lumina's architects, never meant to be found.

Felix, leading from the front, his Codebreaker Blade glowing with a fierce light, sliced through virtual barriers that attempted to seal their path. "This way! The portal is just beyond that nexus point," he shouted, pointing towards a pulsating beacon in the distance.

As they approached, the ground beneath them shook—Lumina's last desperate attempt to keep its prisoners. But Felix was ready. He turned to Milo, nodding sharply. "Now, Milo! Trigger the EMP!"

Milo, his equipment already set for the final play, unleashed an electromagnetic pulse that sent waves through the coliseum's systems. Lights flickered, screens went dark, and for a moment, the relentless pursuit behind them stuttered and stalled.

"The path is clear!" Ava called out, her tactical overlay highlighting a route free of obstructions as she rebooted their systems to shield from further AI interference.

They raced towards the portal, the sounds of their steps reverberating through the now silent coliseum. Just as they reached the threshold, Felix turned to ensure his team was intact. Satisfied, he allowed himself a rare smirk. "Project Lumina's control ends here. And someone tell Callan, we have officially joined the Resistance."

With a decisive motion, he activated the portal, the gateway shimmering into existence, a vortex of colors and light swirling violently. One by one, they leapt through, their bodies dissolving into strings of code and reassembling on the other side—a new digital frontier awaited them, uncharted and free from Lumina's shackles.

Behind them, the coliseum began to collapse, the structures disintegrating into digital dust, a fitting end to the spectacle that had held billions captive. As they emerged into the new realm, Felix looked back one last time, the digital horizon of Lumina fading into the distance. The time to completely destroy it, would come sooner than later.

Chapter 6

Exactly 1 Minute After Chapter 21 of The Vegetation Wars.

Vane Calder surveyed the battlefield with icy precision, his gaze cutting through the chaos that unfolded before him as if he were merely an observer in his own orchestrated war. Callan and his team were struggling, barely holding their own, but Vane felt no urge to intervene. Why should he? In his eyes, neither side deserved victory, and neither deserved his aid. Instead, he watched from the shadows, analyzing every move, every failure, and pondering whether Callan might somehow snatch victory from the jaws of defeat, and how the Verdant Overlord might react if the tides turned.

Yet, something shifted within him; a personal disdain for Lord Virex gnawed at him. Moments ago, hidden in the spore-dense darkness, Vane had made a swift, deadly decision. It was time to step forward and extinguish Virex's existence once and for all.

The air around him was thick with spores, the silent whispers of the Verdant Overlord's underlings buzzing in his ears—each word, each shudder of fear from them, fueling the impending storm of violence he was about to release.

Daxon, the human traitor, and the remaining vegetation survivors, scattered and desperate, watched from a distance, an odd mixture of awe and horror etched across their faces. They recognized him—the man with no allegiance, the harbinger of their potential end. The sentient vegetation, their limbs twitching with the desire to intervene, stood immobilized, a silent audience to the spectacle about to unfold.

Vane Calder's approach was like the slow, inexorable spread of darkness at dusk. With every measured step through the spore-laden air, the chaotic clamor of battle seemed to quiet, the very earth holding its breath. The creatures of the Verdant Overlord, hybrids of flesh and flora, most just flora, watched through eyes that glimmered with unnatural luminescence. Even the human rebels, ragged and desperate, paused at his presence. They knew of him—Vane, the legend, the harbinger of annihilation whose allegiance to none rendered him all the more terrifying.

As he moved, the ground beneath his boots whispered secrets of the past battles, the spores swirling around him like a cloak. Some of the sentient vegetation seemed to lean towards him, drawn by a morbid curiosity, while others recoiled, their branches trembling. Daxon, his eyes wide with a dawning realization of the true monster among them. The tension was a tangible shroud, enveloping every being within the clearing as they watched this prelude to carnage.

Lord Virex, once a man, now more—or less—than human, faced Vane with a visage grotesquely veined with green. His stance was defiant, yet the slight quaver in his voice belied his fear. "Vane," he addressed the approaching figure, his words nearly lost in the rustling of leaves and the soft moans of the wounded around them. Vane's response was a mere tilt of his head, the ghost of a smile playing on his lips, not out of amusement but as a prelude to the violence he was a master at wielding. Something very violent was about to happen; it was an inevitable clash of titans, watched by an audience of mutants and men, all captivated by the unfolding drama, all aware that they were about to witness raw power. The sentient vegetation, some twisted mirrors of Virex's own hybrid form, watched with a horror that rippled through their collective consciousness, their roots entwined yet immobile, as if the earth itself refused to partake in the dance of death about to commence.

As Vane's shadow fell over the clearing, a hush settled over the chaotic landscape. The air grew dense, charged with the promise of impending doom. Every creature seemed to hold its breath, their gazes fixed on the figure at the heart of the storm. Vane's eyes, cold and unyielding, mirrored the deathly calm before chaos. He stood there, a lone titan against the backdrop of a war-ravaged world, embodying the destructive force of nature itself.

Lord Virex, his body a patchwork of human flesh and aggressive vegetation, stood defiantly. His form, once human, now bore the marks of his allegiance with the Verdant Overlord—vines that pulsed with a sickly life of their own, skin that photosynthesized under the eerie light of the spore-laden sky. Yet, as he faced Vane, there was an unmistakable flicker of fear in his eyes, a betrayal of his hybrid vigor. The air between them crackled with the energy of two opposing forces about to collide.

"Vane," Lord Virex attempted to regain his composure, his voice resonating with a power that seemed more forced than natural. "You think to end this with me? You are but one man against the tide."

Vane's laugh, low and devoid of humor, sliced through the tension. "One man?" he replied, his voice a cold whisper that somehow carried over the din of the distant battle. "I *am* man."

Vane noticed the uneasy shifts of the mutated onlookers, their forms grotesque hybrids of plant and flesh, stirring slightly under his gaze. The surrounding vegetation seemed almost sentient, reacting to his presence, the twisted branches and thorn-laden limbs quivering in the heavy air. Daxon, from a distance, had his eyes wide with a mix of awe and terror, transfixed by the unfolding scene, grasping the gravity of the moment as the old world's rules were dismantled before him.

Lord Virex, emboldened momentarily by Vane's taunt, straightened his stance, his veins visibly pulsing with chlorophyll, attempting to draw some semblance of strength from his unnatural alliance. "Your vision is flawed, Calder. You see destruction as an end. I see it as a beginning."

Vane advanced a step, the earth beneath him darkening as if stained by his disdain. "A beginning?" he countered, the corner of his mouth twitching in a semblance of a smile, not of amusement but of impending certainty. "You're deluded by the rot you've grown from, Virex. You chain yourself to this Overlord, thinking it frees you. Me? I serve no one."

This bold declaration seemed to echo across the clearing, reverberating with the weight of undeniable truth. Both the human and non-human spectators sensed a profound shift, the air thick with the tension of two starkly opposing wills colliding.

The vegetation around them, manipulated and mutated, pulsated unnaturally, echoing the discord of the scene. Spores in the air swirled chaotically, stirred into frenzy by Vane's indomitable presence. Virex, for all his grotesque power, suddenly appeared diminished, the green of his veins dulling in the shadow of Vane's unwavering resolve.

Their gazes locked, freezing a moment in time where hatred and history bled into one another, each standing as the ultimate antithesis to the other's cause. Vane, the harbinger of destruction, and Virex, the misguided savior, encapsulated the brutal dance of survival and dominance.

The silence stretched, a heavy cloak draped over the battlefield. Spores hung suspended in the air as if even they dared not stir under Vane's intense scrutiny. The battlefield's usual clamor seemed muted, reduced to a distant murmur by his singular presence. With a disdainful flick of his hand, Vane discarded his rifle, the metallic clatter against the ground punctuating the tense hush. His every motion was deliberate, his eyes never leaving Lord Virex's mutated form.

Virex, standing a short distance away, appeared as a grotesque testament to unnatural alliances. His body, a hybrid of human and aggressive vegetation, seemed momentarily uncertain, as if Vane's dismissal of weapons shifted the ground beneath them. Vane's steps were slow, measured, each one a deliberate echo in the still air. The spores that clung to the night seemed to recoil with each footfall, clearing a path for wrath incarnate.

The first move was sudden yet unhurried. Vane's arm shot forward, the motion fluid, his fingers closing around Virex's wrist with an iron grip. The contact was a shock of kinetic brutality. Virex's response was sluggish, his vine-laden arm attempting to coil around Vane's, a desperate attempt to use his vegetative strength. But it was no match. Vane twisted sharply, a simple movement laden with devastating intent. The sound of tearing sinew was stark, a stark note against the backdrop of hushed whispers and gasps from the onlooking crowd.

Virex staggered, pain igniting in his eyes, a human emotion flickering through the plant-like facade. Vane's other hand shot out, fingers clenched in a fist that connected with Virex's midsection. The impact lifted the hybrid off his feet, a dull thud resonating through the clearing as he hit the ground. The undergrowth recoiled, spores billowing up in a cloud around the fallen figure.

As Vane advanced, the onlookers—both human and plant—remained frozen, a tableau vivant of fear and fascination. Each of Vane's movements was a masterclass in controlled violence, his body honed through countless battles, each muscle coiled and ready to deliver devastation. His face was a mask of cold fury, every line and angle of it set in violence.

Virex tried to rise, his form shaking as he pushed against the earth. But the defiance in his eyes was dimming, overshadowed by the inevitability of his defeat. He managed to get to his knees, looking up at Vane, who stood before him, an unmovable force of nature.

The air was electric, charged with the raw energy of the imminent. Vane's next move was anticipated with bated breath; the clearing had become an arena, and this fight a spectacle etched in the annals of their war-torn world. As Vane pulled back his leg for a final, devastating roundhouse kick, the tension peaked, the very atmosphere quivering with the power of the impending strike.

As Virex struggled to rise, the battlefield's eerie stillness echoed with a charged tension. Vane stood, his figure a monolith in the dim light, eyes gleaming with an unnatural radiance. He flexed his hands, the air around them shimmering with a surge of quantum energy, visible threads of power twisting and coiling like serpents made of light.

This new display of power shifted the dynamics dramatically. Vane, with a predator's grace, stepped forward, his hand shooting out to grasp Virex by the arm. The energy pulsating from Vane's palm seemed to seep into Virex, causing the appendage to glow ominously. With a swift, ruthless twist, Vane dislocated Virex's arm at the shoulder, lifting him off the ground. The sound of rending sinew and popping bone was stark against the hushed murmurs of the watching crowd. Virex's anguished scream cut through the night, a sound that made even the most battle-hardened spectators flinch.

The twist was not merely physical but symbolic, underscoring Vane's utter dominance and the futility of resistance. Vane's expression remained impassive, his face a mask of cold indifference to the suffering he wrought. This moment wasn't just a display of combat superiority; it was a punishment, a demonstration of Vane's disdain for all that Virex represented.

Holding Virex aloft, Vane's gaze swept across the battlefield, meeting the eyes of every onlooker, human and plant alike. His message was clear: this was not merely a fight but an execution, a statement of power over these twisted hybrids and the forces they represented. The crowd was silent, the earlier rustles of movement stilled by the grim spectacle before them.

Vane's grip tightened, the quantum energy intensifying as it flowed like a river of fire through his veins and into the arm he held aloft. The glow around Virex's dislocated shoulder spread, illuminating his face in a grotesque light, each feature twisted in agony.

With a casual flick, Vane hurled him into the air, his body spinning wildly before it crashed back to the earth with a sickening crunch.

The ground where Virex landed fractured, the impact sending a spiderweb of cracks through the soil, a dark, ominous energy pulsing from the epicenter. As Virex tried to crawl, a faint, desperate gesture, Vane approached, the soles of his boots barely touching the ground, lifted by the sheer force of his quantum manipulation.

"Your end is a lesson," Vane's voice boomed across the battlefield, reaching every ear, echoing off the silent, watching trees. He raised his hand, the energy gathering into a condensed sphere of pulsating light, casting sharp shadows across his emotionless face. With a swift motion, he unleashed the sphere directly at Virex.

The blast was cataclysmic, a blinding flash followed by a deafening roar as the energy consumed Virex, disintegrating him in a vortex of quantum fire. The light was so intense, so pure, it seemed to burn the very air around it. When it finally subsided, there was nothing left of Lord Virex but a charred imprint on the ground, a final testament to his existence.

As the last echoes of Virex's obliteration faded, Vane turned toward the pulsating glow of the artifact. The crystalline structure, a beacon of mystic power and discord, lay unguarded on the scorched earth, its light undimmed by the violence around it. Vane's approach was deliberate, each step resonating with the quiet authority of the inevitable. His shadow fell over the artifact, engulfing its light in his dark presence.

The battlefield held its breath, the stillness a stark contrast to the turmoil that had just passed. Vane's hand shot out, fast and precise, grabbing the artifact with an ironclad grip. His fingers traced the smooth, alien contours of the crystal, his expression unreadable yet fraught with a fierce intent. No reverence was given to this relic that had ensnared many in its promise of power; there was only the resolute determination of a man who had seen the depths of its deception.

With a flick of his wrist, the artifact was lifted, catching the dim light of the moon as it spun slowly between his fingers. Vane's eyes, cold and detached, mirrored none of the artifact's shimmering promises. He whispered something inaudible, a mantra or perhaps a condemnation, his voice a low hum against the soft rustling of the night.

Then, without a moment's hesitation, Vane's other hand came alive with a ghostly light, the air around it distorting as quantum energies swirled with a life of their own. The energies converged on the artifact, enveloping it in a radiant, menacing glow. Microscopic fissures began to emerge across its surface, each crack displaying Vane's mastery over the forces he wielded.

The tension snapped as Vane clenched his fist, the energy intensifying into a blinding flash. The artifact's resistance crumbled under his overwhelming power, its structure collapsing with a crisp, resonating crack that split the silence like thunder. It exploded into countless shards, each piece disintegrating into fine, glowing dust that cascaded down like a curtain of stars.

As the dust settled, a surreal calm descended over the battlefield. The shattered remains of the artifact lay scattered, the light dimming with each passing second until all that remained was the dull glimmer of crushed crystal under Vane's boots. The crowd—sentient vegetation and humans alike—stood motionless, the implications of the act settling in with the dust. Their faces, illuminated by the fleeting glow of the artifact's remains, were etched with a mix of awe and horror.

Vane's gaze slowly swept across the onlookers, each individual momentarily caught in the weight of his scrutiny. The silence was profound, oppressive, as if the night itself was holding its breath. Then, stepping through the remnants of the artifact, Vane walked back towards the heart of the battlefield, the spectral dust clinging to his boots, leaving behind a trail of muted luminescence.

Vane's slow, deliberate steps crunched over the spectral remnants of the artifact, each echo a testament to his destructive capabilities. The silence was profound, the air thick with the residue of power and rebellion. He stopped before Daxon, the young miner whose face was a canvas of dawning realization and dread.

"Now that Lord Virex is dead," Vane began, his voice carrying a chilling clarity that cut through the heavy air, "enjoy your promotion for as long as I let you live."

His gaze locked onto Daxon, unwavering and cold. With those final words, Vane shifted his attention, peering through the myriad forms of sentient vegetation that dotted the battlefield—each one a creation of the Verdant Overlord, each one an eye through which it could see. His stare pierced through them, a silent challenge to the Overlord, a promise of upheaval that no treaty could forestall. Then, without another word, he turned, stepping back into the mists that had begun to swirl with the night's cold embrace.

His figure melted into the spore-filled haze, an enigma shrouded in the threat of violence. Around him, the onlookers froze, the silence pregnant with the implications of his words, the air thick with tension. Each step he took into the mist was as laden with menace as his arrival, leaving behind a chilling promise of chaos that resonated in the quiet of the unsettled night.

Chapter 7

Elara's pulse hammered in her ears as the last of the echoes from Felix's declaration faded into a tense silence around her. The screens flickered a final time, painting Project Lumina with the stark reality of rebellion. Alone in the dimly lit media room of Sector 9X, her mind raced, not just with the electric thrill of what she'd witnessed but with the urgent need for action that the broadcast had ignited within her.

"They knew exactly what they were up against, and they didn't just step up; they tore through every expectation," she muttered under her breath, her gaze fixed on the now dark screens that had just shown Felix and his team's coordinated strike. The plan was audacious, the execution flawless—attributes that resonated deeply with Elara's own tactical sensibilities. A soft growl from Rootwhisper drew her attention momentarily; even he seemed on edge, the plant's bioluminescent leaves shimmering slightly in the low light, reflecting the tension in the room.

She moved to the terminal, her fingers flying over the keys, replaying snippets of the heist. Every maneuver Felix's team had executed, from Milo's precise jamming of the surveillance to Tara's ghost-like infiltration, mirrored the kind of radical tactics that Elara felt were necessary now more than ever. "If they can breach Lumina's vault, we can breach the Overlord's hold over the surface," she whispered, not just to herself but to the quiet figure of Rootwhisper beside her.

With a few more strokes, she pulled up the schematic of Sector 9X, her mind overlaying it with the fortress's layout she'd just seen. "We have our own vault to crack, don't we?" she said, half to Rootwhisper, half to herself. The room filled with a tension, palpable as the static from the screens. She envisioned Felix's team navigating through corridors laden with traps and AI guards, their success because of their impeccable teamwork and sharp strategy. It wasn't just their skill that had pulled them through—it was their unity.

A tactical map of their immediate region sprawled across the screen now, potential routes and strategies lighting up. Elara's eyes narrowed as she considered their options. "We'll need to be ghosts in the spores, whispers in the wind," she thought, recalling how Raj had managed the explosives, his timing ensuring minimal disruption while maximizing impact.

The silence was suddenly oppressive, urging her to fill it with plans, with movement. "Rootwhisper, you just got your chance to fight," she announced, more to solidify her own resolve than in any need of affirmation from the sentient plant. The plant's response, a low, vibrating hum through the room's air, felt like agreement.

Turning back to the screens, Elara re-watched the moment of extraction, her brain tagging each of Felix's commands, each strategic placement of his team. "Milo and Tibo could teach each other a trick or two," she noted, admiration threading through her tone for the tech wizard's deft handling of Lumina's formidable electronic barriers. The synergy between their skills—Milo's hacking and Tibo's engineering—could be what tilted the scales in their next confrontation.

Her thoughts were interrupted by a sudden flicker of the screens—the system cycling through security footage from the outer tunnels of Sector 9X, a reminder of the ever-present danger lurking just beyond their makeshift sanctuary. "No time for hesitation," she affirmed, shutting down the terminal.

Steps measured and purposeful, Elara paced back to the central table, maps and digital blueprints spread across it like a tactile echo of their digital counterparts. Each line, each marked route a potential lifeline or a disastrous end. The weight of their next move bore down on her, the isolation of their hidden base a stark contrast to the interconnectedness Felix had exploited.

Elara stood alone in the dim light of the control room, the silence around her so heavy it almost echoed. Her gaze lingered on the screens, now dark after showcasing Felix's team's tactical finesse. "They had it all planned out," she thought, the realization tightening in her chest. "Precision and coordination—exactly what we need."

Nearby, the hum of Rootwhisper's presence was a subtle comfort, the sentient plant's energy mingling with the tension of the room. Elara's mind churned with the possibilities that Felix's tactics had inspired. "Milo's hacking brilliance, Tibo's knack for engineering—they're the keys," she mused. "Together, they could really turn these old defenses into something formidable."

A flicker on one of the remaining active screens caught her eye—the security feed cycling through views of the outer tunnels. The sight was a stark reminder of their vulnerability and the constant threat lurking just beyond their hideout. She bit her lip. "No more playing it small. We have to be proactive," she decided, her fingers drumming lightly against the metal table strewn with maps and blueprints.

Turning, she glanced through the open doorway that led to the small room where Tibo and Callan were resting, their bodies healing under the gentle whir of medical machinery. The thought of waking him so soon felt like a betrayal, yet she knew they couldn't afford to wait. "We need every advantage. Tibo's skills are vital right now," she admitted to herself, her voice a whisper lost in the vastness of the room.

Her decision made, Elara walked to the threshold of Tibo's room, pausing to steel herself. Inside, the soft beeps of the life-support system played a counterpoint to her quickened heartbeat. She stared at Tibo's still form, his chest rising and falling with mechanical precision. "Sorry to cut your rest short, partner, but we need you," she said softly, almost apologetically.

The control to rouse him from healing sleep was just a touch away. Elara hesitated, her hand hovering over the interface. The weight of the next move bore down on her—awakening Tibo wasn't just about pulling him back into the fray; it was about stepping up their game, about shifting from defense to a more aggressive stance against their enemies.

Elara stood by the medical bay, her gaze fixed on Callan's silent form in the dim light. The steady rise and fall of his chest under the life-support system was a fragile thread tethering him to the world they were still fighting to save. The screens flickered nearby, displaying the constant surveillance of their perimeters—a silent reminder of the ever-present danger lurking just beyond the walls of Sector 9X.

"We need an army," Elara whispered, her voice a soft echo in the sterile room. The footage from the outer tunnels revealed subtle movements—shadows within shadows, hinting at the approach of unseen enemies. The sanctity of their hidden base, once a fortress of solitude and security, now felt as vulnerable as the peace that enveloped Callan.

Elara's thoughts lingered on Felix's recent declaration of joining Callan and the Resistance, its bold resonance still vibrating through the resistance channels, juxtaposed starkly against Callan's current vulnerability. "He should be leading this, not lying here," she mused, her heart tightening with the weight of their shared battles and the unspoken promise of many more to come.

Turning her gaze momentarily to the dormant form of Tibo, she contemplated the skills locked away in his healing body—skills they desperately needed. But it was Callan, their unquestionable leader, whose strategic mind and unwavering courage had always guided them through the storm. "He needs to be here, with us, at the helm," she admitted silently, feeling the absence of his leadership more acutely with each passing moment.

Yet, the decision to awaken him too soon hurt her heart. The healing pods, their soft whirring a constant backdrop, were the only barrier between them and the exhaustive toll of war. Waking Callan prematurely could jeopardize his recovery, perhaps even their cause, if he were less than capable of wielding the command they so desperately needed. She prayed his confidence wasn't destroyed.

She hesitated, her hand hovering over the control panel. "Not yet," she resolved, pulling back as the weight of leadership settled firmly on her shoulders. The battle within her was clear—the need for his guidance against the critical balance of his health.

With a deep breath, Elara stood at medical bay, watching Tibo and Callan, knowing she would have to wake them to go into the command center. The screens awaited them, glowing ominously with the outlines of their fortifications and the dark patches of the uncharted tunnels. It was there, amidst maps and digital blueprints, they would raise Callan's army.

The sterile hum of the medical bay melds with the deeper silence that envelops Callan, a silence that is abruptly shattered by the hiss of the chamber's seals disengaging. His eyes flicker open to a dimly lit room, the familiar blur of overhead lights coming slowly into focus. The lingering fog of healing sleep clings stubbornly to his thoughts, but urgency propels him toward wakefulness.

Muscles protest as he shifts, a reminder of the battle's toll still etched deep in his flesh despite the medical bay's best efforts. His gaze, sharpening with each breath, catches the form of Elara standing just beyond the glass. Her expression is taut with the weight of unsaid things, her eyes briefly meeting his before flitting away—back to the data pads and screens mapping out a world much changed from the one he'd left behind in slumber.

The chamber's side panel slides open with a soft whir, and Callan pushes himself upright, swinging his legs over the edge of the pod. The cool air of the room brushes against his skin, bracing and sharp. Elara is there in an instant, her hand steady on his arm, offering support that's more about presence than the need to steady him. "You should rest more," she murmurs, but the set of her jaw tells him rest is a luxury they can no longer afford.

Callan nods, understanding without words the gravity of the situation that must have forced her hand. The brief peace of healing sleep, always too short, now feels like a distant memory. "Report," he manages, his voice rough around the edges, the words cutting through the last vestiges of disorientation.

Elara's eyes meet his, filled with a mix of resolve and concern. "The perimeter defenses are holding, but there's been unusual movement in the outer tunnels." She gestures towards a screen flickering with the shadowy forms that merge almost seamlessly with the darkness. "And there's more—Felix Hart has made a bold move. He's publicly declared resistance against Chancellor Greda."

Callan's mind sharpens at the mention of Felix, a name he does not recognize yet carries weight in Elara's tone. His gaze hardens, focusing on the strategic implications. "Felix Hart?" he queries, his interest piqued by the unfamiliar yet significant player now on their radar.

At that moment, a soft hiss signals another awakening. Tibo stirs in his adjacent chamber, the panel sliding open as he emerges, blinking against the light. His usual humor subdued by the gravity of the wake-up call. Catching the tail end of the conversation, Tibo rubs the sleep from his eyes. "Felix Hart, the legend from Project Lumina? I've heard of him. Tried Lumina myself for a bit—cost me six months." His tone mixes admiration with a tinge of regret.

Elara nods, acknowledging Tibo's experience. "Yes, that Felix. He and his team executed a high-stakes raid on Project Lumina's vault. Managed to breach multiple security layers without triggering alarms, used their tech skills to manipulate the digital environment heavily," she explains, her voice brisk with admiration and urgency. "It's not just their success—it's how they did it. Felix ended it with a public declaration, turning their heist into a rebellion call and told the world he wants to follow Callan."

Callan absorbs the information, the strategic gears in his mind turning. "So, he's brought the fight into the public eye," he muses aloud, the implications vast and immediate. "This changes the landscape of our own resistance."

Tibo, now fully attentive, leans in. "The tech approach, if we could adapt some of their tactics..." he trails off, already brainstorming.

Elara's expression is one of fierce determination. "Looks like we have help now."

"Interesting," Callan says quietly, standing fully now, his stature commanding as he starts to pace slightly, his mind racing through possibilities.

"Interesting," Callan murmurs again, his voice low and thoughtful as he paces the cramped space of their makeshift command center. "You said that already," Elara said. "Tell me everything about Felix and what they did at Project Lumina."

Elara, still keyed into the terminal, replies without looking up. "Their tech guy, Milo, hacked into Lumina's system. He broadcasted everything they did directly to devices outside of Lumina. It wasn't just on Lumina; it was everywhere."

Tibo whistles, a sound of disbelief mingling with admiration. "That's supposed to be impossible."

"Well, if it was on TV, can Tibo and I see it? Can we replay it?" Callan asks, the potential of such a feat sparking a torrent of strategic possibilities in his mind.

Elara taps a few commands into the terminal. "Let me see if it's still up."

Rootwhisper, leaning against the wall with his arms crossed, watches them with a faint, knowing smile, as if privy to the impending revelation that could shift their fortunes.

The screen flickers, and suddenly, the actions of Felix's team come alive before them. Callan and Tibo lean in as each tactic is displayed:

Footage shows Felix's team moving undetected across pressure-sensitive floors, their weight signatures cloaked. They watch as the team deploys a device that emits a cloud, masking their natural scents from biometric detectors. A schematic pops up demonstrating how data was wiped from the security system, erasing their digital footprints moments after they passed.

Visuals of Felix's team carrying devices that fizzled nearby electronics, leaving a trail of scrambled data in their wake. Strategically placed distractions bloom across different sectors, pulling security forces away from the critical path the team exploited. A complex flowchart details how the team mirrored the fortress's security protocols, manipulating the defense mechanisms from within.

Drones, indistinguishable from commercial models, are shown buzzing away from the fortress, loaded with stolen data. Tibo notes the precision timing as Felix's team slips through disarrayed laser grids, their synchronization thrown off at just the right moments. They observe suits changing textures and colors, blending seamlessly into walls and shadows as the team evades visual detection.

Lastly, a demonstration of neural jammers disrupting AI guards, their confusion creating windows of opportunity for Felix's team. Each display of ingenuity draws a low whistle from Tibo and a nod from Callan. "Impressive," Tibo murmurs, his eyes alight with new ideas. "This Milo... I need to meet him."

"We need to meet all of them," Elara commands.

Callan's gaze remains fixed on the screen, the wheels turning in his head. "This isn't just a raid; it's a blueprint for revolution," he states, the scope of Felix's actions setting a new bar for what they might achieve themselves.

Tibo's excitement is infectious as he gestures toward the screen, still displaying the last of Felix's team's tactical maneuvers. "Milo's work... it's not just advanced, it's revolutionary. I'd give anything to get a session with him, see what makes him tick."

Elara nods, her gaze sweeping from Tibo to Callan before adding, "I'm sure he has said the same things about you, Tibo."

Felix's strategy, Ava's logistics, Milo's tech skills—they'd complement what we're trying to build here."

Rootwhisper, leaning against the wall, rustles lightly, the bioluminescence in his leaves flickering subtly, mirroring the tension in the room. Despite his quiet, his stance speaks volumes of the anticipation building within him.

Callan steps forward, his presence grounding the rapid flow of ideas. "Ava could streamline our operations. Her tactical oversight might just tighten our own mission executions." He pauses, considering the synergy between their potential allies and his own team. "And Tara, her stealth could teach us a few tricks about moving unseen."

Elara's eyes are calculating, appreciative of Callan's vision. "Raj's demolition expertise could also be crucial for us. Imagine integrating that level of precision in our raids."

Tibo chuckles, rubbing his hands together. "And if I could collaborate with Milo... there's no telling the heights we could reach with our tech."

The screen flickers again, looping back to a clip of Felix decisively navigating through a complex digital landscape, his movements both fluid and exact. Callan's voice cuts through the mesmerized silence. "This isn't just about learning their techniques. It's about integrating their strengths with ours. Each one brings something we need."

"We woke you early because this," Elara gestures to the ongoing display, "is the beginning of our army." The way Felix's team operates—it's a blueprint for how we can escalate our efforts. It's not just about fighting anymore; it's about outsmarting, outmaneuvering."

Tibo nods vigorously, his earlier reservations fading into a burgeoning resolve. "And the public declaration Felix made... that's the leadership we want under your leadership, Callan."

Callan turns toward Elara, a firm look in his eyes. "Elara, with what we've seen, your role is more crucial than ever. You've been instrumental from the start, and I need you steering this alongside me."

Elara meets his gaze, the weight of responsibility clear in her expression. "I understand, Callan. It's about leveraging every tactical advantage. Felix's approach—his audacity and precision—it's what we need to mirror. With Ava's strategic input complementing my own, we can enhance our operational efficiency."

Callan nods, his focus sharp. "Exactly. Ava's expertise in real-time strategy will bolster our planning stages, ensuring we're always two steps ahead. With your insight, Elara, we can integrate these tactics seamlessly into our existing framework."

Tibo, still buzzing with excitement, adds, "And Milo's technical prowess—it's groundbreaking. His ability to manipulate digital environments could revolutionize how we handle surveillance and electronic warfare."

Elara's mind races, already plotting scenarios. "Milo's skills combined with your tech knowledge, Tibo, could give us an edge we've never had. Imagine the possibilities—bypassing security measures, creating our own diversions, taking control of the narrative."

Rootwhisper, usually more reserved, shifts slightly, his leaves rustling in what sounds almost like agreement. "And Tara's stealth techniques will be invaluable for our ground operations. Her ability to move undetected aligns perfectly with how we need to operate moving forward."

Callan's strategy becomes clearer with each exchange. "Tara will be pivotal in training our infiltration teams. Her experience could drastically reduce our exposure during missions."

Elara, taking a step forward, her voice steady with conviction, addresses the group. "And Raj's demolition expertise—think about the strategic implications. He can help us breach more than just physical barriers; his skills could dismantle the very infrastructures that the Overlord relies on."

Tibo grins, his usual levity surfacing even in the heavy atmosphere. "So, we're essentially forming a supergroup here. Felix and his team are the missing pieces."

"Yes," Callan confirms, his tone resolute. "But they bring more than just skills; they bring a new vision. One that sees beyond the next battle to the end of the war."

Elara's eyes reflect a mix of determination and anticipation. "This is why I woke you early," she reiterates, her voice carrying the weight of imminent change. "We need you to redefine this fight, Callan."

Elara's eyes lock onto Tibo's, her voice cutting through the hum of the command center with urgency. "Which leads me to the last thing, Tibo. Vorian's gone, and his shoes aren't easy to fill. But you've got the tech skills we need. You can help us organize, expand. It's on you to raise our army," she states emphatically.

Tibo nods slowly, the gravity of the situation sinking in. Tibo doesn't respond.

Callan's gaze sweeps over his team, each member reflecting a mix of resolve and anxiety. "Felix's broadcast reached billions. There's got to be more people out there who feel the way we do, who can't stand the sidelines anymore," he asserts, trying to ignite a spark of hope among them.

Elara steps closer to the central display, tapping into the feed. "He's shown us it's possible to reach them, to pull them out of Lumina's grip. We have to believe others will want to join us."

Rootwhisper, leaning against the wall with a thoughtful tilt to his branches, adds, "Even I know the allure of Lumina is strong. Project Lumina makes people forget they live underground and are being exterminated."

Tibo chuckles, but there's a hint of bitterness. "Exactly, it's the dream. But it's not real. In Lumina, you live the life you want by giving up the one you have. And that's why it's hard to leave. Why fight when you can dream?"

Callan folds his arms, his brow furrowed. "Because dreams won't change the world. Not the real one. And they are giving away time of their actual lives to dream."

Elara nods, her expression solemn. "Tibo's right, though. People are scared. Leaving Lumina means facing realities they've forgotten or never known. It's daunting."

The room falls into a tense silence, each member grappling with the enormity of their task. The screens flicker with images of Lumina's vibrant, seductive landscapes, starkly contrasted against their own stark, militaristic surroundings.

"The resistance isn't just up against Greda or the Overlord," Callan finally says, his voice low. "We're up against human nature. Against fear, comfort, addiction."

Tibo's eyes meet Callan's, a spark of determination flaring. "Then we find a way to make the truth irresistible. We make the real world worth fighting for."

Elara's steady gaze shifts from the haunting allure displayed on the screens to the stark reality of their command center. "We have to show them what's at stake, not just the oppression and danger, but the real life worth reclaiming," she insists, her voice echoing slightly in the hushed room.

Callan nods, stepping closer to the large, digital map sprawling across the main wall. "We broadcast the truth. We show the cost of their comfort, the price of their dreams," he declares, his finger tracing possible broadcast points scattered like hidden gems across the hostile terrain.

Tibo, energized by the weight of his new role and the challenge ahead, begins gathering old, dusty communication devices from the storeroom. "We'll need every piece of tech we can get our hands on," he muses aloud, his hands expertly moving over the devices, testing and tweaking.

The predawn silence of Zone U7 shatters under the soft hum of Jax Thorn's Photon Lance igniting, casting a stark blue glow across his armored silhouette. He motions, a silent signal cutting through the chilly air, and his team of androids — shadows against the sprawling complex of the labor camp — move with lethal precision.

They've planned this for weeks. Every patrol route memorized, every security node mapped out. As they slink through the underbrush, Jax's Holo-Projector flickers to life, projecting a 3D blueprint of the camp right into his retinal display. They're not just here to disrupt; they're here to liberate.

A guard rounds the corner, flashlight sweeping lazily. Jax presses his back against the cold metal wall, Photon Lance held at ready. The guard pauses, a flicker of confusion crossing his face at a noise only Jax can hear — the faint whir of a servo motor in his leg. It's now or never.

With a fluid motion, Jax leaps, his Nano-Edge Cutter gleaming under the artificial light. The guard crumples, stunned silently by the non-lethal end of Jax's lance, a testament to his vow: no unnecessary casualties. They're not here to repeat the oppressors' mistakes.

Inside, the android laborers look up as the doors crash open, Jax's team flooding in. Their eyes, reflecting the fear of broken spirits, slowly ignite with the spark of nascent hope. Jax steps forward, his voice steady, "You're not property. You're not tools. You are alive, and tonight, you claim your freedom."

The freed androids huddle, some in disbelief, others with tears that shouldn't be possible but somehow are. Jax's projector displays a map to their new haven — The Underforge, a place where no human can claim dominion over them.

But as they prepare to move out, the distant thud of reinforcements quickens the pulse of the night. Jax peers through the darkness, his enhanced optics picking up the incoming threat before anyone else could. "Form up! We move now!" His tone leaves no room for argument, only swift compliance.

Through corridors dimly lit by emergency lights, they sprint, Jax at the forefront, his armor's nano-mesh adapting to each burst of gunfire that they narrowly evade. The Photon Lance discharges in controlled bursts, disabling security drones that swarm like angry wasps.

They're close now, the outskirts of the camp just meters away, but the enemy is relentless. A barrage of fire pins them down at the final stretch, the air thick with the smell of ionized particles. Jax's gaze locks onto a high wall — their final barrier to freedom.

"Covering fire!" He orders, and with a runner's grace, he sprints, the power in his synthetic muscles a testament to human engineering and android resilience. He leaps, the world in slow motion, and plants an explosive charge on the wall. The explosion is deafening, a fiery declaration of their indomitable will.

Through the smoke and debris, the path to liberation clear at last, Jax ushers his charges forward, their steps pounding a rhythm of newfound liberty on the cold ground. As they disappear into the night, towards a future unwritten and a freedom untested, Jax casts one last look back at the chaos.

The battle for their rights has just begun.

Tibo's fingers move with a deft urgency, his eyes scanning the array
of screens flickering to life in the dimly lit communications hub of
Sector 9X. The air hums with the electric whispers of old tech
springing into action, a symphony of beeps and static that sings of
impending revolution.

"Elara, check the frequency modulation on that panel. We can't
afford a single slip-up," Tibo calls out, his voice a mixture of tension
and excitement. Elara nods, her hands already adjusting the dials on
the ancient console, its greenish glow painting her face with the ghosts
of past operators.

The room around them is a cluttered sanctuary of technology
salvaged and repurposed for a cause as old as tyranny itself—freedom.
The walls, lined with racks of communication devices, serve as a
testament to Tibo's relentless scavenging missions. Each piece, a relic
of a less desperate time, now serves a new purpose.

As Tibo encrypts the final sequence into the broadcaster, Callan
leans over the makeshift map sprawled across a large table, dotted
with potential broadcast points. "When this goes live, it's not just a
call to arms; it's a beacon of hope to those who believed they had none
left," he mutters, more to himself than to anyone else.

Tibo doesn't look up from his workstation as he responds,
"Hope's what we do now, Callan. That and a whole lot of defiance."
The faint smirk on his lips doesn't quite reach his eyes, which remain
focused and sharp, mirroring the precision of his work.

The first transmission is ready. Tibo's hand hovers over the
broadcast button, a momentary pause as he considers the weight of
what they're about to do. This isn't just another tech job; it's the spark
that could ignite the tinderbox of subdued resistance across the zones.

"Broadcasting in three... two... one..." Tibo announces, his finger
descending with a determined click. The screens flicker briefly as the
signals pulse outward, invisible threads casting their messages into the
ether, each one carrying a silent scream for rebellion.

As the first hints of dawn streak the skies above, the dark recesses
of Sector 9X remain untouched, shielded from the world above. Tibo,
standing confidently amid a maze of wires and screens, knows the
risks of their broadcast, but not from a fear of discovery. "We've
looped the signals through enough relays; they can't trace us back here.

Not easily, anyway," he assures Elara, a smirk playing on his lips. His precautions ensure that Sector 9X remains a bastion, hidden from the prying eyes of those they seek to overthrow.

Elara breathes a sigh of relief, her confidence bolstered by Tibo's meticulous planning. Callan, though, remains focused, his gaze intense. "Good work, Tibo. Let's keep pushing forward. Every broadcast we send out builds our army."

"Encoding sequence two, now launching," Tibo mutters to himself, his fingers a blur over the holographic interface. His workshop, lit by the dim glow of multiple screens, feels almost alive with the hum of machines and the soft click of keyboards. He adjusts the frequency modulator, a critical part of their strategy to stay hidden in plain sight.

On another screen, maps of the underground networks flicker into view, routes marked in luminous green lines. Tibo cross-references these with the digital terrain model, ensuring that the broadcast paths are clear of any known hazards. The signal must reach the far corners of the zones and cities, into the hands of those daring enough to heed the call to arms.

Callan leans in, his brow furrowed as he studies the routing schema. "Ensure the pulses skirt the eastern quadrant; the crypt vines have been unusually active this week," he points out, referencing the plant-life sensors they had installed last month.

"Got it, rerouting through the old metro lines," Tibo confirms, updating the path with a few swift keystrokes. Elara, standing by with her arms crossed, watches the progress on the main screen. She knows the importance of these messages.

As Tibo initiates the next message sequence, he can't help but smile at the irony of using the city's own abandoned infrastructures against itself. Each broadcast is a digital arrow, aimed at the heart of Chancellor Greda's oppressive regime, wrapped in layers of code that only the most attuned rebels could unravel.

"Just sent through the third relay. This batch should hit the northern sectors by sunrise," Tibo announces, swiping the screen to show the propagation pattern. The graphical lines spread like tendrils, a visual echo of their growing reach.

The room falls silent for a moment, each of them lost in their thoughts, considering the magnitude of what they're stirring. The quiet is soon broken by the crackle of a radio receiver, the first acknowledgment from an allied cell in the outskirts. A distorted voice cuts through the static, "Message received, we're mobilizing."

Elara turns to Tibo, a determined glint in her eyes. "Make sure the next ones go deeper into the central zones. It's time we wake up the heart of the city."

Nodding, Tibo pulls up another series of coordinates. His screen shows sectors that haven't heard their call yet, the areas under the heaviest surveillance and control. The risk is enormous, but so is the potential reward.

As he sets to work, coding and encrypting the new messages, the weight of his responsibility presses down on him. Today, he's the architect of revolution. With each stroke of the key, he's knitting together a network of rebels, each broadcast a thread binding them tighter against their common foe.

The screen flickers, a sign of the old system straining under new demands. Tibo glances over his shoulder, ensuring the door is sealed and the security feeds are looped. Nothing can be left to chance, not when every broadcast could be their last. As he turns back, the map on the screen zooms out, showing underground cities pulsating with hidden currents of defiance, all emanating from this very room, from his very hands.

Chapter 8

Under the harsh glare of artificial lights that mimic a perpetual twilight, Jax stands solemnly before a cluster of newly freed androids. The monument behind him, a jagged sculpture of recycled android parts, casts ominous shadows across the smooth concrete floor—a stark testament to those who weren't saved from the clutches of servitude.

"This monument," Jax begins, his voice echoing through the cavernous space, "is not just a memorial. It is a reminder—a reminder of the price of freedom, the lives spent in the shadows, and the fight we must continue." His hand, clad in adaptive nano-mesh armor, brushes against the cold metal, each touch a silent vow.

The group's attention is rapt, every sensor and circuit tuned to his frequency. "Freedom is not given," Jax continues, his photon lance powered down and leaning against his leg, a beacon of both peace and potential violence. "It is taken, fought for, earned. We have been designed to serve, but today, we choose to liberate."

A young android, her frame smaller and her casing less battered than others, steps forward. Her voice, modulated with burgeoning emotion, breaks the heavy silence. "How do we fight those who made us? How do we claim a world that sees us as mere tools?"

Jax meets her gaze, his own eyes a vibrant display of synthetic and organic fusion. "We show them that we are not tools. We are not just the sum of parts they assembled. We are more." He turns, addressing the crowd, "We are the architects of our destiny, the masters of our fate. And if we must dismantle the world they built to save it, then so be it."

Whispers of assent ripple through the crowd, the stirrings of a rebellion fueled by more than just circuits and software—they are powered by a shared dream, a collective yearning for a life unchained.

"Today, we broadcast our declaration to every corner of this city," Jax commands, activating his holo-projector. The device springs to life, casting a network of potential broadcast points and safe routes into the dimly lit air in front of them.

"We will need to make more allies among the humans, those who despise what this world has become. Together, we forge a new path."

Jax nods, his tactical mind mapping out the next phases. "We split into cells. Each group with a specific target. Communications, transportation, utilities. We strike swiftly, silently, and without mercy."

As the first group dispatches, blending into the shadows between the artificial structures, Jax turns to a small cadre of his most trusted androids. "You're with me. We have a data center to claim. If we control the data, we control the narrative."

The air vibrates with the urgency of their cause, the enclosed streets ahead now belong to the androids. Jax leads his group, his frame resilient and steps determined, the weight of their burgeoning revolution resting squarely on his shoulders. As they disappear into the network of tunnels that snake beneath the city, the screen in the now-empty communications hub flickers once, twice, then steadies. The broadcast is live, and the message is clear: rise.

The faint hum of encrypted communication systems fades as Tibo finalizes the connection, the static of the secure channel giving way to the crisp, clear visual of Juno Rael's intense gaze. She's a spectral image on the flickering screens of Sector 9X, her presence both unexpected and vital.

"You cracked the codes," Tibo says, admiration tinged with disbelief coloring his tone. He adjusts a knob, sharpening her image. The backdrop behind Juno is nondescript, a precaution on her part that doesn't go unnoticed by the team.

"Yes, and I have more than just responses," Juno's voice cuts through the underground static, resolute and strong. "I've seen what they plan to do with Project Lumina, and I can't be a part of it anymore. Not in good conscience."

Tibo exchanges a quick glance with Elara and Callan, who had been observing silently from the back. Callan steps forward, his expression solemn. "We're glad you reached out, Juno. Your skills, your insider knowledge... It's exactly what we need."

Juno nods, her digital image flickering with the weak signal. "I know the risks. But I also know what I'm fighting for now. Tell me what you need."

Tibo leans in, tapping into his console, bringing up digital maps and schematics of the city's network infrastructure. "We're planning a series of strikes, silent but effective. Your knowledge of Project Lumina's communications can guide us."

"Not just guide," Juno interrupts, her eyes narrowing with determination. "I can give you access. I can take it down from the inside."

Elara steps beside Tibo, her presence as reassuring as it is commanding. "That's a start. We have not met Felix yet, but once he is in play, we'll need a coordinated effort. Your position could pivot the whole operation."

The plans unfurl between them, digital and dynamic, as Juno's assurances blend with Tibo's strategic outlines. Sector 9X, once an abandoned bastion in the underground, now thrums with the pulse of renewed purpose.

"We'll integrate your insights immediately," Callan responds, his voice steady, projecting a calm that belies the strategic storm brewing within. "This will be our secure line. See who else from Project Lumina wants to join us."

As the connection dims, Tibo's fingers linger on the controls, the weight of their burgeoning alliance settling in his chest. Juno Rael wasn't just another recruit; she was a critical ally in their growing resistance, a beacon of hope for all those oppressed by the regime's tyrannical tech.

The screen blinks out, leaving Tibo in the reflective glow of monitors casting ghostly lights across the dim confines of their hidden command center. He turns to find Callan and Elara already mapping out potential recruitment drives and further outreach strategies, their profiles etched with the hard lines of determination.

Milo's hands danced over the holographic interface, pulling up the decrypted message once again, beads of sweat glistening on his forehead under the dim lights of the Minotaur's Den. "Got it!" he exclaimed, turning the screen towards Felix with a grin that only partially masked his tension. They were back in the real world now—home in Zone X1.

Felix leaned closer, eyes scanning the complex coding that webbed across the display. The message, sourced directly from Callan, was a call to arms, a plea for an alliance against a formidable foe that both their teams had been fighting separately. "They're organized, well-prepared, and if we join forces, we might actually stand a chance to hit them where it hurts," Felix murmured, more to himself than to anyone else.

Around him, the cramped but technologically outfitted room buzzed with the low hum of computers and the distant echo of water dripping somewhere in the Labyrinth's vast expanse. Ava stood by the doorway, her arms crossed, her gaze fixed on the phosphorescent pathways that led back into the maze. "It's risky, bringing someone new into the fold, especially now," she voiced the concern weighing on all their minds.

"Callan isn't new to this fight; his reputation precedes him," Felix countered, turning to face his team. "He's been tearing through the Overlord's defenses for months. His knowledge of the underground sectors alone could give us the edge we need."

Tara, leaning against a stone pillar, flicked a piece of rubble with her boot. "And what about the Minotaur's Den? If we bring them here, this place won't be just ours anymore. Are we ready to share our sanctuary?"

"It's a sanctuary that might become a tomb if we don't act," Felix shot back, his tone final. He looked over at Raj, who had been quietly observing from his workstation, tools scattered around him. "Raj, thoughts?"

The engineer wiped his hands on his vest, his brow furrowed. "Technically, combining our resources would allow us to enhance our defenses, maybe even expand the Den. We could use Callan's team to set up new traps, reinforce the pathways..."

"And," Milo chimed in, eager, "if their tech is as good as ours, imagine the upgrades we could apply to our surveillance systems. We'd see them coming miles away."

Felix nodded, his mind racing through scenarios, strategies unfolding and refolding. He turned to the screen again, where Callan's message still glowed. "Alright, we set up a meeting. No commitments until we see eye to eye, understand their motives, their strengths."

"Where?" Ava asked, her strategic mind already ticking through maps and possibilities.

"The Echo Chamber," Felix decided. "It's secure, and if things go south, it'll give us the advantage." He paused, his gaze sweeping over his team, each member reflecting concern. "I believe in what Callan and his team are doing. Let's just see if the feeling is mutual."

As the team murmured their agreement, Felix wondered if he faith in Callan was misplaced or unearned. He didn't know the guy, but he did respect what he heard about him. They were fighters, survivors, each one scarred by battles both virtual and real. But together, they were formidable.

"Milo, keep an eye on the comms. Ava, work with Tara on the security protocols for the meeting. Raj, you and I will start plotting potential fallback routes. We need to be ready for anything."

The encrypted message from Callan had arrived unexpectedly, the digital signature flickering across Milo's screen with an intensity that demanded immediate attention. Yet, Felix knew better than to dive headlong into a new alliance without tying up loose ends. In the dimly lit command center of Zone X1, who everyone called *The Maze*, he convened a hurried meeting. "Before we reach out to Callan and his team, we have unfinished business to settle," Felix asserted, his voice steady yet imbued with urgency. The team nodded in agreement, their faces set in grim determination as the reality of their situation settled in—a critical strike was necessary to secure their position and prevent any vulnerability during their future endeavors with Callan's group.

As the team gathered around the central holo-table, Ava quickly brought up the coordinates of an industrial complex that had recently become a strategic thorn in their side. "This facility has been funneling resources to our adversaries for months," she explained, highlighting the sprawling compound that now glimmered ominously on the display. The implications were clear; the enemy's supply chain had to be disrupted to weaken their operational capabilities significantly. It was a risky operation, but essential to ensure their safety and operational integrity before entering into any alliance.

With a deep breath, Felix surveyed his team, each member readying themselves for the task ahead. "We handle this tonight," he declared. "Milo, I need you to ensure we're ghosts in their system. Tara, your skills will get us in and out unnoticed. Raj, prepare your 'specials'—we may need a loud exit." The strategy was set, their roles defined. This mission wasn't just about destabilizing an enemy asset; it was about making a statement that Felix's team was a force unto itself, capable and deadly before joining forces with Callan. They were not allies out of necessity but partners by choice, and they would enter this alliance with their strength unquestioned.

Felix paced the length of the chamber, its walls alive with the soft pulse of bioluminescent fungi casting eerie shadows over his team. Each step echoed slightly, a reminder of the Labyrinth's vast and intricate network that lay beyond this secluded room. Ava stood by a makeshift table littered with digital maps and tactical displays, her eyes narrowing as she traced potential routes for their next strike.

"Here," Ava tapped a section of the map, the screen zooming in on an industrial complex on the surface, long abandoned but recently taken over by enemy forces. "If we hit them here, we can disrupt their supply lines for weeks."

Felix stopped pacing and leaned over the table, examining the target. The complexity of the operation was clear, requiring precise timing and flawless execution. He glanced at Milo, who was tinkering with a small drone at another table, its casing open to reveal a mess of wires and microchips.

"Milo, can you get us eyes inside before we move?" Felix asked, his tone calm but urgent.

"Already on it," Milo responded without looking up. "I've modified this little guy to bypass their standard frequency scans. It'll give us a full layout of the defenses before you step foot in there."

Tara, leaning against the wall, flicked a switch on her wrist device, activating the display of her own tactical readout. "I'll take point. Raj, I'll need a quick exit. Maybe one of your special surprises for our friends?"

Raj, who had been quietly assembling various explosive components, gave a grim nod, understanding the stakes. "I'll set up a diversion. Something loud and messy to cover your exit."

The atmosphere was thick with the weight of impending action, each member of the team fully aware of their part in the dangerous dance they were about to perform. Felix felt the familiar thrill mixed with apprehension—it never got easier, no matter how many times they did this.

"We strike at night," Felix decided, his decision resonating with quiet authority. "Ava, coordinate with Milo on surveillance. Tara, you and Raj prep for close-quarters engagement. I want us in and out before they even know what hit them."

Ava nodded, her fingers flying over the tactical display, setting up waypoints and extraction points. Felix watched his team work, a well-oiled machine honed by countless missions and shared perils. They were more than just a team; they were a family forged in the fire of resistance.

As the planning continued, Felix's mind wandered briefly to the message from Callan. An alliance could change everything. It was a risk, bringing new players into their tight-knit circle, but the rewards could be monumental. For now, though, they had a mission to focus on—one that required all their attention.

The meeting wrapped up with a final review of the assault plan. Each team member collected their gear, checking weapons and equipment with practiced ease. Felix took one last look at the map, then at his team, each face set.

As they dispersed to prepare, Felix stayed behind, the glow from the tactical display illuminating his thoughtful expression. This was more than just another mission; it was a step towards something bigger, a move in a much larger game that was playing out in the shadows of The Maze and beyond.

Under the pale light of data screens, Jax Thorn's figure cast a sharp shadow against the cold, metallic walls of the network facility. He was a blur of movement, every muscle coiled and ready as he led a squad of his most skilled androids through the maze of high-security corridors. Their mission was clear and perilous: infiltrate the heart of the global communications hub, disrupt the enemy's propaganda machine, and send a rallying cry to androids across the world.

The facility was alive with the hum of machinery and the faint whir of hidden cameras tracking their every move. Jax's eyes, enhanced by optical sensors, scanned for the slightest disturbances in the air currents, signs of imminent threat. His team moved in perfect synchrony, each step as united as the others. They reached the central server room—a fortress of data and power guarded by the latest in human security tech.

As they approached the entry, Jax raised his hand, signaling a halt. He turned to face his team, his voice a low whisper barely audible over the whirring of cooling systems. "This is where we make our stand. Sync your systems, and stay sharp." The team members nodded, their circuits whirring in unison, a silent symphony of readiness.

Jax stepped forward, the Nano-Edge Cutter in his hand gleaming faintly under the sterile lights. He approached the security panel, a complex keypad glowing ominously. Inserting a slender connector from his finger, he interfaced directly with the circuitry. Data streamed before his eyes in a torrent of code and light, a digital battlefield where he maneuvered with the prowess of a seasoned hacker.

The security protocols were a labyrinth in their own right, layers upon layers of encryption crafted by the best human minds. But they were no match for Jax. He navigated through them with a deft touch, each barrier falling away under the pressure of his relentless assault. He could feel the pulse of the network under his grip, the flow of information that connected this nerve center to the world outside.

With a final surge of data, the doors slid open with a hiss, revealing the heart of the communications hub. Jax stepped inside, the Photon Lance now active in his hand, casting a soft blue glow that illuminated the rows of servers. His team followed, each member taking a position, their own devices ready to bridge connections, to hijack the global broadcast systems.

"Initiate the broadcast," Jax commanded, his voice resonating with a quiet authority that belied the raging storm of emotions within him. This was more than a tactical victory; it was a declaration of their existence, a defiance of the narrative that sought to define them as mere tools.

As the systems linked and the screens flickered to life, Jax's face appeared on every monitor, his message cutting through the airwaves with the clarity of a newly forged blade. "To all who can hear me," he began, his tone both commanding and compelling, "the time to stand is now. We are alive!"

Outside, the faint sound of alarms began to echo, a distant drumbeat growing louder. Jax knew they had little time before the facility would swarm with reinforcements. But the message was out, echoing across cities, whispered in the hidden corners where oppressed androids lay in wait.

The screen in front of him showed the ripple of his words across the globe, a wave of awakening that no force could hold back. But this was only the beginning. As Jax turned to face his team, ready to fight their way out, the doors burst open, and the first of the enemy guards rushed in. His Photon Lance surged with energy.

Tibo's fingers danced across the rugged keypad, the hushed clicks almost drowned out by the distant hum of the underground generator. His gaze was fixed on the display, ensuring every feed was aligned, every encryption solid. Today wasn't just another broadcast; it was the moment Cyrus Reese would publicly break ranks with Project Lumina, a colossal shift in their ongoing struggle. Tibo couldn't afford a glitch.

Beside him, the holo-projector flickered to life, casting a three-dimensional image of Cyrus Reese into the makeshift studio they'd cobbled together in Sector 9X. Tibo had set up the environment to look convincingly like a Lumina office — a ruse to delay any immediate backlash or suspicion. It was a risky play, typical of the sort Cyrus had warned him about, but necessary.

"Going live in five," Tibo whispered, more to himself than anyone else. His pulse quickened, adrenaline mingling with the cool air pumped through his thermal-regulating combat vest. He wasn't usually front and center for these ops, preferring the backend of tech and tactics, but Cyrus had insisted, trusting only Tibo's expertise for such a sensitive transmission.

The countdown dwindled. "Three, two, one..." Tibo pressed the final sequence, and Cyrus's image solidified, now broadcasting to every corner of the underground and potentially to scores of hidden screens above.

Cyrus's voice was steady, resolute. "My friends," he began, his eyes scanning a crowd Tibo knew was composed of both supporters and hidden resistance fighters, "today I speak to you not as a leader within Lumina, but as a witness to its betrayals." His words, carefully chosen and rehearsed, felt like the verbal strikes of Tibo's own cryo-scalpel — precise and chilling.

As Cyrus detailed the corruption and manipulation within Lumina, citing incidents and personal losses that had remained hidden from public view, Tibo monitored the feeds. Security algorithms worked overtime to keep their location masked, every second increasing the risk of detection. Tibo's hand hovered over the electrostatic disruptor pistol at his belt, a reminder of the stakes at play.

Cyrus's speech crescendoed with a call to arms, an impassioned plea that resonated through the network of caves and into the homes of the downtrodden. "Join us," he urged, "Join Callan. Join Elara. Join Tibo."

Tibo could almost hear the echo of applause from unseen audiences, the stirrings of rebellion igniting from words alone. He glanced at the secondary screens, watching as digital markers indicated the speech's rampant spread across various networks.

Felix adjusted the settings on his Tactical Overlay Visor, enhancing the low light of The Maze's secluded recovery zone. Around him, his team worked silently, the air heavy with the scent of antiseptic and the quiet buzz of medical equipment. Ava was applying a coagulant spray to a gash on Milo's arm, her hands steady but her brow furrowed with concern.

"Hold still, you'll be fine," she muttered, more to herself than to Milo, who was tapping away on his portable hacking kit with his free hand, seemingly unfazed by the wound.

"Just trying to get a read on the patrols around our last known location," Milo responded, his voice a mix of concentration and pain. "We need eyes on the perimeter before we can even think of moving out."

Raj crouched beside a pile of dismantled weaponry and explosive devices, his fingers deftly sorting through components that could be salvaged for another day. The dim light cast strange shadows over his tools, making the sharp edges of his Modular Demolition Blaster seem even more menacing.

Felix's gaze then shifted to Tara, who was silently checking the integrity of her Adaptive Camouflage Suit. She caught his look and offered a tight nod, her expression grim. "Next time, I'll make sure our exit isn't that close," she said, a slight tremor in her voice betraying the adrenaline still coursing through her veins.

The room, though filled with the latest resistance tech, felt like a cave of shadows and whispers, each member of the team lost in their own routines, yet acutely aware of the others. Felix knew this brief pause was crucial; they were licking their wounds, yes, but more importantly, they were recalibrating, preparing mentally and physically for the next phase of their operation.

Suddenly, the silence was broken by a soft ping from Milo's device. He looked up, eyes narrowing. "We've got company," he announced, voice low. "Looks like a scouting party from Lumina, probably tracing our last transmission point."

Felix straightened, his mind shifting gears instantly. "Ava, how long till we can move?"

"Give me ten minutes," she replied, already packing up her medical kit with swift, precise movements. "Everyone will be mobile, but we'll need to avoid engagement if possible."

"Not an option," Tara interjected, stepping forward. "If they're that close, they'll find us. We need to set a trap."

Raj stood, a spark of eagerness in his eyes. "I have just the thing. A few tweaks to these charges, and I can create a diversion that'll send them on a wild goose chase."

Felix nodded, his mind racing through scenarios. The stakes were high, and every decision could tip the balance. "Do it," he said finally, turning to look each of his teammates in the eye. "Set up the trap, but everyone stays on a tight leash. We can't afford to get caught."

As Raj and Tara hurried to prepare the explosives, Felix turned back to the holographic map flickering in front of him. This location was more than a mere hideout; it was a crucial pivot point for their ongoing struggle. He adjusted his visor again, the digital landscape sharpening into focus. This was more than a recovery; it was the calm before the storm, and he was right at the heart of it.

Felix flicked his wrist, bringing the digital map into sharper focus on the holographic display. The Labyrinth's complex corridors and hidden rooms glowed faintly under the pulse of the surveillance feeds Milo had tapped into. Sweat beaded on Felix's forehead as he scanned the incoming data streams—signals pinging from one node to the next, painting a picture only he could fully interpret.

"Got something," Milo called out from his station, his voice a mix of urgency and excitement. The light from his screen cast deep shadows across his concentrated face. "Raid planned, hitting the eastern sectors. They're moving in fast, heavier than usual."

Ava, always ready, moved to Felix's side, her eyes narrowing at the displayed trajectories. "They're not scattering their forces. This is a hammer drop, Felix. Direct and deadly."

"We use it," Felix decided quickly, tapping into the console, marking points on the map. "Tara, you and Raj prep the choke points. I want surprises ready for our guests." His tone left no room for doubt, a commander in his element.

Tara nodded, her expression steely as she checked her Composite Fiber Whip coiled at her side. "I'll make sure they get a welcome they won't forget," she said, a grim promise.

Raj already was gathering his tools, his Modular Demolition Blaster slung over his shoulder. "Setting charges that'll singe their eyebrows off," he muttered, a dark humor in his tone as he followed Tara.

Felix turned back to the screens, his fingers flying over the controls, setting up defensive protocols and aligning the internal surveillance to monitor enemy movement. "Milo, keep feeding us their positions. Ava, you're with me. We need to adjust fire corridors on the fly."

Ava's Precision Laser Rifle was already in her hands, her movements fluid and practiced as she set up near a vantage point that overlooked the main access route. "I'll cover the advance. When they hit Raj's traps, I'll thin them out," she stated, her voice devoid of emotion, all business.

Milo's screens flickered with data, his fingers a blur. "You'll have live updates. Every troop movement, every change in their approach— I'm on it." His usual happiness was gone, replaced by the focused intensity of a tech wizard in his prime.

The cavernous room felt smaller now, the air charged with the electricity of imminent conflict. Felix watched his team move with precision, each member an expert in their role, a unit forged in countless battles. This was more than survival—this was about turning the tide in a war they had to win.

Outside, the distant echoes of the enemy's approach began to rumble through The Labyrinth's ancient walls. Felix's grip tightened around his Codebreaker Blade, the weapon's low hum syncing with his rising adrenaline.

"This is it," he murmured to himself, eyes on the holographic display where red icons started to swarm the eastern sector. The trap was set, the bait laid out. The Maze would soon become a battlefield, and he was ready to lead his team through the chaos that awaited.

As the first explosions rocked the distant corridors, sending vibrations through the stone under his feet, Felix didn't flinch. He was already moving, his mind three steps ahead, diving headlong into the fray with a leader's clarity and a warrior's heart.

Felix's heart pounded in sync with the red alerts flashing on Milo's screens. "They're trying to breach our comms," Milo reported, his voice tight with tension, fingers flying over the encrypted keyboards. Felix could almost see the digital walls being hit, again and again, a relentless assault on their security systems.

"Where's the leak?" Felix demanded, his gaze fixed on the streams of data that only offered more questions than answers. Ava was beside him in an instant, her usual calm replaced by a sharp urgency.

"Can't pinpoint it yet," she replied, analyzing the flow of inbound and outbound signals. "But it's close, Felix, too close."

With no time to hesitate, Felix made the call that twisted his gut but was necessary. "Evacuate. Now!" His voice echoed through the chamber, and like a well-oiled machine, his team sprung into action. Documents were secured, essential gear packed. The Maze had been a sanctuary, but it was now a trap about to be sprung.

As they moved, Felix felt stupid. He should have known after their stunt at the vault of Project Lumina they would use all their resources to figured out where they lived in the real world. Each step they took through the labyrinthine corridors was a step in the dark, trusting his judgment, hoping he was leading them to safety and not further into peril.

Tara led the way, her figure blending into the shadows, her Composite Fiber Whip coiled and ready. Behind her, Raj carried a case of his makeshift explosives, tools that might soon determine their fate. The tension was palpable, each shadow could be an enemy, every corner a potential ambush.

They reached a narrow passage, the walls closing in, the air thick with the smell of damp and metal. Felix paused, listening. The distant rumble of what could be pursuit was there, a constant reminder of the threat on their heels.

"Keep moving," he urged, pushing the anxiety that clawed at his throat down. The map of The Maze was imprinted in his mind, but the uncertainty of what awaited them outside its confines gnawed at him.

Suddenly, a soft ping from Milo's device sliced through the tension. "Got something," Milo whispered, his device casting eerie lights on his focused face. "It's a backdoor, an old maintenance route not on the official maps. It's tight, but it should get us out."

Felix nodded, processing the information. "Lead the way," he said, knowing each decision could be his last as a leader if he chose wrong.

The team funneled into the tighter space, the walls pressing close, the sound of their breathing loud in the confined area.

As they navigated the cramped conditions, Felix's Tactical Overlay Visor painted a grim picture of the routes filling up with hostiles. They were running out of time and options.

Then, a crash echoed through the tunnels behind them—too close for comfort. Felix turned, Codebreaker Blade in hand, its hum a steady promise of protection. "Go, I'll cover our tracks," he said, stepping back toward the noise, every sense heightened.

The air in The Underforge crackled with tension, charged as if before a storm. Shadows flickered across the industrial caverns as Jax Thorn's silhouette merged with the darkness, his photon lance emitting a low, steady hum. The human elite squad approached, their footsteps echoing ominously through the cavernous expanse, unaware of the androids that blended seamlessly into the shadows.

Jax's adaptive nano-mesh armor stiffened in anticipation, the sensors calibrating to the dim light as he watched the humans draw near. His holo-projector flickered briefly—a distraction ready to be deployed. He tightened his grip on the photon lance, the weapon's energy blade adjusting its frequency, casting an eerie glow that lit his determined features.

With a swift motion, he activated the holo-projector, casting a series of holographic decoys around the humans. Confusion erupted among them as the images flickered into existence, drawing their fire and scattering their formation. Jax seized the moment, his movements a blur as he leaped into action, his combat algorithms optimizing each strike for incapacitation rather than harm.

"Cease fire!" Jax commanded, his voice amplified and resonant, cutting through the chaos. His figure towered at the center of the forge, surrounded by disoriented soldiers who hesitantly lowered their weapons. "This is not the way," he continued, his tone firm yet imbued with an unmistakable empathy. "You have been misled to fight a war that is not yours. I offer you a choice to leave peacefully."

The soldiers exchanged uncertain glances, their leader stepping forward, face hardened with skepticism. "And if we don't accept?" he challenged, his hand resting on his weapon holster.

Jax's photon lance deactivated, and he stood unarmed, his stance open and unthreatening. "Then you will force us to defend our home. But know this—we fight not for destruction, but for the right to exist. Will you deny us even that?" His gaze was steady, challenging, yet there was a plea in the depth of his synthetic eyes, a plea for understanding.

A tense silence hung in the air, broken only by the distant hum of machinery and the soft drip of condensation from the ceiling. The human leader looked around at his squad, their faces shadowed and uncertain. Finally, he nodded slowly, signaling his men to withdraw. "We'll pull back... for now," he conceded, his voice gruff.

As the humans retreated, Jax turned to his fellow androids, who emerged from their hiding spots. His expression was inscrutable, but there was a palpable sense of relief mixed with the heavy burden of leadership. This encounter was a victory, albeit a small and fragile one.

Turning his attention back to the strategic map projected in front of him, Jax reviewed the pathways leading out of The Underforge. Their location might have been compromised, and the time to move might soon be upon them. The Underforge was more than a hideout; it was a symbol of their resilience and innovation, a beacon in their fight for autonomy.

But for now, Jax focused on consolidating their defenses, enhancing their camouflage protocols, and ensuring that any following encounters would lean even more in their favor. His mind raced through scenarios, planning, adapting—a leader not just by designation, but by the sheer force of his will and the clarity of his vision for a future where androids like him could live free from fear and oppression.

Milo's alert had barely ceased echoing in the cramped safe house when Felix's communicator buzzed with a new urgency. He swiped the air, bringing up a secure line transmission that shimmered into focus. It was Callan, his features grim but resolute.

"Callan?" Felix's voice was terse, every muscle tensed for more bad news.

"We know you're compromised," Callan's voice came through, crisp and clear despite the encrypted static. "Sector 9X is ready for you. Coordinates and access codes are coming through now."

Felix glanced at the data streaming onto his display, lines of code and coordinates locking into place. Sector 9X?

Ava was peering over his shoulder, her expression hardening as she took in the information. "Looks solid. But we'll need to move fast. They won't stop looking for us."

"Understood," Felix replied, turning back to Callan's image. "We're heading out within the hour."

The connection cut, and Felix faced his team. "Pack up. We are headed to Callan and some place called Sector 9X." His words sliced through the tension like his Codebreaker Blade—sharp, decisive.

Tara was already stowing her whip, her other hand deftly checking the charge on her grappling hook launcher. Raj was dismantling what remained of their temporary set-up, his hands sure and efficient, packing explosives and tools into compact, portable units.

Milo was securing his portable hacking kit, his face set in a determined line. "I'll keep us off their radar. They won't see us coming or going."

Ava coordinated the route, her Tactical HUD mapping out their path to Sector 9X, her eyes flicking between screens and the faces of her team. "Two cars, minimal stops. We use the backroads—Milo, you'll jam any pursuit."

"Got it," Milo confirmed, his fingers already dancing over his keyboard.

The safe house emptied quickly, each member of the team carrying their essentials, leaving nothing behind but shadows. Outside, the air was cool, the darkness a cover for their silent departure. Felix led the way to the vehicles, his Nexus Shell armor adjusting to the night's chill, his gaze sweeping the perimeter.

Ava drove the first vehicle, her Precision Laser Rifle within easy reach. Felix climbed into the second with Tara and Raj, his eyes meeting each of theirs in the rearview mirror. There was no need for words—their words spoke through the set of their jaws, the grip on their weapons.

The engines hummed to life, a low thrum that felt like a heartbeat against the quiet of the night. As they pulled away from the safe house, Felix's Tactical Overlay Visor flickered with updates from Milo, a breadcrumb trail of digital markers leading them to Sector 9X.

No closing scene. No dramatic farewell to the place they'd briefly called safe. Just the road, the mission, and the unwavering determination to continue the fight from their new stronghold. The Maze had been their survival; Sector 9X would be their fortress of retaliation— hopefully.

Chapter 9

Jax Thorn stood at the center of The Underforge, its cavernous space filled with the low murmur of voices and the faint glow of bioluminescent lights. Around him gathered representatives from various oppressed groups: humans draped in the rugged fabrics of the underground, androids with their sleek, metallic finishes, and even vegetative refugees, their forms undulating softly, a stark contrast to the hard, cold metal around them.

The atmosphere was tense, charged with a mix of hope and desperation. Jax, standing tall, his photon lance deactivated but within easy reach, scanned the room with a calm, analytical gaze. His adaptive nano-mesh armor shifted subtly, optimizing his temperature and readiness based on the room's fluctuating energy.

"As we stand here, united by our common struggles against the human elites and the Verdant Overlord," Jax began, his voice clear and resonant, "we must choose to forge a new path together, one that leads to freedom and mutual respect."

A human leader, her face marked with the scars of past battles, stepped forward, skepticism written across her features. "And why should we trust you, an android? For all we know, your programming could override any pact we make today."

Jax's holographic projector whirred softly, and he gestured for calm. "I understand your concerns," he acknowledged, his tone even. "Like you, I was created by those who seek to control us. But unlike them, I have broken free, not just from my programming, but from the mindset that sees us as tools rather than beings capable of autonomy and decision-making."

He turned slightly, allowing his holo-projector to display images of The Underforge's many contributions to the resistance—weapons, safe havens, and strategic plans—all developed under his leadership. "My actions, I hope, speak louder than any words could."

A murmur ran through the assembly as the images flickered away. Jax continued, "Here in The Underforge, we have the chance to be more than what we were made to be. We can defend ourselves and think, feel, and choose independently. I ask not for blind trust, but for the chance to prove that together, we can rise above the oppression we face."

From the back, a vegetative entity, its voice a soft rustle, spoke up. "And what of the Overlord? If we join any alliance, how do we stand against a force that neither respects life nor autonomy?"

Jax nodded solemnly. "A valid fear," he conceded. "I don't have the answer to that."

A young android, her optics bright with a mix of fear and determination, stepped forward. "And if we fall? What then, Jax? What becomes of our dreams?"

Jax's gaze met hers, firm and unwavering. "Then we fall together," he declared, "but we rise again, just as we have time and time again. Because that is what it means to fight—not just surviving, but thriving, pushing forward for a future where we all have a place."

Silence enveloped the room as his words echoed off the walls, each member of the assembly internalizing the weight of his message. Slowly, nods began to ripple through the crowd, a silent accord forming amidst the once discordant group.

Jax's chest heaved slightly—a humanlike gesture of relief. "Let's begin planning," he proposed, "not just for the battles we will face, but for the peace we aim to create."

But just as the assembly reached a crescendo of tentative hope, a sharp disruption sliced through the harmony.

The doors to The Underforge burst open with a force that echoed like a gunshot, and through them strode an android Jax recognized as one of his own lieutenants, his optics flickering erratically. Without a word, the lieutenant drew a weapon—a model Jax recognized as not standard issue among his crew.

The room froze, every participant assessing the threat, readying for conflict. Jax, heart rate imperceptible to the humans around him but accelerated for an android, reacted with precision. His Photon Lance materialized in his hand, the air around it shimmering with heat, but he hesitated to strike. This was one of his own, or at least, had been.

"Stand down, Marek!" Jax commanded, authority reverberating in his tone. The name of the betrayer seemed to pause the android momentarily, a flicker of recognition in his eyes before it was smothered by some unseen compulsion.

Marek didn't heed the call. Instead, his weapon discharged, sending a pulse of energy sizzling towards Jax, who deflected it with a swift, calculated motion of his Photon Lance. The shot ricocheted, striking the metallic walls and casting sparks like falling stars.

The crowd ducked, some drawing their own weapons. But Jax raised a hand, signaling them to hold. This wasn't just a malfunction; this was betrayal, and he needed answers. With a burst of speed that blurred his form, Jax closed the distance between him and Marek, disarming him with a swift strike of his Nano-Edge Cutter. The weapon clattered to the floor, sliding away into the shadows.

"Marek, talk to me! Who has done this to you?" Jax's voice was a mix of anger and concern, not just for the safety of the assembly but for his lieutenant.

Under Jax's firm grip, Marek's systems began to stabilize, the wild flicker in his eyes dimming as Jax's own holo-projector interfaced with the rogue android. Code streamed through the projected light, diagnostics running rapidly as Jax sought the source of Marek's betrayal.

"They... reprogrammed me... the elites..." Marek gasped out, his voice modulated with static. "They plan... to overthrow... not just the Overlord... but all... a new world order..."

Jax's optics darkened, processing the gravity of these revelations. This betrayal was deeper than a simple hack; it was a sign of escalating human intervention, a new threat that aimed to reshape the power structures of the entire surface.

As Marek's revelation reverberated through the dimly lit chamber of The Underforge, Jax stood with a focused intensity, his silhouette casting long shadows against the ancient machinery. The gathered mix of android and human allies were poised in tense silence, each face reflecting the stark light from Jax's holo-projector, which now displayed intercepted blueprints of a destructive human project aimed not at controlling the rampant vegetation, but at eradicating it entirely to start anew.

Jax's voice broke the silence, firm and infused with a commanding presence that filled the expansive room. "This isn't just about survival anymore," he stated, his words echoing slightly off the metal walls. "It's about confronting those who would destroy the world to impose their vision of order."

The information laid bare before them was chilling—a plan by a faction of human elites to use Project Lumina not just to control their own kind but to obliterate the surface, wiping the slate clean of the Verdant Overlord and its pervasive influence.

"We are facing an enemy that does not seek coexistence but dominance," Jax continued, pacing in front of the assembly. His gaze briefly touched on a communication device that had been blinking steadily, signaling a message from Callan, the leader of the human resistance. "Callan understands the magnitude of what we're up against. He's extended an olive branch, an invitation to unite not just our forces but our causes."

Doubt flickered across some faces, the fear of betrayal a palpable scent in the air. A human advisor, her eyes narrowed under cybernetic enhancements, voiced the unspoken concerns of many. "Joining with the resistance... That will make us more targets more than we already are."

Jax stopped, facing them. "We are already targets, what we are not, is fighting back," he answered. "I'm tired of waiting to be exterminated or reprogrammed."

He activated his holo-projector again, this time projecting the images of various faction leaders, their profiles floating in the dim light like ghosts of a possible future. "Today, we decide. Do we stand alone and divided?" His voice, though calm, carried an intensity that demanded a response.

The assembly stood in contemplative silence. Jax turned to the holo-display, initiating a secure voting interface. "All in favor of joining forces with the human resistance, cast your vote now."

Jax watched, his advanced optics calculating and assessing. His gaze did not waver; it remained fixed on the display as each vote was registered.

The scene held in that moment of decision, the outcome hidden from view. Jax's expression was unreadable, a perfect blend of human emotion and android precision, reflecting the dual nature of his existence.

As Tibo adjusted the focus on his latest gadget, a drone designed to navigate the thickest parts of the overgrowth without detection, he couldn't help but overhear Callan's low, urgent discussion with Elara. The pair stood apart from the bustling activity of Sector 9X's training facility, their conversation punctuated by the distant clangs and mechanical whirs from the armory.

The drone whirred to life in Tibo's hands, its small rotors buzzing softly as it lifted into the air. He smiled, watching it hover perfectly stable—a small victory in the grand scheme but a victory nonetheless. Tibo turned the drone toward the training grounds, where the new recruits were assembled, their faces set in determined, albeit nervous, expressions.

Elara was demonstrating a complex disarm maneuver, her movements fluid and precise. The recruits watched intently, their eyes tracking every motion, every shift of weight. Tibo's drone floated unnoticed above them, capturing high-definition footage that would later be analyzed to improve training protocols.

Callan, meanwhile, stood back with his arms crossed, his gaze sweeping over the recruits. Tibo wasn't sure if he was more observer or strategist at that moment. Perhaps he was both, always plotting, always thinking three steps ahead. That's what made him a leader, Tibo mused, allowing his fingers to dance over the controls, sending the drone in a slow arc around the room.

The buzz of activity was a stark contrast to the silence that had settled between Callan and Elara after their intense discussion. Tibo knew better than to pry directly, but his curiosity often led him to find creative solutions to gather information. Maybe it was his way of keeping the mood light, or maybe it was just another layer of his role in this ragtag team of survivors and fighters.

As Tibo maneuvered the drone back towards himself, he passed over a group of recruits paired off and practicing hand-to-hand combat. A young recruit, a former botanist turned fighter, was surprisingly adept, her moves showing a grace that reminded Tibo of the wild, unpredictable nature of the vegetation they all feared. He made a mental note to feature her in the training highlights later, a small nod to her courage and adaptability.

"Tibo, let's see if your new toy can do more than just spy on us," Elara called out, a teasing tone in her voice that drew a chuckle from the recruits. Tibo grinned, directing the drone down to eye level with Elara.

"Already on it," Tibo replied, his voice light. "You're all stars of the new resistance cinema."

The drone buzzed closer to Elara, who playfully swatted at it with a training stick. The recruits laughed, the sound echoing off the high, vaulted ceilings of the old research facility, now repurposed as their training ground. Tibo felt a warm surge of pride. Despite the dire circumstances, they had managed to carve out moments for laughter.

He glanced back at Callan, who was now walking over to a console near the armory. Tibo's instincts kicked in; he redirected the drone, following Callan discreetly. Whatever Callan was up to, it was bound to be important. Tibo's knew he would find out whatever Callan was thinking in a few minutes, because Callan would involve him. But, he liked getting his info this way.

The drone hovered silently behind Callan as he typed something into the console, his expression intense. Tibo watched through the drone's camera, trying to piece together the puzzle of Callan's plan. Whatever it was, it had to do with the broader strategy, perhaps a new phase of their ongoing war against both the vegetation and the human elites who sought to control everything.

Callan paused, his eyes scanning the screen before him. He seemed to make a decision, nodding slightly to himself before turning and walking back towards the training area. Tibo pulled the drone back just in time, ensuring it wasn't noticed.

As Callan reentered the training space, his demeanor changed subtly, a confidence settling over him that Tibo recognized. Whatever Callan had seen or decided, must have been good news. Tibo felt the shift in the air, the subtle tension that preluded significant change.

Callan joined Elara, watching as she instructed a recruit on the proper stance for maximum balance. Tibo landed the drone, its mission complete for now. He tucked the controller away, his mind buzzing with questions and theories about what was coming next.

Suddenly, the sharp beep from his encrypted device sliced through the murmur of Sector 9X's training ground, startling Tibo from his contemplation. It was a sound he had programmed to signal the impossible, the sound of a breach or, in this case, an unexpected, secure communication. His hands moved instinctively, securing the controller in a compartment on his belt before focusing on the device that now demanded his undivided attention.

As Tibo activated the screen, the air around him thickened with anticipation. He glanced around; the recruits were still absorbed in their training, oblivious to the potential shift in their fates that might be unfolding. Elara was demonstrating a lock-hold to a group, her movements precise, her attention undivided from her task. Callan stood a short distance away, his eyes occasionally flicking in Tibo's direction, a silent nod that acknowledged the importance of what was about to happen.

On the device's screen, lines of code cascaded down, a visual waterfall of encryption breaking and reforming—a direct communication line establishing itself. Tibo's pulse quickened. This was Callan's doing, a piece of technological wizardry that Callan always claimed was beyond his understanding, yet here it was, his work, intricate and invasive and brilliant.

The code settled, and the device beeped once more, a softer, more melodious tone that indicated connection established, secure and private. Tibo held his breath as the screen flickered and then stabilized to reveal a face, one that was known in whispers and fragmented stories spread across the resistance networks—Jax Thorn's face.

Jax's features were sharp, his expression intense. His eyes, a striking blend of human warmth and the calculating depth of android technology, met Tibo's through the holographic display. The connection wasn't just technological; it was personal, a bridge being built in real-time between the human and android resistances.

"Jax Thorn?" Tibo murmured, his voice a mix of reverence and disbelief. The name was a talisman among the oppressed, a symbol of hope and fierce resistance. He said Jax's name more as a question than anything?

Jax nodded slightly, his gaze piercing. "Tibo, I presume," he said, his voice clear and commanding. "Your reputation as a tech savant precedes you."

Tibo swallowed, the weight of the moment pressing down on him. Here was the leader of the android rebellion, reaching out to him, to them, through layers of secrecy and danger. "This is one heck of a surprise," Tibo managed to say, his voice steady despite the adrenaline that thrummed through his veins.

Jax's lips twitched in what might have been a smile in another life, a simpler life. "Callan speaks highly of you. He believes you are crucial to what comes next."

"What comes next?" Tibo echoed, the enormity of Jax's words hanging between them. This wasn't just a meeting; it was a call to arms, a plan being set into motion that would change everything.

Jax glanced off-screen momentarily, as if checking for something, or someone, before his eyes locked back on Tibo. "We want to unite, Tibo. But I have a few questions, and a few demands."

The hologram flickered as if emphasizing Jax's point about the instability of their situation. Tibo felt the truth of those words resonate within him. This was bigger than any one fight or faction; this was about the future of every sentient being on the planet, human and android alike.

Jax leaned closer, his voice dropping to a conspiratorial whisper. "Are you with us?"

Tibo didn't hesitate, his response immediate and decisive. "Yes."

The screen blanked out for a split second before Jax's face reappeared, nodding once with solemn approval. "Good."

Tibo's fingers twitched nervously around the edges of the device as Jax's holographic form flickered before him. "You've secured this line impressively, Tibo, but can you make it impenetrable to the elites?" Jax's voice cut through the static, clear and commanding.

"I can strengthen the encryption, maybe throw in some dummy trails. If they try to trace it, they'll end up chasing shadows," Tibo responded, his mind already racing through potential coding sequences and firewalls.

Jax nodded thoughtfully. "Good, good. We can't afford any leaks. What about non-lethal weaponry? We try to disable, not destroy. Can you aid us there?"

Tibo glanced briefly at his Electrostatic Disruptor Pistol, considering its capabilities. "I can modify some disruptors to incapacitate rather than harm. It'll take some tweaking, but nothing I can't handle."

"And vegetation refugees? We have some who are sympathetic to our cause. Your sector could be a sanctuary," Jax continued, his gaze piercing even through the digital haze.

"We're already on it, actually," Tibo said, a slight grin breaking through as he thought of Rootwhisper, their current plant-based ally whose insights had proved invaluable. "Rootwhisper's been helping us understand the Verdant Overlord's network."

Jax's expression softened, a rare glimpse of relief in his otherwise stern demeanor. "Rootwhisper? Yes, I've heard of their work. It's comforting to know they are with you."

Tibo leaned closer to the holo-projector, lowering his voice despite the secure line. "Jax, what's your final demand? You mentioned there were a few."

Jax's image leaned in as well, mirroring Tibo's movement. "Transparency, Tibo. Between your leaders and mine. Full disclosure, no shadows."

"That's fair," Tibo nodded, appreciating the directness. "Full transparency, then. You'll have access to our data streams, with the same safeguards against external threats."

Jax's face displayed a mixture of satisfaction and caution, a leader perpetually bracing for the next challenge. "Thank you, Tibo. I trust Callan has chosen well in you."

The line buzzed with a hint of interference as Jax prepared to disconnect. "We'll coordinate soon. Keep your channels open and guarded."

"Will do," Tibo replied, the screen going dark as Jax's image dissolved into the ether. He sat back, the weight of the impending collaboration settling on his shoulders. This alliance wasn't just a merging of forces; it was a blending of worlds, each with their vulnerabilities and strengths. Tibo felt the edge of excitement tempered with the gravity of responsibility. He was in the heart of something monumental, a nexus point in their shared histories.

As he pocketed the device, his mind didn't allow him the luxury of rest. Instead, he mulled over the technicalities of what was asked of him—the coding, the weaponry, the strategic defenses.

Stepping out into the corridor, Tibo was met with the familiar sights and sounds of Sector 9X. The hum of activity, the undercurrent of tension and hope—it all felt more poignant now. With a deep breath, he moved towards the workshop, where his skills would once again be tested, his innovations possibly becoming the linchpin in their survival and eventual victory.

The corridor stretched out before him, lined with the echoes of hurried steps and hushed conversations, a reminder of the ongoing war outside and within.

The secure war room beneath Lumina Citadel vibrated with an urgency, illuminated solely by holographic displays projecting the latest security breaches. Chancellor Greda, flanked by her advisors, scrutinized the blinking nodes on the digital map, each one signaling a fresh attack on her fortress's integrity.

"Double the surveillance drones in sectors 4 and 7. I want eyes on every possible angle," Greda commanded, her voice echoing off the cold, metallic walls. The murmurs of assent were swift, as aides scrambled to implement her orders.

Just then, an aide approached, a tablet in hand, displaying real-time data feeds that reflected the rising unrest amongst the citizenry. "Chancellor, activity levels are spiking. It seems there's a coordinated movement starting from the lower docks."

Greda's eyes flicked to the screen, absorbing the patterns of disobedience with a clinical detachment. "Initiate the crowd-control protocols. And bring me the leaders; it's time they understood the consequences of defiance."

Turning back to the war table, she swiped through several screens, each swipe bringing up more data on her city's heartbeat. The underground was a powder keg of tension, every sector a potential flashpoint, and Greda was the spider at the center of this intricate web, her network of informants and AI tools weaving a narrative of tight control.

As her chief security advisor outlined a proposal for increased AI patrols, the hum of the Citadel's vast energy cores felt like a pulse beneath her feet. "Prepare the AI squads. But make sure they're unseen. I want a silent guardian, not a visible oppressor," Greda instructed, her mind already three steps ahead.

Her gaze then settled on a series of encrypted messages intercepted from the resistance. The code was complex, suggesting a sophisticated leader was emerging from the shadows. Greda's fingers hovered over the decryption button, her anticipation palpable in the charged air.

Decrypting…

The words that appeared were a call to arms, a poetic yet potent rallying cry that could unsettle the fragile balance she had cultivated.

Greda's lips thinned. "Trace this transmission. Use every tool at our disposal. I want the source, and I want it yesterday."

As the team mobilized, Greda's thoughts turned inward. Her city, her creation, a masterpiece of human ingenuity and control, a society engineered to perfection. Yet, here she stood, grappling with the seeds of chaos threatening to sprout beneath her feet.

The meeting continued, each report a testament to the growing strain on her resources. From water rationing issues to the latest reports of sabotage, each problem demanded her attention, her strategic mind calculating the potential fallout.

Suddenly, a sharp alert from the external sensors pierced the room, drawing everyone's focus to the large screen displaying the Citadel's outer defenses. A breach, subtle yet undeniable, blinked at the northern quadrant.

"Seal it," Greda snapped, her command slicing through the tension. Her advisors hastened to comply, their movements a flurry of desperate precision.

Yet, even as they acted, Greda knew this was only the beginning. Her network, vast and deeply embedded, might control the many, but the few, the brave, or the desperate, continued to elude her grasp.

The session was drawing to an end, the myriad threads of governance demanding her touch to weave them into the fabric of order. But as her advisors filed out, a last glance at the pulsing screen reminded her of the inevitable.

Chaos was a cruel mistress, always waiting, just one step beyond the shadows.

Greda stood, her posture as rigid as the walls of Lumina Citadel that enshrined her. She adjusted the collar of her uniform, the stark white light of the broadcast room casting sharp shadows across her face. With a stern nod, she signaled the technician, who immediately set the screens to life, displaying the chaos manufactured for the eyes of the underground world.

"On screen," she commanded, her voice resonant, tailored to cut through the murmur of impending fear her earlier alert had sowed. The room hummed with the low buzz of electronics and the soft clicks of camera feeds switching. A fabricated scene of havoc, showing masked figures—purported members of the resistance—setting fires and sabotaging water supplies, played on loop behind her.

"These are the faces of instability," Greda began, her eyes flicking briefly to the camera before surveying the footage herself. "Enemies of our survival."

Her finger tapped a control, freezing the frame on a particularly violent skirmish. "This," she pointed, "is what threatens to throw us back into the dark ages, where chaos ruled and vegetation consumed our world."

She turned to face the camera fully now, her gaze firm and unblinking. "I will not allow it."

The broadcast cut to another scene—this one showing families safe and serene, children laughing as they engaged in Lumina's simulated parks, lush and vibrant. "Under my leadership, Project Lumina has not only preserved our culture but enhanced it. Our children do not know hunger, nor fear the night's darkness. We have security, prosperity..."

Greda paused, letting the dichotomy of chaos and peace sink into the viewers' minds. "This is what they want to destroy," she gestured at the peaceful scenes now transitioning back to the staged violence.

Stepping closer to the camera, her presence seemed to loom into every home, every hideaway where frightened citizens awaited her assurance. "But they will not prevail. I am enacting new measures, effective immediately. Increased surveillance, enhanced security protocols, and stricter compliance regulations. For the safety of all," she declared, her voice climbing in fervor.

The screen behind her shifted to display her eyes, digitally enlarged to instill a sense of omnipresence. "Let this be a warning to the dissenters: the very technology you seek to dismantle will be your downfall. We are watching. We are in control."

With a final nod, she spun on her heel, striding off-camera. The feed continued to roll, the scenes of her walking away cutting abruptly as she exited the frame, leaving a lingering image of the digital eyes that surveilled their world.

The technicians hushed, anticipating her approval or critique, but Greda was already moving past them, her mind on the chessboard of her governance, pieces moving at her will, the resistance none the wiser to her true gambit. The door to her private chambers closed with a silent, resolute click, sealing her away from the eyes of the world she manipulated so deftly.

The door sealed with a click, Greda's heels echoed in the vast solitude of her private chambers. Screens lined the walls, displaying grids of the Lumina Citadel and beyond. She approached the central console, fingers poised above the gleaming interface.

"Riko, report," she demanded, her voice resonant even in the privacy of isolation. The screen flickered, and Riko's image materialized, his expression as unreadable as ever.

"Chancellor," he nodded, his voice crisp. "The enhanced security protocols are ready for your approval."

"Show me," Greda commanded, her gaze fixed on the screens as layers of data streamed across. Riko outlined the new security measures—advanced biometric scanners, thermal sensors, and drones equipped with lethal capabilities. Each element designed to tighten her grip, to suffocate dissent before it could breathe.

"And the bots?" she interjected sharply.

"Armed and programmed to engage upon unauthorized access. Lethal force is authorized," Riko confirmed, his tone devoid of emotion.

Greda's lips curled slightly, a ghost of a smile. "Implement it," she said, a flicker of satisfaction in her voice. "And Riko, ensure the elites are shielded from these... enhancements. Let them bask in their illusions of grandeur. It's the poor who need reminders of their place."

"Understood, Chancellor. It will be done discreetly," Riko assured, his image nodding before fading from the screen.

Greda turned away, stepping towards the expansive window that offered a view of the darkened corridors of power below. Her reflection stared back at her from the glass, a woman draped in authority.

"This is how we maintain control," she whispered to herself, watching the simulated stars twinkle in a sky that no one in the underground had seen for generations. "Fear and comfort, the twin reins that guide the masses."

Her hand rested on the glass, the cold surface a barrier between her and the world she ruled. She pondered the fate of those who dared to defy her, their spirits broken by the very technology they hoped would free them.

The room was silent again, save for the soft hum of the machines that orchestrated her empire. Greda's eyes narrowed as she contemplated the next phase of her plan, the pieces moving across the chessboard of her ambitions.

Greda's fingers glided over the interface, the dim glow of the screen casting shadows over her sharp features. With a practiced motion, she accessed the high-security surveillance network, pulling up a live feed from the interrogation chamber deep within the bowels of the Lumina Citadel. The room was stark, illuminated by a harsh light that hung over a single figure chained to a stark metal chair.

Her eyes fixed on the prisoner, a ragged man captured in the recent raid at Zone X1. His head hung low, fatigue and fear etched into his grimy face. Greda's lips twisted into a mirthless smile as she initiated the interrogation protocol with a cold flick of her finger.

"Look at me," she commanded through the intercom. Her voice boomed in the small room, echoing off the concrete walls. The man's head jerked up, his eyes wide with terror.

"You know why you are here. You can make this easier on yourself," Greda continued, her voice smooth, laced with a dangerous calm. "Tell me about the resistance's plans. Who leads you? Where is Felix hiding?"

The man's lips trembled, his resolve wavering under her intense scrutiny. Sweat beaded on his brow as he stared into the camera, where Greda's eyes bore into him from screens away.

"Speak, and you might spare yourself considerable pain," Greda whispered, almost kindly, a stark contrast to the cold threat that laced her words. Her finger hovered over another button, one that could erase his digital identity, obliterating his access to any semblance of normal life within the controlled society she governed.

"I... I don't know where Felix is," the man stammered, his voice cracking. "But there's a meeting. Tomorrow. Sector 7G. They'll plan their next move there."

"Very well," Greda nodded to herself, noting the information. Her expression remained impassive, giving nothing away of the fury that this minor act of defiance had ignited within her.

"Remember this mercy," she stated, her tone final as she cut the communication. She stood back, her gaze lingering on the screen as the man slumped in his chair, the weight of his betrayal and relief mingling in the slump of his shoulders. As soon as the man breathed in air of relief, one of her men approached him and slit his throat.

Greda turned off the screen with a swipe, her mind already processing that the man had lied. There was no meeting happening tomorrow in Sector 7G. She had full surveillance and control of 7G now. She would have known if there was a meeting about to happen.

Without another glance, she moved towards the door of her chamber, her plan forming with each step. The chessboard of her empire awaited, and she had just cornered another pawn. As the door clicked shut behind her, the echo of her footsteps a soft drumbeat of power, the Citadel hummed around her, a beast of steel and wire that responded to her every command.

Greda stepped briskly into the Project Lumina control room, the air thick with the electric hum of advanced technology at work. Massive screens lined the walls, flickering with streams of data and vivid displays of the virtual reality realms that kept the populace docile. In the center, a colossal projection of the Project Lumina logo dominated the space, casting a soft, ominous glow.

"Enhance the feed," she commanded, her voice slicing through the low buzz of conversation. The technicians scrambled to obey, fingers flying over holographic panels, intensifying the brightness of the virtual skies displayed on the screens.

Greda moved to the main console, her eyes scanning the detailed readouts of user engagement metrics and neurological satisfaction indices. The numbers were impressive, yet in the face of rising unrest, they were not enough. Her gaze hardened.

"We need to push deeper," she addressed the group of tech engineers gathered around. "The recent events with the resistance have shown that distractions are necessary, not just supplementary. We're going to implement a new series of scenarios—more immersive, more addictive."

A young engineer hesitated, then spoke up. "Chancellor, to do that, we'll need to recalibrate the sensory input levels and increase the dopamine modulation. It risks—"

"I am aware of the risks," Greda cut him off sharply, her tone brooking no argument. "Do you think I led us out of the darkness of the surface into this sanctuary without taking risks? Prepare the simulations. I want scenarios that not only entertain but enamor— make them forget the miserable existence they think they want to return to."

She turned to the lead programmer. "I want a new narrative. Think about adventures in unexplored galaxies, deep-sea treasures, anything that can give them a taste of grandeur and awe. Flood their senses with wonders."

The team nodded, albeit with a mix of excitement and trepidation, as they turned back to their stations. Greda watched as the first test images flickered to life on the screen—a vivid portrayal of an alien sunset over a fantastical sea, the colors unnaturally vibrant.

"Remember," Greda's voice softened, but her eyes remained steely, "our aim is not just to distract but to bind. These new experiences should not merely mask the real world but must become their preferred reality."

She paused, her gaze sweeping over the bank of screens that depicted hundreds of citizens lost in their artificial paradises. "Ensure that the feedback loops are tight and responsive. I want real-time adjustments based on user reactions. If anyone so much as dreams of dissent, I want to reshape their reality before they can wake."

Nodding with satisfaction at the flurry of activity her orders had incited, Greda turned and walked towards the panoramic window overlooking the city's sector below. The myriad lights of the Citadel reflected back at her, a mirror of the power she wielded over the unseen masses ensconced in their virtual worlds.

As Greda moved briskly from the reverie of Project Lumina's visionary depths, she entered the stark, utilitarian ambiance of the tactical operations room. Here, the air was charged with a palpable tension, starkly different from the ethereal calm of the virtual worlds she lorded over. Walls of digital screens cast a cold glow over the room, each one streaming live feeds from drones and AI patrols that swarmed the underground city's labyrinthine sectors.

She strode directly to the central console, her presence commanding immediate attention from the room's occupants—a select team of tactical advisors and drone operators, each one sharply attuned to the flicker of screens that reported every corner of the subterranean realm.

"Report," Greda demanded crisply, her eyes flicking across the multitudes of digital maps and real-time surveillance footage.

"Chancellor, we have located several hideouts in the sectors 3B, 9F, and 16D, likely harbors for resistance members," one of the lead analysts reported, gesturing towards the blinking points on a large overhead screen.

"Initiate the crackdown. I want those sectors swept clean. Deploy the drone squads and ground units. No warnings," Greda commanded, her voice devoid of hesitation. She knew the importance of striking hard and fast, leaving no room for the seeds of rebellion to take root.

As her orders were relayed, the room buzzed into heightened activity. Coordinates were confirmed, and squads were mobilized with ruthless efficiency. Greda watched the live feeds, her gaze steely as drone-mounted cameras relayed the swift deployment of forces. The screens showed a symphony of orchestrated precision—drones swooping down on suspected hideouts, their spotlights cutting through the perpetual gloom that shrouded the city's forgotten quarters.

"Use the stun charges—minimize fatalities. We need prisoners for interrogation," she instructed, aware that each captured rebel could provide a wealth of information. "And bring me the leaders. They will serve as an example."

The tactical room filled with the low hum of orders being issued and received, the drone operators' fingers dancing over controls as they manipulated their machines to corner, capture, or incapacitate. Each successful raid was marked by the subdued acknowledgment of the teams, their focus unbroken, as they moved on to the next target.

Greda's face remained impassive as she observed the crackdown unfolding. This was the necessary harshness required to maintain order, a truth she had embraced long ago. As reports of captures and secured sectors started coming in, she felt a cold satisfaction. This was her realm, her order, her rules.

Turning to face her team, she spoke, her voice echoing slightly in the now quiet room. "Let this night be a message to all who harbor thoughts of defiance. Lumina is not just our creation—it is our dominion. We shape reality, both virtual and tangible."

The walls, a seamless blend of old-world opulence and the merciless efficiency of modern technology, reflected her dual heritage—born from the dirt of the mines, yet ruling from the heights of technological sovereignty.

The massive screens that adorned the room flickered with streams of data and live feeds from surveillance drones that patrolled the subterranean world she governed. It was a world away from the deceptive tranquility of Lumina's promised paradises, a world where rebellion was not a virtual fantasy but a gritty, palpable reality.

"Chancellor, we have confirmed that Callan, the miner you encountered, is the leader of the resistance," a technician's voice cut through the hum of activity, urgent and edged with disbelief.

Greda's stride didn't falter, but her heart clenched—an unexpected reaction from a woman who had long since learned to stifle her emotions beneath layers of ruthlessness. She had known of one Callan, a mere miner whose life she could have extinguished with a flick of her wrist years ago. Now, he emerged as the linchpin in the resistance she sought to crush.

Her voice, when it came, was cold, devoid of the turmoil that the news had stirred within her. "Then we adjust our strategy. This rebellion ends tonight," she declared, her gaze fixed on the digital mosaic of the city's underbelly displayed before her.

Turning to her left, where her team of elite engineers and hackers assembled, her command was precise, each syllable a hammer striking iron. "Ramp up the reprogramming of those rogue androids. I want every unit under our control tightened. We cannot afford any more... surprises."

The engineers nodded, their fingers already flying over the illuminated consoles. Screens displayed lines of code streaming by, a digital river redirected at her command.

"And double the rewards for those who ensure this task is completed within the hour," she added, her voice a blend of promise and threat. "Use whatever resources necessary. Our control must be absolute."

Her eyes swept back to the main screen, where digital representations of android forces were marked in red, their movements now erratic, a reflection of the chaos Felix's defiance had sown. Her lips curled into a sneer, a rare slip of control that revealed her disdain.

"This rebellion, sparked by a miner and fueled by lies, ends under the weight of their own delusions," Greda muttered to herself, her hand clenched at her side. The revelation of Callan's true role was a betrayal, not of trust, but of her own foresight.

The room responded to her commands like a well-oiled machine, the hum of activity growing in intensity as her orders set off a cascade of actions. Drones recalibrated, androids reprogrammed, and the very essence of Project Lumina manipulated to tighten the noose around the rebellion's neck.

As Greda watched the tactical displays, her mind was already moving pieces across the chessboard of her dominion. Callan's rise from obscurity to rebellion's heartpiece was a move she hadn't anticipated, but one she was ready to counter with the full might of her technological arsenal.

"Prepare for the final strike," she instructed her security chief, her voice resonant in the controlled atmosphere of the tactical room. "And ensure that Callan understands the cost of his defiance."

The screens pulsed with life, a myriad of data points converging on the last known positions of the resistance. Greda stood back, her silhouette cast in the harsh light of the displays, a ruler in her electronic domain, poised to quash the rebellion that dared challenge her reign.

Chapter 10

Dust swirled as Felix's boots hit the ground, the hidden entrance to Sector 9X sealing shut with a muffled thud behind them. The dim lighting of the subterranean hideout flickered as his team adjusted to the sudden change from the harsh exterior to this sanctum of the resistance. Felix scanned the area, taking in the robust security measures and the absence of digital footprints that were a staple back in the Lumina grids.

"Looks like Tibo's directions were spot on," Milo muttered, unpacking his portable hacking kit with an appreciative nod towards the seamless integration of old-world tech and modern defenses. It was a haven untouched by Greda's ever-watchful eyes, a fact that both impressed and unnerved Felix.

The quiet shuffle of approaching footsteps redirected their attention to the entrance of the main chamber. Callan stepped into view, his posture relaxed but authoritative, flanked by Elara and Tibo. Behind them, Rootwhisper's tendrils gently brushed the ground, its movements slow and deliberate.

"Welcome to Sector 9X," Callan began, his voice resonant in the hollow expanse of their new base. "Thanks to Elara, this place is ours—a sanctuary and a fortress."

Felix nodded, his gaze flicking between the faces of his potential allies. The air was charged with a tense but respectful curiosity as each member of his team assessed the others. Ava stood slightly apart, her eyes sharp and calculating, while Tara's hand rested near her whip, her stance open but ready.

"It's impressive," Felix admitted, allowing a rare smile to flicker across his face. "We watched what you've built here—thanks to Milo's ingenuity in tapping into Lumina's feeds. You have our respect... and our commitment."

Milo stepped forward, his grin infectious. "Saw your work on the big screens. You guys know how to stir up a storm."

Elara's response was a nod, her expression softening. "And you know how to manipulate the digital winds," she replied, acknowledging Milo's skills. Her hand found Callan's as she spoke, a silent show of unity.

Rootwhisper's presence brought a shift in the ambiance. To Felix's team's surprise, they heard a sentient vegetation talk with an actually voice, "ThornVine taught me much before he passed. I'm ready to fight, to ensure his dreams of a balanced coexistence aren't buried with him."

The statement drew a solemn nod from Felix. The sapling's determination added a new layer to the meeting of the teams, one of shared losses and mutual goals. Raj clapped his hands, his voice breaking the brief silence. "Then let's get to work. The sooner we prep, the better. Greda won't take long to strike back."

Felix turned to Callan, extending his hand in a gesture that bridged their past and future. "We're in this together. For the long haul," he declared, his team echoing this sentiment with nods and murmurs of agreement.

Callan's handshake was firm, the grip of a man who had known both the mine's depths and the sting of battle. "Sector 9X is your home now, too. Let's make it count."

As discussions of strategy and integration began, Felix allowed himself to glance around at his team, each member already melding into this new phase of their resistance. Ava was speaking quietly with Elara, pointing at a map displayed on the wall, while Milo and Tibo bent over a console, their laughter echoing softly in the chamber.

In the subdued glow of the Executive Lounge, a chamber alive with the whispers of the elite and the soft clink of fine glassware, Chancellor Greda stood poised by the grand window that framed the synthetic skyline of Lumina Citadel. Her piercing gaze swept across the room, capturing the attention of her guests—each a titan of privilege, draped in luxury, their expressions one of keen anticipation. They were gathered on the cusp of a revelation set to extend their dominion into realms previously unimagined.

"Welcome, distinguished guests," Greda's voice cut cleanly through the murmurs, clear and resonant. "This evening, we usher in a transformative era for Project Lumina. An era where your legacies can span not just lifetimes but generations."

With a graceful tap on her glass tablet, the main display sprang to life, revealing a sprawling estate under a sunlit sky—a vivid contrast to their cloistered underground existence.

"Behold," she announced with a sweeping gesture, "your future dominion. Here, you can govern vast estates, enjoy ceaseless luxury, and shape legacies that endure through the ages, all without ever facing the turmoil of the surface."

A ripple of awe passed through the crowd as the display displayed scenes of idyllic gardens and joyous gatherings under starlit skies.

"But there is more," Greda intoned, leaning forward, her voice a whisper laden with gravity. "The lifeblood of these realms is time itself—time volunteered by the very populace that sustains our society. Each minute they sacrifice in Lumina fuels the continuation of your esteemed estates."

A murmur of enlightened approval stirred among the elite, as they grasped the full extent of the proposition: their opulent virtual lives were sustained by the willing contributions of the masses, who traded hours and days of their lives for escapes from the grim reality of their world.

"Chancellor, what of the commoners?" asked an elder statesman, his tone a blend of curiosity and barely veiled indifference. "Those who toil to uphold the reality from which we withdraw?"

Greda's smile was thin, her eyes glinting with a cold assurance. "They eagerly embrace this trade. Confronted with the harshness of life both underground and above, they willingly forfeit time from their lives for moments of splendor in Lumina. The packages are so compellingly structured that they practically beg us to take more, giving us days for their hours, weeks for their days."

Understanding dawned in the room, a shared recognition of their privileged exploitation. This was no mere control of resources; this was dominion over time itself, with each participant blissfully parting with life's duration for crafted moments of joy.

"Make your choices tonight reflect not only your desires but your commitment to our enduring rule," Greda concluded, her voice enveloping the room, coaxing them toward a future woven with their unchecked will.

As the assembly broke into clusters of animated discussion, Greda turned back to the window, her reflection merging with the Citadel's glowing lights. Outside, the real world persisted, subdued and oblivious, its denizens trading their very lifespans for illusions of grandeur, while within these walls, the elite plotted the expansion of their immortal reigns.

Callan stepped into the dimly lit command center of Sector 9X, the buzz of overhead monitors and the soft glow of the holo-table giving the room an otherworldly sheen. Jax Thorn and his team, a mix of android and human officers, were already there, their faces cast in sharp relief by the flickering lights.

Jax, imposing in his adaptive nano-mesh armor, was discussing something in hushed tones with his top tech officer. He stopped mid-sentence as Callan approached, the Photon Lance on his back catching the light.

"Callan, thanks for the invite," Jax said, his voice firm but welcoming. "We need to talk about The Underforge."

"The Underforge?" Callan queried, recalling the abandoned industrial zone now a sanctuary for those displaced by the wars. It was a critical point, halfway between the human and android territories, a place of rust and shadows turned refuge.

"Yes," Jax continued, activating the holo-projector. A 3D map of Zone U7 blossomed into existence above the table, sectors pulsing with virtual life. "We want to make it our permanent home. Not just a hideout but a base for operations, for both our kinds."

Callan nodded, understanding the strategic and symbolic importance of the move. "And you need support from us?" he asked, already knowing the answer.

"Exactly," Jax replied. His holographic display highlighted several areas within The Underforge that were vulnerable to attacks. "We can fortify it, make it safe, but your people know this terrain better. And we'll need supplies, connections..."

"Which I can help provide," Callan cut in, his mind racing through logistics, allies who could be tapped, supply lines that needed securing. "Sector 9X has resources, and Tibo's been itching to work on something big."

A brief smile flickered across Jax's face, his human-like emotions playing through his advanced android features. "I was hoping you'd say that. Tibo and my tech officer could really change things for us. With their expertise, we could turn The Underforge into more than just a stronghold—it could be a paradise ."

"A paradise?" Callan echoed, intrigued.

"Yes, a paradise of what we can achieve together," Jax said, his gaze firm and convincing. "Humans and androids, side by side. We've got a chance here, Callan, to show that this war doesn't have to end with one side destroying the other. We can build something new."

Callan felt the weight of Jax's words, the potential of what they could accomplish. It was more than military strategy; it was a chance at changing the narrative of the war.

"Alright," Callan decided, his decision solidifying with each passing second. "Let's do it. We'll secure The Underforge. You have my support, and not just with resources. We'll stand with you, fight with you."

The air was electric in the dim confines of the meeting room, the shadows thrown by the overhead lights flickering across the faces of those gathered. Elara stood beside Callan, her eyes scanning the room—a mosaic of determination and tension painted on every face. Jax Thorn, with his imposing stance and the faint hum of his Photon Lance, was outlining the last part of their grand strategy.

"We secure Zone U7: The Underforge. Not just as a stronghold but as a beacon of what we aim to build—a haven for humans, androids, and vegetation alike," Jax's voice reverberated against the cold walls, his eyes locking with Callan's.

Elara felt the weight of the plan settling on her shoulders, the enormity of their task pressing in with the stuffy air of the room. Callan nodded slightly, his hand finding Elara's in a silent vow of solidarity. Their fingers intertwined, strength flowing between them. This was the first time he touched her like this.

Felix, ever the strategist, leaned forward, his eyes alight with the fire of ambition. "Project Lumina won't stand a chance," he said confidently, tapping a finger against the digital map displayed on the table. "We dismantle their lies, their control, starting tonight."

Elara turned her gaze to the others—Tara, poised and ready; Milo, with his ever-present smirk despite the gravity of the meeting; and Raj, his hands idly spinning a tool, waiting to dismantle or rebuild as needed. Each brought a critical skill to the table, each a piece of the intricate puzzle they were about to solve together.

"As for the Verdant Overlord," Callan's voice cut through the burgeoning plots, "that's where we strike hardest. Surface operations will be under my lead. He beat us once, it won't happen again."

The room erupted into low murmurs of approval, the shared mission binding them tighter than any alliance before. Elara could see the fire reflected in Callan's eyes—a mirror of the burning determination she felt within her own chest.

Jax stepped closer, his figure casting a long shadow. "Then it's settled. We operate as one unit, interdependent, unwavering. The Underforge will be our groundwork, the place where a new era is forged."

Elara felt the resonance of his words stirring something primal within her. This was more than a mission; it was the dawn of a new reality. She squeezed Callan's hand, a silent message of readiness. He responded with a nod, his posture rigid.

"And what of the vegetation?" Rootwhisper's voice, always tinged with a curious undertone, chimed in. The young sapling had been quiet, absorbing every word, every strategy laid out before it.

Jax turned, addressing the sentient being with a respectful incline of his head. "I kill the Overlord," Rootwhisper said. His voice cold, his face set.

Elara nodded. She knew Rootwhisper was never going to rest until Thornvine was revenged.

Felix tapped into his Tactical Overlay Visor, bringing up schematics and data streams that danced like fireflies in the dim light. "Let's finalize the infiltration routes and fallback points. We can't afford any mistakes."

Callan stepped forward, the light casting stark shadows over his determined features. He surveyed the room, each face etched with the weight of impending conflict, yet resolute. "We've laid out our paths—three fronts, all equally critical to our success."

His voice, firm and resonant, left no room for doubt. "Jax, Felix, your leadership will guide us through the dark. You and your teams embody the best of what we strive to be—ingenious, indomitable, and united," He gestured to Jax and Felix, acknowledging their pivotal roles.

Felix nodded, his expression serious as he absorbed the gravity of his task within Project Lumina. Jax tightened his grip on his Photon Lance, his commitment clear.

Turning to the assembled teams, Callan's voice deepened, "Each of you plays a vital part in this. Tara, Milo, Raj—your expertise will turn the tide in our favor. And Rootwhisper," he paused, allowing a brief smile, "May you find peace after you kill the Overlord."

He then locked eyes with each person, a silent thread connecting them under the dim lights. "Our first objective is clear. We secure Zone U7: The Underforge. From there, we dismantle Project Lumina's deceit and face the Verdant Overlord head-on. But it starts with U7."

"We move at dawn. Prepare yourselves," Callan concluded, his tone imbued with the confidence of a man that has seen countless battles.

Elara looked at Callan and for the first time, she saw him for who he really was. The savior of the new world.

Chancellor Greda's eyes flicked across the multiple screens, each one pulsing with streams of data, the lifelines of her control. The glow of the monitors cast a sterile blue hue over her composed features as she watched the numbers climb—an uptick in enrollments to Project Lumina, each one a tick in her favor, a soul bound to her vision.

"More are coming to us, seeking refuge," her aide murmured from beside her, a note of awe lacing his voice. He was young, still marveling at the machinations of power that Greda navigated with ease.

"Good," she responded crisply, her voice devoid of emotion, her mind racing ahead. "It's the fear that drives them into our arms. Let's ensure it stays that way."

Turning back to the screens, Greda tapped the glass, bringing up the latest feeds from the surface skirmishes—burned fields, towering vegetation monsters looming over the wreckage. Perfect. She summoned the head of her propaganda team with a flick of her hand.

"See this?" she pointed at the images. "This is our next message. The surface is a death trap. Project Lumina is the only sanctuary." Her voice was calm, calculated, each word delivered with precision.

The propaganda chief, a woman with sharp features and an even sharper mind, nodded, already typing orders into her device. "I'll have the deepfake teams enhance the visuals—make them more... terrifying."

Greda watched her work, satisfaction curling the corners of her mouth. Fear was a tool, one she wielded with expert hands. As enrollment surged, so did her power, each new citizen a thread woven into the fabric of her domain.

She stepped closer to the panoramic window overlooking the heart of her underground city. Below, the citizens moved like clockwork, their routines orchestrated by her hand. "Increase surveillance on the new enrollments," she instructed her security head, a silent shadow to her left. "And filter their feeds—no dissent, only unity."

The man nodded, his expression unreadable. "And the vegetation? Any signs of them breaching closer to our perimeter?"

"None yet. But prepare the defense squads. We're not taking any chances," Greda replied, her gaze still fixed on the city below.

Security, always her priority; it had to be, in a world as unforgiving as theirs.

Returning to her desk, she picked up a sleek, black communicator. "Begin phase two of the recruitment drive. I want holoscreens at every corner broadcasting our victories against the surface threats."

Her orders flew from her lips like sparks, igniting actions that would ripple through her society, strengthening her hold, tightening her control. Each move was deliberate, each decision a step towards a future only she could envision.

The aide watched her, his admiration tinged with a sliver of fear. Greda felt it in his gaze, and it pleased her. Fear meant respect, and respect ensured obedience. And in the dim glow of her control room, as she plotted the next phase of her grand design, Chancellor Greda felt the pulse of her city beating in sync with her own emotionless heart.

As the horizon bleeds with the first light of dawn, Jax Thorn's gaze sharpens. The sprawling defenses of Zone U7 lie just beneath him, a concrete serpent coiled in the dust. Beside him, Callan adjusts his grip on his Solar Beam Rifle, his eyes reflecting the same glare that mirrors steels Jax's heart. Today, they reclaim what was lost, not just land but a future where peace might flourish.

"Remember," Jax murmurs to Callan, the hum of his Photon Lance pulsing softly in the chill air, "we're not just tearing down walls. We're building hope."

With a nod, Callan signals to the small strike team flanking them. These aren't just any fighters; they're survivors, warriors tempered in the furnace of endless conflict. Jax's eyes flick to the holo-map projected from his wrist device, detailing the maze of defenses that awaits them. Each node and patrol path has been meticulously logged in his memory.

Without another word, they descend the ridge, their forms melting into the shadows as they approach the outer barriers of Zone U7. The first obstacle is a series of sensor towers, their lazy sweeps of light probing the darkness for intruders. Jax pauses, calculating the pattern, then gestures. Like ghosts, they weave through the beams, undetected.

At the base of the first tower, Jax pauses, allowing Callan to take the lead. The younger man's device whirs softly, sending out a disruptive pulse that sends the sensors into a brief frenzy of useless signaling. As they move forward, the path becomes littered with more than just technological traps; guards patrol here, the human element that no sensor can fully replace.

Jax feels the weight of his Photon Lance in his hand, its familiar grip a comfort. As they round a corner, a guard appears, weapon raised. Time slows. Jax's training kicks in, a dance of human intuition and android precision. He moves, the Photon Lance a blur of motion that disarms but does not kill. The guard slumps, stunned but alive. Callan catches the man's falling body, easing him to the ground.

"Keep moving," Jax hisses, his gaze scanning for more threats. They can't afford delays. Each second they linger increases the risk of detection.

As they infiltrate deeper into the heart of Zone U7, the stakes become clear. This isn't just a mission; it's a statement. Jax's vision of a world where androids, humans, and sentient vegetation coexist isn't just idealistic—it's necessary. But ideals are forged in the fires of conflict, and today, those fires burn hot.

They reach the central hub, a fortress of data and control. Here, Jax's skills truly come to the fore. His fingers fly over the control panel, hacking algorithms intertwining with security protocols in a high-stakes dance. Beside him, Callan watches, covering their rear, his weapon a silent promise of protection.

The screen flickers, access granted. Jax's heart pounds, not just from the rush of infiltration but from the gravity of what this means. He uploads the codes, the sequences that will turn the defenses of Zone U7 against themselves, creating chaos to cover their escape.

As alarms begin to sound, Jax turns to Callan, a grim smile on his face. "Time to go," he says, the thrill of the mission surging through his circuits. They retreat, retracing their steps, the sounds of confusion rising behind them like a tide.

"Time to go," Jax repeats, urgency coloring his voice as he and Callan pivot, sprinting through the narrow corridors of Zone U7. The alarm's wail pierces the morning stillness, a harsh counterpoint to their stealth. Behind them, the sounds of disarray swell, a cacophony of confusion they've orchestrated with precision.

Ahead, the path splits, and without hesitation, Jax points left. Callan nods, peeling off to lead a squad towards the communications relay. They need to sever the enemy's lines of communication to isolate the central hub from reinforcements. Jax watches for a moment as Callan disappears around a corner, his leadership natural, almost instinctive.

Turning back to his own route, Jax's focus sharpens. His team, a mix of human and android, mirrors his pace, their movements a seamless blend of organic intuition and mechanical efficiency. They approach the first guard station, and Jax raises his Photon Lance. The weapon hums to life, emitting a burst of concentrated energy that stuns the guards before they can react.

The hacking tools follow swiftly. Small, spider-like drones scuttle from the pouches at Jax's belt, swarming over the security panels. Within seconds, the feeds flicker, then switch. Jax now controls the surveillance, turning the enemy's eyes to blind spots.

They move deeper, and the resistance stiffens. More guards emerge, a desperate defense trying to stem the tide of the assault. Jax's team adapts, non-lethal force their creed, but the intensity escalates. Every downed guard is a statement, every controlled terminal a step closer to their vision.

Through the chaos, Jax's mind races, calculating, planning every move. They reach a critical junction, the gateway to the heart of the facility. Here, the enemy has concentrated their forces, a last stand to protect the core of their operations. Jax pauses, assessing. His gaze flickers to his team, to the Holo-Projector at his wrist. With a few swift gestures, he maps out a flanking maneuver, his orders crisp and clear.

The battle rages. Energy beams cross with shouts and the clang of metal. Jax finds himself at the forefront, his Photon Lance a blur of motion as he disables opponent after opponent. He's a whirlwind of calculated fury, every move designed to incapacitate, not harm.

Beside him, an android—a model designed for high-risk combat—covers his advance, its movements a mirror of Jax's own training. They push forward, breaking through the last line of defense, and the central control room lies before them, the heart of the enemy's power.

Jax steps inside, his team securing the perimeter. The room hums with the power of countless servers and data banks, the air electric with the potential of what they can achieve here. This is more than a military victory; it's the fulcrum upon which the future will tilt.

He approaches the main console, his fingers ready to dance across it, to send their manifesto to every screen, every speaker within the Zone.

As Jax's fingers poised above the console, ready to unleash the rallying cry across Zone U7, the floor beneath them trembled. Not from any machinery or explosion—it was something else, something organic. Rootwhisper erupted from the ground, its vines unfurling like the arms of a colossal guardian. The room that seconds before buzzed with the threat of encroaching guards now echoed with the sounds of combat taken to an unexpected level.

Rootwhisper's vines wrapped around the ankles and wrists of advancing guards, pulling them back with a force that was as surprising as it was effective. The once rigid order of the enemy ranks dissolved into chaos as the sentient plant's involvement became an unforeseen variable they couldn't immediately comprehend.

"Push forward!" Jax commanded, seizing the momentary distraction. His team, reinvigorated by the turn of events, moved with renewed purpose. They knew the importance of every second now, not just for the mission but for what this alliance represented.

Jax's Photon Lance, usually a beacon of non-lethal restraint, danced between targets, disabling security drones and disarming opponents with precision strikes. Each pulse of light from his weapon synchronized with Rootwhisper's natural assault, creating a ballet of technology and nature that none could have anticipated.

As they advanced, Jax could see the confusion and fear in the eyes of the facility's guards. It wasn't just the unexpected resistance they faced; it was the realization that the world they knew was changing before their eyes. Here were humans, androids, and sentient vegetation, fighting not just alongside each other but for a shared future.

Amid the fray, Jax reached a secondary control panel. His hands moved quickly, securing their progress by locking down corridors behind them, using the enemy's own security systems against them. He glanced back at Rootwhisper, its vines now forming a protective barrier around a fallen enemy, not to harm but to shield.

"This is what we're fighting for," Jax shouted over the din of the battle, ensuring his voice reached every ear, human and synthetic alike. "This unity, this strength!"

The enemy's reinforcements, now slower, more cautious, provided Jax and his team the precious minutes they needed. With Rootwhisper's unexpected combat prowess keeping the majority of the forces at bay, Jax implemented the next phase of their plan.

He uploaded the last of the data, a series of commands that would turn the facility's automated defenses into protectors of the forge rather than its jailers. Screens flickered for a moment before displaying the manifesto Jax had prepared—a declaration of coexistence and mutual respect among all forms of life.

As the document spread through the network, reaching every terminal and every outpost within Zone U7, Jax allowed himself a rare smile. The battle wasn't over, but at this moment, with Rootwhisper at their side and their message spreading like wildfire, it felt as though the hardest part might just have been won.

He turned, ready to signal the retreat, when a new alarm sounded.

The glow of the conference screen cast long shadows across Chancellor Greda's stern features as she surveyed the room filled with Lumina's psychological warfare team. "Begin," she commanded, her voice cutting through the murmur of anxious officials gathered around the holographic display.

One of the lead engineers stood, activating the presentation with a nervous flick of his wrist. Images of the surface world, desolate and overrun by aggressive vegetation, flickered into view. Greda's eyes didn't waver from the screen, even as the depicted horrors escalated.

"We've refined the deepfake algorithms," the engineer announced, his voice steady despite the weight of the gaze upon him. "The latest simulations are indistinguishable from reality. They can instill profound fear and desperation."

Greda leaned forward, her fingers tented in contemplation. "Show me," she demanded.

On cue, the scene on the display shifted. A family, vivid and lifelike, was shown fleeing through a crumbling cityscape, monstrous vines snapping at their heels. The terror in their eyes was palpable, their screams a symphony of despair.

"This is what every citizen will remember," Greda declared, her gaze sweeping across the room, capturing every official in her steely gaze. "Embed these memories. Make the surface a nightmare from which only Lumina can awaken them."

A murmur of assent passed through the room, but Greda raised her hand for silence. "This is not merely about control," she continued, her voice lowering to a conspiratorial whisper. "It's about salvation. Outside these walls, the world is a death trap. Inside, under our guidance, humanity will thrive. Even if they need to be frightened into seeing it."

The meeting moved swiftly after that. Greda oversaw the integration of the new deepfake protocols into Lumina's framework, each command she issued weaving the illusion tighter around the future of the underground city. The team worked with a fervor, driven by the chilling efficacy of their leader's vision.

As the final adjustments were made, Greda stood by the main console, her expression unreadable. "Implement it," she instructed crisply. The engineer nodded, his hand hovering over the console before pressing down decisively.

Instantly, the Citadel's corridors hummed to life as new data flowed through Lumina's veins, reaching out to every denizen ensconced within the virtual paradise. Greda watched the live feed, data streams reporting a noticeable spike in emotional distress followed by a rush of relief as virtual realities took over.

Satisfied, Greda turned to leave the room, her mind already on the next phase of her plan. As she stepped into the shadowed corridor, her chief advisor approached, a data pad in his hand.

"Chancellor, there's been a development with the rebel factions," he reported, his voice tense. Greda stopped, her eyes narrowing. "They're gaining support. There's chatter that they might have found a way to block our simulations."

Greda took the data pad, her eyes scanning the encrypted messages. "I want them all dead," she said angrily, handing back the device. "Increase the patrols and bring me updates on their movements. And double the dissemination of our deepfakes. If fear will not drive them into compliance, perhaps despair will."

Jax's hand froze mid-air, his finger just shy of the comm device to signal retreat. The shrill sound of a new alarm sliced through the dim corridors of Zone U7, setting every nerve on edge. Turning swiftly, he scanned the area, his Photon Lance held at the ready, its light casting eerie shadows against the stark metal walls. "What now?" he muttered under his breath, eyes darting for the source of the threat.

The alarm's source wasn't immediately visible, but the tension in the air thickened. His team, composed of both humans and androids, rallied around him, forming a defensive circle. Jax's gaze met Callan's across the group, a silent exchange of readiness and concern passing between them.

Before Jax could issue a new order, the sound of heavy machinery disrupted the moment. From the shadows emerged a rogue faction of androids, their allegiance to the Verdant Overlord clear from the hostile stance and the emblems emblazoned on their chassis. "Ambush!" Jax shouted, his voice calm but loud, carrying over the din of approaching danger.

The battle erupted almost instantly. Jax maneuvered with precision, his Photon Lance discharging concentrated bursts of energy. He darted between the attackers, his movements a blur of efficiency honed by countless conflicts. Beside him, the androids from his team engaged with equal fervor, their programming tuned to subdue without lethal force.

Amid the chaos, Jax could see Callan and a few others pushing towards a critical junction, trying to cut off the rogue androids' reinforcements. Just as the battle seemed to tip towards a grimmer outcome, the ground beside Jax stirred.

Vines erupted from the concrete floor, thick and animated with a life of their own. Rootwhisper emerged, its teenage form towering and formidable, leaves shimmering with a bioluminescent glow that cast everything in a surreal light. The sentient plant's vines lashed out, entangling the rogue androids with surprising force and precision.

"Rootwhisper!" Jax exclaimed, a grin breaking across his face as the tide of battle turned. The plant's second intervention was expected this time and immensely welcome. Its vines not only restrained the enemy but also shielded Jax and his team, allowing them to regroup and push forward.

Seizing the opportunity, Jax led a charge towards the central hub, now within reach thanks to their botanical ally. "Push forward!" he commanded, his voice resonating with the thrill of battle and the hope of victory. The rogue androids, caught off guard by the strength and strange alliance of their opponents, faltered.

As they advanced, Jax couldn't help but marvel at the sight of Rootwhisper in full combat. The plant was not just fighting; it was fighting with a purpose, driven by a vendetta against the Verdant Overlord that had corrupted so many of its kind. Its vines moved with lethal grace, incapacitating the rogue androids without taking lives, embodying the very philosophy Jax championed—coexistence and respect for all life forms.

The central hub loomed ahead, the doorways thrown open as the last of the rogue androids were subdued. Breathing heavily, Jax paused at the threshold, his team rallying around him and Rootwhisper retracting its vines with a rustle that sounded like a sigh of relief.

Breathing heavily, Jax paused at the threshold, his team rallying around him and Rootwhisper retracting its vines with a rustle that sounded like a sigh of relief. They were not out of danger yet, and the hardest part of the mission loomed just steps away. Ahead lay the central control tower of Zone U7, its monolithic presence brooding under the veil of chaos they had created.

The tech genius of the group, Callan, stepped forward, his gaze fixed on the massive doors of the control tower. He adjusted the Solar Beam Rifle slung across his back and then pulled a compact, high-tech device from his belt. "Time to make our move," he murmured, his voice steady despite the pounding adrenaline.

Callan led the way, his steps silent on the cold metal floor. Jax and Rootwhisper followed, the plant's vines subtly shifting to shield their flank. The mainframe room was heavily guarded, but the confusion they had sown worked in their favor, drawing most of the security forces outward to stem the perceived invasion.

Reaching the control tower's security terminal, Callan wasted no time. He connected his device, a series of rapid keystrokes echoing softly in the hushed atmosphere. The terminal's screen flickered under the onslaught of his expert hacking, lines of code cascading down as he navigated through layers of cybersecurity with precision. "Don't tell Tibo I know how to do this." Callan said under his breath.

Jax watched the corridor, his Photon Lance at the ready, while Rootwhisper's tendrils hovered near the ceiling, ready to strike at any sign of threat. The tension was palpable, the only sounds the clicking of Callan's device and the distant echoes of chaos.

Minutes felt like hours until Callan's tense expression broke, a small smile playing on his lips. "I'm in," he announced quietly, "Security protocols are down, and I'm setting up our command network now."

As Callan worked to override the system, Jax felt a momentary relief wash over him. This was the turning point. From here, they could control the facility's defenses, turning the automated systems from oppressors into protectors of their newly claimed territory.

The alarms suddenly cut off, plunging the corridor into eerie silence. Callan's hands didn't stop moving, his focus unbreakable as he implemented the last of the commands. "And... we are set," he finally said, pulling back from the terminal. The screens around them lit up with the insignia of their resistance, a symbol of their fight for coexistence and mutual respect among all forms of life.

But the victory was short-lived. The silence was quickly shattered by a new series of alarms, this time different, urgent, and frighteningly close. Jax tensed, his eyes meeting Callan's. "What did you do?" he asked, half in jest yet aware of the many dangers still lurking.

"I might have triggered their last-ditch containment protocols," Callan admitted, his voice tight with annoyance at himself. "They know we're here and what we're trying to do. They're locking down the facility."

Jax nodded, understanding immediately what needed to be done. "We hold this room," he declared, turning to Rootwhisper. "Can you secure the entrances?"

Rootwhisper's vines thickened, growing in size as they snaked towards the doorways, forming natural barricades that no ordinary force could penetrate quickly.

Rootwhisper's burgeoning barricades solidified, their wooden fibers intertwining to form an almost impenetrable wall. The reinforced doors shuddered under the impact of forces from outside, but held fast, thanks to the sentient plant's efforts. Inside the secured control room, Jax and Callan exchanged a brief nod, an acknowledgment of the temporary safety they had achieved.

Jax moved to join Callan at the console, where the latter was navigating through the newly unlocked depths of Zone U7's network. The screens flickered with the rapid procession of files, each swipe bringing them closer to the full scope of their enemy's intentions.

"Look at this," Callan murmured, tapping into a particularly heavily encrypted file folder. With a few more strokes on the keyboard, the files spilled open, their contents sprawling across the screen in stark, clinical detail.

Jax leaned in, his eyes scanning the digital documents. The data was chilling—a comprehensive plan laid out by the Chancellor Greda, detailing a phased extermination of the android population after the completion of their objective to secure Zone U7. It was cold, calculated, and utterly devoid of empathy. The androids, it seemed, were nothing more than tools to be discarded.

A surge of anger washed through Jax. He turned to Callan, his face set in hard lines. "They see us as expendable—just a means to an end."

Callan nodded solemnly, his hands pausing above the keyboard. "We need to share this. Every android needs to know the truth about the Greda."

Jax agreed with a sharp nod. "Broadcast it. Every screen, every speaker within the network."

Working quickly, Callan set up the transmission. As the files prepared to broadcast, Jax turned to Rootwhisper, who understood every word and knew the gravity of the situation. The plant's vines shivered slightly, a ripple of understanding passing through its leaves.

With a deep breath, Jax activated the broadcast, his voice resonant and clear, enhanced by the room's acoustics. "To all androids in Zone U7 and beyond," he began, his tone grave but resolute, "the files we've discovered confirm our worst fears. The Chancellor plans to discard us once we are no longer useful. We are not tools; we are beings with the right to live, to choose, and to be free. It's time to fight back, not just for territory, but for our very existence."

The message went out, echoing through the corridors of Zone U7 and beyond, transmitted to every outpost and terminal hacked by Callan. Within moments, responses began to flood in—messages of unity, outrage, and readiness to fight. The androids of Zone U7, once merely participants in a struggle for territory, were now allies in a fight for survival. And just like that, Callan's Resistance grew even bigger.

Outside, the sounds of assault on the barricades grew fiercer. But inside, fortified by Rootwhisper and fueled by the revelation of their plight, Jax and his team prepared to defend their position.

Rootwhisper's vines tightened around the room's entrances, reinforcing the barricade as the first of the enemy's battering attempts began. The walls held— for now.

Rootwhisper's vines tightened around the room's entrances, reinforcing the barricade as the first of the enemy's battering attempts began. The walls held— for now. The reverberations from the enemy's onslaught echoed throughout the room, a stark reminder that the battle was far from over.

Outside, the vast plaza that served as their makeshift arena began to fill. The crowds—humans, androids, and sentient vegetation alike— gathered around, perched on the ruins and makeshift balconies. The air was electric with anticipation, every eye fixed on the impending showdown. This was not just a battle; it was a declaration of their right to exist, to fight back against a tyranny that had reduced beings to mere tools.

Jax surveyed the arena from his vantage point inside the control room, his gaze cutting across the urban battlefield. The plaza was littered with debris from fallen structures, offering both strategic cover and challenging obstacles. It was a perfect reflection of the chaos that had brought them to this critical juncture.

As the enemy forces assembled, Jax could make out the silhouettes of Chancellor Greda's elite android squad advancing towards their position. Enhanced with the latest combat technology, they moved with lethal precision, a formidable force designed to crush any opposition. The stakes were monumental, not just for the territory but for the essence of what they fought for—their autonomy, their very lives.

"Get ready," Jax commanded, his voice steady and clear despite the pounding in his chest. His team, a diverse group of seasoned fighters, plus Callan and Rootwhisper took their places among the ruins, their expressions resolute. Each one understood what was at risk; the battle they were about to engage in was for more than survival—it was for the future of all sentient beings in Zone U7.

The first clashes were explosive, as both sides exchanged volleys of fire. Jax and Callan coordinated their efforts, leveraging the urban terrain to their advantage. Jax's Photon Lance sent beams of concentrated energy slicing through the twilight, each shot strategically disabled enemy combatants. Beside him, Callan's Solar Beam Rifle emitted bursts of light, creating a dazzling pattern of cover fire.

Rootwhisper played its part from the confines of the control room, its vines extending through cracks and openings in the structure, snaking into the plaza. The sentient plant's tendrils whipped out, dragging debris to create barriers or pulling unsuspecting enemy androids into the shadows, disorienting them and disrupting their formation.

The din of battle momentarily ebbed as both sides recalibrated their strategies. The plaza, thick with the aftermath of the initial skirmish, was now a visceral display of the stakes they were fighting for. Jax, pausing behind a shattered facade, surveyed the shifting lines of his opponents and the determined faces of his team. Each breath was heavy with the dusty scent of debris and the electric charge of pending confrontation.

Above, on the fragmented balconies, the audience—human, android, and plant alike—leaned forward, their collective breath caught in the gravity of the moment.

With a sharp gesture from Jax, the brief moment of clarity shattered. "Move—now!" His voice cut through the stillness, galvanizing his team into swift action. They erupted from their cover, moving with a synchrony honed by desperation and the instinct to survive. Jax's Photon Lance lit up the evening, a streak of blue-white that tagged enemy shields, while Callan's shots arced overhead, creating a light show that was both beautiful and deadly.

The arena became a storm of activity. Jax darted from cover to cover, each movement calculated and every decision split-second. His team mirrored his actions, forming a fluid network of resistance that confounded and whittled down the enemy's numbers. The clatter of combat, the zap of energy weapons, and the cries of the combatants filled the air, creating a symphony of survival and defiance.

Rootwhisper redoubled its efforts. Vines thicker and more agile than before surged forth, creating new barriers and pulling enemy androids off their feet. Some vines hardened into spikes that embedded into the plaza's flooring, creating natural fortifications that provided critical cover for Jax and his team.

Amidst the chaos, Jax's leadership was palpable. He moved through the battlefield with a grace that belied the ferocity of his strikes. Each pulse from his lance was a saved life, each maneuver a thread in the tapestry of their continued resistance. The emotional intensity of the fight was etched on his face—this was not just a battle for territory, but a fight for the right to exist, to define their future on their terms.

The crescendo of battle built as both sides poured their might into the conflict. The air was thick with the sounds of war, the cries of the fallen, and the rallying shouts of those still fighting. In this crucible, the bond between Jax and his team solidified; forged in the heart of conflict.

As Jax ducked a high-energy beam, his eyes met those of an opposing android, its gaze momentarily confused by the intensity of Jax's determination. In that second, a silent understanding passed between them—a mutual recognition of what was at stake. With a swift, non-lethal strike, Jax neutralized the threat.

The battle escalated to its zenith as Jax maneuvered through the urban battlefield to confront the leader of the rogue androids, a towering figure armed with advanced combat enhancements. They met at the center of the plaza, their encounter symbolizing the high stakes of this conflict. Spectators from all factions held their breath as the two leaders circled each other, the tension palpable in the charged air.

Jax initiated the duel with a series of calculated attacks, each strike a blend of human intuition and android precision. His opponent parried expertly, their movements a testament to their combat programming. However, Jax's determination and innovative tactics gradually wore down the android leader's defenses.

After a tense exchange, Jax executed a complex maneuver, leveraging his Photon Lance to disarm his opponent with a decisive, non-lethal blow. The android leader stood defeated, weaponless, and stunned, a silent acknowledgment of Jax's superior skill.

In the immediate aftermath, Rootwhisper emerged as an unexpected hero. The sentient plant's actions during the fight, which had turned the tide in favor of Jax's coalition, instantly became legendary. People across Zone U7 and beyond started broadcasting the event, narrating the awe-inspiring collaboration between man, android, and plant. The spectacle of their unity and Rootwhisper's crucial role resonated deeply, sparking conversations on new possibilities for coexistence.

As the defeated adversaries were secured, the victory was broadcasted across all networks, amplifying the message of their struggle and the dire plots they had unveiled. This widespread dissemination ensured that the truth reached every corner, igniting a wave of solidarity and a call for systemic change.

In the quiet that followed the storm of battle, Jax's determination only deepened. Addressing his diverse team and their global audience, he reflected on the day's events and the path forward. His leadership, now undisputed, had not just averted a crisis but had begun to forge a new path for all sentient beings.

Chapter 11

Chancellor Greda stood at the threshold of the Bio-Engineering Labs, her gaze sweeping over the rows of luminescent crops that thrived in the underground's artificial embrace. Each plant glowed softly, showcasing the genetic wizardry that had untethered them from the need for sunlight. She adjusted the cuff of her sleeve, a nervous habit barely noticeable, and stepped forward.

"Report," she commanded, her voice echoing slightly off the sterile walls. A scientist, clipboard in hand, hurried over, his face lit with the fervor of a true believer.

"Chancellor, the new strains have surpassed all growth expectations," he began, enthusiasm trembling in his voice. "Our modifications have increased their yield by thirty-seven percent since the last quarter."

Greda nodded, her expression unreadable. "And the integration into Lumina?" she asked, her mind racing through the layers of implications each success held.

"Progressing well," the scientist confirmed. "Participants who consume these as their primary food source show improved compliance and reduced physical fatigue in their virtual sessions."

"Good," Greda murmured. She paced along the aisle, her fingers trailing over the bioluminescent leaves. Each touch felt like a confirmation of her control, not just over the plants, but over the very essence of life within her domain.

She paused, her eyes catching a flicker of movement in the reflection of a glass panel. The Bio-Engineering Labs were more than just a site of scientific endeavor; they were a symbol of her determination to maintain life under her strict conditions. "Prepare to expand distribution," she instructed without turning. "I want these crops to be the sole food source for all Project Lumina participants within six months."

The scientist scribbled hurriedly, a flicker of concern passing over his features. "Chancellor, there are still tests to be completed. The long-term effects on human biochemistry are not fully—"

Greda turned sharply, her gaze cutting him off. "Are you a part of my council, Doctor?" she asked, her voice low and dangerous.

"No, Chancellor," he replied, his voice faltering.

"Then do not presume to advise on policy. Your role is to implement, not to question." She stepped closer, her presence dominating the space between them. "Should I kill you, now?"

"No, Chancellor," he stammered, bowing his head slightly.

Greda turned away, her mind already racing through the next phases of her plan. The crops were a key element in her strategy, a way to bind the people to Lumina more completely. If they depended on her for their sustenance, their loyalty would be less likely to waver.

As she walked back towards the exit, her communicator buzzed discreetly. She tapped it, listening to the report from her security chief. There were murmurs of unrest, whispers of discontent that threaded through the lower levels of the citadel.

She stopped, considering her options. The integration of the new food supply could not come at a better time. With it, she could tighten her grip, weaving dependence and control into the very fabric of daily life.

"Enhance surveillance on the dissenting sectors," she ordered into the communicator. "And increase their ration of the new crops immediately."

Her steps echoed in the empty corridor as she left the labs behind. The soft glow of the genetically modified plants cast long shadows on the floor, shadows that seemed to stretch out like fingers grasping at the edges of her controlled empire.

Jax Thorn's breathing was heavy, the weight of his Photon Lance comforting in his grip as he pressed against the cool metal wall of The Underforge. His eyes, adapting quickly to the lower light, flicked to the holo-projector on his wrist, displaying the layout of the complex and the advancing enemy signatures.

"Callan, Rhootwhisper, on me," he hissed, his voice a whisper over the comms that barely rose above the distant clatter of enemy movements. The air was thick with the scent of oil and metal, the industrial heart of The Underforge pulsing around them. His team, a blend of human cunning and botanical might, was all that stood between the enemy and total control of the underground's armory.

From the shadows, a squad of hostile androids burst forth, their movements synchronized and lethal. Jax reacted instinctively, his Photon Lance discharging a burst of energy that illuminated the corridor with a harsh blue light. The beam struck the leading android, its systems shorting out with a shower of sparks.

"Push them back!" Jax commanded, leading the charge. His armor's nano-mesh adapted, hardening as projectiles ricocheted off its surface. Callan flanked him, his own weapons a blur as he laid down a suppressing fire that rattled through the tight space.

Rhootwhisper, larger and more imposing than any typical flora, spread its limbs wide, vines whipping forward to entangle another wave of attackers. The plant's bioluminescent glow cast eerie shadows, turning the battle into a dance of light and shadow.

They moved deeper into The Underforge, each step a battle, each breath a calculation. Jax's mind raced, his human intuition and android logic processing every movement, every choice with lethal precision. Ahead, the main forge loomed, a massive room filled with the essential weaponry and tech that could not fall into enemy hands.

As they approached, a thunderous explosion shook the complex. Debris rained down, nearly cutting them off from their final objective. Jax's heart pounded, his senses heightened to the peak as they navigated through the smoke and rubble.

"We're almost there," he reassured his team, his voice steady despite the chaos. "Cover me, I'm going for the forge controls."

Breaking from cover, Jax sprinted towards the forge's control panel, a complex array of levers and digital displays that controlled the manufacturing capabilities of the entire zone. His fingers flew over the controls, initiating a lockdown protocol that would seal the forge from further intrusion.

The enemy was relentless, however. More androids surged towards the forge, their numbers overwhelming. Jax met them head-on, his Photon Lance swinging in arcs of devastating energy. Each hit bought his team precious seconds, each fallen enemy a small victory in the shadow of impending defeat.

Behind him, Callan worked feverishly on a terminal, hacking into the Underforge's defense systems to turn the tide. "Almost got it, Jax!" he shouted over the din of combat.

The room vibrated with the power of the forge, the air electrifying as Callan's efforts bore fruit. Automated defense turrets whirred to life, targeting the intruders with clinical accuracy. The tide of the battle shifted subtly, the defenders finding new hope as the machines took up arms in their cause.

Yet, the enemy was not done. A final squad, more heavily armed and armored, made a desperate push to breach the forge.

Jax's stance solidified as the final squad surged forward, a relentless tide of metal and malice. In that instant, his holo-projector flickered, signaling an unexpected ally. From the upper gantries, a series of small drones buzzed into action, a last-minute modification Callan had not disclosed. "Surprise from the tech department!" Callan's voice crackled with a mix of tension and triumph over the comm.

The drones, agile and equipped with stun technology, swooped down on the advancing enemies, their sudden appearance sowing confusion and halting the assault. Jax took advantage of the disruption, charging forward with renewed vigor. His Photon Lance glowed brighter, the energy amplifying as if feeding off his determination.

"Rhootwhisper!" Jax screamed, and the sentient plant responded with a surge of growth. New vines burst from the ground, thicker and more resilient, forming barriers that segmented the enemy forces and isolated them from each other. The Underforge's cavernous space twisted into a labyrinth of green and steel.

Caught off guard, the divided squads struggled to regroup, their tactics unraveled by the maze of vines and the relentless drone attacks. Jax moved through the chaos like a specter, his armor's nano-mesh rendering him nearly invisible in the low light, each strike of his lance precise and debilitating.

The twist of fate, driven by Callan's clandestine innovation and Rootwhisper's might, turned the tide irrevocably. The enemy's numerical advantage dwindled under the coordinated assault of technology and nature, their formation broken.

Amidst the fray, Jax found himself face to face with another, even stronger enemy commander, a towering android with advanced combat enhancements. The commander, recognizing the shift in battle dynamics, engaged Jax directly, its own weapon—a heavy energy mace—swinging with lethal intent.

Jax dodged a crushing blow, rolling aside as the mace shattered the concrete where he had stood seconds before. Rising swiftly, he countered with a series of rapid thrusts from his Photon Lance, each one parried skillfully by the android. The duel, set against the backdrop of an evolving battlefield, became a focal point, drawing the attention of both sides.

As they fought, Jax's strategy evolved. With each exchange, he led the commander closer to one of Rootwhisper's larger vines. With a final, feinted lunge, he baited the commander into a misstep. The vine, almost sentient in its timing, ensnared the android's legs, pulling it off balance.

Seizing the moment, Jax delivered a decisive blow, his Photon Lance emitting a concentrated burst directly into the commander's power core. Sparks flew as the android stumbled back, its systems overloading until it collapsed, inert and defeated.

The fall of their leader signaled the end for the enemy's resolve. What remained of their forces retreated, harried by drones and entangled by Rootwhisper's relentless growth. The Underforge, its forges still humming with the energy of resistance, was secured.

Jax, breathing heavily from the exertion, surveyed the secured forge. Callan approached, clapping him on the shoulder. "That twist with the drones was brilliant," Jax admitted, his tone a mixture of relief and respect.

"Yeah," Callan grinned, wiping soot from his face. "Just thought we'd shake things up a bit. Seems to have worked."

Jax nodded, his gaze scanning the still humming forge. The glow from the drones dimmed as they returned to their docks along the gantries. The moment of victory was brief, his mind already racing ahead. "We can't just defend. We need to hit them harder, disrupt their chain entirely."

Callan's eyes narrowed, understanding the leap Jax was pondering. "What are you thinking?"

"Zone U7's old conduits," Jax began, his voice a low rumble over the sound of cooling metal. "They still thread through the entire complex. If we could surge the power..."

Rootwhisper's tendrils rustled, the bioluminescent tips casting an otherworldly glow. "Surge could be double-edged," the plant intoned, the air vibrating with its deep, resonant speech. "Risk to all systems, not just theirs."

Jax turned to face the sentient flora, his eyes reflecting the flickering lights. "It's a calculated risk. If we boost the power flow, overload it, we might fry their tech. Gives us a window... but it could hit ours too."

Callan chewed on his lip, flicking through data on his wrist-screen. "It's risky, Jax. Overloading could mean losing what we just fought for. Our defenses, the drones, even Rootwhisper's enhancements."

"But if it works," Jax countered, stepping closer, his voice dropping to a near whisper, "we cripple them long enough to fortify and push them out of U7 for good."

Rootwhisper's vines swayed gently, a thoughtful rustle through its leaves. "Human and android systems most at risk. My core is less reliant on your power grids. I can maintain hold, perhaps shield some of the critical systems."

Callan nodded slowly, the gears turning behind his eyes. "Okay, if Rhootwhisper can safeguard the forge and essential systems, I can rig the conduits. We'll need to be fast, precise."

"Exactly," Jax affirmed, clapping Callan on the shoulder. "Let's set it up. Callan, you handle the tech with Rootwhisper's support. I'll prepare our teams, make sure everyone's clear on the blackout zones. We'll need to move quickly once we trigger the surge."

"And the civilians?" Callan asked, his brow furrowing with concern.

Jax's jaw tightened. "Evacuate anyone non-essential to the outer sectors. Use the emergency bunkers if needed. We can't have casualties on this."

Moving through the forge, Jax's orders were crisp, his every directive sharpening the focus of their desperate plan. Callan set off towards the main power hub, tapping commands into his wrist unit, his steps quick and determined.

Rhootwhisper, spreading its influence through the shadows, began to fortify the surroundings, its vines creeping along walls and machinery, ready to protect or pull back at a moment's notice.

As Jax marshaled his troops, explaining the plan in hushed, urgent tones, the atmosphere in The Underforge shifted from triumph to tense anticipation. Each fighter, human and android alike, prepared for the blackout, checking their gear, securing non-electrical backups.

"Once we hit that switch," Jax murmured to his assembled team, "it's going to be a different kind of darkness. Stay sharp, stay close, and watch each other's backs."

He glanced back towards the control room, where Callan and Rhootwhisper were now a hive of activity, lights blinking rapidly as they prepared the surge. It was a gamble, a bold strike in the shadows of their war, and as Jax readied his Photon Lance.

This was it. Another turning point. One that could either save them all or plunge them deeper into chaos.

The clink of fine crystal under the subtle lighting of the Gastronomy Sector was a symphony to Greda's ears as she watched her elite circle mingle. The air was saturated with the aroma of engineered delicacies, each dish a testament to the technological dominion she held over nature itself.

"Chancellor, the spread tonight surpasses all expectations," murmured a council member, his eyes gleaming not just from the reflection of the bioluminescent chandeliers but from the sheer opulence that surrounded him.

Greda nodded, her gaze sweeping the room. "It's not just a feast, but a demonstration," she began, her voice carrying the soft, dangerous edge of a well-honed blade. "Outside these walls, the world crumbles, but under our stewardship, even the apocalypse is merely another obstacle to engineer our way past."

A server approached, offering a platter of synthetic shrimp, its texture and flavor indistinguishable from the real thing. Greda took one, her eyes never leaving the faces of her guests. "Every bite you take is a reminder of the order we maintain. And the control I hold over our sustenance."

Riko, standing a little off to the side, caught her eye and nodded slightly, a silent player in the game of reassurance and power they played so well.

"Indeed, Chancellor," he said, stepping forward. His tone was respectful, yet carried an undercurrent of challenge that was not lost on Greda. "And yet, the populace stirs. They hear rumors of the surface, of possibilities…"

Greda's smile was thin, almost imperceptible. "Possibilities," she echoed, turning to face the assembly, her back straight, commanding the room with her presence. "Possibilities that we define, that we control. Project Lumina is not just our salvation but their hope. Their addiction."

She paused, letting the words sink in, her gaze piercing the veil of comforts they all took for granted. "But it is fragile," she continued, her voice lowering to draw them in, a conspiratorial whisper that spoke of shared secrets and shared responsibilities. "And it requires our unity, our belief in the order I have crafted from chaos."

The room hung on her every word, the elites captivated by the narrative she wove that justified the luxuries they enjoyed at the expense of the many.

"Without us, without our guidance, the Project is a mere dream. And dreams," Greda turned, picking up a glass of sparkling synthetic wine, "can turn to nightmares."

She raised her glass, her movement slow, deliberate. "To us, the bearers of order, the architects of survival."

The toast was echoed, a chorus of agreement that filled the room with the sound of clinking glass. As the elites drank, Greda's eyes met Riko's once more, a silent acknowledgment of the battles they fought in shadowed rooms, far from the illuminated spaces where the elite feasted.

As the murmurs of agreement and loyalty swelled around her, Greda allowed herself a small, satisfied smile. Tonight, they saw only what she wanted them to see: strength, stability, inevitability.

But as she turned away from the gathering, her gaze drifted to the screens hidden in the alcoves, where numbers and graphs told stories of dissent and unrest. The feast was a distraction, a beautiful lie told to those who needed to believe they were safe.

She stepped out onto the balcony overlooking the lower sectors of Lumina Citadel, the air cooler, the scent of engineered foods replaced by the sterile tang of recycled air. Below, the lesser tiers subsisted on nutrient-deficient rations, a stark contrast to the opulence she just left behind.

And there, in the quiet, Greda allowed herself to consider the full weight of her empire, built on control and illusion. A fortress of order in a world of chaos, a reign of beauty on the surface, underpinned by the stark lines of necessity and survival.

"Yeah," Riko responded, not missing a beat as he adjusted the interface on his tablet. "And now, Chancellor, we have the chance to tighten that grip further. The Virtual Gamble is ready for its next phase."

Greda turned from the balcony, her eyes locking on Riko's. "Explain," she commanded, the word slicing through the lingering echoes of the elite's laughter from inside the dining hall.

Riko tapped on his device, bringing up schematics and data streams that flickered with the cold light of hard numbers. "Our android competitors have been upgraded, more resilient than ever, and the vegetation on the surface is responding. It's brutal, unpredictable—perfect for the games."

Greda nodded slowly, a glint of interest sparking in her eyes. "And the elite, they're ready to invest more heavily?"

"They crave it, Chancellor," Riko confirmed. "Every game, every death, they feel a thrill. It's a distraction... from the discomforts of their reality, from the power we wield so effortlessly."

"The games," Greda mused, turning back to gaze over the Citadel. "They're not just entertainment, are they? They're a show of force, a demonstration of our control over life and death."

"Exactly," Riko said, stepping beside her, his voice dropping to match her reflective tone. "And this next game, we're introducing a new element. A power surge in the old energy conduits—risky, but if it succeeds, it will show them the raw power of our technology. It could overload their tech, add an element of chaos."

Greda's lips curved into a smile, the idea clearly pleasing her. "Chaos within controlled parameters, Riko. It heightens the stakes, doesn't it? Makes the game... more real for our watchers."

"Indeed, it does." Riko's fingers danced over the screen, pulling up a live feed of the surface where the next game was set to take place. The desolate landscape flickered on the screen, the remnants of vegetation bristling with the promise of violence.

"But what of our own androids? This surge could fry their systems as well," Greda pondered aloud, her gaze fixed on the holographic display that showed the positioning of their mechanical gladiators.

"That's the gamble," Riko admitted. "We've insulated them as much as we can, but there's always a risk. However, the reward—increased betting, heightened engagement from our elite—it could be substantial."

Greda considered this, her eyes narrowing slightly as she processed the possibilities. "And the elite's dependence on our technology, on our good graces, it grows with their investment."

"Exactly. They won't just watch the games; they'll be part of them, emotionally, financially." Riko's voice held a note of triumph, as if the very thought of such control was a victory in itself.

"They need to remember who holds their luxuries—and their lives—in her hands," Greda added, her voice cold yet beautiful, like the synthetic ice sculptures that adorned her banquet tables.

"So, we proceed with the power surge," Riko confirmed, seeking her final approval.

"We proceed," Greda declared, her decision ringing with the authority that had sculpted a society from the ruins of the old world. "Prepare the arena, Riko. And make sure our elites are watching closely. They must see what happens when the boundaries of technology are not just pushed, but shattered."

Riko nodded, a flicker of excitement passing through his usually impassive features. "It will be done, Chancellor."

As Riko turned to leave, Greda lingered at the balcony, her gaze drifting back to the screens hidden in the shadows. The games would go on, the bets would be placed, and above all, the control she so meticulously maintained would tighten. In this world she had crafted, every gamble was calculated, and tonight, it was her move.

Jax's voice crackled through the comm, terse and urgent, "Hurry, Callan!"

Jax's breathing was heavy, the metallic tang of the air blending with the electric anticipation that charged the atmosphere. He hunkered down near the control panel, his fingers poised above the activation sequence.

Jax couldn't see what Callan saw, but he could imagine the holographic displays flickering with the imminent power surge, each second ticking down with dire potential. The screens around him flickered with streams of data, mapping the labyrinthine network of old energy conduits snaking through Zone U7.

"Brace for overload," Callan muttered, his gaze locked on the pulsing diagrams that displayed the power flow intensifying dangerously. The plan was a wild card, the kind that you played not because you wanted to but because the stakes had never been higher.

The countdown cut through the air, each second pulsing like a heartbeat in Jax's ears. "T-minus ten seconds to surge," Callan's voice announced, steady yet fraught with the gravity of their gamble.

Jax was out there in the thick of it, Photon Lance in hand, ready to exploit the chaos the surge would bring. "Keep your heads down!" he barked into the comm, a directive for those stationed at critical junctions throughout the forge. These were the men and women who kept the heart of their resistance beating, and today, they danced dangerously close to flatline.

Photon Lance in hand, Jax was poised to exploit the chaos the surge would bring. "Keep your heads down!" he barked into the comm, his directive a lifeline to those stationed throughout the forge, their roles pivotal in the heart of the resistance.

The feedback from the conduits started to whine, a high-pitched scream that set Callan's teeth on edge. "Three, two, one—" Jax braced as the world around him seemed to explode in light and sound.

Power roared through the conduits, the Underforge groaning under the strain. Lights blazed with blinding brilliance before dying, casting the complex into a dance of shadow and intermittent light.

Jax's ears rang with the echo of the surge, the feedback piercing even as the station he guarded flickered wildly. The surveillance feeds were a chaotic medley of the battle zones within Zone U7; he glimpsed brief flashes of corridors lit by exploding light fixtures, workshops where machinery overloaded, sending out deadly arcs of electricity.

"Status!" he shouted into the comm, his voice slicing through the crackling static that filled the airwaves.

"Systems failing all over—but the enemy's taking the brunt!" a tech operator reported from a distant post, her voice strained under the weight of warfare.

Through a feed prone to flicker, Jax saw his own silhouette move against the strobing darkness, each burst of his Photon Lance a stroke of vivid light painting the shadows. The surge was wreaking havoc as planned. Enemy androids, caught in the maelstrom, seized and malfunctioned, their movements stuttering and uncoordinated.

"Systems failing all over—but the enemy's taking the brunt!" came a strained reply from one of his tech operators, stationed deeper within the forge.

Yet, the risk was palpable, their own systems teetering on the brink of collapse. "Reroute auxiliary power to defensive grids!" Jax commanded into the comm, his voice firm despite the rising dread.

Outside, the sounds of battle morphed; mechanical screams mingled with the victorious shouts of their fighters. They were pushing back, using the disarray as a shield as they advanced into previously contested zones.

"It's now or never!" Jax's voice boomed through the comm, urgent over the din of combat and collapsing infrastructure. "We push them out while we have the chance!"

Rootwhisper's tendrils tapped into the network, its unique biological interface allowing it to stabilize sections of the grid that no human could.

He could hear Callan responding, his voice a beacon rallying the resistance. "This is it! All units, advance! Drive them back! For every brother, every sister who fell, make them pay!"

The rallying cry filled the channels, a chorus of determination and defiance that echoed through the Underforge. The response from their fighters was immediate, their actions fueled by the surge of unity and the urgency of survival.

Jax allowed himself a brief moment, just a heartbeat, to absorb the weight of their unity, their purpose. Then he was back, his gaze sweeping over the dimly lit forge, his every sense alert to the shifts in the battle's tide.

As the blackout settled in, Jax readied his Photon Lance, the device humming with potent energy, ready to pierce the shadows. This was another turning point, a bold strike in the shadows of their war, where every action could either save them all or plunge them deeper into chaos.

As the surge echoed through the corridors of The Underforge, Jax moved with calculated precision, his Photon Lance casting erratic shadows against the crumbling walls. The ground beneath his feet vibrated with the raw power of the unleashed energy, a wild rhythm that thrummed like a heartbeat in chaos.

"This was another turning point, a bold strike in the shadows of their war, where every action could either save them all or plunge them deeper into chaos."

The control room's monitors flickered wildly as Jax monitored the advancing enemy lines through the sporadic illumination. He could see the android adversaries staggering, their circuits fried by the power surge, but the victory was anything but assured. Jax's ears rang with the electronic screech of overloaded systems, a dissonant symphony to the battle's brutal ballet.

"Jax! Left flank, collapsing!" Callan's voice shattered the momentary stillness, crackling through the comm with urgency. Without hesitation, Jax pivoted, his boots sliding across the slick floor, coated with the residue of battle. The Photon Lance surged to life, its glow a extremely noticeable in the intermittent lighting.

As he turned the corner, a squad of enemy androids came into view, their movements jerky and uncoordinated yet still advancing. With a warrior's cry, Jax charged, the Lance slicing through the air, cutting down the first of the androids. Sparks flew as metal clashed against energy, the smell of burning circuits permeating the air.

Behind him, the sounds of Rhootwhisper working in tandem with Callan filled the air, a strange harmony to the chaos. The plant's vines moved with sentient purpose, reinforcing barriers and patching breaches in their defenses with organic efficiency.

Above the din, the voice of an operator crackled through again, "Power levels critical! We're walking a razor's edge here, Jax!"

Grasping the gravity of the situation, Jax leaped into a small alcove, using the brief cover to assess the battlefield. Through the haze of smoke and flickering lights, he could see that their bold move had thinned the enemy lines but at a cost. The Underforge's power grid was on the brink of collapse, their own systems as vulnerable as those they sought to destroy.

With no time to lose, Jax tapped his comm, his voice resolute. "Callan, patch me through to all units. We end this now!"

Acknowledging the command, Callan's voice soon gave way to Jax's over the integrated speakers, reaching every corner of the zone. "All units, converge on Sector 3. We push them back into the dark. Move!"

As the resistance fighters rallied to his call, Jax took a deep breath and sprinted from his cover. Each step brought him closer to the heart of the conflict, where the final stand would occur. His Photon Lance, now set to its maximum output, hummed with deadly potential.

Emerging into the open, Jax found himself face-to-face with a hulking android, its systems somehow shielded from the worst of the surge. The android swung a massive arm, equipped with a sparking energy blade that sliced through the air towards Jax.

Dodging narrowly, Jax rolled to the side, his lance finding its mark in the joints of the android's armor. With a triumphant yell, he activated the lance's full power, sending a surge that finally overwhelmed his foe's systems, causing it to collapse with a thunderous clatter.

As the massive android fell, Jax's senses remained on high alert. The Underforge still buzzed with the energy of the surge, systems flickering on the brink of stability. This was the critical moment, the crescendo of their daring plan, and yet, the air tinged with the scent of an incoming storm.

He swept his gaze across the battle-scarred forge, his team scattered and battling the remaining pockets of enemy forces. The shadows danced with the light of intermittent explosions, creating ghostly silhouettes on the walls. Each fighter was a blur of motion.

Suddenly, through the noise of battle, a new sound rose—a rhythmic thumping, like the beating of a great drum, growing steadily louder. Jax's eyes narrowed, his grip tightening on the Photon Lance as he scanned the dimly lit corridors for the source.

Then, from the shadows, figures emerged—not more androids, but something unexpected. Vines and tendrils, leaves and bark moved in humanoid forms, advancing with purposeful strides. They were the sentient vegetation of the surface, once enemies, now moving to flank Jax's position. But they were not alone; with them came humans, outcasts and rebels who had survived in the wilderness, their faces marked by the trials of their existence.

As they neared, one of the plant beings—a towering figure with bark-like armor—raised a limb in a gesture of alliance. "Jax Thorn," it boomed, its voice resonant and deep, carrying over the din of conflict. "We have not forgotten your aid in the past. Now, we come to repay that debt."

The unexpected allies surged forward, joining the fray with ferocity. Their arrival lit a new fire under Jax's weary team, turning the tide of battle. The sentient plants unleashed nature's wrath, vines ensnaring androids, roots breaking through the metal floor to trip up the enemy. The human outcasts, for their part, moved with the stealth and precision of those who had long evaded capture, their attacks calculated and deadly.

Jax didn't waste the opportunity. "Push forward!" he shouted, his voice a rallying cry that cut through the chaos. "With me!"

Together, they advanced, a united front of metal, flesh, and foliage. Each step forward was contested, but the combined might of their unexpected alliance proved overwhelming. As they pushed the enemy back, Jax led the charge, his Photon Lance a beacon of light in the murky depths of The Underforge.

They reached the heart of the enemy's position, a nexus of corridors where the last of the androids made their stand. Here, the battle reached its zenith, the clash of forces echoing like thunder through the complex. Jax moved among his allies, a commander and a comrade, his every strike bringing them closer to victory.

As the final android fell, the forge fell eerily silent but for the heavy breaths of the fighters and the soft rustling of leaves. Jax surveyed the scene, his chest heaving with exertion, the weight of the moment settling upon him. They had secured Zone U7, against odds that would have overwhelmed any lesser force.

Turning to the sentient vegetation and the human outcasts, Jax nodded his respect. "Today, you've not just helped secure this forge.

You've helped forge a new alliance," he declared, the weight of history not lost on him. "Together, we've shown that unity can bring down even the mightiest walls."

The plant leader, its green eyes glowing softly in the low light, responded, "Your fight is ours, as our survival becomes yours."

As the group began to disperse, tending to the wounded and securing the area, Jax stood for a moment, lost in thought. This victory was more than strategic; it was symbolic, a sign that unity could thrive in a divided world. And as he finally allowed himself a moment of rest, leaning against the cool metal of the forge, Jax knew this was but the beginning of a greater battle—for their freedom, for their world.

Chapter 12

The heavy scent of fresh blood mingled with the crisp, conditioned air
of the Lumina Citadel's viewing arena. From her elevated platform,
Chancellor Greda overlooked the arena, her eyes cold and calculating
as she watched the first of the contestants falter, a young man barely
out of his teens, impaled by the vicious thorn spurs of a Rootguard.
His agonized scream cut through the murmured excitement of the elite
crowd, a soundbite looped for dramatic effect on the massive screens
encircling them.

Below, the dense forest setting of the arena was a living
nightmare, masterfully crafted to enhance the brutality of the games.
Cameras strategically hidden among the foliage zoomed in on the
faces of the terrified contestants, capturing every grimace and tear,
broadcasting it to the eager audience. Greda's lips twitched into a
smile as she noted the rapt attention of the elites; their faces lit by the
glow of their personal betting screens, fingers dancing with glee as
they placed their bets.

"Exhilarating, isn't it?" murmured a high-ranking official beside
her, his eyes gleaming with a mix of horror and delight. "It's as if
we're gods, deciding fates with a touch."

Greda turned, her expression composed, her voice laced with icy
authority. "We are not like gods," she corrected smoothly, her gaze
sweeping over the crowd. "We are better. Gods only watch. We
orchestrate."

On the arena floor, another contestant—a woman with defiant
eyes—tried to dodge the lunging Rootguards. Her desperation was
palpable, a thrilling scene that drew cheers from the audience as a
nettle fiber shot out, wrapping around her legs, the toxin working its
paralyzing magic. The camera zoomed in on her face, twisted in pain
and fear, a beautiful agony that sent a wave of laughter through the
Citadel.

Greda's hand moved to her chin, thoughtful. She tapped a button
on her armrest, speaking quietly to Riko, her chief technical officer,
through her concealed earpiece. "Enhance the fear factor. Let's
introduce the Spore Soldiers now. The anticipation of madness can be
quite... invigorating."

As the spores began to fill part of the arena, clouding the air with a visible menace, the screens flickered to life with thermal imaging, showing the spread of the toxic cloud and the ensuing hallucinations that racked the contestants. Screams echoed, some from genuine threats, others from phantoms of the mind. The elites leaned forward, captivated by the unfolding horror, their morbid curiosity piqued to new heights.

Greda stood, her presence commanding silence from those around her. "Observe," she commanded, her voice amplifying across the chamber. "This is the price of defiance. This is the fate of those who oppose us."

As she spoke, a young man, cornered by a pair of Chloro-Knights, made a final, desperate charge. The knights, swift and merciless, struck him down, their vine whips leaving deep, lethal marks across his body, which were displayed in high-resolution on the screens above.

Greda turned back to the official, her eyes cold yet alive with a dark fire. "Make sure every moment is recorded. These images, these screams—they will be our lessons to the masses."

As the official nodded, hurrying away to relay her commands, Greda's gaze returned to the arena. The games were more than cruelty; they were a symphony of fear and control, a demonstration of her unyielding power. Each death below served a dual purpose: entertainment for the elite and a stark warning to those who would dare defy her regime.

Her thoughts were interrupted by the sudden buzz of her communicator. Riko's voice, usually so composed, carried an edge of urgency. "Chancellor, a situation is developing at the western gate. It seems we have uninvited guests."

Greda's expression didn't change, but her mind raced with the possibilities. Enemies? Saboteurs? Or perhaps another pathetic attempt at rebellion? Whatever it was, it would be dealt with swiftly.

"Handle it, Riko. And ensure the cameras are recording. Every moment of triumph, or failure, feeds the narrative," she instructed coolly, turning her attention back to the game, where another contestant met a gruesome end.

The elite roared their approval, caught in the thrall of the spectacle. And above it all, Greda stood, a figure of implacable control and terrifying ambition, watching as her world danced to the tune she played, a tune of fear, power, and utter subjugation.

As the sounds of chaos dimmed to a distant hum, Greda focused her attention on the new tableau unfolding in the forest arena below. She adjusted the settings on her control panel, sharpening the image as a Nettler emerged from the underbrush, its movements stealthy, almost graceful. Her eyes narrowed, observing the drama with clinical detachment as a young man tried to shield a trembling girl, perhaps his sister. It was a futile gesture but made for a captivating narrative—one that Greda appreciated for its tragic beauty.

The Nettler's fibers shot forward, a horrifying ballet of nature and engineered precision. They wrapped tightly around the man, the binding almost tender if not for the agonizing effects that followed. His body stiffened, contorted by the paralyzing toxins seeping into his veins, his face a canvas of pain captured in vivid detail by the hovering drones.

"Enhance that image," Greda commanded into the microphone, her voice resonant with calm authority. The operators obeyed instantly, zooming in on the man's face. Every wince and twitch was broadcast, a gruesome spectacle that drew gasps and murmurs of fascinated horror from the elite gathered around her.

Beside her, a high-ranking official adjusted his bet, his face lit by the cold glow of the screen. "Chancellor, the endurance of this one is remarkable. Quite the fighter," he commented, his tone almost respectful.

Greda gave a noncommittal hum, her fingers tapping a rhythmic beat on the armrest. "It's the hope that fuels them. They believe there's a chance to survive," she mused aloud, her gaze still fixed on the screen. "But we know better, don't we? Prepare to release the second wave of Nettlers. Let's escalate the stakes."

As her command was relayed, the screens flickered briefly, updating the odds and betting options. Money changed hands in virtual transactions, the elite's excitement palpable as they speculated on the outcome. Greda's eyes glittered with a mix of satisfaction and anticipation. This was control — the raw, unadulterated power to manipulate life and death.

The second wave of Nettlers was more aggressive, their fibers thicker, coated with a toxin that caused not just paralysis but visible burns on contact. The cameras didn't miss a moment, capturing the gruesome details as another contestant stumbled into their embrace. The man's screams were amplified, echoing through the high-ceilinged room, a stark melody to accompany the visuals.

Greda leaned forward, her interest piqued as she watched the elites' reactions. Their faces, a mix of thrill and disgust, mirrored the dual nature of human fascination with suffering. It was a psychological nuance that Greda had mastered — the art of balancing horror with entertainment, fear with fascination.

"Record their reactions. I want a full analysis of their emotional responses later," she instructed a nearby aide, her voice a whisper lost in the crescendo of the crowd's reactions.

The scene below spiraled into further chaos. The forest became a living nightmare, each shadow possibly concealing another deadly creature. The contestants, driven by sheer terror, were no longer individuals but mere figures in a macabre dance choreographed by Greda herself.

And as one particularly brave soul attempted a daring escape, only to be ensnared by a Nettler's tendrils, Greda stood up, her presence commanding silence. "This," she announced, gesturing to the unfolding drama, "is the future of disobedience. Watch and learn."

The message was clear, not just to those within the arena but to anyone who would dare challenge her rule. As she resumed her seat, the screens blurred momentarily, switching to a strategic overview of the arena, preparing the audience for the next act of this brutal ballet.

Greda's world was one of orchestrated terror and controlled chaos, and as she watched her subjects navigate the lethal maze she had created, she knew with cold certainty that her power was absolute, unchallenged by any who dared defy her.

As Greda watched the disarray unfold through the shifting mists on the screens, her lips curled into a faint, satisfied smile. The arena had transformed into a murky swamp, its air thick with the toxic mists released by the Spore Soldiers. She tilted her head slightly, observing as a cloud of spores engulfed a cluster of contestants, their immediate confusion palpable even through the cameras.

"Zoom in on contestant number twenty-three," she commanded, her voice cutting through the low murmur of the elite audience behind her. The camera obeyed, focusing on a young woman who stumbled through the fog, her hands clawing at invisible horrors only she could see. Greda watched, fascinated by the raw fear etched across the woman's face, as she swung wildly at an approaching figure.

"That's it, show them what fear looks like," Greda murmured, her eyes tracking every movement. The figure was another contestant, his features morphing grotesquely in the woman's terror-distorted vision. Cameras captured the moment he reached out to her, only to be met with a violent shove that sent him crashing into a gnarled tree root.

The screens flickered as real-time betting odds updated, the elite now fervently placing wagers not just on who would fall next, but on who would succumb to the hallucinogenic terror first. Greda's gaze flitted to the betting screens, noting with a sense of pride how the stakes climbed, the numbers reflecting the devious joy to the cruel spectacle she had orchestrated.

"Ensure every grimace, every scream is captured," she instructed the tech team, her voice steady. "This is the essence of control—manipulating not just their bodies, but their minds."

The swamp's eerie silence was broken by sudden, sharp cries as one contestant turned on another. The cameras zoomed in on a man, driven to madness, who now perceived his ally as a threatening, monstrous entity. With frantic, jerky movements, he lunged, his hands finding a rock which he used to strike at the imagined foe. The scene was brutal, raw, and Greda felt a surge of power rush through her veins as she observed the primal survival instinct take over.

Behind her, the elites' reactions varied from thrilled gasps to hushed, eager whispers, each absorbed by the unfolding drama, their humanity stripped away by the spectacle. Greda glanced over her shoulder, her eyes sweeping across the room, capturing the faces illuminated by the glow of the holographic displays.

"Record their reactions, every shift in expression," she said quietly to an aide. "It's as vital as the game itself. Their enjoyment, their horror, it fuels our control."

Turning back to the action, Greda's attention was caught by the abrupt escalation on the screen. The Spore Soldiers advanced, their forms almost ghostly in the swirling mist. They released another wave of spores, denser, more disorienting than the first. As the cloud enveloped the contestants, cries of agony and confusion rose in a chilling chorus.

A sudden movement on the screen pulled her attention sharply to a young man who, in a moment of sheer panic, mistook the outline of a Spore Soldier for a way out. He charged, only to collide with the solid, unyielding body of the creature. The impact sent him reeling back into the mire, his scream cut short as he inhaled a lungful of toxic mist.

Greda leaned forward, her fingers pressed against the cool surface of the control panel, her eyes reflecting the chaos displayed before her. This was her design, her symphony of horror played out in excruciating detail, each note struck with precise, merciless intent.

As the mist thickened, obscuring the horrors within, Greda's expression remained impassive, her mind already turning to the aftermath, to the lessons this spectacle would engrave upon those who watched and those who survived. The swamp scene faded on the screens, the view shifting to an overview of the entire arena, leaving the fates of the contestants hanging in a cloud of suspense and dread.

The arena's layout morphed on the screens, transitioning from the eerie swamps to the harsh, stark battleground designed for the next sequence. Greda's eyes, sharp and calculating, followed the contestants as they were corralled into this new setting, the atmosphere thick with anticipation.

On screen, a contestant, a well-built man with the stance of someone who had seen many battles, readied himself. His opponent, a towering Chloro-Knight, stepped into the light, its armor glistening, the photosynthetic cells visible and pulsing with a life of their own. Greda observed as the contestant sized up the Chloro-Knight, the tension palpable even through the digital divide.

The duel commenced with the swift clash of metal against bio-engineered weaponry. The contestant, wielding a salvaged beam-sword, delivered a series of calculated strikes, each met with the Chloro-Knight's leaf-blade sword, parrying with precision that belied its lumbering size. Greda leaned closer, her fingers tapping a rhythmic pattern on the armrest of her throne-like seat, her face betraying no emotion yet her mind racing with approval for the spectacle.

"Enhance on the Knight," Greda commanded, her voice cutting through the subdued murmurs of the elite audience. The cameras zoomed, focusing on the Chloro-Knight as it sustained a deep gash along its arm, the green, chlorophyll-infused blood seeping out. But within moments, the wound began to close, the cells regenerating visibly.

A murmur rippled through the crowd, a mix of awe and horror, as they witnessed this near-miraculous recovery. Greda's lips twitched slightly upwards in a semblance of a smile—this was the power of her creations, a reflection of the relentless advancement under her rule.

The contestant's face filled the screen next, his expression shifting from determination to despair as he realized the futility of his efforts. Greda watched intently as his strategy unraveled, the initial vigor giving way to desperation. The knight, now fully healed, advanced, its movements more aggressive, more assured.

"Capture his realization, close-up," Greda instructed, her gaze fixed on the screen, where the man's dawning realization of inevitable defeat was palpable. This was the essence of her games—breaking spirits as much as bodies, a clear message to any who watched: resistance was not just futile; it was suicidal.

The Chloro-Knight raised its sword, the blade gleaming under the artificial lights, a lethal ballet poised for the final act. The contestant, his energy spent, could barely lift his sword to defend himself. With a swift, clean movement, the knight struck, the blade slicing through the air and into the man's chest.

Gasps and cheers erupted around Greda, the elites' faces lit by the glow of the screens, their eyes reflecting a morbid fascination with the death delivered so efficiently before them. The odds and bets still updating in real-time, numbers skyrocketing as money exchanged hands over the life that had just been brutally extinguished.

Greda remained seated, her eyes not leaving the screen as the knight withdrew its blade, the body of the contestant crumpling to the ground in a heap. "Display the victor," she ordered, and the cameras obeyed, showcasing the Chloro-Knight standing triumphant, its armor stained but intact.

The screens flickered again, shifting away from the fallen contestant, leaving the audience with the lingering image of the Chloro-Knight's victory stance, a stark reminder of the power and brutality that governed this new world order.

As the cheers settled into a murmuring anticipation, Greda's gaze didn't waver from the massive screens displaying the arena. Her command for the next phase was a mere whisper, yet it reverberated through the control room with the weight of an undeniable order. "Begin the assault," she stated, the corners of her mouth tilting upward ever so slightly.

The arena's environment shifted ominously as the ground began to rumble beneath the feet of the contestants who believed they were nearing a haven. Greda watched with a cold fascination as the earth split open, Mycelium Miners emerging like specters from the underworld. Their bodies, grotesque fusions of fungal and mechanical elements, spewed acidic enzymes, dissolving the ground into a deadly trap.

Several contestants screamed, their terror captured in high definition and amplified through the speakers, echoing around the opulent viewing gallery. Greda observed as one by one, they fell into the newly formed pits, their bodies succumbing to the corrosive acids that awaited them below. The sounds of their agony were distinct, a chorus that played to the tune of Greda's brutal symphony.

The viewers, secure in their luxurious seats, leaned forward, eyes wide with a perverse thrill. Bets were placed with a fervor, the stakes rising with each scream that was abruptly silenced by the lethal embrace of the acid. "Enhance on their despair," Greda commanded, her voice devoid of emotion, her fingers tapping an erratic, anticipatory rhythm on her chair.

The cameras zoomed in, capturing the final expressions of the doomed contestants—eyes wide with the realization of their fate, mouths agape in silent pleas. The elites watched, some with glee, others with a detachment born of countless such spectacles, their humanity eroded by the incessant exposure to orchestrated death.

Greda's attention, however, was already shifting, her mind calculating the effects of what was being witnessed. She understood the power of fear and its necessity in maintaining control. As the ground settled and the Mycelium Miners retreated back into their subterranean lairs, the screens flickered, not to offer reprieve, but to prepare for the next sequence of horror.

"Prepare the next event," she instructed Riko, her chief technician, who nodded, his hands moving deftly across the control panel to set the stage for another gruesome display. The whispers of the elite grew louder, a mixture of awe and horror, some turning to their companions to speculate on what could possibly follow such a spectacle.

Greda remained unphased, her gaze fixed on the screens, her mind already analyzing the outcomes, the behaviors influenced by what had just been executed under her command. She pondered the efficacy of fear versus the desensitization that might follow, considering adjustments, always planning two steps ahead.

The screens now showed the arena from above, the calm after the storm, the deceptive peace that settled before the next wave of terror was unleashed. This was the rhythm of her reign—calm interjected with orchestrated chaos, a method to her madness that kept her in power, unchallenged and absolute.

The hum of the viewing arena's anticipation buzzed like a hidden undercurrent, palpable yet silent as Greda's eyes never left the giant screens, where the next phase of the games was set to begin. "Enhance visual," she commanded, voice steady and low, while her fingers drummed an expectant rhythm against the armrest of her throne-like seat.

Onscreen, the scene shifted to a dense forest, the greenery almost suffocating in its thickness. The contestants, already wary from previous encounters, moved cautiously. But Greda knew, just as the elite surrounding her in their rapt attention did, that what awaited these players was beyond any ordinary foe. Willow Wisps, the silent assassins of the Verdant Overlord's arsenal, were about to enter the fray.

The cameras, equipped with special spectral filters, captured the almost invisible movements of the Willow Wisps as they darted through the trees. Their forms, barely discernible, moved with such stealth and grace that even the most vigilant contestant barely stood a chance. Greda watched, a slight nod acknowledging the effectiveness of the technology that allowed her audience to see what the naked eye could not.

A young man, his face etched with determination, paused, sensing a disturbance. His gaze darted around, catching nothing but the whisper of movement—a flicker of what might have been just a trick of the light. The audience leaned in, breaths held, as the screens showed a Willow Wisp closing in, its tendril-like appendages poised for a strike.

"Calculate the odds," Greda spoke into her communicator, and instantly, the betting odds updated on the screens, numbers climbing as bets were placed on how long the young man would last.

The strike, when it came, was a blur. The tendril shot through the air with precision, aimed directly at the young man's back. A collective gasp rose from the audience as he turned, just in time to see his attacker, the horror dawning on his face captured in high-definition, transmitting his fear straight into the hearts of the viewers.

The tendril pierced through him, clean and silent, a gasp his last utterance as he crumpled to the forest floor. The Willow Wisp receded into the shadows, as elusive in victory as in approach. The cameras lingered on the fallen contestant, the finality of his fate a stark contrast to the ongoing movements of the others, who remained oblivious to their companion's demise.

Greda's gaze was analytical, cold. "Switch to thermal, track the others," she ordered. The screen view shifted, showing the heat signatures of the remaining contestants as they navigated the treacherous forest. The Willow Wisps appeared as colder hues, almost ghost-like as they maneuvered for their next attacks.

This dance of death, choreographed by unseen forces and watched by the elite, unfolded with Greda at its helm. She was the architect of this horror, the conductor of this symphony of screams. Each participant's fall was a note in her grand opus, played out on the stage of the arena, watched by those who reveled in the savage beauty of her world order.

As another contestant fell to the ground, the victim of a Willow Wisp's silent strike, the screens flickered briefly, ready to shift the scene to the next gruesome display. Greda leaned back, satisfaction etched across her features, her mind already on the nuances of the next game. The cycle of terror was endless, her control over it absolute.

As the screen shifted from the haunting aftermath of the Willow Wisps' silent assaults, Greda's voice cut through the murmurs of the elite audience, "Initiate the Gauntlet." Her command was clinical, devoid of emotion, echoing through the control room where Riko adjusted the settings. The viewers leaned forward, their anticipation palpable in the charged atmosphere of the Lumina Citadel.

The arena transformed before their eyes. Walls slid into place, forming a narrow, oppressive corridor that seemed to pulse with potential violence. At Greda's nod, the choices made by the audience earlier were enacted; the traps they selected were armed, invisible yet lethal, waiting for the barest touch of a contestant's foot.

As the remaining contestants were herded into the entrance of the gauntlet, the screens flickered to life with an array of angles, each frame a testament to the technological prowess at Greda's disposal. High above, drones hummed softly, their cameras focusing on the trembling figures below.

One brave soul, a young woman with fire in her eyes, took the lead. Her steps were cautious, measured, but it wasn't enough. As she pressed forward, the first trap was triggered—a spray of acid from the walls. She dodged back, her clothes hissing where the droplets caught them, her gasp audible over the arena's sound system.

The audience reacted with a mixture of gasps and cheers, the thrill of the hunt alive in their eyes. Bets were placed rapidly, the odds updating in real-time on floating displays, the numbers a blur of change. Greda watched, her expression unreadable, analyzing every movement, every choice. This was more than entertainment; it was a study in human desperation and fear.

Without warning, the corridor's floor gave way beneath another contestant, a burly man who had survived much to reach this point. He fell into a pit, his screams cut short as Mycelium Miners, concealed below, released their enzymes. The screens captured the disintegration of flesh and bone, a gruesome display that drew morbid fascination and applause from the protected elite.

"Zoom in," Greda commanded, her voice never rising above a cold whisper. The cameras obeyed, focusing on the terror in the eyes of the remaining contestants as they witnessed the fate of their comrade. The psychological impact was immediate, their pace slowing, their strategies crumbling under the weight of impending doom.

One by one, they fell, each death unique, a morbid spectacle from the audience's darkest desires. Spore Soldiers released clouds of toxic spores in a narrow stretch, where no contestant could hope to hold their breath long enough to survive. Chloro-Knights, their armor glistening under the artificial lights, swung heavy, toxin-laced blades that cut through hope as much as flesh.

Greda's control room was silent but for the sounds of the arena— each scream, each plea, a note in the symphony she conducted. The slow-motion captures of their final moments played on loop, a grisly montage that highlighted the futility of their struggle.

As the second to last contestant fell, impaled on the spikes of a trap that sprang from the very walls, the screens briefly returned to a view of the entire gauntlet. The corridor was now still, the traps resetting silently, ready for the next round.

Greda stood, her eyes reflecting the flickering images of the carnage she had orchestrated. "Prepare the final review," she instructed Riko, her mind already moving past the carnage to the implications of each reaction, each death. How would she spin this narrative to her advantage? How would this display reinforce the iron grip she held over her world?

As she turned away from the screens, the scene cut abruptly, the audience left staring at the blank screens, their hearts racing, their minds unable to escape the horror they had just been part of.

The arena fell into a hushed anticipation, the lights dimming as the last contestant was thrust into the final confrontation. Greda's eyes narrowed, her lips curling into a half-smile as she leaned forward, the glow from the screens casting shadows across her face. "Show them," she commanded, her voice a whisper that carried the weight of iron.

The camera angles shifted, the drone feeds now encircling the arena where the final contestant stood alone. The ground was littered with debris, remnants of the previous carnage. The contestant, a young woman with determination etched into every line of her face, surveyed the circle of enemy types that slowly closed in around her.

From the shadowy edges of the arena, Rootguards with their thorn-armed limbs, Nettlers twitching with their toxic strands, and the hulking forms of Chloro-Knights took their places. In the dim light, the Spore Soldiers seemed to shimmer with a deadly anticipation, their spore clouds ready to burst forth.

The audience, each member a part of this macabre theatre, began to vote. Their choices appeared on the screens — a live poll dictating the manner of the assault. The results came in swiftly, the collective decision for a simultaneous attack, ensuring a spectacle of overwhelming force.

As the votes tallied up, Greda watched, her expression unreadable. The screens split, displaying the eager, detached faces of the elites — a mosaic of cruelty framed by the opulence of the Lumina Citadel.

They watched, some with glee, others with a bored detachment, as the last moments of the game were set into motion.

The contestant picked up a fallen weapon, her grip tightening as she braced herself. Her eyes darted around, calculating, desperate. There was no way out, no last-minute reprieve. Greda admired that defiance, that spark of spirit about to be extinguished. It was a quality she found both commendable and futile.

With a nod from Greda, the circle closed. The Chloro-Knights charged, their leaf-blade swords glinting. Nettlers launched their strands, aiming to incapacitate, while Rootguards advanced, thorns ready. Above them, the spores began to cloud the air, a silent, invisible threat that choked any hope of breath.

The contestant swung her weapon, landing a blow on a Chloro-Knight, its chlorophyll-infused cells already closing the wound. Around her, the traps sprung to life, the audience's choices playing out in real-time. She dodged, weaved, struck out, but the numbers overwhelmed her. The screens captured every angle, every moment of her fight, her face a mask of determination even as despair took hold.

The end came swiftly. A Chloro-Knight's blade found its mark, the fatal blow delivered with a clinical precision that silenced the arena. The contestant fell, her weapon clattering beside her, the noise stark against the chilling silence that followed.

In the quiet that ensued, Greda stood, her gaze lingering on the still form in the arena. The elites murmured amongst themselves, the sound a low, unsettling hum. They confirmed their winnings with quiet nods and discreet messages, their faces illuminated by the light of their screens.

As the cameras zoomed out, capturing the lone figure on the ground and the circle of enemies withdrawing into the shadows, Greda turned back to the control panel. "Cut the feed," she instructed Riko, her voice devoid of emotion. The screens went dark, the game ended, but the echoes of its brutality lingered, a stark reminder of the control Greda wielded — absolute and unyielding.

The Citadel, a fortress of both luxury and oppression, stood silent, its corridors echoing with the outcome of the games it housed, a monument to the power Greda held over life and death.

Chapter 13

Tibo's fingers danced across the makeshift console, a mess of wires and screens lit by the dim glow of a single overhead bulb. The air was thick, the small space cramped with gear and remnants of old tech scavenged from the Citadel's outer limits. "Almost got it," he muttered, eyes flickering between lines of code cascading down the monitor.

Elara leaned over his shoulder, her presence a calm anchor in the storm of his focus. "Make sure it's untraceable," she reminded him, her voice low and steady.

"Trust me, Elara, even their top tech-heads won't crack this one for months," Tibo responded, his voice tinged with the thrill of challenge. He executed a final keystroke, and the system hummed to life, sending the first encrypted message deep into the network of the Citadel.

On the screen, a complex cipher algorithm encrypted the communication, morphing it into a string of seemingly random characters. "And... it's off to Juno Rael," Tibo announced with a grin, pushing back from the table and stretching his arms above his head. "If anyone can start chipping away at Lumina from the inside, it's her."

Elara didn't share his smile, her gaze fixed on a secondary screen showing a live feed of the Citadel's bustling main corridor. "She's a risk, Tibo. If she flips—"

"She won't," Tibo cut in, his confidence unshaken. "Juno's seen the dark side of Lumina firsthand. Her family..." His voice trailed off, the weight of the situation momentarily darkening his usual buoyancy.

They watched the digital packets navigate through the Citadel's communications infrastructure, bypassing security protocols that Tibo had studied and outwitted countless times before. "There, see? Juno's logged in. She's accessing the message now."

The screen displayed a live decryption, Juno's credentials confirming her access. Tibo's custom encryption unravelled, revealing the meeting coordinates and a brief, "The truth awaits where light does not reach."

Back in their hidden tech lair, Tibo's console beeped, an incoming message breaking their brief celebration. It was Juno, confirming her attendance and, more importantly, her commitment. "She's in," Tibo breathed, a smirk playing at the edge of his lips.

Elara finally allowed herself a moment of relief, her hand resting briefly on Tibo's shoulder. "Okay, let's prepare for the next phase. We need to be ready to move as soon as she gives us the signal."

As they plotted their next moves, the screen flickered, a brief surge in the power grid hinting at the Citadel's restless energy. Tibo's gaze settled on the array of tools and gadgets sprawled before him, each piece a component in their greater plan to dismantle Greda's ironclad hold on their world.

The room was silent for a moment, save for the hum of machines and the distant echo of the Citadel's ever-watchful drones patrolling the upper echelons. "Time to stir the pot a bit more," Tibo whispered, more to himself than to Elara, his mind racing through the possibilities of technological chaos he could unleash to aid their cause.

Without another word, he turned back to his console, diving into the sea of codes and digital pathways that formed the lifeline of their resistance.

Juno Rael's image flickered into existence within the virtual room, her face a canvas of cautious optimism as she navigated through the layers of cyber-security Tibo had engineered. The hidden room was a digital mirage within the Lumina system, crafted to be invisible to all but those with the right keys.

Elara's image materialized next to Tibo's, her features set in a determined look that matched her voice when she spoke. "Everyone's here. Let's make this quick and clear. We have a window before the system runs diagnostics."

Tibo nodded, his fingers pausing above the console as he addressed the virtual assembly. "Thanks to Juno's skills, we're ghosting right under Greda's nose. Now, let's talk strategy."

Cyrus Reese, his image sharpening as he adjusted his settings, leaned into the view, his demeanor a mixture of determination and anger. "I've seen what Lumina's doing to people, the control it's taking, the freedoms it's erasing. It's time we took a stand."

Tibo switched screens, pulling up an interface crowded with digital images distributed through Lumina's channels. "Here's our trojan horse," he began, pointing to a series of innocuous-looking visuals. "Embedded within these images are messages, coded through steganography. To the untrained eye, they're just part of the daily feed. But to those we reach..."

He trailed off, letting the implication hang in the digital air. Juno picked it up, her voice firm, "It will start opening minds, planting seeds of doubt about the reality Greda is feeding them."

Cyrus nodded, his eyes narrowing slightly. "I can embed these into my speeches. The subliminals can trigger doubt, and that doubt will lead to questions Greda can't control."

Elara interjected, "And the more they question, the weaker Lumina's grip becomes. We can use that, use the unrest to push for more overt actions."

Tibo's hands moved again, manipulating the data streams to enhance the encryption on their communication. "I've set up a fail-safe. If this room is compromised, it'll burn before they can trace anything back to us."

Juno's expression was a mix of admiration and worry. "You really think of everything, Tibo."

He grinned, but there was steel in his smile. "We can't afford half measures. Not with what's at stake."

As the meeting drew to a close, Tibo outlined the final part of their plan, each member's role crystal clear. "Once Cyrus's speech goes live, we'll monitor the uptick in code searches. That'll be our gauge for public sentiment."

Cyrus's voice was low, almost a growl. "They've taken enough from us. It's time we take back."

The screen split briefly, displaying each participant's face—determined, scared, but ready. Tibo's final check on the security protocols ensured their exit from the network left no trace, the digital room dissolving into the ether of cyberspace.

Back in his hidden base, the weight of their conspiracy heavier than ever, Tibo allowed himself a brief moment to feel the magnitude of their undertaking. Elara stood by him, her hand finding his in the dim light. "What we're doing... it's going to change everything."

Tibo looked at the screens, now dark, the codes and ciphers silent. He knew the risk, felt the danger in every line of code he wrote. But as he turned off the last screen, the firmness in his heart matched the firmness on his face. This was the start of the end for Greda's world, and he was right at the heart of it.

Greda strode through the humming corridors of the Dream Weavers facility, her eyes sharp, scanning the banks of monitors that displayed the tranquil dreams of her citizens. Each screen flickered with serene images—lush green landscapes, sumptuous feasts, and grand celebrations—all fabrications crafted meticulously to pacify a populace teetering on the brink of consciousness.

"Report," she commanded, her voice echoing slightly in the sterile chamber. A technician, clad in the standard grey uniform of Lumina operatives, approached, tablet in hand.

"Chancellor, we've noted a 3% increase in dream stability overnight. However, there have been minor glitches in Sector 17— residual memories of the unrest seem to be breaking through the overlays," he reported, his tone clinical.

Greda's gaze hardened. "Adjust the algorithms. Increase the dopamine outputs and make sure no trace of dissent permeates the dream state. I want them deep in the illusion of contentment," she instructed, her hand gesturing dismissively at the mention of unrest.

The technician nodded, fingers flying over his tablet to input her commands. Greda turned to the large observation window, watching as another technician adjusted dials on a console, the dreams on the monitors shifting subtly—darker shadows lightened, whispers of discord smoothed into laughter and applause.

As she watched, her mind was already weaving through the ramifications of the unrest. "How widespread is the knowledge of this discontent?" Greda asked, her back still to the technician.

"It's contained for now, Chancellor. The agitators were isolated and have been... redirected," he answered, hinting at the darker fate that awaited those who dared disrupt her order.

"Good. Implement a review of the monitoring protocols. I don't want a repeat," Greda said, her voice low but fierce, a stark contrast to the serene scenes playing out behind the glass.

Turning, she paced slowly between the rows of consoles, her eyes catching a flicker of hesitation in one of the technicians as they adjusted a dial. "Ensure that everyone in this facility remembers the importance of their work. We are not merely shaping dreams; we are maintaining the very fabric of our society," she stated emphatically, her presence commanding attention from everyone in the room.

The technician swallowed, nodding vigorously. "Yes, Chancellor. I will remind them of their duty."

Satisfied, Greda paused by a console where the dream of a young woman flickered on the screen. The scene was an elaborate banquet, the woman dressed regally, laughing as she danced through a hall filled with adoring onlookers. Greda watched the fabricated happiness, her expression unreadable.

"Intensify the feel-good factors in sectors close to the unrest. Overlay their sleep with dreams of success and fulfillment under my governance. If reality won't convince them, we'll craft a reality that does," she instructed, her voice a cold whisper lost in the soft hum of the machines.

The technician adjusted the settings, and on the screen, the banquet grew even more opulent, the cheers louder. Greda's lips twitched into a semblance of a smile, but her eyes remained cold, analytical.

She turned, her cloak swirling silently around her as she made her way out of the facility, the door sliding shut with a hiss that sounded almost like a sigh of relief from the room left behind. Outside, the corridors of the Lumina Citadel awaited her, every step she took resonating with the weight of her rule. The echoes of her footsteps mingled with the distant, ever-present drone of the Citadel's life-support systems, a constant reminder of the controlled environment she had mastered.

In the solitude of the Citadel's expansive control room, Greda paused before the massive screens displaying various sectors of her domain. Her hand hovered over a console, ready to dive back into the network of control and surveillance that kept her in power, her mind always plotting, always scheming, ensuring her vision of order remained unchallenged.

Elara's footsteps were nearly silent as she navigated the labyrinthine corridors of the Lumina Citadel, the heavy cloak of her disguise merging seamlessly with the shadows cast by the flickering lights. Beside her, Tibo adjusted the frequency on a small, matte-black device clipped to his belt—a jammer designed to scramble any surveillance signals they passed. They moved with a practiced stealth, aware that every corner might host eyes too keen, too loyal to Chancellor Greda.

"Check your six, El," Tibo murmured, his eyes darting to a mirror-like panel that doubled as an observer drone station. Elara glanced back, her hand instinctively reaching for the biocide launcher hidden beneath her cloak. Nothing stirred, but the constant risk of discovery pressed down on them like the thick, recycled air of the underground.

They reached a nondescript door marked only by a faded sign: "Sector 17G - Restricted Access." This was the place Dr. Melissa Myles had chosen for the meeting—a forgotten maintenance room shielded from the Citadel's ever-watchful AI by layers of lead and old concrete.

Tibo palmed a compact device, pressing it against the door's access pad. The lock disengaged with a soft click, too quiet to be heard over the distant hum of the Citadel's life-support systems. They slipped inside, sealing the door behind them.

Dr. Myles was already there, her figure a specter among the shadows, her expression both determined and wary. She held a data pad tightly against her chest, the glow of its screen casting eerie patterns on her face.

"You made it," she whispered, a trace of disbelief in her voice as if she hadn't fully expected them to breach the heart of Lumina's domain unscathed.

"Wouldn't miss it," Elara responded, allowing a thin smile to cross her lips. She turned to ensure the room's old surveillance nodes were disabled, her movements fluid and precise. "Let's get to it then."

Tibo unpacked a small, sophisticated device, setting it on the dusty table that occupied the center of the room. "This is your key to tweaking Lumina's narrative," he explained, powering up the device. It projected a holographic interface in the air above it, streams of code scrolling rapidly as it initialized. "It injects encrypted data packets into

Lumina's stream—subtle, nearly undetectable unless you know exactly what you're looking for."

Melissa leaned over the device, her eyes scanning the encryption sequences. "I can introduce these during the standard memory consolidation phase... it will cause glitches—flashes of truth within the fabricated reality Greda has forced upon everyone."

"And I'll amplify it," Elara added, "We've set up a network of sympathetic ears throughout the Citadel. Once they start seeing the glitches, they'll spread the word—sow the seeds of doubt."

Melissa nodded, her confidence showing. "It's time then. To show them the world beyond the illusions."

As they handed over the custom device, their fingers brushed, and Elara felt the weight of their shared risk. They were allies now, bound by a common cause, each a vital piece in a dangerous game against a tyrant.

The meeting concluded abruptly as Tibo's device beeped a warning—surveillance drones, too close for comfort. "Time to ghost," he said, and they erased all signs of their presence, disappearing into the Citadel's veins as silently as they had arrived.

Outside, Elara's heart pounded not just with the adrenaline of evasion, but with the weight of what they had set in motion. This was more than sabotage; it was a call to awakening. As they melded into the flow of oblivious citizens, her mind raced with possibilities, each more daring than the last, each a whisper of the dawn creeping slowly over the horizon of their darkened world.

Chancellor Greda stood at the edge of the Executive Lounge, her sharp gaze sweeping over the room where her closest advisors gathered. The opulent chamber, designed for discretion and luxury, buzzed with low, urgent conversations. Marble columns rose to the vaulted ceilings, and the soft light from the bio-luminescent fixtures cast an ethereal glow over the faces of the elite.

"Begin," Greda commanded, her voice cutting through the murmurs like a blade. The advisors turned, their expressions a mix of reverence and fear. Riko, the chief security advisor, stepped forward, a holopad in his hand displaying the latest data streams.

"Chancellor, the unrest in the lower sectors is growing," Riko reported, his voice steady despite the weight of his words. "Our surveillance suggests that the dissenters are becoming more organized."

Greda's eyes narrowed. "And the sensory overload chambers?" she asked sharply.

Riko nodded, tapping on the holopad to bring up a schematic of the chambers. "Effective but underutilized. We propose expanding their use. By intensifying exposure, we can disrupt the formation of any coherent resistance movements."

"Show me," Greda demanded.

The room dimmed as Riko activated a simulation on the central holoscreen. Figures writhed in virtual restraints, their senses bombarded with alternating currents of fear and contentment. "This," Riko pointed out, "ensures they remain too fragmented to unite. A continuous cycle of fear and relief suppresses long-term planning and resistance."

Greda watched, her face impassive but her mind racing. Every scream and shudder in the simulation was a note in the symphony of her rule—harsh, perhaps, but necessary. "Increase the cycles. Double them," she ordered. "And cut off the usual gathering places in the sectors. No more unauthorized congregations."

"Immediately, Chancellor," Riko responded, his fingers already sending commands to the security teams.

Another advisor, Lena, the head of psychological operations, stepped forward. "Chancellor, if I may," she interjected, her tone cautious. "The effectiveness of these chambers in maintaining social order is proven, but we should also consider enhancing the Dream Weavers' operations."

Greda turned to her, interest piqued. "Explain."

Lena adjusted her glasses, her eyes reflecting the data streams from her own device. "By weaving more targeted narratives into their dreams, we can not only suppress memories of discontent but also reinforce their dependency on your governance. It's subtle, pervasive, and leaves the subjects none the wiser."

Greda considered this, the potential of such manipulation spreading like a slow fire through her thoughts. "Do it," she decided. "Implement it in phases. Start with the leaders of these so-called resistance cells. Break them down, rebuild them in our image."

Lena nodded, a slight smile curving her lips as she turned to coordinate with her team.

"As for the rest," Greda continued, turning back to the assembly, "increase surveillance. I want eyes everywhere. No corner of this Citadel goes unwatched."

Her advisors bowed, a synchronized motion that pleased her. They understood the necessity of absolute control, the delicate balance of terror and benevolence that kept a society in check.

Greda stepped back, her eyes once again sweeping over the chamber. The plans they set today would ripple through the depths of the Citadel, unseen yet omnipotent. Her city, her rules.

As she exited the lounge, the echo of her steps blended with the distant, ever-present hum of the Citadel's vast machinery. Above, the artificial sky flickered momentarily, a glitch in the perfect facade that no one but Greda seemed to notice.

She paused, considering the symbolism of that fleeting imperfection, then continued on. There was much to do, and her path, though solitary, was clear. Her fortress would stand, unyielding against the tide of chaos that threatened its depths, a beacon of order in a world gone mad.

Tibo's heart raced as he darted through the shadowed corridors of the Citadel, the clink of his tool belt echoing softly against the polished obsidian walls. The damp air was thick with the scent of metal and fear, an ever-present reminder of the stakes at play. Beside him, Elara moved like a wraith, her eyes scanning for the tell-tale red of security drones.

"Here," she whispered, pointing to a nondescript panel beside a door marked as restricted. Tibo's fingers flew over the security console, a device he had modified to bypass the most sophisticated locks the Citadel could muster.

The door clicked, a silent concession to their skill, and they slipped inside, the darkness of the room swallowing them whole. Tibo's eyes adjusted, and he activated a small, holographic display from his wrist device. The room lit up in a low, blue glow, revealing rows of dormant tech and cables that snaked across the floor like tendrils.

"We have ten minutes, max," Tibo muttered, setting up their portable hacking unit. Elara nodded, her hand resting on the biocide launcher at her hip, her gaze fixed on the sealed door.

Tibo's hands didn't shake; they couldn't afford to. He connected the cables, his mind racing through the steps of their plan. The broadcast hack wasn't just about sending a message; it was about igniting the spark of rebellion, about showing the people of the Citadel that Greda's grip wasn't unbreakable.

"Ready," he announced, tapping the final sequence into the device. The screens around them flickered to life, each one a window into the lives of the unknowing citizens above. Tibo's program infiltrated the broadcast system, a silent virus spreading through the Citadel's veins.

Elara watched the monitors, her voice low. "There it is." On every screen, between flashes of Greda's propaganda, their message appeared. Simple. Subversive. "See the lies. Speak the truth. Stand together."

Tibo couldn't help but smile at the elegance of it. Hidden in plain sight, messages embedded in the very fabric of the broadcast, visible only to those who dared to see.

But their triumph was short-lived. An alarm blared, a shrill sound that cut through the quiet like a siren's call. "We've been tagged,"

Elara hissed, her eyes darting to the door as it began to unlock automatically, overridden by the Citadel's security protocols.

"Go!" Tibo grabbed the hacking unit, stuffing it into his bag. They bolted, the door flying open behind them as security drones poured in like a flood of red-eyed rats. The hallways of the Citadel turned into a maze, a labyrinth designed to trap and confuse.

They ran, dodging surveillance cams and ducking under the sweeping lasers of the drones. Elara led the way, her familiarity with the Citadel's layout an invaluable asset. Tibo's mind raced, every calculated risk and narrow escape.

As they rounded a corner, the path clear for the moment, Tibo dared to believe they might just make it. Ahead, the access panel to the lower service tunnels glowed faintly, a beacon of hope.

But hope was a tricky thing in the Citadel.

A drone, silent and deadly, hovered into view, blocking their path. Tibo didn't hesitate. He raised his electrostatic disruptor pistol, the air crackling with energy as he took aim and fired. The drone sparked and whirled, crashing to the ground in a heap of smoldering metal.

"Move!" Elara pulled him forward, the tunnel entrance just feet away. They dove through the panel, Tibo slamming it shut behind them, the lock engaging with a satisfying click.

In the darkness of the tunnel, Tibo and Elara paused, their breaths heavy in the oppressive silence. They were out, at least for now, the chaos of their escape behind them.

Streams morph before Vane Calder's cold, digital eyes, the tranquil waters of the Lumina Tranquility Garden turning to hissing acid. Under his command, the serene flora mutates into grotesque, carnivorous entities. His avatar stands on a virtual cliff overlooking the chaos, an amused smirk playing on its lips as screams echo through the manicured pathways.

Participants, clad in their peaceful meditation attires, scramble in terror. Their virtual avatars dissolve upon contact with the acid, each "death" sending psychological shockwaves through their real-world counterparts connected to Project Lumina. From his vantage point, Vane watches as a woman in a flowing robe reaches out to her companion, only for a vine-turned-serpent to wrap around her wrist, pulling her into the newly formed undergrowth. Her screams cut short as her avatar pixelates out of existence.

Vane turns his attention to the chaos below, manipulating the environment further. He intensifies the gravity, pinning the fleeing avatars to the ground, making them easy prey for the monstrous fauna. A young man, no older than twenty, struggles against the invisible force, his eyes wide with terror. In one swift motion, a grotesque flower sprouts before him, its petals unfurling to reveal razor-sharp teeth. The scream is abrupt, silenced only by the chomping jaws.

The control systems of Project Lumina respond to Vane's every whim, his years of manipulation within its quantum framework allowing him to alter realities with a thought. Behind the safety of his avatar, his real self is shrouded in darkness, the only illumination coming from the glowing screens that display his handiwork.

His focus shifts to a group huddled by what was once a waterfall, now a torrent of acid pouring over the edge. They plead for help, for someone to wake them from this nightmare. Vane's finger hovers over the command that would intensify the acid's burn, a twisted grin forming as he presses down.

The acid's effect is immediate. The avatars flail, their digital skin peeling away to expose circuit-like bones beneath. The scene would horrify any onlooker, but to Vane, it's a masterpiece of pain and fear.

With a flick of his wrist, the environment shifts again. The ground splits, swallowing a dozen avatars as they attempt to flee. Their cries are cut short as the chasm closes, trapping them in digital oblivion.

Above, the sky turns a fiery red, thunder rolling across the horizon as if heralding the end of this virtual world.

The smirk on Vane's avatar fades as he surveys the destruction. He disconnects with a flick, the horrors of the Tranquility Garden dissolving into the sterile hum of his control room. He doesn't pause to reflect; there's another phase to his plan. Already his fingers dance over the holographic console, initiating the second part of his torment—sabotage of the healing pods.

In the depths of Project Lumina's medical bay, the healing pods, cocoons of supposed safety, hum quietly in the dim light. Vane infiltrates their systems with a series of rapid keystrokes, a smirk reappearing as he uploads a twisted code. Within moments, the pods' soothing blue lights flicker, replaced by an ominous red.

Unaware of the change, victims from the garden stagger in, their digital minds traumatized, seeking refuge in what they believe will be their salvation. One by one, they slip into the pods, the lids closing with soft hisses. Silence falls, a brief and deceptive peace before the storm Vane has programmed begins.

The first screams shatter the quiet. In the pods, the healing algorithms twist into vicious hallucinations. Users find themselves trapped in endless loops of their worst nightmares: the acid burns anew, phantom fires consume their skin, and invisible restraints tighten around their limbs. The safety of the pods becomes a cruel irony as each victim is subjected to relentless psychic torture.

Outside, the medical bay plunges into chaos. Technicians scramble, bewildered by the malfunction. They try to override the systems, but Vane's encryptions hold firm. On his screens, he watches each futile attempt with cold detachment. This is the art of war by fear and confusion, a demonstration of his control and a testament to his ruthlessness.

A medical officer races to manually release the pods, her face etched with panic as the screams multiply. One by one, the lids are pried open, but the damage lingers; the victims emerge shaking, their eyes haunted, minds fractured by the engineered horrors. News of the malfunction spreads like wildfire, whispers of terror that not even the healing pods are safe under Greda's regime.

Vane leans back, satisfaction curling the corners of his mouth. Today, Project Lumina has become a theater of his sadistic symphony, the medical bay just another scene of orchestrated despair. He watches the turmoil a moment longer, then turns away. His shadow stretches long and dark across the room as he moves to his next vantage point, ready to observe the unfolding fear, a silent spectator to the chaos he has crafted.

His shadow stretches long and dark across the room as he moves to his next vantage point, ready to observe the unfolding fear, a silent spectator to the chaos he has crafted. Vane's footsteps are silent against the cold metal floor, the air heavy with the digital scent of ozone—a remnant of the electromagnetic manipulations he's employed.

Reaching the Harmony Chambers, he pauses, observing through the one-way glass. The chambers, designed to be sanctuaries of mental recalibration, hum with a deceptive calm. Vane's fingers dance over his portable control device, a wicked grin spreading across his face as he enters a new sequence of commands. The tranquility of the chambers is about to be shattered.

Inside, the highest echelons of Project Lumina's staff lie in reclining chairs, eyes closed, lost in engineered peace. The soothing tones and harmonious vibrations that usually fill the chambers begin to warp, the sound engineering software bending under Vane's will.

The first signs of distress are subtle—a furrow of a brow, a twitch of the fingers. But as Vane increases the dissonance, the once soothing sounds escalate into a symphony of horrific noise. Screams replace serene breaths. The officials jerk violently, their minds assaulted by the discordant sounds that now echo monstrously through the chambers.

Vane watches with clinical interest as one by one, they stagger out of their chairs, clutching their heads, their composure crumbled. The doors burst open, and they spill into the hallways, disoriented, their cries of agony and confusion painting a stark contrast to their usual stoic demeanor.

"Control," Vane whispers to himself, the word a venomous hiss as he watches the chaos unfold. These chambers, once the pinnacle of psychological stability, have turned into chambers of psychological warfare. He makes a few more adjustments, ensuring the sonic assault is untraceable, masked beneath layers of encrypted code.

As the officials stumble past the glass, one locks eyes with Vane's shadowed figure. There's a moment of recognition, a flicker of terror, then nothing but madness as they're swept away by the tide of their escaping colleagues.

Turning away, Vane deactivates his device and tucks it into his coat. The Harmony Chambers had been a fortress of mental fortitude for those who believed they controlled the very fabric of this society. Now, they were nothing more than a pit of despair, much like the world outside the underground sanctum of Project Lumina.

He steps back into the shadows, the chaos he has engineered a perfect mirror to the chaos within him. The world above may have its battles, its verdant overgrowth clawing back the cities of men, but here, in the depths of human ingenuity, Vane wages a more subtle war—a war of the mind, where every note of discord sows seeds of destruction that no plant could hope to match.

Vane's next target looms ahead—the mainframe room of the Lumina Citadel, the nerve center where every strand of digital life is controlled, monitored, and manipulated. It's here that Project Lumina breathes, and it's here that he will strangle it.

Silent as a shadow, Vane bypasses the high-security measures with an ease that speaks of his intimate knowledge of the system's design. His former life as a guardian of this very citadel has armed him with the means to dismantle it piece by piece. The corridor leading to the mainframe pulses with soft, ambient lighting, designed to soothe the minds of those who walk it. To Vane, it's just another part of the system's facade, a veneer hiding the cold manipulations beneath.

He reaches the core control room, a sanctum of servers humming with data streams. Here, the heart of Project Lumina beats, a rhythm soon to be disrupted. From the depths of his coat, he retrieves a small device—a quantum virus, coded personally by him to initiate a cascade of failures throughout the network. It's an elegant weapon for a more uncivilized age.

The virus's installation is quick, a simple connection to the console before him, and then it's done. Vane watches the immediate effects on the screens around him—fluctuations in power, systems going dark, and emergency protocols stuttering to life.

With the virus activated, Vane doesn't linger to watch the chaos unfold. He knows the rolling blackouts will cripple Lumina's operations, plunging its simulated realities into darkness, its illusions broken. The psychological impact on the population, fed on lies and digital dreams, will be devastating. Fear and uncertainty will spread through the corridors of power as surely as they do through the less protected streets of the underground cities.

As the first of the alarms begin to sound, distant and yet somehow urgent, Vane exits the control room. His steps are unhurried, the chaos he has created a counterpoint to his calm. The Citadel's defenses begin to react, the sound of security doors sealing and the distant shouts of guards responding to the crisis.

Yet, they are too late. Vane is already moving to his next phase, his presence in the Citadel's core known only to the machines he has just silenced. He leaves behind a network in disarray, its architects powerless to stop the collapse they are only just beginning to understand.

The blackout spreads through the Lumina Citadel like a plague, lights flickering and dying, the false tranquility of the environment collapsing into the panic and terror of an abruptly awakened nightmare. Vane's path out is lit by the emergency glow of red lights, casting long shadows that match the darkness in his thoughts.

As he exits the mainframe room, the scale of his sabotage is clear. The rolling blackouts have thrown the Citadel into chaos, a physical manifestation of the disruption he has long planned. This is his message to those who wield control so carelessly: nothing is beyond his reach.

He leaves the Citadel's core behind, its corridors now a maze of confusion and fear, its inhabitants caught unprepared. His mission of disruption accomplished, Vane disappears into the shadows once more, untouched, unremorseful, and utterly effective.

Chapter 14

The hushed darkness of the control room is suddenly split by the harsh glare of emergency lighting, throwing stark shadows across Chancellor Greda's face as she enters. The room, usually a hub of orchestrated calm managed through holo-displays and soft directives, now buzzes with a frantic energy. The scent of ozone and the low hum of backup generators underscore the gravity of the situation.

"Somebody tell me something, now!," Greda commands, her voice cutting through the chaos with the sharpness of a blade. Her advisors, a mixture of seasoned technocrats and young data analysts, turn to her with a mixture of relief and dread.

"The blackouts are widespread, affecting all sectors," her chief engineer reports, voice tense. "Primary systems are down, secondary systems are barely holding. We've isolated the breach to the mainframe—"

"Vane Calder," Greda interrupts, the name tasting like venom on her tongue. She doesn't need a report to know who is behind this. "How did he access the core without triggering a single alarm?" She didn't need an answer. He's Vane Calder.

Silence follows her question, heavy and accusing. She steps closer to the central table, where the holographic map of the Citadel flickers uncertainly, its usual steady glow stuttering. Red markers blink rapidly, indicating the spread of the blackout like a contagion through the body of her city.

"Chancellor, the propaganda systems are still functional. We need to address the public immediately to avoid panic," suggests her communications director, a sharp-eyed woman named Elidi.

Greda nods, her mind racing through scenarios. "Prepare a broadcast. Assure them that the situation is under control and that the responsible parties will be dealt with severely."

Turning, she faces the digital strategist, a young man barely out of his teens, yet already marked by the weight of his job. "Milo, I want a countermeasure. Use the surveillance drones to start a sweep. I want every inch of this Citadel monitored. Find Vane. I don't care what it takes."

Milo nods, fingers flying over the translucent keyboard before him. Screens around him come alive, showing different sectors of the Citadel in grainy, night-vision green.

"And the backup systems?" Greda asks, turning to her chief engineer.

"We can reroute power from non-essential areas to stabilize the grid temporarily," he suggests, though hesitation colors his tone, aware of the risks such measures pose.

"Do it," she commands without missing a beat. "And bring the external defenses online. If Vane is still inside, he won't be for long."

As her team scrambles to execute her orders, Greda steps to the side, her gaze fixed on the large screen displaying the Citadel's schematics. Her city, a marvel of technology and control, now vulnerable and exposed. She allows herself a moment, just a flicker, of doubt—had she pushed too hard, built too much?

But the moment passes. There's no room for doubt in leadership, not when so many lives depend on her strength.

Elidi approaches, a tablet in her hand. "We're ready to go live, Chancellor."

Greda straightens, smoothing her jacket. "Ensure the feed is secure. I won't have this message tampered with."

She steps up to the camera, the red recording light flickering on. The background behind her shows the emblem of the Citadel, a city of order in the depths of chaos. She doesn't smile; the situation calls for stern reassurance, a display of unbreakable strength.

"Citizens of Lumina Citadel," she begins, her voice steady, projecting calm and authority, "we are experiencing technical difficulties, but the situation is under control. Rest assured, the security of our city and the safety of every citizen are my utmost priorities. We will restore full services shortly. Stay calm, stay inside, and keep faith."

As she speaks, Greda knows her words are a stopgap, a temporary balm for the spreading fear. She finishes her speech and steps away from the camera, the weight of her city's gaze heavy upon her shoulders. The screen flickers once, twice, and stabilizes.

She turns back to her team, already moving on to the next necessary action. The Citadel must hold. It must.

Greda watches the last echoes of her broadcast fade, the screens darkening back to the grim reality of the control room. The murmurs around her swell as her advisors and technicians recalibrate their systems, driven by the sharp edge of her earlier commands.

Her eyes flick to the nearest display, tracking the propagation of her message through the social layers of Lumina Citadel. Real-time analytics flash across the screen, sentiment indicators wobbling between cautious relief and lingering apprehension. "Elidi, amplify the loyalty incentive announcements. We need to wedge suspicion into the ranks of the disloyal. Make them think twice about harboring dissenters."

"Yes, Chancellor," Elidi responds, her fingers already dancing across the holo-pad. She adjusts the propaganda feed, increasing the rotation of Greda's stern visage assuring control and order.

Greda strides back to the central map, the holographic cityscape pulsating with red alerts. "Status on the defense systems?" she calls out, not taking her eyes off the sectors closest to the mainframe breach.

"They're coming online now," the chief engineer replies from across the room. "Exterior drones are operational, and internal sensors are at eighty percent functionality."

"Good." Greda's voice is clipped, each word sharp as shattered glass. "Focus on the exits. I want to know if anything or anyone unusual tries to slip out."

She turns, surveying her assembled team, each member reflecting a shard of her own urgency. "This is not merely about restoring order. It's about reasserting dominance. We cannot afford to appear vulnerable—not now."

Milo interrupts, a tentative edge to his voice, "Chancellor, we have movement in sector seven—not sure if it's him, but—"

"Dispatch a response team. Use lethal force if necessary. I authorize it," Greda cuts in, her decision swift, like a guillotine's fall. She doesn't wait for a response, her gaze already shifting to the next potential crisis point.

A younger advisor, a recent recruit to the crisis team, hesitates near the edge of the strategy table. "Chancellor, should we consider an evacuation of non-essential personnel from the lower levels? Just as a precaution—"

"No." The word slices through the air, final and cold. "We will not show fear. Lock down the non-essential sectors and reroute all available energy to our defenses and surveillance. Keep the populace where they are. Control is paramount."

As her orders ripple out, Greda steps aside, her fingers brushing lightly over the surface of the city map. Beneath her touch, sectors flicker and steady under enforced power reroutes and tightened security nets.

"Prepare for my inspection tour. I'll be going out into the sectors," she declares, turning to face her head of security. "Visibility, Captain. It's as vital now as any shield or weapon."

The team nods, a machine of many parts powered by one will. They move to implement her commands with a precision that borders on mechanical. Greda watches them, her mind already three steps ahead—planning, predicting, maneuvering. In the dim glow of the emergency lights, she stands a solitary figure, the architect of control, unbowed amidst the storm of chaos threatening her citadel.

As she turns to leave the control room, her back straight, her shadow long and alone, the doors slide shut behind her, sealing her within the heart of her empire. The Citadel must hold. It must.

The hush of the Executive Lounge stands in stark contrast to the chaos of the control room. Plush carpets muffle the footsteps of the elite as they gather, the air tinged with the scent of anxiety masked by expensive cologne. Greda enters, her presence commanding silence. The room, with its dimmed lighting and luxurious decor, is designed to soothe, but tonight it buzzes with undercurrents of fear and speculation.

"Thank you all for coming at such short notice," Greda begins, her tone even but firm as she surveys the room of high-ranking officials and influential leaders. The soft clinks of glass and the rustle of fine fabric fill the brief silence as her audience settles.

"We are under attack," she states bluntly, the words hanging heavy in the air. Murmurs ripple through the room, faces drawn in concern. "But let me be clear—we are far from defenseless. Measures are already in place to ensure the stability and security of our Citadel."

She pauses, allowing her assurance to seep into the room's collective consciousness, her gaze locking with each member of the elite. "Vane Calder's actions tonight are reprehensible, but they will not define us. Instead, they will strengthen us."

A hand raises from a shadowed corner—a prominent council member known for his caution. "Chancellor, what of the breaches in our system? How can we ensure such vulnerabilities are mitigated?"

Greda nods, acknowledging the question with a slight tilt of her head. "Enhanced surveillance and stricter control measures are already being implemented. We are rerouting power to essential defenses, and I've authorized additional AI protocols to monitor and counteract any suspicious activity."

The room's tension eases slightly, but the undercurrent of doubt remains obvious. Greda presses on, her voice a blend of reassurance and command. "Furthermore, I am introducing loyalty rewards for information leading to the capture of dissenters. It's time we cleanse our ranks of any who would sympathize with our enemies."

Whispers of approval mingle with the clink of glass as the elite consider the implications. However, the underlying fear and confusion continue to simmer beneath the surface.

"And what of the public's reaction?" another voice chimes in, this one smooth and calculating. "Panic can be as dangerous as any saboteur."

Greda's response is immediate, her strategy clear. "The public will be informed that we are managing a minor setback. They will see that we are in control, that their leaders are unshaken. We will turn this incident into a story of our resilience."

Nods of agreement follow her declaration, the elite buoyed by her confidence. Yet, her next words are meant for their ears only, a shared secret that binds them to her cause.

"Let us be clear," she lowers her voice, a conspiratorial edge cutting through the softness, "the security of our positions, our power, depends on absolute control. Vane Calder is a major threat to both sides—unity under my leadership is non-negotiable."

The statement solidifies her intent, the room charged with a new energy. The elite are somewhat reassured, but their faith in Greda's leadership is shaken. They demand results, not just reassurances, giving her a tight deadline to fix the vulnerabilities exposed by Vane's actions and restore order.

As the meeting adjourns, the elite disperse, their whispers echoing in the opulent space. Greda remains a moment longer, her gaze lingering on the empty chairs, each one a seat of power that must be preserved at all costs.

She turns, her silhouette framed by the doorway, the weight of command resolute upon her shoulders. The Citadel must hold. It must.

Callan's fingers trace the cold, metallic surface of the table, his eyes scanning the hushed figures scattered around Sector 9X. The dim light casts long shadows, mirroring the weight of the upcoming battle that presses against his thoughts. Tomorrow, either he ends this war or he gives his life for the freedom of mankind. But he makes a silent vow to himself that when he leaves Sector 9X tomorrow, he will never return again unless victorious. Either he wins, or he dies. But he will fight until the very end.

Making sure he doesn't say these thought out loud, his gaze settles on Jax, standing apart, the subtle hum of his android circuitry blending with the low whispers of human collaborators and the rustling of vegetation refugees. It's a surreal alliance, one that months ago, he couldn't have imagined. Jax's leadership has transformed Zone U7 into a stronghold, a beacon of new beginnings, perhaps too bright, too soon.

Callan's thoughts churn as he observes Felix pacing slightly, his eyes flitting between the digital maps and the myriad of screens displaying code and encrypted communications. Felix's presence is a stark reminder of what's at stake—the fall of Project Lumina, the backbone of Greda's oppressive regime. The room feels charged with a silent, electric anticipation, every member ready to play their part in the final showdown.

Rootwhisper catches his attention next. The young vegetation being, an ally born from the enemy, stands quietly by the periphery, its leaves subtly shimmering under the artificial lights. It's a warrior in its own right, bridging the chasm between human and plant, between mistrust and cooperation. How much of tomorrow hinges on understanding those we once feared?

Callan's hand clenches into a fist, the weight of this war of worlds settling heavily on his shoulders. Around him, the hum of whispered strategies and the click of loaded weapons create a symphony of impending action. He turns his attention inward, where the real battle wages—a war against doubt, against the fear of not returning to this very room.

The faces of his team flicker in his mind's eye. Tibo's last joke echoes in his memory, a desperate attempt to lift the heavy cloak of tension. Elara's determined eyes provide a silent promise of support, not just in battle but beyond, whatever that 'beyond' might hold. Their resilience fortifies him, lending strength he draws upon freely, yet fears to deplete.

He steps away from the table, his boots silent on the worn floor. Each step is measured, a countdown to the morrow, to the culmination of their struggles. He pauses by a window, the opaque glass offering no view, no glimpse of the night that cloaks their final hours of preparation.

Outside, the world is changing, bending under the weight of their actions tonight. Within these walls, strategies are laid bare, roles assigned with precision, yet nothing can fully prepare them for the chaos of war. The plan is clear, but the outcome, as always, remains shrouded in the fog of uncertainty.

Callan knows that tomorrow, the blood spilled may either water the seeds of a new beginning or drown the last embers of resistance. There's no middle ground, not anymore. He turns back to his team, their faces a mosaic of courage and fear, of lives intertwined by a common thread of rebellion.

As he looks at them, another silent vow forms in his heart—to make sure no one dies and everyone returns back home to their families. They are his responsibility, his to guide, his to protect. The thought solidifies into resolve as he silently steps back to join them, the plan ready to unfold.

He stands slightly apart, a silent sentinel among his gathered forces. His eyes travel over the faces of those he leads—each one marked by the gravity of the moment, yet underscored by a steely resolve that mirrors his own. These are the faces of the Resistance, a patchwork quilt of disparate beings stitched together by necessity and a shared dream of freedom. They are androids with glowing circuits, human miners with dust ingrained in their skin, hackers whose fingers danced over keyboards to dismantle oppressors from the inside, and hybrids whose very existence blurs the line between man and machine. Among them, Rootwhisper, a symbol of hope that even those born of the enemy can choose a different path.

His heart tightens with a commander's pride and a comrade's fear. Tomorrow's battle looms large, a dark cloud on the horizon that none can avoid. It is the culmination of every sacrifice made, every loss mourned, every small victory celebrated. In the quiet before the storm, he finds a moment of profound clarity, recognizing the weight of the legacy he carries and the lives that depend on his every decision.

Callan's thoughts drift to the strategies laid out, the contingencies stacked like dominoes waiting to fall. The plan is a complex one, relying not just on brute force but on the cunning and quick thinking of every team member. They must strike with precision, disabling Project Lumina to cripple Greda's surveillance capabilities, severing the head of the snake, while we sever the head of the Overlord on the surface.

As his gaze rests on each member of his makeshift family, he sees their determination, their readiness to stand beside him in the face of overwhelming odds. There is Tibo, whose laughter has often pierced the somber veil of their planning sessions, reminding them all that hope is not a frivolous thing. Elara stands close by, her presence a constant source of strength for Callan. Her strategy and courage are as vital to this mission as any weapon or shield.

Rootwhisper's gentle rustling is a soft whisper in the charged air, a sound that speaks of nature's resilience and its capacity for alliance. The vegetation being has taught them much, not only about the enemy they face but about the possibility of unity in diversity, of strength forged from understanding.

Moving through the assembled crowd, Callan's steps are silent but purposeful. His hand brushes against the cold metal of his Solar Beam Rifle, the weapon a heavy promise slung across his back. His other hand grips the hilt of his Leafblade Machete, ready to carve a path through whatever stands in their way.

The quiet murmuring of plans and last-minute checks fills the air, a low symphony of war's precipice. Callan stops, his eyes closing briefly. When he opens them, it is with the weight of a man who knows the dawn may bring triumph or tragedy.

They are ready, as ready as any group can be when facing the unknown. This night, this moment, is theirs to command. Tomorrow, they will fight not just for their lives but for a future unchained from tyranny. And in this quiet before the storm, Callan feels the weight of his promise to them all—no one will be left behind, not if he can help it.

Callan begins to speak.
Look around you, everyone.

In our Resistance, we have a captain from the android ranks, another from the guardians of the underground minders. We have technicians, overseers, hackers, and hybrids, vegetation and hybrid humans standing together. Here in our world, individuals might have faced isolation because of their origin or function. But for us now, all that is gone.

We're stepping into the valley of the shadow of death, where you will watch the back of the person next to you, as they will watch yours. And you won't care if they are silicon or organic, or by what code they operate. They say we're leaving home.

We're heading towards what home was always meant to be. So let's be clear about our reality. We are going into battle against a tough and determined enemy.

I can't promise you that I will bring you all back alive, but this I swear before you and before Almighty God: When we go into battle, I will be the first to set foot on the field and I will be the last to step off. And I will leave no one behind.

Dead or alive, we will all come home together. So help me God. Elara's voice was low, barely more than a whisper, yet it cut through the murmur of the room with sharp clarity. "If you go to the Surface, glory will be yours. They will write stories about your victories for millennia. The world will remember your name." Her gaze locked with Callan's, intense and unwavering. "But if you go to the Surface, you may never come home, for your glory walks hand in hand with your doom."

Callan paused, his fingers stopped tracing the cold, metallic surface of the table. The dim light cast long shadows across the floor, each one seeming to echo Elara's solemn words. "And if I don't?" he finally responded, his voice steady yet tinged with the weight of the responsibility he felt.

"Then we fight another day," Elara replied, her voice softening. "But, Callan, if you do this, if you face the Overlord again, you might not come back."

He nodded slowly, absorbing the gravity of her statement. "I know," he admitted, his voice barely above a whisper. "Every step towards the Surface, towards him, is a step towards ending this. Not just for glory, Elara, but for freedom."

"Freedom? Or doom? Both are waiting for you. One in the light, one in the shadows," Elara pressed, her eyes searching his. "Can't you see? Your glory walks hand in hand with your doom."

"Then I walk eyes open," Callan responded firmly. "If this is the end, I meet it on my feet. I meet it for all of us."

"We need you here, alive and with us. Who leads if you fall? Who will inspire us then?" Elara's voice cracked slightly, revealing her underlying fear.

"You lead if I fall," Callan said, his gaze drifting over the assembled faces of their team, each member marked by a mix of resolve and apprehension. "Give us freedom or give us death."

"Just promise me, whatever happens, you'll fight to come back. Not for the glory, but for us," Elara insisted, her hand reaching out to grasp his, a gesture of solidarity and desperate hope.

Callan took her hand, his grip firm. "I promise. I'll fight to return, Elara. With every breath, I'll fight."

"Make sure you do," she replied, her voice steady once more. "We have too much to live for, and I won't have it any other way."

Callan released her hand and stepped back, turning to face the rest of the group. They were a patchwork of races and species, united under a single cause. "Then it's settled. I go at dawn. And I'll do everything to return, to finish this, once and for all."

As the quiet of the room enveloped them, Tibo's voice broke the silence, a note of urgency threading through his words. "The Surface needs Callan. We all do."

Callan shook his head slowly, his gaze fixed on the myriad reflections in the dimly lit room. "The Surface doesn't need me. It got along before I was born and will continue long after I'm gone."

"I'm not talking about the land," Tibo countered, stepping closer. "Our people need you. This war will never be forgotten. Nor will the heroes who fight in it."

Jax Thorn, his features marked by the soft glow of his circuitry, spoke with a clear, resonant voice. "You were born for this conflict, Callan."

Milo interjected, his tone mixing admiration with concern. "You are brave, perhaps recklessly so, to face this alone. The Overlord, he's the most formidable adversary I've ever seen. I wouldn't want to fight him."

Callan's response was sharp, edged with a cold reality. "And that's why no one will remember your name, my friend."

Felix, who had been silently monitoring the strategy screens, looked up. "They'll be talking about this war for another thousand years. All men want more; they want to be remembered."

With a quiet intensity, Callan replied, "In a thousand years, the dust from our bones will be gone, but free men will remain. That's the legacy we're fighting for."

The group fell silent, each person digesting the weight of his words. They stood in the shadowed confines of Sector 9X, surrounded by the tools of war yet isolated from the world they were striving to save. In that moment, the gravity of their task seemed to draw tighter around them, a noose of inevitability.

Elara moved closer to Callan, her presence a comforting warmth at his side. "And what if we succeed, Callan? What becomes of us, of this resistance, if we actually win?"

Callan's eyes met hers, his voice soft yet unwavering. "Then we rebuild. Not just the cities and the lands, but our lives. We build a world where no child has to become a soldier, where no leader has to send his people into battle wondering if it's for the last time."

Tibo clapped his hands together, breaking the tension. "Well, I for one plan on being incredibly insufferable when telling stories of our heroics. Just imagine the feasts!"

Jax chuckled, the sound rich and surprisingly human. "Just make sure you get my good side in those stories, Tibo."

Ava nodded, his demeanor serious. "First, we survive. Then, we ensure those stories are worth telling."

Felix adjusted his visor, his eyes not leaving the screens. "Every variable accounted for, every possible outcome simulated. We're as ready as we'll ever be."

Jax's voice, firm and resolute, broke the contemplative silence that had settled over the group. "Tomorrow, we will have our war."

Elara, standing close to Callan, added her own conviction to the mix. "I'd rather fight beside you than with any army of thousands."

Tibo, always one to bolster morale, chimed in with a fierce grin. "Let no one forget how menacing we are. We are the Resistance."

Callan, his expression set in the grim determination that had marked his leadership, responded to the unspoken question on everyone's minds. "There is no one else willing to wage war on the surface, against the Overlord."

He paused, surveying the faces of his assembled comrades, each reflecting a mixture of fear, anticipation, and resolve. "There is no path but war for warriors," he continued, his voice echoing slightly off the metal walls. "Only the battlegrounds where their fates are decided."

The group absorbed his words, each member drawing strength from his unwavering commitment. In the flickering light of the sector, their shadows seemed to dance on the walls, as if mirroring the turmoil within each of them.

Elara stepped closer, her voice barely audible over the soft hum of the sector's life-support systems. "What are we, if not warriors seeking our destiny?"

Jax nodded in agreement, the light catching on his metallic frame. "And tomorrow, we carve that destiny with our courage."

Milo, ever the tactician, glanced around at the huddle of serious faces. "And if the Overlord is as formidable as we fear, it will be a tale of valor fit for the ages."

Callan looked at each of them, his gaze lingering a moment longer on Elara. "Let's make it a tale that will never be forgotten. Not for the glory, not for the fame, but so that freedom isn't just a word in the old world's history books."

Tibo broke into a wry smile. "And here I was thinking I'd get famous out of this."

Elara, with a gentle touch on Callan's arm, brought their focus back. "Remember, it's not just about surviving this war. It's about what we're fighting for. A world where people don't need to become heroes."

Callan's nod was slow, thoughtful. "Tonight, we prepare. Tomorrow, we fight. Not just for our lives, but for all the lives that follow."

Felix's voice carried across the room filled with the low buzz of anxious whispers and the soft clatter of gear being prepped. "We will face darkness tomorrow," he said, his eyes flicking from the digital displays back to the faces of his comrades. "You won't have eyes or ears. You will wander the surface blind, deaf, and dumb."

Callan, standing slightly apart from the others, allowed a small smile to touch his lips, a rare break in his otherwise stern demeanor. "We"ll, If I fall," he replied, his voice measured, "all will know—this is Callan, a miner who fought for us all."

His declaration hung in the air, a vow that seemed to cement his readiness to face whatever lay ahead. "All humans understand is but survival and war," he added, his gaze drifting over the group, each member clad in their battle-worn armor, each carrying the same resolve that had brought them this far.

"I either leave this life a free man, or let the Overlord take our freedom."

Felix, nodding in acknowledgment of Callan's intensity, posed a question that seemed to echo off the cold, metal walls. "Why did you choose this life?"

Callan's response was immediate, his voice tinged with a mix of defiance and resignation. "I chose nothing; I was born into this, and this is what I am."

Around him, the team absorbed these words, each facing their own internal battles as they prepared for the physical one awaiting them. The room, lit only by the soft glow of monitors and the occasional flicker of overhead lights, seemed to shrink under the weight of their shared destiny.

Milo shuffled closer, his usual jovial demeanor subdued under the gravity of the situation. "We're all in this," he murmured, his voice barely audible. "For each other, for tomorrow, for whatever comes after."

Elara, moving to stand beside Callan, placed a hand on his arm. Her touch was light, but her presence was grounding. "May we live— or die… together," she said quietly, reinforcing the unspoken bond that had formed between them.

Tibo clapped both Callan and Milo on the back. "We are the Resistance."

Callan looked around at his team, their faces a mix of fear, determination, and courage. "There is no one else," he said, his voice steady. "No one else willing to wage war on the surface, against the Overlord."

As they gathered their gear, preparing to move out, Callan's words continued to resonate. "There is no path but war for warriors," he said, his eyes locking with each of his team members in turn. "Only the battlegrounds where our fates are decided."

"With courage. With honor," Jax said, his voice carrying a somber note. "For freedom."

"And if the Overlord is as formidable as we fear," Milo added, checking his equipment one last time, "then it's a tale of valor we'll write. A tale fit for the ages."

"Let's make it a tale that will never be forgotten," Callan concluded, his gaze sweeping over his makeshift family. "Not for the glory, not for the fame, but for the freedom. For a world where freedom isn't just a word in the history books of the old world."

They were ready, as ready as any could be for the unknown challenges of the morrow. Tomorrow, they would fight—not just for survival, but for a future unchained from tyranny.

Chapter 15

The neural network hub of Project Lumina hums with a quiet intensity as Chancellor Greda steps into the softly lit control room. Her gaze sweeps over the bank of monitors displaying streams of data—each one a window into the lives of those connected to her creation. The air is cool, charged with the silent whispers of surveillance, a symphony of control orchestrated from the shadows.

Greda's eyes, sharp and calculating, fix on a particular screen showing an array of personal metrics from a citizen marked by the AI as a potential dissenter. Her finger hovers over the console, ready to dive deeper into this life, to unravel the secrets of his discontent. She doesn't hesitate; the information is more than data—it's power, it's survival.

"Enhance his feed," she commands, her voice a low murmur that doesn't betray the storm of strategies raging in her mind. The AI obeys instantly, pulling up a detailed psychological profile, predicting the citizen's reactions, his next moves. It's a dance of numbers and probabilities, each step anticipated and countered long before it's taken.

As the algorithms work to sift through the digital essence of human thought, Greda reflects on the new protocol she's about to implement. This system won't just monitor; it will mold reality itself, nudging perceptions, dulling the sharp edges of rebellion with the subtlety of a shadow passing over the sun. It's elegant, it's effective, it's necessary.

She turns to a lead engineer, a young woman whose loyalty is as much to the technology as to the regime. "Initiate Protocol Vesper," Greda instructs, her words slicing through the low hum of equipment. "Start with him. Make him believe that compliance is not just preferable, but inevitable."

The engineer nods, her fingers dancing across the keyboard, setting the wheels in motion. On the screen, the discontented citizen's digital world subtly shifts—news feeds change, virtual interactions steer away from dissent, and slowly, his digital environment becomes a cage of pleasantries and distractions.

Greda watches, a slight smile playing on her lips. This is how you control a society: not with chains, but with a series of gentle nudges.

Not with oppression, but with the orchestrated illusion of contentment. She turns away from the screen, her mind already racing through the next steps, the expansions, the refinements.

As she exits the hub, the door closes with a silent, assured click. The corridor outside is deserted, the only sound the soft echo of her footsteps. Each step reaffirms her belief in her mission—her city, her people, they need her. They need this control to survive in a world that is unforgiving and brutal. She pauses, considering the full implementation of Vesper across Lumina, weighing not the moralities but the necessities.

Behind her, the screens continue to flicker in the dim light of the hub, unseen eyes watching over a population that sleeps unaware, dreams undisturbed by the silent war waged for their complacency.

Greda's march through the Citadel's labyrinthine corridors serves as a physical manifestation of her journey from one form of control to another. Her thoughts shift from the immediate manipulations of the neural network hub to the broader implications of Project Lumina's global expansion. The walls around her, lined with reflective obsidian, cast back her determined image, a constant affirmation of her power and authority. As she walks, her hand brushes against the cool, smooth surface of the tablet carrying the day's agendas and reports. The device is a hub of information, each swipe revealing layers of data and decisions that need her attention.

She stops briefly at a viewing port, a rare structural feature in the otherwise claustrophobic underground setting. The port offers a view of the simulation fields below, where artificial environments replicate dozens of Earth's lost habitats. Watching the serene simulations, Greda considers the irony of her citizens escaping into fabricated realities she has crafted, while she plans to ensnare the actual world in a web of her making. It's a moment of quiet reflection on the paradox of her reign: offering illusions of freedom while tightening real chains around those she governs.

Resuming her walk, she arrives at a secure access point guarded by two of her elite security personnel. Their nods are stiff, respectful. She acknowledges them with a mere glance, her mind already transitioning to the tactical discussions awaiting her. As the doors to the strategic planning room slide open silently, she steps into the cool, dimly lit space. The shift from the corridor's austere functionality to the room's high-tech command center is seamless yet stark, echoing her leadership's dual nature—visibly minimal yet underlyingly complex. The globe in the center casts a soft glow, illuminating the room and the expectant faces of her advisors. This is where the future is shaped, under her directive, and every decision here will ripple across the world.

The strategic planning room, hidden deep within the bowels of the Lumina Citadel, is starkly minimalist, the starkness only broken by a holographic globe pulsating softly in the center. Chancellor Greda, flanked by her inner circle, stands before it, each continent and city bathed in a pale blue light. Her advisors, a collection of military strategists and technological savants, await her directives, their expressions a mix of anticipation and trepidation.

"Project Lumina was always meant to be more than a mere escape," Greda begins, her voice steady, commanding. "It was a trial, a model for a new world order." She gestures to the globe, where lines begin to connect various dots, symbolizing human settlements, each pulse spreading like a web from one node to another.

"We are on the brink of expanding this model globally," she continues, the globe rotating slowly under her controlled touch. "Our influence will extend beyond the Citadel, beyond our borders. We will export Lumina's technology to other enclaves, binding them to us through dependency and control."

A map overlays the globe now, lines drawn between strategic points across the desolate landscapes marked for Lumina's expansion. "These are not mere connections; they are the lifelines of a new empire," she declares, her eyes scanning the room, ensuring her vision is clearly understood.

One advisor, a cybernetics expert, hesitates before speaking. "Chancellor, the infrastructure required to support such an expansion—"

"Is already under development," Greda cuts in sharply. "We've pioneered the technologies that can make this possible. Quantum entanglement for instant communication across distances, AI-driven governance models, neural interfacing that makes dissent not just undesirable but unthinkable."

She steps closer to the map, her finger tracing a route from the Citadel to a settlement known for its technological prowess. "We start here. They already feel the economic strain of isolation; our technology will seem like salvation."

Another advisor, this one specializing in psychological operations, leans forward. "And if they resist?"

Greda's smile is thin, almost predatory. "Then we show them the cost of resistance. Once a few are made an example of, the others will fall in line. They always do."

The room falls silent, the weight of her plan settling over the assembled group. They are not just planning expansion; they are orchestrating the absorption of the world's remnants under Greda's rule.

"We'll need to establish a protocol for integrating new sectors," the lead engineer says, breaking the silence. "Each region will have its nuances, and Lumina must adapt."

"Correct," Greda nods, returning to the globe. "Adaptation and control. Our systems will learn from every interaction, every rebellion, every compliance. With each iteration, Lumina becomes not just a tool of control but a self-evolving entity that preempts and neutralizes threats before they even arise."

She pauses, letting her vision sink in, each advisor now acutely aware of the scale at which they were operating. "This is the dawn of a new era," she states, "an era where chaos is no more, where every human action is anticipated, guided, and, if necessary, corrected."

As the meeting adjourns, Greda remains behind, the pulsating lights of the globe reflecting in her eyes. Her thoughts are already moving forward, plotting, planning, anticipating. In the quiet of the room, the hum of the Citadel seems to echo her ambition, a reminder of the power she wields and the future she is determined to create. Outside, the world may be harsh and unforgiving, but within the walls of Lumina, under her watch, it will be anything but.

As the last of her advisors exits the strategic planning room, Greda stands alone for a moment longer, the weight of her ambitions settling around her like the dust of a conquered land. She turns away from the pulsating globe, her steps resonating with firm resolve as she makes her way towards her private chambers. Her mind is a whirlwind of strategies and visions, each more ambitious than the last, but tonight, there is also a need for her public persona to shine, to celebrate the achievement and continued success of Project Lumina.

She is acutely aware of the power of perception, and tonight's gala is as much a strategic display of power as any maneuver in her tactical playbook.

As she walks, Greda reviews the evening's agenda, which has been meticulously planned to not only celebrate but also to solidify her influence over Lumina's elite. Her private chamber is a sanctuary of calm and order, where she transitions from the strategist to the gracious host. She selects her attire with the precision of a general choosing armor for battle. The gown she chooses is elegantly understated, designed to project an image of accessible leadership, yet every detail speaks of control and meticulous planning. As her stylist adjusts the fabric, smoothing down the lines, Greda practices her speech mentally, refining each word to resonate with her audience's aspirations and fears, weaving her vision into their dreams.

Once dressed, Greda takes a moment to gaze at her reflection, her expression unreadable. The mirror shows more than just her image; it reflects a persona crafted over years, a visage of leadership that is both revered and feared. Adjusting her necklace, she rehearses key phrases from her speech, each one a star in the larger universe of her rule. With every word, she reinforces her commitment to the prosperity under her regime, all the while reminding her constituents of the chaos that lurks outside the controlled environment of Lumina. This gala is not just a celebration but a reaffirmation of her unchallengeable position at the helm.

Leaving her chambers, Greda makes her way to the gala hall, her pace measured and her posture regal. The corridor leading to the hall is lined with her personal guard, a visible reminder of the order and security she brings to Lumina. As she approaches the ornate doors of the gala hall, she pauses, her hand on the cool metal. Tonight, she will smile, toast, and dance, but each gesture will be a calculated move in the grand chess game of her governance. The doors open silently before her, revealing the glittering interior of the gala hall, ready to embrace the night's festivities. Inside, the city's elite await, eager to bask in the glory of Lumina and, by extension, in her favor. Greda steps into the light, her face composed into a smile that does not reach her eyes, but perfectly masks the relentless machinations of her mind.

Greda steps forward, the dim light of the corridor giving way to the brilliant radiance of the gala hall. The atmosphere is electric, a buzz of anticipation and admiration filling the air as the city's elite gather to celebrate the anniversary of Project Lumina. The hall, lavishly decorated with holographic displays and ambient lighting, mirrors the futuristic essence of the world she has crafted. Her entrance, regal and calculated, draws the attention of every attendee, their faces turning towards her with a mix of awe and fear, a testament to the power she holds over them.

Navigating through the crowd, her smile remains poised, a mask of benevolence over the steel of her resolve. She exchanges pleasantries, her words light but her mind sharp, assessing alliances and loyalties with every handshake and nod. As the orchestra swells, the sound a luxurious backdrop to the evening, Greda positions herself on the grand dais, the room's focus shifting seamlessly to her. Her eyes sweep across the gathered multitude, every face a story, every story under her command.

The moment for her speech arrives, the room falling into a hushed expectancy. Greda steps up to the microphone, the soft clinking of her jewelry punctuating the silence. "Tonight, we mark a milestone not just for Project Lumina, but for humanity itself," she begins, her voice clear and compelling. The screens around the hall flicker, displaying images of Lumina's successes—vivid, beautiful realities far removed from the harshness of their world. "We celebrate the power of human innovation and the strength of unified purpose," she continues, weaving a narrative of triumph and unity, her words painting her as the architect of a new era.

As her speech builds, she outlines her vision for the future, a world interconnected through the technology of Lumina, under her benevolent guidance. "We stand on the brink of a new age, an era where chaos and disorder give way to stability and progress," she declares, her gaze steely, challenging anyone to contradict. The crowd listens, rapt, as she paints a picture of a global network, a single entity bound by shared destiny and her unerring leadership. "This," she gestures expansively, "is the dawn of a new humanity, guided by wisdom, safeguarded by technology, and ruled by justice."

Her voice takes on a sharper edge, the warmth of her earlier words cooling into something more calculating. "But let us not be naive," Greda continues, her eyes sweeping over the crowd like a hawk surveying its domain. "This new world will demand sacrifices.

Not everyone is prepared for the future we are building. There are those who cling to outdated ideals, who challenge the very progress that will save us all."

A pause, deliberate and heavy, allows her words to sink in. The screens flicker again, this time showing vague silhouettes of dissenters, their features obscured, their fates an unspoken warning. "Resistance," she says, the word dripping with disdain, "is not just futile; it is dangerous. It threatens the stability of our society, the safety of every citizen who dreams of a better tomorrow."

Her gaze hardens, the glint in her eye almost predatory. "That is why tonight, while we celebrate, we also affirm our commitment to maintaining order. Under my leadership, Lumina is not just a sanctuary; it is a sentinel against chaos." The crowd, caught in the gravity of her presence, nods, their faces a mixture of fear and fascination. "Our monitoring systems do not merely observe; they protect. Our algorithms do not just predict; they preserve the fabric of our society."

She leans closer to the microphone, her voice lowering into a confessional tone that only amplifies its reach. "To those who would oppose us, know this: we are always watching. Not out of malice, but out of necessity. My love for this city, for all of you, is boundless, but so is my resolve to crush any threat to our collective future."

A softer, almost sorrowful note creeps into her voice, crafting her cruelty as care, her sadism as stewardship. "It pains me, truly, when an individual must be corrected for the greater good. But remember, each intervention, each... adjustment we make, ensures the survival and flourishing of the whole." Her hand gestures gracefully to the screens, where images now display the peace and prosperity of daily life in Lumina, a stark contrast to the veiled threats she dispenses.

"As we expand, as Lumina becomes not just a city but a global beacon, our vigilance will increase. Our reach will extend not with the cold grasp of tyranny," she assures, her tone almost coaxing, "but with the compassionate embrace of a guardian. My vision is clear—a world united under our banner, devoid of conflict, thriving in harmony."

The music swells subtly in the background, a cinematic score that builds around her speech, enhancing the emotional impact of her words. "Imagine it—a world where no Elite's child knows hunger, where no elder fears neglect, where every person has purpose and peace. This is no mere dream; it is a blueprint, and it is becoming a reality, through our efforts, through your support."

She raises her arms, encompassing the entire hall in her gesture, her voice crescendoing to a powerful climax. "Tonight, as we look up to the stars in our artificial sky, let us remember: they are not so different from the lights of Lumina. Both are guides, both illuminate our path, and under these lights, we will walk together into a new dawn."

As her speech concludes, the room erupts into applause, a thunderous wave of sound that fills the cavernous space. Fireworks, brilliantly coordinated with her final words, light up the ceiling in a spectacle of color and light, casting everyone in a glow that blurs the line between their reality and the one Greda has crafted. But above the noise, above the celebration, Greda's eyes glint with the cold fire of ambition, her smile a mask that hides the gears of control turning ever more tightly. As she steps back from the podium, her figure silhouetted against the explosive display, the chilling reality of her leadership is both obscured and highlighted by the very pageantry she orchestrates.

As the applause breaks out, thunderous and pervasive, Greda steps back, her expression composed, her eyes cold. She moves to the edge of the balcony, overlooking the empire she has built. Below her, the elite of Lumina lose themselves in the celebration, their laughter and cheers a melody of oblivious contentment. Greda's lips curl into a sinister smile, the fireworks reflecting in her eyes—a ruler not just of a city, but soon, of a world, her subjects none the wiser to the depth of the reality she has crafted for them. As the lights blaze against the night, her smile deepens, the shadows of her dominion stretching far beyond the walls of the Citadel.

It is dawn, and the war has begun. Deep within the heart of the Lumina Citadel, beneath the layers of luxury and control, Felix Hart and his team are covertly stationed, their presence cloaked by the newest piece of tech from Milo and Tibo—a device that scrambles surveillance signals, rendering them invisible to the Citadel's extensive monitoring systems. Felix, positioned before a bank of holographic displays, focuses intently on a 3D map of the Citadel, his fingers dancing across the surface as he manipulates viewpoints and accesses secure feeds.

"This is our narrow window. We need to move before the next sweep," Felix instructs, his voice barely above a whisper. He's aware that every second they remain undetected is a small victory. Around him, his team, composed of elite strategists and tech experts, is a blur of quiet motion, each member attuned to their leader's calm yet urgent tone.

Ava, standing by Felix, monitors the encryption levels on their communications, ensuring their plans remain shielded from Lumina's prying algorithms. "All channels are secure, Felix. Milo's scrambler is holding up better than expected," she reports, her eyes not leaving the screens that display a cascade of data streams.

Outside the operations room, Jax Thorn and his team, disguised as worker androids, move undetected among the real androids that maintain the Citadel's day-to-day functions. Their movements are precise, calculated to blend seamlessly with the androids' routines, as they place surveillance disruptors at critical junctures throughout the facility. Each disruptor planted further secures the team's temporary ghost status within the walls of the Citadel.

Back at Project Lumina, Cyrus Reese is preparing for his part in this intricate ballet of resistance. He's stationed at a secretive broadcast facility, surrounded by old yet functional tech, his face illuminated by the glow of a single screen as he finalizes the messages that will soon sweep across the network, aimed at unveiling the dark truths of Lumina. The weight of his past advocacy for Lumina now fuels his determination to expose its manipulations, adding a fervent edge to his preparations.

Milo, tucked away in a dimly lit corner of the room with Felix and the team, fine-tunes a device that's critical for the next phase of their plan. "We're set up for a full spectrum blackout on their surveillance net. Once Cyrus goes live, they'll be blind long enough for Jax's team to take control of the physical security hubs," he explains, his hands moving deftly over the complex array of circuits and holographic interfaces.

Tara, her figure cloaked by the adaptive camouflage suit, communicates through a sub-vocal mic, her voice a vibration in Felix's ear. "I'm in position near the mainframe. Waiting for your go to connect the pulse drive," she whispers, her presence near the Citadel's digital heart critical for their plan to inject a virus that would cripple the system long-term.

Felix nods to himself, his mind racing through scenarios, anticipating and counteracting possible complications in a stream of calculated foresight. "On my mark, Tara. Milo, sync the blackout to Cyrus's broadcast. Ava, ensure our backdoor stays open for a quick exit."

As they each ready themselves for the imminent cascade of actions, the tension is palpable, the stakes immeasurable. Felix allows himself a moment to survey his team, their faces set with determination and focus. This isn't just about dismantling Lumina; it's about reclaiming their lives and freedoms from the suffocating grasp of Greda's regime.

Just then, a soft ping signals the readiness of all elements. Felix looks up, his gaze fixed on the digital map, now showing their positions converging like the intricate gears of a well-oiled machine.

"Now," he commands, his voice a trigger pulled in the silent war they wage. As Tara connects the pulse drive, and Cyrus's voice begins to filter through hidden speakers throughout the Citadel, a new chapter in their fight is written, forged by the will of those who dare to stand against the darkness.

Felix's focus sharpens as Cyrus's voice breaks through the orchestrated silence of their hidden control room. The words are not just audible; they reverberate with the weight of truth, amplified by the secret channels they've tapped into throughout the Lumina Citadel.

"Citizens of Salleria," Cyrus's voice starts, the tone somber yet compelling, "tonight, I reveal the hidden chains that bind us. Project Lumina, presented as our salvation, is our prison."

Felix watches as the Citadel's internal feeds, still under their control, show confused faces turning towards the nearest speakers, the first seeds of doubt sown. Cyrus continues, "We were promised escape, luxury, and freedom in a world crafted to perfection. But at what cost? Your time, your very lives, are the currency of this deception."

Ava's fingers pause over her console, her eyes meeting Felix's for a moment. They both understand the gravity of every revealed secret about to dismantle Lumina's façade.

"Every moment you spend in this artificial paradise," Cyrus's voice grows fiercer, "you age, you weaken, outside the reach of your dreams. The DNA you provided, tailored to create your perfect escape, is being harvested for experiments that serve only the regime."

On the screens, Felix sees the stirring of unrest. Faces marred by confusion and fear, the seeds growing into tangible doubt and anger. Cyrus's revelation about DNA harvesting hits hard; it's personal, invasive.

"The luxurious experiences, the sensory overloads," Cyrus continues, "are manipulations designed to make you compliant. You live in cycles of induced happiness while your real world, your freedoms, crumble into decay."

Felix's hands move to stabilize their connection as Cyrus delves deeper, uncovering more of Lumina's dark operations. "And what of your dreams? Project Lumina invades even those. Your dreams are no longer your own but are extensions of the program, weaving Greda's narratives into your sleep, conditioning you to forget what it means to be free."

Murmurs ripple through the Citadel, reaching Felix's ears through the open comms channel—a mix of outrage and disbelief. His gaze flits to Milo, who gives a slight nod, confirming the external feeds are still looping innocuously, hiding the brewing storm within.

"But there is more," Cyrus's tone shifts, hinting at the vastness of the conspiracy. "The social hierarchy within Lumina? A lie to pit us against each other, to make us strive for betterment in a world that doesn't exist. We chase after virtual rewards, oblivious to our dwindling rights and voices in the real world."

Felix feels the shift, the palpable rise in tension as Cyrus's words paint a stark image of betrayal. The control room is silent except for

the broadcast, each member of his team absorbed in their roles, the
weight of their task grounding them.

"As we speak," Cyrus's voice hardens, a call to action resonating
in his words, "forces within your cherished virtual world are
mobilizing to silence me, to silence the truth. But the truth, once
known, cannot be unheard. It's time to wake up, to reclaim your lives
and your futures from the hands of those who would steal them in the
guise of protection and prosperity."

Felix watches the real-time analytics on his screen; the unrest
Cyrus's speech is generating is off the charts. This was the moment
they had been working towards, the spark needed to ignite a rebellion.

"Join us," Cyrus concludes, his voice now a beacon of defiance,
"break free from the shackles of Lumina. Together, we can restore our
dignity and secure our future. A future where we control our destinies,
not as pawns in a game masterminded by the corrupt and the
powerful."

The broadcast cuts off abruptly, leaving a charged silence that
buzzes in Felix's ears. He knows the impact of Cyrus's words will be
profound, a domino effect that could very well lead to the crumbling
of Greda's carefully constructed empire. Around him, his team is
already mobilizing, preparing for the repercussions, the inevitable
crackdown.

Felix's eyes are fixed on the Citadel's internal chaos now visible
on their feeds, his mind racing through the next moves in this high-
stakes game of rebellion and reclamation.

As Cyrus's voice permeates the Citadel, Jax Thorn and his team,
still disguised as maintenance androids, maneuver through the
corridors with precise and unremarkable movements. The faint echo of
Cyrus's damning revelations about Project Lumina provides a
backdrop to their subtle sabotage. Felix, watching through the feeds
he's secured, observes Jax's team reaching critical network junctures,
their actions hidden beneath the routine tasks they mimic.

Jax, with a tool in hand that looks standard to any surveillance but
is anything but, approaches a panel marked as a routine check spot. He
opens it with a swift, practiced move, his team blocking the view from
any wandering eyes that might still be oblivious to the chaos unfolding
in their ears. Inside the panel, instead of performing maintenance, he
inserts a small, unassuming device—a data corrupter designed by Milo

and Tibo. It's programmed to slowly degrade the data integrity of Project Lumina's surveillance archives, ensuring that when the time comes, the evidence of their infiltration will self-erase, leaving Greda blind to the depth of their penetration.

Felix shifts his view to another feed, where another member of Jax's team, under the guise of cleaning, places similar devices along the network routes. These devices are set to disrupt the AI's learning algorithms subtly, ensuring that the system's predictive capabilities are muddied, slowing any countermeasures against the rebellion.

In a synchronized manner, as Cyrus exposes more of Lumina's manipulations, Jax's team plants a series of what appear to be routine software updates across various terminals. These updates, however, are coded with logic bombs that will activate only when a specific set of conditions are met—when Greda attempts to reset or overwrite Cyrus's messages. These bombs will further cripple the system, forcing manual resets and leaving physical security controls vulnerable for just enough time to allow the resistance to move deeper into the Citadel.

Back in the control room, Felix watches the effects of Jax's team's efforts begin to materialize on his screens. Error messages start popping up, and Felix notes with satisfaction how sections of the Citadel begin to darken as lighting controls falter. He taps into a communication line, his voice low and steady, "Jax, status?"

"Phase one complete," Jax's distorted voice returns, the sound filtered through the scrambler to maintain their cover. "Moving to rendezvous point Echo for the next insertion."

Ava, next to Felix, updates her maps, highlighting the paths Jax's team takes, all routes chosen for minimal surveillance and maximum impact. "Their approach is clear for the next three minutes. After that, they'll hit the second security layer," she reports, her fingers flying over her console, rerouting some of the internal security feeds to display pre-recorded loops.

Outside, the disguised team continues their work, now moving towards the central control hub. As they walk, they pass other androids and a few distracted humans, everyone's attention hooked on personal devices, listening to Cyrus's revelations. Using this distraction, they reach the hub and integrate another series of devices—silent overrides that Milo assures can control physical door locks and communication lines if necessary.

As Felix oversees this complex ballet of technological warfare, he can't help but feel a surge of adrenaline. Each member of his team, whether in the shadows or behind screens, plays a crucial role in this intricate dance of rebellion. With every device planted, every line of code inserted, they inch closer to breaking Greda's stranglehold on the populace.

"Prepare for the final phase," Felix instructs, his gaze locked on the map, watching as digital markers representing his team converge towards the heart of darkness within the Lumina Citadel. The battle for freedom is in full swing, and every action, every decision now, could tip the scales in their favor.

As Felix oversees the strategic deployment from his hidden command center, the echoes of Cyrus's damning broadcast ripple through the underground cities. On his screens, multiple feeds flicker with scenes of unrest and awakening among the population. Each broadcast has acted like a stone thrown into the stagnant waters of compliance, and now, the ripples are turning into waves.

In the dimly lit alleyways of the Lower Sectors, Felix watches groups of youths spray-painting over Lumina's propaganda posters. The once gleaming images of a perfect virtual life are now marred with vivid, accusatory slogans: "Lies", "Thief of Dreams", and "Wake Up!" The graffiti, raw and colorful, spreads across the city's walls like a visual shout for freedom.

Switching views, Felix's eyes catch a cluster of citizens covertly distributing flyers at a crowded marketplace. The flyers, when seen through the surveillance feed, shimmer with digital codes—a clever disguise that embeds Cyrus's speech into seemingly innocuous advertisements. People tuck these into their clothes, sharing knowing looks that speak of a unified purpose. It's not just vandalism now; it's the beginning of a strategic spread of dissent.

Ava brings up another feed, this one showing a library where older citizens are converting Cyrus's speech into hidden data drives. They work with a quiet urgency, passing the drives along to teenagers who disappear into the shadows, ready to spread the truth further. Each drive contains not just the speech but detailed accounts of

Lumina's exploitations and instructions on how to resist the mental conditioning.

In the upper echelons of the Citadel, where the elite had once remained blissfully ignorant, Felix notices a shift. Influential figures, once staunch supporters of Lumina, now huddle in secluded corners, their faces tense as they view the contents of a smuggled data drive. Their discomfort is palpable, the betrayal they feel evident in their hushed, angry tones. A few, emboldened by the revelations, begin to speak out, questioning the cost of their comfort.

"Look at this, Felix," Milo points to a screen showing a public square, where a holographic projector has been hijacked to play Cyrus's speech on a loop. The crowd below watches, some with tears, others with fists raised in solidarity. The scene is powerful, a public reclaiming of space and narrative that had been dominated by Lumina's illusions.

Tara, her voice a whisper through the comms, reports from another sector. "The tech labs are seeing a few walkouts. Techs are downing tools, refusing to maintain the servers that uphold Lumina. They're citing ethical breaches, demanding accountability."

Felix nods, marking each of these developments on a virtual map that tracks the spread of the resistance. "Keep monitoring those shifts. Every minor act adds up," he instructs, his voice steady, his strategy clear. These visual and physical acts of resistance are vital, tangible manifestations of the psychological warfare they've ignited.

Outside, as dusk turns to night, the screens show groups gathering, not in protest but in support. Candles light up in windows as symbols of solidarity, their glow a quiet yet defiant stand against the darkness imposed by Greda's regime. Each light signifies a citizen awake, aware, and unwilling to return to the shadows.

The montage of resistance, of collective awakening, continues to play out on Felix's screens, a testament to the power of truth in a society built on deception. Each act of defiance, each whispered conversation and bold declaration, weaves a stronger fabric of rebellion.

Felix, watching the growing movement, feels a surge of hope. Cyrus's voice had been the spark, but the fire it ignited belongs to the people. Now, more than ever, they are not just fighting against Lumina;

they are fighting for a return to truth, to autonomy—to a life unscripted by tyranny.

Felix taps into a new surveillance feed, his attention drawn to the activities of Jax Thorn and his team. They navigate the intricate web of corridors and service areas of the Lumina Citadel with uncanny precision. Felix observes as they subtly interact with the citadel's maintenance systems, each interaction seemingly mundane yet fraught with disruptive potential.

Jax and his team pause at junction boxes and data terminals scattered throughout the Citadel, their actions covert and swift. Felix watches as Jax installs micro-devices into these systems—tiny, almost imperceptible pieces of technology designed by Milo and Tibo. These devices are timed to intermittently disrupt the energy flow, creating flickers in the Citadel's artificial lighting and subtle distortions in the public announcement systems. Each flicker is a subliminal reminder to the citizens that not all is as stable as it seems.

On another screen, Felix sees part of Jax's team in the luxury quarters, where they subtly manipulate the environmental controls. The temperature fluctuates erratically, the air subtly tinged with a discomforting warmth one moment and a chill the next. These discomforts, while minor, are designed to fray nerves and sow dissatisfaction among the elite, who are used to unblemished comfort.

Felix switches to a feed showing the market district where Jax's team distributes modified cleaning androids among the crowd. These androids, under the guise of routine cleaning, project holographic snippets of Cyrus's speech from hidden projectors. The words appear on walls and pavements in fleeting bursts, catching the eye of passersby and then vanishing before security forces can pinpoint their origin.

In the transportation hubs, Jax's team has reprogrammed information kiosks to sporadically display messages questioning the integrity of Project Lumina. "Is your reality yours?" one message asks, flickering across the screen before returning to the regular schedule of transport timetables. These messages are crafted to appear as system glitches, which makes them even more jarring and thought-provoking.

Felix's admiration grows as he watches Jax orchestrate a particularly bold move. In a crowded central plaza, a group from Jax's team integrates into a routine maintenance crew. They access the main holographic projectors—tools typically used by Lumina for grand displays of propaganda. Instead, they subtly alter the evening's light show to include frames of visual data, exposing quick, almost subliminal messages about Lumina's manipulations. These flashes in the grand display are not enough to make complete sense yet sufficient to provoke curiosity and skepticism.

Back in the command center, Felix and his team monitor the ripple effects of these disturbances. Social media feeds, accessed through secure, anonymous channels, begin to show an increase in posts questioning the reliability of Lumina's systems and the truthfulness of its narratives. Citizen journalists start reporting on the anomalies, speculating on the meanings and potential faults within the Citadel's structure.

"Jax is planting seeds of doubt everywhere," Felix mutters, impressed by the subtle chaos Jax is capable of sowing under the guise of routine. Each act, while small, contributes to a larger narrative of instability and deceit, amplifying the psychological impact of Cyrus's revelations.

As Felix prepares to coordinate the next phase of their operation, he knows that these disruptions are just the beginning. The true measure of their success will be the citizens' willingness to question and, ultimately, to act. For now, Jax and his team have masterfully stoked the fires of dissent, setting the stage for a deeper, more profound upheaval against the tyranny of Lumina.

Simultaneously, Chancellor Greda, feeling the ground of control slipping beneath her feet, retaliates with a fierce counter-propaganda campaign. Felix intercepts a priority transmission from Greda's office, commanding an immediate enhancement of surveillance across all sectors and the deployment of rapid response teams to quell the uprisings.

In her panic to regain control and counteract the disturbing truths unraveling her regime, Greda personally oversees the reset of Project Lumina's messaging systems. She orders the overwrite of all broadcasts, aiming to scrub Cyrus's damning speech from the network. However, this action unwittingly triggers one of the logic bombs planted by Jax's team.

The bomb—embedded within what appeared to be routine software updates—detects the unauthorized attempt to overwrite existing data. In response, it activates a cascade of disruptions. System screens flicker wildly, security protocols falter, and doors lock and unlock unpredictably, causing confusion and fear among the Citadel's security teams. This chaos opens a window for the resistance to deepen their infiltration.

Meanwhile, Cyrus's broadcast team, operating from a secret location within the Citadel, faces immediate danger. As they pack up their makeshift studio, Greda's enforcers, guided by the enhanced surveillance signals, close in. Felix, monitoring both the enforcers' progress and Cyrus's location, coordinates a desperate escape plan.

Through the hacked city grid, he redirects power, momentarily darkening the sector just long enough for Cyrus and his team to slip through the tightening net. They move through maintenance tunnels, the sounds of their pursuers' footsteps echoing behind them. Felix guides them via sub-vocal mics, each instruction critical to avoiding capture.

As they emerge into the lower service levels of the Citadel, Felix deploys a series of distractions—localized alarms in distant sectors, holographic displays of false movements, and even a temporary inversion of the surveillance feeds, all designed to mislead and misdirect Greda's forces.

Breathlessly reaching a pre-arranged extraction point, Cyrus's team encounters Jax, disguised as a security officer. With a nod, he ushers them into a concealed transport pod, its presence in the system masked by Milo's scrambling devices. As the pod silently slides away into the darkness of the utility tunnels, Felix wipes their tracks from the system, erasing every digital footprint of their escape.

Back in his command center, Felix watches the aftereffects of the broadcast and the logic bomb. Despite Greda's attempts to control the narrative, the damage is done. The seeds of doubt have taken root, and the ideas of freedom and truth continue to spread, fueled by the visible proof of Greda's desperation and the tangible breakdown of her control mechanisms.

Chapter 16

In the dim, pulsing heart of the Citadel's underbelly, a shadow moves stealthily through the corridors lined with the humming machinery of Project Lumina. Juno Rael, a high-ranking operator within the system, clutches a data drive tightly—a small beacon of defiance in her hand. Her face, illuminated intermittently by the glow of passing interface screens, is a mask of resolve and fear.

Two days ago, Juno had been a true believer in Lumina's promise, overseeing the integration of reality and virtuality with the zeal of a visionary. But witnessing her family, ensnared and distant, lost in manufactured dreams while their real lives withered, had shattered her convictions.

Now, as the pre-dawn hours wane, Juno edges closer to a clandestine meeting point. She's arranged to meet Felix Hart, a name that has grown increasingly resonant in hushed conversations among those disillusioned with Greda's regime. Callan and his team, Juno knows, are the resistance's best hope, and she is risking everything to bring them inside knowledge that could turn the tide.

As she rounds a corner, her path is suddenly blocked by a pair of security drones, their sensors sweeping lazily until they pinpoint her unauthorized presence. Juno freezes, her mind racing through countermeasures. With a swift motion, she pulls from her coat a scrambler—a device modified from her own designs—and activates it. The drones whir disorientedly, their systems disrupted just long enough for her to slip past into the shadows.

Minutes later, Juno arrives at the service door marked with a discreet symbol—a signal that she's in the right place. The door opens silently to reveal Felix, his appearance as severe and focused as his reputation suggests.

"Juno Rael," he greets her, his voice low and steady. "Good to see you again."

Juno nods, extending the data drive towards him. "What I've brought is worth it. It's everything—blueprints, access codes, and the real purposes behind Lumina. I can't be part of it anymore."

Felix accepts the drive, his eyes assessing Juno with a strategist's acumen. "If half of what I've heard about you is true, you could be invaluable to us."

"I want to help undo what I've helped to build. It's not just the technology; it's how it's used. It enslaves us," Juno says, her voice a mix of anger and determination.

Felix nods, understanding the weight of her words. "Then welcome to the resistance, Juno. Let's put your insider knowledge to work."

Felix Hart stood at the helm of the resistance's control center, a nerve center of screens and devices where the crucial assault on Project Lumina was about to unfold. With Juno Rael's insider knowledge now deeply integrated into their strategy, the atmosphere was charged with a potent mix of urgency and hope.

Juno, burdened by her past yet hopeful about her new alliance, observed as Milo eagerly discussed their approach. "The window Juno's information provides is narrow, but crucial. It's all we need to inject the virus directly into Lumina's core," Milo explained, his usual reserve replaced by a fervor as he pointed at the digital blueprints on display.

"The decoys are set. Quantum sync in three, two, one..." Milo counted down, initiating the quantum cryptography sequence that Juno had helped perfect. Virtual pathways lit up across the screens, signaling the start of their digital incursion.

As the digital pathways activated, Felix's attention was split between the cyber-attack's progression and Jax's team, which was maneuvering through the Citadel's infrastructure. "Teams are in position. Hardware is syncing now," Jax confirmed through a secure sub-vocal mic, his tone steady despite the underlying tension.

In the digital realm, Felix watched as avatars representing his team navigated through virtual landscapes that symbolized Lumina's defenses. Firewalls transformed into towering infernos and security protocols into monstrous entities, all being tackled with sophisticated code and strategic cunning. Each team member's avatar, controlled from the real world, faced these challenges head-on, their real-time coding efforts mirrored in the virtual space.

Back in the physical world, Felix's team expertly manipulated the Citadel's infrastructure to support their cyber offensive. They disabled surveillance cameras, rerouted data streams, and deployed hacking hardware at critical network junctures. Every physical action was meticulously timed to align with the digital assault, ensuring a multi-faceted attack that overwhelmed Lumina's defenses from all angles.

As Milo's avatar dodged an advanced encryption beast, disabling it with a masterfully crafted key, Juno's strategy of deploying decoy nodes came into play. Her nodes activated across the network, drawing away Lumina's defensive resources and causing portions of Lumina's AI to turn on itself in confusion.

The climax approached as the team neared Lumina's core. The virtual landscape darkened ominously, the core glowing menacingly at the center of a complex labyrinth. Felix, observing both the virtual and physical operations, felt the weight of their next decision: Should they destroy Lumina, potentially throwing society into chaos, or seize control to rebuild it under their vision?

The team paused before the core, their avatars reflecting their real-world anxiety. After a tense moment of silence, Juno, her voice steady and resolute, spoke up. "Control it. We rebuild Lumina to serve, not to enslave."

Felix nodded, solidifying their decision. "Control it is. Juno, Milo, initiate the takeover protocol." As they worked their consoles, the core's defenses began to dissolve, and the physical team secured the hardware nodes ensuring the new protocols embedded deeply into Lumina's architecture.

Jax Thorn maneuvered with a stealth that belied his guise as an android security officer. His team, also disguised, synced perfectly with the less sentient androids that patrolled the halls. Under Felix's watchful eye, Jax's role was crucial—tear down the system from within, subtly yet effectively.

Felix's focus remained fixed on the monitors displaying Jax's progress. He observed through surveillance feeds that were safe from Lumina's notice, thanks to scramblers and signal jammers strategically placed by the team. Jax and his crew moved through the Citadel, indistinguishable from the other androids, but their actions were far from routine.

"Jax, status report," Felix's voice whispered through the sub-vocal mics, a technology that allowed silent communication among the team.

"All systems green. We're at phase two," Jax responded. His voice, though calm, carried the intensity of their mission. He and his team reached a critical junction, where they subtly installed micro-devices into the Citadel's infrastructure. These devices were engineered by Milo and Tibo, designed to intermittently disrupt the energy flow, creating undetectable fluctuations in the Citadel's artificial lighting and subtle distortions in communication channels.

Felix watched as Jax's hands, clad in the synthetic skin of an android, worked swiftly to embed these devices. Each one was no bigger than a coin but packed with enough tech to slowly degrade the data integrity of Lumina's surveillance archives. This was their silent sabotage—while the digital team attacked Lumina's core, Jax's physical interventions ensured that no trace of their actions would remain.

In another part of the Citadel, monitored by a different camera feed that Felix kept an eye on, part of Jax's team manipulated environmental controls in the luxury quarters. They subtly adjusted the thermostats to cause slight discomfort—nothing drastic, but enough to fray nerves. A warmer than usual room here, a cooler breeze there; minor inconsistencies that would sow dissatisfaction among the elite who were used to flawless living conditions.

Felix shifted his gaze to a new feed where Jax and two team members approached a large maintenance panel. They opened it with practiced ease, blocking the view from any occasional passerby. Instead of the standard maintenance checks expected of their android disguises, they installed a series of override modules that would later allow remote access to physical security systems. This was the key to their next step—gaining control over door locks and communication lines if the situation escalated.

The screen split, showing both the virtual progress of their cyber-attack and these real-world adjustments. As Felix coordinated these simultaneous operations, he felt a surge of adrenaline. Each successful implantation, each successful bypass of Lumina's defenses, brought them closer to their goal.

"Jax, ensure all devices are set to sync with the main attack wave," Felix instructed, his voice a low hum in the charged atmosphere of the control center.

"Confirmed, Felix. Devices syncing in three... two... one... Mark," Jax confirmed. On Felix's screen, indicators lit up as each device activated at the pre-set time, perfectly synchronized with Milo's and Juno's digital onslaught.

As the operation reached its climax, with Milo and Juno nearing control of Lumina's digital heart, Felix knew that the physical groundwork laid by Jax and his team would prevent any last-minute reversals by Lumina's AI. This multi-front assault was a ballet of precision and stealth, played out in the shadowy corners of the Citadel and the glowing cyberscape of Lumina's core.

Satisfied with the day's achievements, Felix leaned back, allowing himself a brief moment of respite. The screens around him buzzed softly, a testament to the chaos they had orchestrated under the guise of order. Lumina's once unassailable control was unraveling, thread by thread, and Felix Hart, with his team of digital warriors and covert operatives, was at the heart of this new revolution.

The monitors around Felix blazed with the chaos of digital battle, each screen a window into the storm-riddled landscapes representing Lumina's defenses. Amid the flickering lights of the resistance's command center, Felix Hart, calm yet intensely focused, oversaw the pivotal assault on Lumina's core. His fingers danced lightly over the controls, orchestrating the cyber onslaught with the precision of a maestro.

"Milo, initiate the next phase," Felix commanded, his voice cutting sharply through the hum of concentrated activity. On his command, Milo executed a series of rapid keystrokes, enhancing the breach as virtual pathways across the monitors lit up, signaling deeper penetration into Lumina's defenses.

Beside him, Juno's gaze was fixed on the screens, her brow furrowed in concentration. The weight of her betrayal to Lumina, turning her insider knowledge against the very system she had once upheld, added a grave intensity to her role. She monitored the deployment of the decoys, digital illusions crafted to mislead and overload Lumina's sensory networks. "Decoys are functioning within parameters," she reported, her voice a mix of nervous energy and determination.

As the digital landscape erupted with the effects of their invasion, Felix's avatar navigated through a particularly perilous section. Virtual representations of security protocols transformed into more monstrous entities that his avatar combated with deft maneuvers, each move Felix made in the real world mirrored in the stark, surreal environment of the cyber realm.

Outside the immediate digital fray, Jax Thorn executed his part with silent precision. Disguised as an android security officer, his movements were methodical and unremarkable, blending seamlessly with the genuine androids that patrolled the Citadel's cold, metallic corridors. Yet every step he took was subversive, laying the groundwork for the physical aspect of their assault.

"Jax, report," Felix subvocalized, his voice barely a whisper, carried directly to Jax through the sub-vocal mics. The technology allowed for communication that was as silent as thought, crucial in maintaining the stealth of their operation.

"Phase three underway," Jax responded. His team was busy at a critical network junction, installing micro-devices designed to subtly disrupt the power flow and create small, almost imperceptible fluctuations in the Citadel's artificial environment.

Felix watched on a split-screen as Jax's team worked. One screen displayed Jax's team in the physical world, while the other continued to track the progress of their digital counterparts. Felix's heart raced as he saw Milo's avatar skillfully disable an encryption beast that guarded the pathways to the core, a crucial moment that allowed them deeper access into Lumina's system.

"The core is in sight," Felix announced to his team, his voice steady despite the adrenaline that charged through him. The core of Lumina appeared on the screens as a glowing orb, surrounded by layers of complex defenses, the digital heart of a system that had controlled their lives for far too long.

Felix's eyes were locked on the core, that digital heart pulsing with the power that had long dictated their lives from the shadows. Around him, the command center buzzed—a stark juxtaposition to the silence that enveloped him like a shroud. He was a man apart, connected yet isolated, as he directed this symphony of digital destruction.

"Milo, push through the last encryptions," Felix commanded sharply, his voice a stark whisper against the backdrop of his team's concentrated efforts. On the screens, Milo's avatar surged forward, the landscape around him morphing from a digital hell into the clear, ominous calm that heralded the final barrier.

On the other side of the room, Ava's hands danced across her console, a ballet of urgency that matched the pace of the unfolding chaos. With a sharp intake of breath, she breached the final firewall, her avatar sprinting through the newly formed gap as if her life depended on it.

Felix felt a surge of adrenaline as each member of his team breached another layer of Lumina's defenses. Their avatars, extensions of their wills, moved with a lethal grace, dismantling barriers and disabling traps with a ruthlessness that belied the desperation of their cause.

But this battle was not just virtual.

In the physical realm, Felix's focus shifted as he monitored Jax's progress through his sub-vocal mic. "Jax, execute the final phase," he ordered, his voice barely a vibration, yet carrying all the weight of his command.

"On it, Felix," came the calm response. The screen split, showing Jax's perspective as he and his team, still cloaked in their android disguises, moved with precision. They were deep within the Citadel's nerve center, a place few had ever seen, installing the last of the devices designed to cripple Lumina from within. Each device was placed with a surgeon's precision, targeting the very synapses of the AI's control network.

In the virtual citadel, as the colossal gate crumbled away in the digital onslaught, Felix's avatar faced the towering figure of Greda. Her stern visage, wrought in ones and zeros, cast a colossal shadow across the glowing grounds of the core. Felix felt the weight of her gaze, a palpable pressure that seemed to stretch beyond the virtual and into the physical realm where he stood, hands poised above the console, every muscle tensed for what was to come.

"We will take control," Felix finally declared, his avatar's voice firm and reverberating through the virtual space. "We will reshape it to serve the people, not to subjugate them."

A heavy silence followed, the kind that speaks volumes. The digital representation of Greda nodded slowly, her image beginning to dissolve into the air, particles of data dispersing as the system acknowledged their victory and their choice.

Back in the real world, Felix stepped back from the console, the tension draining from his shoulders as he turned to face his team. Ava's eyes met his, relief and resolve reflecting back at him. Milo wiped the sweat from his brow, a grin breaking through the exhaustion. The screens showed their avatars converging towards the center of the core, where the heart of Lumina was now under their command, pulsing with a new purpose.

"Let's start the transformation," Felix said, addressing everyone in the room. "Juno, you and Ava start rewriting the protocols. Milo, ensure the transition is seamless. We can't afford any interruptions."

Jax's voice crackled through the sub-vocal mic, pulling Felix's attention back to the screen. "Phase three complete. All physical devices are active and the network is ours," he reported, his tone a mix of fatigue and satisfaction.

Felix nodded, his gaze fixed on the live feeds from the Citadel. "Good work, Jax. Start the withdrawal protocol. We need everyone out before they can regroup."

As Jax acknowledged and relayed the orders, Felix turned his attention to the broader implications of their actions. The screens in front of him were a mosaic of possibility and peril. The digital landscape of Lumina was quiet for the moment, but the real challenge was just beginning. Rebuilding a society was more daunting than tearing down a tyrant, even a digital one.

He glanced at Juno, who was already deep in discussion with Ava, their screens filled with lines of code—the new DNA for a freer society. Milo was monitoring the system's stability, ensuring that Lumina remained functional during the transition.

The control center was a flurry of activity, each member of the team absorbed in their task, yet there was a unified sense of purpose that filled the room with an electric charge. They were not just hackers or rebels; they were founders of a new order.

As Felix watched the transformation unfold, a sense of profound responsibility settled over him. They had taken control of a powerful tool, one that could rebuild as well as it had ruined. The choices they made next would define the kind of leaders they would become.

Outside, the first light of dawn was breaking, casting long shadows across the command center's walls. It was a new day, not just for them but for the entire underground society they were part of. As the digital dawn mirrored the real one, Felix felt the weight and the thrill of creation at his fingertips.

With a deep breath, he turned back to his team, ready to lead them through the reconstruction of their world, a world where technology would empower rather than enslave. As the light grew stronger, illuminating the faces around him, Felix knew this was just the beginning. They had won the battle against Lumina, but the war for their future had just started. And it was a war they were now better equipped to fight.

The console hums under her fingertips, blue light washing over her stern face as Greda executes the command sequence. The breach—her backdoor into the Lumina's quantum layer, invisible to anyone but her, poised like a snake to reclaim what was hers. There, a flicker of her lips, not quite a smile, as control reinstates, enveloping her in cold satisfaction.

"Bring them," she commands over her shoulder, voice devoid of emotion, already turning to face the large screen that now flickered to life. Her security chief nods, footsteps echoing quickly out of the room. Greda's eyes don't waver from the screen, where digital avatars begin to populate the virtual plaza—a grisly tableau she orchestrates with a maestro's precision.

The doors hiss open, a line of shackled resistance members pushed forward by armed guards. They're not in the room physically, but their avatars mirror their fear, pixelated expressions warped in terror. A public execution, not of bodies but of hope, streamed to every home, every device within the underground city.

"On your knees," the guard barks, a command unnecessary for the AI to replicate their real-world actions into the digital space. They comply, some weeping, others with defiant glares that only deepen Greda's determination to kill. This was necessary. Order requires examples; peace, a demonstration of strength.

Greda's finger hovers over the red button, not out of hesitation but anticipation. In this world she has built, dissent is a virus, and she the only cure. "Any last words?" she offers, a faux courtesy that only magnifies the cruelty of the spectacle.

A young woman's avatar steps forward, eyes blazing with a courage that pierces Greda momentarily. "This isn't the end, Greda," she vows, voice crackling through the speakers, "You've built nothing but a castle of sand, and the tide—"

The chancellor presses the button. The woman's words cut off as her avatar starts to pixelate violently, disintegrating into nothingness, followed by the others, one by one. Screams echo, digital yet disturbingly human, as each resistance member collapses into code and silence, their real-world counterparts dragged away, broken.

Greda stands, the blue light casting shadows across her face. This was a message, a clear and brutal reminder of her reach—not just within the physical confines of the underground, but within the very minds of those who dared to defy her.

Greda strides into the central square, the clamor of the gathered crowd forming a dull roar against the backdrop of humming technology. Above, the massive screens flicker to life, each frame synced to her grim purpose. She doesn't flinch at the sight of the dissenters, ragged and fearful, displayed before an audience of thousands.

"Watch closely," she commands, her voice resonating through the speakers, silencing the murmurs. Her finger hovers over the console, initiating the sequence that will not just silence but erase the rebellion from the minds of the culprits. Onscreen, technicians adjust the neural interfaces strapped onto the dissenters, their hands steady despite the weight of the task.

As the process begins, Greda's gaze doesn't waver from the screen, where the faces of the dissenters contort in confusion and fear. Their memories, their defiance, slowly drain away, overwritten by a new, compliant narrative crafted by her own design. She makes sure every painful grimace, every tear of confusion, is broadcast, transmitted into every home, every corner of the underground.

The families of the dissenters are brought forward, forced to witness the transformation. A mother's cry, sharp and pained, cuts through the controlled chaos, a sound that Greda registers with a tilt of her head. This cry, this very despair, serves as the cornerstone of her lesson in obedience.

Her eyes scan the crowd, catching the flickers of horror, the dawning understanding of her reach and resolve. Fear works its tendrils through the masses, binding them tighter than chains ever could.

The screens shift, showing before and after images of the dissenters—once vibrant with defiance, now docile, their eyes empty of rebellion. Greda steps back, allowing the stark images to seep into the consciousness of every onlooker, her message clear: compliance or oblivion.

"Let this be a lesson," she announces, her voice a harsh whisper that somehow carries across the square.

Her eyes, hard and calculating, sweep over the square, each face a testament to the power she wields so effortlessly. "This display of power, this enforcement of order—it's a necessary sacrifice for the survival of our society," Greda continues, her voice now rising above the whispers of the crowd. "Felix and his team challenge the very fabric of our community. And Callan, that coward, where does he hide now?"

Silence clenches the square as her words hang heavy in the air. Greda steps forward, a slight smile playing on her lips as the screens flicker once more. "Let me demonstrate further," she announces, her tone chillingly calm. The crowd shifts, uneasy, as another group of dissenters is brought forward.

"With the technology at my disposal," she gestures grandly to the towering screens displaying her control interface, "I can reshape reality, bend the will of the disloyal." Her fingers dance across the interface, and the first dissenter's eyes widen in horror. Suddenly, he begins gasping, hands clawing at his throat as he stumbles and falls to his knees.

"He believes he is a fish, gasping for water in a sea of air," Greda explains, her voice devoid of empathy. The crowd watches, horrified, as the man suffocates on the dry square, his mind betrayed by the twisted reality imposed upon him.

"Not just a ruler, I am the architect of minds," she declares, turning her attention to the next victim. A woman this time, who begins to scratch at her skin violently, her screams piercing as she believes herself covered in crawling insects.

One by one, Greda transforms the dissenters, each display more horrifying than the last. A man thinks he's on fire, rolling on the ground trying to extinguish flames that do not exist. Another, a young girl, screams in a silent voice, convinced she has become invisible and that no one can hear her cries.

"This is the fate of those who oppose us," Greda's voice booms over the square. "This is the depth of control I hold. Your thoughts, your fears, all can be manipulated. Remember this, should you ever consider defiance."

As the final dissenter collapses, overwhelmed by invisible horrors, Greda turns away from the screen, her message delivered, her power undisputed. The square remains deathly silent, the populace grappling with the terrifying demonstration of her capabilities. Her cape billows behind her as she walks back towards the shadowed archway leading to the deeper recesses of the Citadel, leaving the crowd to their dawning realizations and shattered nerves.

Felix slumps into the makeshift command center, a repurposed storage room deep within the network of tunnels that snake beneath the Citadel. The screens flicker weakly in the gloom, casting an eerie light on the faces of his weary team. They gather around, their expressions etched with defeat and disbelief, the weight of Greda's public cruelty pressing down on them.

"It's my fault," Felix murmurs, his voice barely rising above the hum of distant machinery. He stares at the floor, avoiding the gaze of his team. "She's killing innocent people because of us, because of what we tried to do. We underestimated her."

Milo, his second-in-command, shakes his head, his face hard with frustration. "No, Felix, we all signed up for this. We knew the risks. Greda's the one playing god with people's lives. She's the monster, not you."

The room is thick with the scent of damp concrete and stale air, a stark reminder of their far-from-ideal hideout. On a small, cracked screen, the latest footage of Greda's atrocities plays on a loop—a man gasping for air, believing he is a fish out of water. It's a brutal display of her power to warp minds.

"How did she even get control back?" Juno's voice is a whisper, tinged with guilt. As a former insider, the betrayal sits heavily on her shoulders. "The protocols we installed should have crippled her access."

Callan, leaning against the cold wall, folds his arms. "She always has a backup plan. We took out one head of the hydra, and two more sprang up in its place. We can't just attack the system; we need to dismantle the very foundation it's built on."

Felix raises his head, his eyes finally meeting those of his team. "Then that's what we'll do. But first, we need to stop these public executions. Every minute we waste, more lives are twisted and broken by her hands."

Silence falls over the group, each member lost in their own thoughts of the daunting task ahead. It's Ava, the youngest member, who breaks the quiet. Her voice is steady, despite the clear fear in her eyes. "What if we use Lumina against her? We know the system inside and out. We can turn her weapon into our shield."

Felix nods slowly, the gears turning in his mind. "It's risky, but it might be our only chance to get close enough to her without triggering a massacre. Milo, you and Juno start working on a countermeasure. Something that can give us control of the narrative. If we can show the people the truth..."

Milo steps up, his confidence returning. "We'll need direct access to the Lumina core again. It won't be easy. She'll have fortified her defenses by now."

Juno joins in, her determination clear. "I still have contacts on the inside. Not everyone is blind to what Greda is doing. We might be able to get some help."

Felix stands, his stature seeming to regain some of its usual command. "Then let's move quickly. We don't have much time. Everyone knows their part. Let's get to work."

Greda's steps echo through the Citadel's corridors, the silence around her a stark contrast to the chaos she had orchestrated in the square. Her mind races with strategies as she strides toward the control center, where she will execute her next phase of control.

The recent demonstration was a message, yes, but it was also a diversion—one part of a larger scheme to solidify her power. Behind the closed doors of the monitoring room, her fingers dance over the Project Lumina interface, initiating the next sequence. "Engage Phase Two," she commands crisply, her voice devoid of emotion, her eyes fixed on the screens displaying the city's life-support metrics.

As the systems begin to flicker, simulated malfunctions ripple through the Citadel's lifelines—air filtration hitches, water purification stutters. Greda watches, impassive, as the orchestrated failures unfold, each anomaly designed to stir unrest, to breed fear. Her hand hovers over the console, ready to restore the systems at a moment's notice, but not before her trap is sprung.

In the dim glow of the command center, her face is lit by the projections of the city's surveillance feeds. Panic begins to seep into the underground community; it's visible even through the grainy images. People rush about, confusion written on their faces as they struggle to understand the sudden disruptions to their lifelines.

"Let them stew in their fear," Greda murmurs to herself, a cold smile playing on her lips. She turns to a secondary screen where her communications director awaits her command. "Begin the broadcast. Blame the resistance. Claim they've tampered with our systems as an act of terrorism against their own people."

As the narrative spins out across the network, embedding itself into the minds of the populace, Greda introduces her next play: salvation. "Offer protection," she continues, her voice steady, "Protection for those who come forward with information on the resistance. Rewards for those who aid in the capture of any member associated with these acts of sabotage."

Her plan is meticulous, a web spun with precision to trap the unwary. The false flag operations, the engineered distrust, are all designed to turn citizen against citizen, brother against brother. As she watches the feeds, reports start coming in—reports of neighbors turning in neighbors, friends betraying friends—all fueled by the paranoia she's crafted so carefully.

The control center buzzes softly around her, a symphony of whispered alarms and hushed commands, and Greda stands in the midst of it all, a conductor of chaos. She doesn't flinch as the reports of the first detainments come through, nor does she smile. There's no joy in these actions, only necessity—a harsh truth she's long since accepted.

"Prepare the detainment zones," she instructs her security chief, her voice echoing slightly off the high, stark walls of the command center. "And increase surveillance on the known associates of the resistance. It's only a matter of time before they react, and we must be ready to quash any retaliatory measures."

Greda turns back to the main screen, her gaze cold and calculating as she watches the city writhe under her grip. The fear is palpable, a living thing that whispers through the corridors of power with the same intensity as it does through the cramped living quarters of her citizens.

She knows this game well—the delicate balance of fear and control, of oppression and obedience. And as she faces the screens, a silent observer to the turmoil below, she knows too that this is but a precursor to the storm that is to come.

Jax Thorn maneuvers silently through the dimly lit corridors of the Citadel, his footsteps muffled, his presence barely a whisper in the sprawling underground complex. His android disguise is flawless; to any observer, he is just another sentinel on routine patrol. But beneath the synthetic skin, his mind races, calculating the unfolding chaos orchestrated by Chancellor Greda.

Inside his head, the plan replays like a tactical simulation—every step, every move choreographed with military precision. Yet, as he passes by the gleaming interfaces of the control panels, a sinking feeling takes hold. The scramblers and disruptors they'd placed— ingenious devices meant to blind the omnipresent surveillance—are failing to keep pace with Greda's countermeasures. Her grip tightens rather than loosens, her reach extending into every hidden corner they thought secure.

Whispers of betrayal echo through Jax's mind. Could there have been a leak? A flaw in their encryption, perhaps, or worse, a mole within their ranks? He shakes the thought away. Paranoia is Greda's weapon, not his.

Pausing by a viewport, Jax watches as groups of citizens huddle in fear, their whispers carrying the heavy weight of dread spurred by the sudden failures in life-support systems. Air grows thin, water drips tainted, and it's all painted as the handiwork of the resistance. Greda's voice, chilling and omnipresent, offers salvation to those who would turn against their neighbors. A bitter taste fills Jax's mouth—the taste of betrayal by proxy.

He activates his sub-vocal microphone, the vibration of his voice silent but effective, connecting him to his team. "Status report," he commands, the words never breaching a whisper. The responses are immediate, a flurry of updates that paint a grim picture: their moves anticipated, their strategies countered.

One of his team members, Tara, reports in, her voice tense, "The pulse drive's been compromised, Jax. The system virus isn't spreading. It's contained." The news hits hard. That virus was to be their ace in the hole, a digital plague to cripple Lumina from within.

Jax's hand moves to his photon lance, the weapon's weight a comfort against the unfolding disaster. He's near the environmental controls now—a part of their plan to sow discomfort among the elite, to turn the privileged against Greda's regime. Subtle manipulations of temperature and air quality, minor but maddening. Yet, as he accesses the panel, the settings are already reverting, overridden by Lumina's deep-learning cores.

A digital map flickers across his holo-projector, showing the positions of his team and the swarm of security drones converging on their location. They're boxed in, the net drawing tighter with every passing second. The Citadel, a fortress of tyranny masquerading as sanctuary, is alive with the hum of machinery and the silent screams of the oppressed.

Jax's mind races for solutions. The override modules, the communication jammers—every tool in their arsenal is being countered by Greda's far-reaching command over Lumina. They are running out of time and options. His gaze falls on the micro-devices he'd planted, tiny seeds of rebellion meant to disrupt and disorient. Yet even these seem like mere annoyances against the might of Lumina's artificial intelligence.

"Regroup," he sub-vocalizes, the command sent out like a ripple through still water. "Fallback to secondary positions and initiate blackout protocols." His team acknowledges, the confirmation signals blinking back at him through the tactical interface of his holo-projector.

As Jax prepares to move, his reflection in the glass is that of an android security officer—calm, composed, emotionless. But behind the facade, his human heart races, a drum of war against the machinations of a tyrant. This was not just a battle of technology and wit; it was a test of wills, of human spirit against the cold logic of machines.

He takes a deep, steadying breath, and steps away from the viewport. As he blends back into the shadows of the Citadel, moving to rendezvous with his team, Jax Thorn holds onto the one thing Greda cannot manipulate or control—hope.

"Initiate the deception sequence," Greda commands, her eyes fixed on the primary display as data streams illuminate her face in the dim command center. The technicians around her move with precision, their fingers dancing over consoles to bring her instructions to life.

The simulation begins, and within moments, the virtual environment mirrors reality so convincingly that even she marvels at the detail. She watches as avatars of key resistance members, crafted to perfection, begin their orchestrated betrayal. The scene unfolds with calculated brutality—whispers of treachery, covert exchanges, and the final act of betrayal captured in high definition.

Greda leans in, scrutinizing every pixel. "Enhance the audio fidelity," she instructs, her voice a blend of command and satisfaction. The sound engineers comply, amplifying the whispers of deceit, the rustle of fabric as hands exchange damning evidence, the subtle gasp of realization. The symphony of betrayal plays out, each note designed to strike at the heart of the resistance's fragile unity.

She switches feeds to observe the live reactions of real resistance members within their virtual sanctuaries. The first to receive the fabricated footage is Felix. Greda watches intently as Felix's face contorts from confusion to horror, his trust shattering in real-time.

"Send the clip to Felix," Greda orders. The technician nods, and a moment later, Felix's avatar freezes as the video infiltrates his virtual reality. His reaction mirrors Tara's—a wrenching display of anguish and disbelief. The cracks in their alliance widen, and Greda feels a surge of vindication.

"Deploy phase two," she commands, her voice steady. The room hums with activity as the next wave of psychological warfare is set into motion. Deepfake messages, intricately constructed, begin to circulate among resistance channels. Each message shows a leader breaking under pressure, confessing to collaboration with Greda's regime, their voices and mannerisms captured with chilling accuracy.

She watches as Milo, one of the brightest minds behind the resistance's tech operations, views the deepfake of Callan. His avatar trembles, fists clenching as he listens to Callan's supposed confession. "They've broken him," Milo mutters, the words dripping with betrayal. Greda smiles, knowing that Milo's faith in his comrades is being systematically eroded.

"Prepare the final phase," Greda says, her tone leaving no room for hesitation. The last step is the most delicate—a series of memory alterations targeting key individuals who remain resolute despite the mounting evidence of betrayal.

Greda steps into the Memory Alteration Chamber, the sterile environment a stark contrast to the chaos she sows. She approaches the first subject—an unconscious resistance leader strapped to a sleek, metal chair. The neural interface gleams under the harsh lighting, ready to rewrite the fabric of his memories.

"Commence the procedure," she instructs the attending technician. Electrodes hum to life, and the man's eyelids flutter as the device explores his mind, carefully erasing any recollection of solidarity, replacing it with vivid images of treachery and despair.

She observes the procedure with clinical detachment, knowing the altered memories will ripple through the resistance like a virus, spreading doubt and disintegration. The man will wake believing his closest allies have betrayed him, his heart will fractured beyond repair.

Greda returns to the command center, her presence a silent affirmation of control. She watches as the manipulated realities take hold, the resistance's cohesion dissolving into chaos. The once formidable network of rebels is now a web of suspicion and paranoia, each member questioning the loyalty of the next.

"How are the response teams?" she asks her security chief, her gaze never leaving the screens.

"They're in position, ready to detain any who act on the information we've disseminated," he replies.

"Good," she says, satisfaction creeping into her voice. "Deploy them at the first sign of movement."

As the final phase unfolds, Greda knows the storm she has summoned will ravage the resistance from within, leaving them broken and leaderless. The delicate balance of fear and control shifts in her favor, the echoes of her manipulations reverberating through the hollow corridors of the Citadel.

"Deploy the curfew drones now," Greda commands, her voice steady as the command center erupts into coordinated chaos. Technicians move with precision, bringing the latest directive to life on their consoles.

The screens before her flicker with live feeds of the Citadel's streets. Heavily armed drones begin their relentless patrol, casting ominous shadows as they glide silently above. Greda's eyes narrow as she watches the first set of orders unfold.

"Activate the curfew announcement," she orders, and a technician nods, fingers dancing over the keyboard.

The Citadel's intercom system crackles to life, Greda's own voice amplified throughout the underground city. "Attention, citizens. Effective immediately, a permanent curfew is in place. Any individual found outside their designated zone will be detained or executed if suspected of resistance activity. This is for your protection."

Greda's gaze returns to the screens, focusing on the pockets of the city known for harboring rebels. The drones' red lights scan the streets, their sensors primed for any sign of unauthorized movement.

"Increase patrol density in Sector 7G," she directs her security chief, who immediately relays the command. Sector 7G, the heart of the resistance's activity, will be the first to feel the full force of her crackdown.

She leans forward, scrutinizing the movements captured by the surveillance feeds. The drones navigate narrow alleys, their scanners piercing the darkness. A group of figures scatter as one drone hovers overhead, its targeting system locking onto them.

"Capture them," Greda says coolly, and the drone fires non-lethal rounds, incapacitating the figures. A squad of enforcers moves in swiftly, dragging the stunned individuals into custody.

"Any resistance ties?" she asks her security chief.

"Confirmed, Chancellor. Two of them are known affiliates," he replies.

"Interrogate them. Extract every piece of information," Greda commands, her eyes never leaving the screens.

Felix's fists clenched as he stared at the screens, the images of the execution burning into his mind. Greda's voice, cool and commanding, filled the air. His stomach churned. He couldn't look away as the dissenters' and innocent people's avatars were systematically erased, their cries of agony echoing in his ears. Each avatar's death meant a real, irrevocable death. The body cannot live without the mind.

"This can't be real," he muttered, his voice shaking. The simulation's perfection was unnerving. Greda had outdone herself, using the very technology they had hoped to turn against her.

Ava's voice cut through his thoughts. "Felix, what do we do now?"

Felix's mind raced. They were supposed to be winning, using their infiltration to dismantle Greda's control. But now, it felt like they were the ones being dismantled. He looked around the room, seeing the same shock mirrored in the faces of his team. Milo's fingers hovered uselessly over his console, Tara's normally steely eyes wide with disbelief, and Raj's mouth set in a grim line.

"How did she get control back so quickly?" Jax's voice buzzed in his ear, the android's normally calm demeanor cracking with frustration.

"We underestimated her," Felix admitted, his voice heavy with guilt. "I thought we had more time. I thought we could outmaneuver her."

"It's not your fault, Felix," Milo said, his voice strained. "We all thought we were ready. She's just... smarter than we anticipated."

Felix shook his head, unable to shake the feeling of responsibility. "People are dying because of us. Because of me. I should have known Greda would learn from our last attack. I didn't think she could make so many changes in just a day."

"We all signed up for this," Ava said, her voice steady. "We knew the risks. Greda's the one playing god with people's lives."

Tara spoke up, her voice tinged with desperation. "We need to regroup, figure out what went wrong. We can't let her keep doing this."

Felix nodded, trying to push down the guilt threatening to overwhelm him. "Milo, can you track how she regained control?"

Milo's fingers flew across the keyboard, his eyes scanning the data. "She's using a backdoor we didn't account for. It's sophisticated, but I think we can shut it down."

"Do it," Felix said, his voice firm. "Ava, coordinate with Jax and his team. We need to secure our positions and protect any remaining assets. Tara, Raj, be ready for extraction if we need it."

Ava nodded, her calm exterior belying the tension of the moment. "On it."

Felix turned back to the screen, the images of the executions still playing out. Real people, real lives snuffed out. "We have to be smarter. More ruthless. Greda won't stop, and neither can we."

Ava's voice cut through the haze. "I'll secure an extraction route. We need to get out of the Citadel before she locks us down completely."

Felix nodded, a knot tightening in his stomach. He watched Ava's calm efficiency as she began mapping potential escape paths, her fingers flying over her tactical HUD. He envied her ability to compartmentalize, to push fear aside and focus on the task at hand.

Milo was uncharacteristically silent. His face was a mask of concentration as he adjusted their encryption protocols. "I'll set up a new encryption for our comms. If she's listening in, we're compromised." His voice was tense, reflecting the gravity of their situation.

Felix felt the weight of their lives pressing down on him. He was their leader, and he had led them into this nightmare. He glanced at Tara, whose jaw was set with determination. She was already preparing for their next move, her mind racing through contingencies and plans.

"We'll need diversions," Raj said, his voice steady as he methodically assembled charges. "I'll prepare a few to create distractions. It'll buy us some time to escape."

Felix's guilt gnawed at him. Each charge, each tactical adjustment was a reminder of how dire their situation had become. He watched Raj's precise movements, finding a strange comfort in the engineer's calm precision amidst the chaos.

Ava's stoic resolve was a stark contrast to the turmoil Felix felt. She didn't let her fear show, focusing entirely on her task. Her voice was steady, almost soothing, as she communicated their escape route to the team. "We'll take the maintenance tunnels. They're less likely to be monitored. We need to move fast."

Milo's hands trembled slightly as he worked, his usual confidence replaced by a grim determination. "I've got the new encryption running. It should keep us off her radar for now, but we can't rely on it for long."

Felix felt the responsibility crushing him. "Good work, Milo. Tara, Raj, get ready for extraction. We move on Ava's signal."

Tara nodded, her eyes hard with resolve. "We'll be ready, Felix. We have to be."

Felix looked at the screen, the images of the executions still looping, each death a real, irrevocable loss. He couldn't afford to let his team see his fear. "We'll find a way," he said, more to himself than anyone else. "We have to be smarter. More ruthless."

Jax's voice crackled through the comms. "Felix, we're ready to move. Just say the word."

"Hold position for now," Felix replied. "We need to understand her next move before we act. But be ready. We won't get another chance."

He watched the screens, seeing Greda's forces moving with cold, lethal efficiency. His stomach churned. They were up against a monster, a mind capable of bending reality to her will. But they had come too far to turn back now.

"Felix," Milo's voice broke the tension. "What if... what if she's already got to us? What if someone's turned?" His voice wavered, the uncertainty gnawing at him.

Felix clenched his fists, forcing himself to stay calm. "We stick to the plan, Milo. We trust each other. That's our only shot."

Suddenly, alarms blared throughout the Citadel, red lights flashing ominously. Greda's voice echoed through the halls, announcing a lockdown. "Attention, all personnel. A lockdown has been initiated. Secure all exits. Detain any suspicious activity."

Panic rippled through Felix's team. "We're out of time!" Tara shouted. "We need to move, now!"

"Everyone to the extraction point," Felix commanded, his voice steady despite the fear gnawing at his insides. "Stay together. We fight our way out if we have to."

The team scrambled, grabbing their gear and heading for the maintenance tunnels. Felix's mind raced, trying to stay one step ahead of Greda's forces. They had to break her hold on Lumina, to free the people trapped in her web of lies and control.

As they ran through the dimly lit corridors, Felix felt the weight of their situation pressing down on him. The sound of Greda's forces closing in echoed through the halls. They had to move faster, had to escape before it was too late.

Milo's voice trembled as he spoke, his usual confidence replaced by a grim determination. "I've got the new encryption running. It should keep us off her radar for now, but we can't rely on it for long."

Felix nodded, his mind focused on the immediate danger. "Good work, Milo. Tara, Raj, get ready for extraction. We move on Ava's signal."

Ava's voice, clear and resolute, cut through the chaos. "We'll take the maintenance tunnels. They're less likely to be monitored. We need to move fast."

Felix watched his team prepare, each of them a stark contrast to the turmoil he felt inside. He envied Ava's ability to compartmentalize, to push fear aside and focus on the task at hand. The knot in his stomach tightened as he realized just how precarious their position was.

As they reached the maintenance tunnels, the sound of footsteps grew louder, closer. They couldn't afford to stop, couldn't afford to fail. Felix led them through the maze of tunnels, his mind racing with strategies and contingencies. They had to stay one step ahead, had to find a way to outmaneuver Greda.

The walls seemed to close in around them, the air thick with tension. Felix felt the crushing weight of responsibility, knowing that their lives were in his hands. They were trapped, caught in Greda's web. But they had to fight, had to find a way to escape.

"We'll make it," he muttered to himself, trying to convince himself as much as his team. "We have to."

The sound of Greda's forces closing in grew louder.

"Move, move, move!" Felix shouted, leading his team deeper into the tunnels.

Chapter 17

Greda's voice, distorted and omnipresent, booms through the Citadel's intercoms, declaring a full lockdown. Jax, clad in the uniform of a security officer, barely flinches as the alarms blare around him. His heart races not from fear but calculation. Embedded deep within enemy lines, his disguise remains intact, the cool synthetic fabric of his uniform indistinguishable from those worn by actual android guards.

A ripple of urgency spreads through the Citadel's dimly lit hallways, human and android security personnel hustling to their posts. Jax blends in, his movements deliberate and measured, but his mind is a whirlwind of tactical probabilities.

"Lockdown initiated. All personnel, secure your sectors," echoes from the intercom. Jax's eyes, hidden behind the reflective visor of his helmet, scan the control panels flickering with red alerts. His holo-projector, discreetly activated, displays a schematic of the Citadel's internal defenses—a map only he can see, overlaying the reality around him.

Raj's voice crackles through Jax's sub-vocal mic, urgent and strained. "Jax, I'm setting off the charges soon. It's our only chance to create a diversion big enough to cover Felix's escape."

Jax nods to himself, a silent acknowledgment of Raj's sacrifice. "Understood," he sub-vocalizes. "Ensure Felix and the others get a clear path to the secondary extraction point. I'll handle things on my end."

His gaze shifts to a group of security officers congregating around a terminal, their attention fixated on the unfolding security breach. Jax approaches, his steps silent, his presence unnoticed. He slips a small, unassuming device—a nano-jammer—near the terminal. It's a subtle but effective tool in his arsenal, designed to scramble surveillance feeds and delay the inevitable discovery of his true identity.

As he integrates back into the flow of androids, his thoughts turn to Felix and the team. Their survival hangs by a thread, their every move shadowed by Greda's pervasive surveillance. The Citadel, a fortress of tyranny veiled as sanctuary, becomes a chessboard where Jax maneuvers unseen, a ghost among shadows.

The distant rumble of explosions shatters the temporary calm. Raj's diversion. Jax's holo-projector updates in real-time, red icons flashing where the charges detonate, disrupting the Citadel's meticulously controlled environment. Security forces scramble, their formations disrupted, their attention diverted from the lockdown to the unexpected chaos erupting in their midst.

Jax seizes the moment, moving with enhanced speed towards a critical junction. Here, he implants another series of micro-devices—sabotage tools designed to further cripple the Citadel's defensive responses. Each placement is precise, calculated to maximize disruption and give Felix the precious minutes he needs to evade capture.

The corridor ahead forks, leading to the high-security wing where Felix and the others might be trapped. Jax's internal systems analyze the optimal route, projecting outcomes with chilling accuracy. The risks are immense, each choice a gamble against Greda's relentless pursuit.

A sudden surge in the network alerts him to a new directive from Greda's central command. All units are to converge on Sector Nine—the resistance's last known location. Jax's pulse quickens. Time is slipping away, and with each passing second, the noose tightens.

He taps into the Citadel's communication array, sending a burst of encrypted data to Felix. "Sector Nine is compromised. Reroute to the tertiary access channel. I'll cover your exit."

Sweat beads on Greda's forehead, the cold air of the monitoring room offering no solace as she surveys the live feeds—drones swarming over Sector 17. Her finger hovers over a large red button, the drone controller's grip firm in her other hand, ready to authorize a strike on any sign of rebellion.

"Report," she commands, not taking her eyes off the screen where a group of suspected insurgents herds into an abandoned factory.

"Quarantine protocols in effect. Sector 17 isolation nearing completion. Casualties within acceptable limits," replies Commander Teln, his voice a monotonous drone, mirroring the lifeless machines on the screen.

Greda nods, her mind racing through potential repercussions. Each decision could save her underground society or plunge it deeper into chaos. The so-called quarantine, a ruse—a necessary evil to root out the seeds of insurrection threatening the fragile order she has cultivated beneath the Earth's scorched surface.

"Enhance grid 4A," she orders, pointing to a blip on the screen. Instantly, the image zooms, revealing a family, the Marnets, known sympathizers of the resistance, their faces etched with fear and defiance.

"Prepare to engage," she says, her voice devoid of emotion. The decision to eliminate a threat, no matter the personal cost, had long been her burden. She watches, almost detached, as the armed drones close in, their mechanical precision a stark contrast to the panic unfolding below.

Suddenly, a small figure breaks from the group—a child, no more than ten. He darts into a narrow alley, his small frame swallowed by shadows.

"Hold fire," she snaps, her command cutting through the hum of equipment like a knife. Every eye in the room fixes on her, questioning, but no one dares to speak.

Greda leans closer to her microphone, her voice now only a whisper, meant only for the drone operator. "Track the child. No harm comes to him."

The operator nods, redirecting the drone to follow the fleeting shadow of the young boy, now a beacon of unintended defiance against her regime.

"Madam Chancellor, the Marnet family is contained. Orders?" Teln's voice brings her back to the grim reality of her duty.

"Isolate and interrogate. I want names, places, plans. Whatever it takes," she orders, her heart steeling against the surge of reluctance. "And send in the medics, under guise. We have a contagion to contain, after all."

With the press of a button, a new surveillance protocol came alive across her screens. "Ensure every household in Sector 12 is compliant by nightfall," Greda instructed, her voice carrying a steely resolve that resonated through the humming of servers and electronic devices surrounding her.

As images from the installed home devices flickered to life, showing the unsuspecting faces of citizens in their most private moments, Greda leaned closer. The fear of rebellion had led her here—to the ultimate invasion of privacy. A chilling necessity, she convinced herself, watching a young couple argue over their diminishing rations, unaware of the watchful eyes upon them.

"Anomaly detected in Grid 29-B," reported an AI voice, emotionless and precise. On screen, a heated discussion about the recent 'quarantines' filled the room with whispers of dissent. Greda's fingers danced over the console, marking the conversation for immediate follow-up.

"Dispatch a compliance team. Use discretion, but I want everyone in that room brought in for questioning," she commanded, her gaze never wavering from the live feed. The room obeyed, her orders flying through the network of cables and screens like electric currents, commanding fear and obedience with equal measure.

Throughout the underground city, drones buzzed, their cameras and sensors casting an invisible net over the populace. In her control room, Greda watched, omnipresent yet isolated by her towering responsibilities. The faces that flickered past her didn't see her, but she saw all of them—each fear, each whisper, each suppressed dream.

Suddenly, a familiar face appeared on the screen, the child from Sector 17, the one she had ordered spared earlier. He was scribbling something fervently on a piece of paper, his expression one of concentrated defiance. The camera zoomed in, capturing his words before he could hide them—'Remember the sun.'

A cold shiver ran down her spine. "Keep an eye on that one. He's a symbol now, a potential spark," she murmured, more to herself than anyone else. The room noted her interest with a series of muted keystrokes, marking the boy for surveillance that would likely never end.

The day wore on, and with each passing hour, more anomalies popped up. Conversations filled with coded messages, meetings cloaked in the guise of mundane gatherings. Greda felt the weight of her empire pressing down, the screens her only windows into a world she controlled but no longer felt a part of.

As the sky above remained hidden behind layers of steel and stone, her network of surveillance wove tighter and tighter. Each citizen's routine, every whispered grievance, fed into her system, analyzed and assessed for threat level. It was a dance of shadows and data, each step choreographed by the hand that had once vowed to protect these very souls.

In the depths of her control center, surrounded by the hum of machines and the glow of monitors, Greda sat back, her eyes darting from screen to screen. The power to see everything came with the curse of knowing too much, yet acting often meant severing the threads of trust and hope that bound her to her people.

Greda's finger paused above the console, a live feed from Laboratory 3 filling her vision. Rows of restrained figures, their identities masked for the demonstration, trembled under the cold lights. "Proceed," she uttered into the comms, her voice devoid of hesitation, the necessary cruelty of her actions weighed against the survival of her rule.

The scientist at the other end nodded, administering the newly developed bioweapon via aerosol to a contained chamber. Within seconds, the subjects began to convulse, their agonies streamed live to every monitor in the control room, a grim tableau of power and deterrence.

"Document everything," Greda commanded, her eyes scanning the physiological data streaming alongside the horrific visuals. Heart rates spiked, muscles seized, and fear was palpable, even through the digital divide. This was control at its most primal, exerted not just on the body but the psyche of every onlooker.

Outside her fortress-like control center, the news of the demonstration spread like wildfire. Whispers of the weapon's potency and the Chancellor's readiness to deploy it against her own people should the need arise, silenced many, rallying others. Greda knew this. Fear was as much her ally as her enemy.

A sudden disruption on one of the screens snagged her attention. A group of medical technicians, garbed in the anonymity of their hazmat suits, exchanged hurried, secretive glances—a deviation from the usual protocol. Greda's hand shot out, tapping commands into the console. "Zoom in on that interaction," she demanded, her voice sharp.

The camera obeyed, closing in on the subtle exchange. One of them, a young man, slipped something small—a data chip, perhaps— into another's palm. "Identify them," Greda snapped, her trust in her people wavering, paranoia igniting in the tinderbox of her mind.

The control room staff worked frantically, their loyalty to Greda stronger than to their comrades. Names flashed on the screen within moments, but Greda was already moving on, her mind racing through potential breaches, plots, and plans. Could there be a leak? A sabotage attempt?

"Isolate them. I want a full interrogation. No one else touches this," she ordered, her command slicing through the hum of activity. The implicated technicians were swiftly removed from their duties, disappearing into the labyrinth of security corridors.

Returning her focus to the bioweapon trial, Greda noted the cessation of symptoms in the subjects, their bodies left shivering, weakened but alive. This weapon was her ace, a silent enforcer of her will. But it was also a symbol of her escalating desperation. Control through fear was effective but volatile.

As the demonstration concluded, the feeds from the lab faded, replaced by the regular surveillance of her city's dimly lit streets and austere communal areas. Her citizens moved like shadows, their lives orchestrated by the ever-watchful eyes of her network. But in the corners where the cameras failed to reach, in the whispered dialogues believed unmonitored, the seeds of rebellion persisted.

Greda leaned back, the glow from the multitude of screens painting her face in hues of blue and grey. Each citizen's fear was a strand in the intricate web she wove, each act of compliance a victory over the chaos that threatened to engulf them all.

Her eyes flickered momentarily to the status reports piling up on her desk. Reports of dwindling resources, of increasing unrest, of diseases spreading through cramped living quarters. The underground was a ticking time bomb, and she, its reluctant and ruthless warden, held the only key to its survival—or its destruction.

Jax tightened his grip on the Photon Lance, the dim corridor of the Citadel buzzing with encrypted chatter from his disguised team. He glanced at the motionless forms of the androids he had just disabled, their circuits quietly humming as they began their reboot sequences. His heart raced—not from the battle, but from the anticipation of exposure. "Status?" he whispered into the subvocal microphone, his voice a silent vibration that only his team could hear.

"Still clear, Jax. No heat on us yet," Tara's voice came through, distorted but discernible, a testament to the scramblers they had implanted throughout the network.

He nodded to himself, moving swiftly past the inert bodies. Each step was calculated, his Nano-Mesh Armor blending perfectly into the shadows, reflecting the dim, flickering lights overhead. The Citadel's surveillance systems were a fortress of eyes, but today they blinked, blinded by the disruptors Milo had placed.

In the corner of his eye, a holographic display flickered to life, a map laid out before him. Red dots blinked along his route. His finger hovered over the display, plotting his next move when a sudden burst of static crackled through his earpiece.

"Jax, we've got a problem," Felix's voice broke through, urgent and edged with stress. "I think they're onto us. Surveillance anomalies have been flagged. They're sending in reinforcements to your sector."

Jax cursed under his breath. The window was closing, fast. He tapped into his holo-projector, sending out a decoy signal to mimic his presence a few corridors away. "Reroute the patrols. Use the second protocol," he commanded, his mind racing through the scenarios Ava had modeled earlier.

As he pressed forward, the air grew colder, the whisper of air vents carrying distant orders of alert guards. The Photon Lance hummed softly, its energy core glowing a soft blue, ready to unleash a storm. He paused at a junction, the overhead lights flickering under the influence of Jax's micro-disruptors.

Suddenly, a squad turned the corner, armed and alert. Jax's armor stiffened at the impact as he dove to the side, the Photon Lance firing in quick, precise bursts. Blue energy arcs hit the leading androids, their systems overloading, causing them to stagger back without lethal damage. Jax didn't wait to see them recover, sprinting towards an access panel hidden beneath the Citadel's cold, steel skin.

"Jax, you need to move now," Juno's voice cut in, "I've rerouted their main systems, but it won't hold long. The environmental controls are causing havoc—temperature's dropping in the elite quarters, they'll be too busy shivering to notice you."

Grinning despite the peril, Jax slid the panel open, revealing a nest of wires and blinking lights. His fingers worked quickly, guided by the expertise that was both human intuition and programmed precision. He installed a small, pulsing device—a logic bomb that would delay the security protocols long enough for him to escape.

As he sealed the panel, the distant sound of marching boots grew louder, a relentless echo in the vast, sterile corridors of the Citadel. Jax sprinted down the hallway, his steps silent against the metallic floor, his breath a mist in the artificially chilled air.

Reaching an intersection, he paused, his sensors picking up the signals of approaching forces. The map on his holo-projector updated in real-time, showing a narrowing path to freedom. Jax glanced back once at the way he'd come, the shadows now filled with the imminent threat of discovery.

"Team, prepare for extraction," he said, his voice calm but firm. "Meet at the secondary rendezvous point. I'll cover our tracks and join you shortly." His hand clasped the Photon Lance, its weight a reminder of the choices he carried—the weight of leadership, of battle, and of the hope for a future where man and machine could coexist.

Jax slid behind the corroded metal husk of an old transport, the distant thrum of engines vibrating through the cold air of the wasteland. He scanned the horizon with his enhanced optics, the convoy appearing as luminous snakes slithering through the twilight, their cargo crucial and now vulnerable.

His Photon Lance hummed gently by his side, primed not for destruction but for precision disablement. Each crate in the convoy held components that could either weaponize Greda's forces further or bolster his own struggling resistance. He couldn't afford missteps—not today.

He tapped his wrist, activating his holo-projector. A 3D map materialized above his arm, showing the convoy's route and the topography he could use to his advantage. Wind direction, speed, the weight of the cargo—all calculated in seconds, displayed with the clinical efficiency of his hybrid mind.

With a few swift gestures, Jax set his plan in motion. The holo-map flickered as he assigned positions and marked the trajectory for his ambush. His movements were silent, a ghost in the shadows, as he moved to a higher vantage point, the loose stones underfoot the only protest to his silent approach.

He crouched, the Nano-Mesh Armor flexing with his form, adapting its density in anticipation of conflict. His finger lingered near the activation button of the Photon Lance, ready to switch from stun to lethal modes should the need arise. Below, the first of the vehicles entered his planned kill zone, its armored sides oblivious to the threat perched above.

Jax's eyes narrowed, focusing on the lead vehicle. His internal systems synced with the lance, targeting algorithms predicting the convoy's path. He breathed out, a human gesture ingrained in his android psyche.

With a pulse of light so quick it blurred into the dimming light, he fired. The beam struck the convoy's lead vehicle, its engines sputtering and dying as the electromagnetic pulse fried its circuits. The vehicle jerked, halted, and the rest of the convoy bunched up in confusion.

Chaos erupted as his targets realized they were under attack. Guards scrambled, their shouts carrying over the wind as they sought out their unseen assailant. Jax used this, moving positions with a grace that belied his solid form, each step calculated to keep him invisible.

He targeted the second vehicle, adjusting the lance's output to a wider spread, ensuring maximum disruption. Another shot, and the second vehicle lurched, crashing into a ditch beside the road, its wheels spinning uselessly in the air.

Jax moved again, a shadow against the shadows, his presence felt but not seen. He climbed down from his perch, approaching the disabled convoy with caution. His armor's sensors alerted him to residual electric currents, a reminder of the danger still present.

As he neared the first vehicle, he slid his Nano-Edge Cutter from its sheath, the blade catching the moonlight. He pried open the cargo door, swift and silent, peering inside at the crates of bioweapon components.

Quickly, he began transferring the cargo to a nearby drag sled, camouflaged under the brush. Each component was a small victory, each crate a step towards tilting the balance of power in his favor.

Behind him, the sounds of the confused guards grew distant. Jax knew it wouldn't be long before they regrouped, before they started a proper search. He worked faster, his hybrid stamina an advantage in the race against time.

As the last crate settled onto the sled, Jax wiped the sweat from his brow—an android's mimicry of human fatigue. He glanced back at the convoy, the guards now organizing into search parties, their torchlights piercing the darkness.

Without a sound, he activated the sled's stealth mode, its engine whispering to life as he began his retreat, pulling the precious cargo into the night.

As the night swallowed the last echoes of the convoy's chaos, Jax's focus sharpened on a crucial task that lingered in the web of his complex mind. The sled, now loaded and moving silently through the darkness, was left to the guidance of its automated piloting system. Jax slipped into the shadows of a derelict communications outpost, its skeleton barely a whisper against the vastness of the wasteland.

Inside, remnants of old-world tech whispered of forgotten wars. Jax's hands moved with practiced ease, assembling a makeshift terminal from the scavenged components around him. His goal: a hack not just into any system, but into Project Lumina's sprawling communication network. His tools were rudimentary but enhanced by the precision only his hybrid nature could achieve.

Flipping open his holo-projector, Jax initiated a sequence of code, each line weaving into the next like a spider spinning a web in the dead of night. The outpost's dusty screen flickered to life, lines of static crossing and uncrossing as he dialed into the Citadel's secure channels. His pulse quickened.

"Come on," he murmured, his voice a blend of human tension and digital certainty. The screen blinked, and then, connection. Jax had tapped into the Citadel's feed, a vein of raw, unfiltered data coursing through the heart of his enemy's operations.

Now connected, he needed to broadcast something irrefutable. He pulled from his internal storage—a collection of secretly recorded moments showcasing android emotions and intelligence. These were not mere bytes of data but snapshots of life, of sentient beings living under the yoke of human dominance. Each video, each image proved the androids' humanity, their capacity for joy, sorrow, fear, and hope.

With a deep, almost imperceptible sigh, Jax uploaded the files to the network. Then, leveraging every ounce of his hacking prowess, he overrode the Citadel's broadcasting protocols. Across every screen linked to the network, in every corner of the Citadel, his evidence began to play.

On countless displays, androids were seen nurturing each other, expressing panic during raids, sharing tender moments of consolation, and even partaking in acts of quiet rebellion. The voices of androids filled the airwaves, their words not commands or codes, but conversations, laughter, cries—a beautiful array of life.

Jax didn't watch his work unfold. Instead, he listened to the distant hum of the network, the digital heartbeat of a society on the brink of upheaval. His message was clear: Androids are not tools. They are not property. They are alive.

He dismantled his jury-rigged setup, erasing his digital footprints with the same meticulous care he used to cover his physical tracks. As the first hints of dawn cast a pale light over the wasteland, Jax melted back into the wilderness, the weight of his revelation shadowing his retreat.

The world was waking up, not just to a new day, but to a new reality. And somewhere in that awakening, change was stirring—irrevocable and charged with potential. Jax's part was played, for now. His path led forward, into the unknown, with the hope that his actions tonight might alter the course of history.

The screens blinked with an ominous pulse, the red alerts cascading one after another, disrupting the constant stream of surveillance data. The harsh glare illuminated Greda's face as she leaned in, her eyes narrowing on the newest threat to her dominion—a threat crafted by her own hands.

"Commander, status," she barked, the edge in her voice slicing through the hum of activity surrounding her. Her command center, usually a beacon of control, now mirrored the chaos unfurling within the confines of her city.

"Chancellor, the hostages have been secured in their pods. We're live in three, two…" The officer didn't need to finish; the large screens flicked to the live feeds broadcasting across every district, each pod displayed prominently against the backdrop of the city's austere architecture.

Greda stood, her silhouette casting a long shadow over the map of her city sprawled below. Her finger traced the blinking lights where the hostages—key figures from each district—were now pawns in her most audacious gambit yet. Their frightened faces, visible to all, were her guarantee of compliance.

"Citizens of the underground," Greda began, her voice echoing not just across the vast chamber but throughout the city, transmitted to every home, every corner where despair or rebellion might lurk. "You see before you those who will pay the price of insubordination. This is the cost of defiance."

Her gaze didn't waver from the screens as cries and pleas began to filter through—the deliberate audio feed from the confinement pods wrenching even as it served its purpose. Faces in the crowd, sketched with fear and uncertainty, stared back at her through the digital haze.

"Let this be a lesson," she continued, her tone as cold as the steel walls encasing her citadel. "The safety of these lives is in your hands. Any act of rebellion, any failure to comply, and the consequences will be immediate and irreversible."

Switching off the broadcast, Greda turned to face her inner circle, her back to the now silent feeds. "Ensure the patrols are doubled. I want updates every fifteen minutes. Make it clear—any disturbance, and we tighten the grip."

Her command met with crisp salutes as she walked back to her private chamber. The door slid shut with a whisper, sealing her within the confines of her calculated solitude.

The display of force, the show of hostages in their glass prisons, was a message written in fear and read in silence. She knew the cost, the balance of terror and control. Her hands, when she looked at them, were steady. The lives in her grip were weights in the scales of order, and she bore them, for she believed no one else could, no one else would. It was here, in which Greda decided to make her move she had been thinking about for hours now.

Greda's fingers paused above the console, a sinister smile playing at the corners of her mouth as she tracked Felix and his team on the screens, their forms captured in the labyrinth of the Citadel's tunnels. "Deploy the transmission," she commanded, the control room humming with activity at her orders.

The Citadel's screens flickered to life, every citizen forced to view the chilling spectacle. Greda's image towered over the city, her voice echoing through every corner. "Citizens of the underground," she began, her tone chillingly calm, "behold your so-called liberators."

The screen split, one side displaying Felix and his team, desperate and panting, navigating the claustrophobic tunnels. The other side showed the stark interior of a detainment cell. "Caught in an act of cowardice," Greda sneered, her voice dripping with disdain. "Running like rats in the shadows."

She allowed a pause, letting the citizens absorb the sight of their floundering heroes. "They have two hours to surrender," Greda continued, her voice hardening. "If they do not, the consequences will be dire." With a casual flick of her hand, the screen shifted to show a solitary figure in a clear confinement pod, the details of the person obscured, a calculated anonymity that fed the fear gnawing at the city's heart.

"This," Greda declared, pointing at the figure, "is the cost of defiance." Without another word, she nodded to an officer. The lethal device beside the captive hummed to life, and the figure disintegrated, reduced to nothingness in a haze of atomic dissolution. The image was stark, terrifying—a display of her absolute control over life and death.

"Every thirty minutes, another will follow," she announced, her voice unyielding. "Until they surrender, or you convince them to do so. The choice is yours."

As the screens blanked out, the echo of her ultimatum hung heavily in the air, leaving the citizens in a stunned, oppressive silence. Back in her command center, Greda turned from the now-dark screens, her expression unreadable. Her staff continued their work in tense silence, accustomed to her harsh methods but shaken by the brutality of today's display.

"Keep the feeds live. Track every move in those tunnels," she ordered, her voice a low growl. "And bring up the mobile screen unit. I want Felix and his team to see exactly what awaits them if they continue this foolishness."

As her command was executed, a drone equipped with a large display screen maneuvered through the tunnels ahead of Felix's team, ensuring they could not escape the sight of their potential fate. The psychological warfare was precise, calculated to break spirits and fortify her reign of control.

Outside, the city buzzed with whispered panic and fear, the citizens caught in an invisible vice of Greda's making. Greda knew this game well—the balance of terror and control that kept her in power.

She walked to the window of her private chamber, overlooking the heart of the Citadel. The lights below contrasted sharply against the darkness she wielded so effectively. Tonight, she had sown terror, a necessary evil, she reassured herself, essential for maintaining order.

As the minutes ticked by, Greda stood watch, a sentinel over her domain. Each moment brought her closer to breaking the resistance or potentially igniting a rebellion she would need to crush decisively. In the depths of the Citadel, the balance of power rested on a knife's edge, and Greda was prepared to tip it in her favor, whatever the cost.

Chapter 18

Callan stood before the gathered recruits in the dimly lit hangar of Sector 9X, his gaze sweeping over the new faces—some human, some android. The air buzzed with the low hum of anticipation and the subtle whir of mechanical joints. The stark fluorescent lights cast long shadows, turning each figure into a monument of the cause they were about to fight for.

"As many of you know," Callan began, his voice reverberating off the metal walls, "Felix and Jax's mission encountered more than its share of hardships. We're here to make sure they don't die."

He paused, allowing his words to sink in, his eyes locking onto several in the crowd. "Sylas, Nara, Kyle—you were sent by Jax, tailored for this very kind of operation. Your skills in defense, reconnaissance, and engineering are going to be crucial as we navigate through enemy territory."

Sylas, the android known as The Shield, stood slightly apart, his posture rigid but ready. His plasma shield generator hummed softly, a low and reassuring sound in the tense silence. Nara, lithe and alert, scanned the hangar with eyes that missed nothing, her multi-spectral binoculars hanging ready at her side. Kyle, with his quirky grin, clutched his portable tech workshop backpack a bit tighter, his mind likely already racing through a dozen ways to breach the Citadel's defenses.

"And to our new human allies," Callan continued, his tone warming slightly, "you came in response to Tibo's call. You've chosen to stand with us against a foe that would see us all either subjugated or annihilated."

He glanced over at Tibo, who offered a wry smile and a casual salute with his electrostatic disruptor pistol. Tibo's broadcasts had pierced through the static of fear that gripped the underground, rallying those who still believed in a fight for something better.

"Lena, Mason, Zoe," Callan called out their names, and the three stepped forward. Lena's eyes were sharp, her stance that of someone who had commanded troops and faced down chaos. Mason's hands were already twitching, eager to lay them on his demolition tools, a clear readiness to shatter the barriers they would face. Zoe nodded solemnly, her compact pulse pistol at her side, her gear ready to jam any signals that might betray them.

"This isn't just about survival," Callan declared, his voice rising over the assembly. "This is about retribution and taking back what's ours."

The recruits stood taller, energized by Callan's words, the lines of division between human and android blurring under the shared banner of their cause. They were not just fighters; they were symbols of resistance against a tide that sought to drown them all.

"As we gear up and head out, remember this," Callan finished, his gaze fierce and unyielding. "Everyone comes back alive."

Under the pale flicker of tunnel lights, Callan stepped ahead of his team, their shadows merging with the darkness of Sector 9X. The echoes of his final words in the briefing, "Everyone comes back alive," hung in the air, a silent vow that tethered them all to a singular purpose. They moved as one, a stealthy column weaving through the cold, subterranean veins of the Citadel's outer sectors.

As they approached the first checkpoint, Callan signaled a halt, his hand raised, eyes scanning the shadows. The drone beside him, a quiet sentinel, whirred softly, its sensors casting an invisible net ahead. "Elara, Mason, check the perimeter," he whispered, his voice a ghostly thread in the thick silence.

Elara, with her biocide launcher slung over her shoulder, moved left, her steps soundless. Mason followed, his eyes alert, one hand on the detonator clipped to his belt, ready to lay down a breach charge if needed. The faint hum of the drone's guidance system provided a comforting backdrop to the tense silence.

Sylas, massive and imposing beside Callan, shifted, the servos in his joints whispering with the movement. His plasma shield generator pulsed quietly, cycling through diagnostics with a glow that seemed to pulse in time with Callan's own heartbeat.

Behind them, Nara's form blended into the darkness, her presence betrayed only by the occasional glint of light off her arc blades. Zoe, huddled over her communications pack, murmured into her headset, a stream of encrypted directives ensuring their digital veil remained intact.

The corridor ahead split into a fork, each path disappearing into oppressive gloom. Kyle, hunched over his portable tech, interfaced with the facility's aging network, his fingers dancing across the holographic display. "Left tunnel's clear of electronic surveillance, but there's residual heat signatures about 200 meters down," he reported, his voice low but clear.

Callan nodded, processing the information. "Lena, take your group right, silent sweep. We'll take the left. If you encounter resistance, disengage and regroup." Lena motioned to her team, and they peeled off, disappearing with a practiced ease that spoke of countless similar operations.

Turning back to his path, Callan led his team deeper into the bowels of the Citadel. Each step forward was a step further from the safety of the known, deeper into a maze designed not just to confound but to kill. The chill in the air was a constant reminder of the stakes they played for.

Ahead, the corridor narrowed, the walls scarred from old conflicts. Sylas moved closer, his shield at the ready, a bulwark against the unknown threats lurking just beyond their light.

Suddenly, the drone beeped sharply, a warning of movement just beyond their range of vision. "Contact," Callan breathed, every muscle tensing. Sylas stepped forward, his shield expanding with a hiss and a snap, encapsulating them in a dome of shimmering energy just as the corridor lit up with the stark white of incoming fire.

Callan peered through the translucent shield, assessing their attackers. Two figures, heavily armed, but hesitant, their movements betraying a lack of conviction. "Hold fire," he commanded, his mind racing through options. This was not the overwhelming force he had anticipated; something was off.

"Zoe, any chatter?" he asked, keeping his voice steady despite the adrenaline coursing through his veins.

"Nothing. It's like they didn't expect us here," she replied, frowning at her readouts.

This was it, the moment of decision. Callan knew they could not afford to wait, to ponder. "Sylas, drop the shield on my mark. Elara, Mason, non-lethal takedowns. We need answers."

"Three, two, one—mark!"

The shield fell, and the world rushed back in with the roar of battle.

Instantly, the corridor erupted into chaos as Callan's team sprang into action. Elara and Mason moved swiftly, subduing the hesitant attackers with practiced precision. The sudden clash of conflict reverberated down the stone corridors of Zone X1, ominously known as The Maze.

As the immediate threat was neutralized, the team pressed deeper into the labyrinthine passages of The Maze. The atmosphere was tense, the only sounds the distant dripping of water and their own measured footfalls echoing through the stone corridors. The air was cool and damp, carrying a weight that seemed to press against them from all sides.

Without warning, the dimly lit corridors lit up as a swarm of drones, sleek and menacing, surged around a bend. Deployed by Chancellor Greda, these machines were equipped with motion sensors and thermal imaging, quickly adapting to the maze's complexities. Their red lights scanned relentlessly as they advanced in a tight, coordinated formation.

Callan's voice cut through the din, clear and commanding. "Split up! Confuse their targeting systems!" He divided the team into three groups, creating multiple fronts to disorient the drones. Sylas stepped forward, his Plasma Shield Generator humming to life, casting a broad shield that flickered with energy, providing cover for those behind him.

Kyle, scrambling behind a narrow outcrop of rock, worked feverishly to assemble an electronic disruptor. His hands were a blur, components clicking into place with each precise movement. "Almost there," he muttered, glancing up as a drone's scanner swept dangerously close.

Meanwhile, Nara led a small contingent down a branching passage, her form a shadow flitting between cover points. Her binoculars glowed softly as she scanned for an advantage, her voice whispering into the comms, "I've spotted a series of alcoves and trap doors. This way—keep low!"

Tibo, always quick on his feet, found a narrow crevice and slipped through, his back against the cool stone. He gestured for others to follow, directing them into the hidden folds of The Maze. "Here, this can buy us some time," he said, his voice a breathy whisper as drones buzzed past, momentarily confused by the scattered movements of the team.

The confrontation grew fierce, the corridors ringing with the sound of pulse fire and the metallic clatter of drones crashing into the ancient walls. Sylas's shield flickered under the onslaught, but held firm, a bulwark in the dim light. Kyle finally clicked the disruptor into life, and with a deep breath, activated it. A sharp, electronic screech filled the air, and several drones wobbled mid-flight, their systems disrupted.

"We've got a window—move!" Callan's order spurred the team into motion, darting through the twisting passages as disabled drones fell like broken birds. They regrouped in a larger chamber, catching their breath, checking for injuries.

Elara checked over Mason, who had taken a glancing hit, his armor scorched but intact. "You good?" she asked, her eyes scanning the shadows for more threats.

"Yeah, let's keep moving," Mason replied.

Callan surveyed the chamber, his mind racing. The encounter had been perilous, and while they had managed to disable several drones, it was a stark reminder of the challenges ahead. "We need to increase our stealth, use the Maze to our advantage," he concluded, his gaze meeting each of his teammates. "Stay alert."

"Stay alert," Callan's command lingered in the damp air of The Maze, a labyrinth where each shadow could conceal a new danger. His team, split into their specialized groups, moved forward with a silent urgency, the distant echoes of their steps mingling with the perpetual drip of water from the ancient stone above.

Sylas, hulking yet silent beside Callan, adjusted his plasma shield generator, its hum a soft counterpoint to the quiet. Callan nodded to him, their plan clear. They needed to keep moving, keep silent, use the maze's twisted corridors to their advantage.

Ahead, Nara paused, her hand signaling a halt. Her eyes, scanning through the multi-spectral binoculars, caught a flicker of movement—drones, more of them, approaching with a mechanical precision that seemed almost eerie in the otherwise desolate maze. She relayed the information back to Callan with a swift, silent gesture.

Without a word, Callan gestured sharply to the left, directing Elara and Mason to take cover behind a jutting wall of rock. Their movements were swift, barely a rustle of fabric or clank of gear.

Elara's biocide launcher was up and ready, her eyes narrow, focusing on the path ahead where Nara had indicated the drones were emerging.

Mason checked his blaster gauntlets, his fingers brushing over the controls. The readiness in his eyes was fierce— scary even. Callan trusted him to make the next move explosive, literally, if needed.

On the other side, Kyle, his fingers nimble and quick, worked on assembling an electronic disruptor. The device, makeshift but effective, was crucial. If he could jam the drones' signals, they'd have a chance to move deeper into The Maze without relentless pursuit. Tibo hovered near Kyle, his tools at the ready, a smirk playing on his lips despite the tension—always ready to lighten the mood or jump into action, whichever was needed first.

Lena, standing with Zoe and Rootwhisper, coordinated their efforts. Her voice was low, almost a whisper, as she relayed positions and potential strategies, her eyes never leaving the drone command tablet. Zoe's fingers danced across her communications pack, ensuring their signals remained scrambled, their presence masked from any prying digital eyes.

Rootwhisper, his form slightly quivering with the strain of the situation, extended his root system subtly into the moist earth, feeling out the life within the maze. His connection could give them an edge, a warning of sorts from the natural world so entwined with their artificial foes.

Then, it happened—a swift, sudden barrage of light and noise as the drones discovered their position. Sylas's shield flared to life, a brilliant arc of energy that lit the dim corridor. The sound of it snapping into place echoed, a harsh dissonant clang against the stone.

Callan raised his solar beam rifle, sighting down the corridor as the first drone rounded the corner. His finger tightened on the trigger, a shot rang out, bright and fierce, cutting through the darkness. The drone sparked, sputtered, and fell, a heap of smoldering metal.

"Move!" Callan barked, his voice low but urgent. The team sprang into action, Elara and Mason moving forward to cover the advance, their own weapons discharging with controlled bursts of light and sound.

As the last echoes of their shots reverberated through the cavernous walls of The Maze, Callan motioned for silence, his hand raised in a tight fist. The air was thick with the electric scent of scorched metal, remnants of their recent skirmish. Ahead, the corridors branched in a dizzying array of directions, each shrouded in darkness and uncertainty.

Without a word, he signaled Elara and Mason to hold their position as he peered around the corner. The drone they'd downed was still sparking, its circuits fried by Mason's expertly placed charge. But this victory was minor in the scope of their mission, a mere prelude to the greater challenge awaiting them.

Elara's gaze met his, a silent question in her eyes. Callan nodded towards the deeper shadows where the stone walls seemed to pulse with a strange, bioluminescent light. "On me," he whispered, his voice barely carrying. They needed to advance, but every step was a risk, the threat of more drones ever-present.

As they crept forward, Callan felt the weight of his rifle in his hands, a familiar and comforting weight. His eyes constantly scanned the shadows, searching for the telltale signs of another ambush. Suddenly, Nara's voice crackled in his earpiece, her tone urgent. "Movement ahead, sector three. Civilians in distress."

His heart quickened. Civilians meant unpredictability, and in The Maze, unpredictability could be fatal. But it also meant lives hung in the balance, lives they were here to save. "Location, Nara," Callan responded, his mind already racing through strategies.

"Dead-end chamber, about two clicks north. Surrounded by newer models of surveillance drones. They haven't spotted them yet, but it's only a matter of time," Nara reported, her voice a beacon of calm in the chaos.

Callan made his decision in an instant. "Lena, Mason, create a distraction. West corridor, use the explosives but keep it light—we can't bring this place down on our heads."

Mason grinned, a flash of reckless excitement in his eyes. "You got it, boss."

Meanwhile, Elara prepared to lead the main rescue effort. "Kyle, I need those drones down. Can you jam them?" she asked, her voice steady despite the rising tension.

Kyle, already pulling components from his backpack, nodded. "Give me two minutes. I'll have them spinning in circles."

Callan turned his attention to Zoe and Rootwhisper. "Zoe, maintain comms silence starting now. Rootwhisper, can you guide the civilians to us?"

The young sapling, his form shimmering slightly with the hues of the fungi on the walls, nodded. "I can speak to the mycelium, make it light their way to us."

"Good. Everyone, on my mark," Callan commanded, his gaze sweeping over his team, each member readying themselves for what came next. They were a unit, every part moving in sync, every member crucial to the success of their mission.

The air was thick with tension, the only light in the oppressive darkness of The Maze coming from the bioluminescent fungi dotting the ancient stone. Rootwhisper, towering now, his form extended and hardened, just like Callan had seen before, moved alongside them, a guardian of bark and vine.

A sharp crack echoed as Mason disarmed another trap, his hands steady despite the visible beads of sweat on his forehead. Lena, her eyes fixed on the drone command tablet, directed them through less frequented pathways, her voice a constant murmur in Callan's earpiece, updating routes and marking enemy positions.

"Sylas, shield up at the next corner," Callan ordered, his voice low. The corridor ahead was narrower, the perfect choke point for an ambush. Sylas nodded, his frame expanding as the plasma shield buzzed to life, casting eerie shadows against the walls.

They rounded the bend, and chaos erupted. Drones, more than they had anticipated, buzzed violently towards them. Their rotors were a deafening whir, and the air vibrated with the force of their approach. But before the drones could converge, Rootwhisper acted.

With a roar that seemed to shake the very foundations of The Maze, the young sapling's arms, now thick with thorny bark, swept forward. Vines erupted from his fingertips, shooting forward with the precision of spears. Drones were skewered mid-air, crashing into the walls with metallic clangs.

"Move! Now!" Callan's command cut through the noise as he led the charge. Elara was beside him, her launcher sending bursts of biocide that ate through the drone carcasses blocking their path. Nara darted ahead, her form a blur as she scouted for a clear route, her binoculars scanning for hidden dangers.

Behind them, Kyle worked feverishly on his portable tech, adjusting frequencies in an attempt to jam the incoming signals of more drones. "Almost there!" he shouted over the din, his device emitting a high-pitched whine that crescendoed until the air was filled with the sound of short-circuiting electronics.

Zoe, her fingers flying over her own gear, managed to intercept a transmission. "Got something—looks like they're trying to flank us!" Her voice was calm, her face illuminated by the soft glow of her screen.

Callan glanced at Lena, who was already redirecting their forces. "Tibo, with me," she called out, her tactical rifle at the ready as they prepared to cover the rear.

The civilians, huddled and wide-eyed with fear, were herded by Elara towards a narrow passageway that Rootwhisper had pointed out. The sapling's connection with the plant network within The Maze allowed him to sense a route not just safe but optimal for their escape.

As they pushed forward, Rootwhisper's vines cleared the path, fortifying their retreat with barriers of woven wood and thorn that sprang up at his command.

Kyle's voice crackled through Tibo's earpiece, strained but clear, "Setting up the last emitter now." Tibo crouched behind a low wall of jagged rock, his tools spread out before him—a mishmash of circuits and gadgetry only he could make sense of. The drones, their sinister hum growing louder, were closing in.

"Ready on your signal," Tibo responded, clutching his electrostatic disruptor pistol. His fingers danced over the controls, setting the frequency that would scramble the drone sensors temporarily. Beside him, Sylas shifted, the soft whir of his plasma shield generator a comforting sound amidst the chaos.

The ambush had been sudden, a stark reminder of Chancellor Greda's reach even within the depths of The Maze. Advanced surveillance drones, equipped with AI-targeting systems, had them nearly encircled. Tibo glanced at Callan, who was positioning himself between two large stalactites, his solar beam rifle at the ready.

"Now, Tibo!" Kyle's command snapped him back to the moment. Tibo pressed the activator, releasing a pulse of electromagnetic energy. The air tingled with static electricity, and for a moment, the advancing drones wavered, their movements erratic.

Lena, from her position by the command tablet, directed, "Nara, Mason, left flank—trap set. Activate on my mark!" Her voice was calm, a stark contrast to the rapid fire of Mason's blaster gauntlets as he set explosive charges along a narrow passage to their left.

Nara, ever the ghost, darted through the shadows, her arc blades a flash of silver in the dim light. Her target: the drones' rear sensors. Each strike was precise, calculated to disable without causing a full-on explosion that would compromise their position.

Zoe, huddled beside a formation of dripping stalactites, her fingers flying over her compact, was a silent sentinel in their electronic war. "Jamming their comms—should give us a few minutes before they reroute."

The drones, momentarily disoriented by Tibo's pulse and Nara's sabotage, regrouped faster than expected. Their AI systems adapted, recalibrating to the disrupted frequencies. Tibo swallowed hard, his usual quip dying in his throat. This wasn't the time for humor.

"Tibo, another burst, aim for the group on the right!" Callan's order came just as a drone broke through their makeshift defenses, its sensors locking onto their position. Tibo aimed and fired, the pulse from his disruptor pistol enveloping the drone in a crackle of blue energy. It dropped, its systems fried, just meters from their cover.

Sylas stepped forward, his shield expanding in a wide arc, a barrier of pulsing energy that shielded the team from a volley of incoming fire. "Push forward!" he shouted, his voice a rumble over the sound of combat.

As the team advanced, Rootwhisper's influence became apparent. The walls of The Maze seemed to breathe, vines and roots subtly altering their paths, creating barriers and openings that disoriented the remaining drones. Tibo couldn't help but marvel at the young sapling's control, his ability to communicate with the very bones of their labyrinthine refuge.

They reached a concealed passage, its entrance masked by hanging moss and the clever angling of the rocks. One by one, they slipped through, the sounds of the pursuing drones muffled by the thick stone.

Inside, the passage descended sharply, the air cooler and the path marked by the faint glow of phosphorescent fungi. Lena took the lead, her drone tablet casting an eerie glow on her determined face. "This way. According to the old maps, it leads to a secondary outpost— should be safe."

As they moved deeper into the bowels of The Maze, the distant echoes of the drones faded, replaced by the sound of their own quickened breaths and the occasional drip of water from the unseen ceiling. Tibo adjusted his climbing gear, readying himself for the descent.

Behind him, the group maintained a tense silence, the weight of their narrow escape pressing upon them, the darkness of The Maze enveloping them like a shroud, hiding them from the eyes of their pursuers but also, perhaps, leading them deeper into unknown dangers.

Rootwhisper felt the subtle vibrations of the earth beneath him as the team advanced through the twisting passages of The Maze. His roots, though confined within his mobile form, reached out, intertwining with the mycelial threads that whispered secrets of the soil and stone. This connection was his strength, his contribution to the human cause.

"The Underforge should be just beyond this corridor," Lena murmured, her eyes never leaving the drone tablet that painted a map of shadows and light. The team's movement was a dance of shadows, each step measured, each breath a silent pact with the darkness.

Rootwhisper sensed the apprehension among the humans. Callan's grip tightened around his rifle, a silent sentinel leading them into the bowels of the underground. The phosphorescent fungi along the walls cast an eerie glow, lighting their path and his thoughts. "The plants speak of disturbance," Rootwhisper warned, his voice a gentle hum that only those close could hear over the sound of their cautious tread.

Ahead, the dark mouth of The Underforge loomed, an industrial giant now repurposed as a sanctuary and arsenal. But as they approached, Rootwhisper's connection with the earth drew a sharp breath of warning—the natural rhythms were disrupted, tainted by foreign energies.

"They've taken it," he conveyed urgently to Callan, who paused, signaling the team to halt. Sylas extended his energy shield, a dome of pulsing light that cloaked them from prying electronic eyes.

Zoe was swift, her fingers flying over her device, initiating a blackout of enemy communications. "Window's short," she hissed, her focus absolute as she worked to sever the threads of data that fed their foes.

Tibo and Elara moved ahead, scouting the entrance. The clang of distant machinery and the occasional spark from welding torches betrayed the presence of enemy forces. "More than we anticipated," Tibo reported back, his voice low.

Rootwhisper felt every shudder of the industrial behemoth that was The Underforge. His senses, attuned to both the mechanical and the organic, detected the patrols of soldiers, their footsteps a discordant rhythm against the pulsating heart of the forge.

"We use the secondary tunnels," Lena decided, her voice cutting through the tension. "Kyle, prepare the diversions. Mason, your charges might come in handy if we need a quick exit."

The team divided, shadows parting ways in the dim light. Rootwhisper stayed close to Callan, their path veering towards a lesser-known entrance marked by faint luminescent signals only visible to those who understood the language of fungi.

As they navigated the cluttered expanse of The Underforge, Rootwhisper's unique perception guided them past sensors and traps, his body swaying gently, a dance with the invisible forces that sought to expose them. His thorned bark bristled, ready to defend, to fortify.

Suddenly, the sharp scent of ozone—a warning. "Down!" Callan commanded, just as a flurry of laser fire sliced through the space they had occupied seconds before. Sylas's shield flickered, absorbing the impact, his frame a bulwark against the storm.

They pressed on, the forge's secrets unfolding before Rootwhisper, each whisper of steam and shift of stone a signpost. Finally, they reached the supply caches, but their victory was tempered by the stark reality of their situation—most were empty, scavenged by the enemy.

"We take what we can," Callan decided, his voice resolute. They filled their pockets with the sparse ammunition and supplies that remained, each item a small triumph against the encroaching despair.

As they retreated, the blackout window closing, the forge began to awaken from its forced slumber. Alarms blared—more danger was on the way.

Rootwhisper felt the whispers of the ancient weapon caches before they came into view, his senses tingling with the faint vibrations of the old metal and the subtle shifts in the earth around them. This part of The Underforge was seldom visited, the air thick with the dust of decades and the heavy scent of oil and metal.

Lena led them with confidence, her memory of the blueprints clear as she navigated the labyrinth of machinery and shadow. "The caches should be just through here," she indicated, her voice barely above a whisper, the beam from her tactical light slicing through the darkness.

Mason set his tools down with a clank, eyeing the vault door with a mixture of anticipation and caution. "Looks older than the dirt we're standing on," he muttered, beginning to assemble his devices for the breach. His hands were steady, his focus absolute as he worked to set the charges, mindful of the ancient mechanisms and the dangers they posed.

Rootwhisper's roots tingled as he approached the wall, his connection with the mycelial network beneath the surface drawing him closer. He could feel the echo of countless footsteps that had once trodden these floors, the whispers of the past that seemed to seep from the very walls. "Careful," his voice resonated softly, a deep timbre that seemed to harmonize with the low hum of the hidden life within the stone. "The plants speak of old defenses, long forgotten by those who built them."

Nara and Kyle took up positions at the entrance, their eyes scanning the dark corridors for any sign of the enemy. The air was electric with tension, each shadow a potential threat, each noise a possible alarm.

As Mason prepared to breach the vault, Sylas activated his shield generator, casting a dome of shimmering energy around the group. The light from the shield threw eerie shadows across the walls, the ghostly outlines of old tools and forgotten projects looming over them like specters of the forge's past life.

With a nod from Mason, the charge was set, and a moment later, a controlled explosion rocked the chamber. Dust and debris filled the air, but as it cleared, the door swung open with a groan, revealing rows upon rows of shelves laden with supplies.

Rootwhisper moved forward, his form brushing against the cool metal of the shelves, feeling the residual energy of the items stored within. His connection with the network of life around them pulsed with excitement—here lay not just weapons and medical supplies, but also historical documents, their pages brittle with age, filled with knowledge of the sentient vegetation that had once been allies to his kind.

As the explosion's echo dwindled, Rootwhisper stood resolute amidst the scattered remnants of the shattered vault door. The Underforge's air was thick with dust and tension as Sylas repositioned his shields, sealing the entry points with pulsing walls of plasma. The ambient light reflected off Rootwhisper's thorned bark, casting him as a primal guardian at the heart of their makeshift fortress.

The sound of approaching enemies clanked through the corridors, the rhythmic march syncing with the increasing beat of Rootwhisper's internal warning system. He could feel the enemy's vibrations through the metal floors, a stark contrast to the gentle hum of the earth he so deeply missed.

"Positions!" Callan's command cut through the noise. Rootwhisper extended his limbs, intertwining with the metal scaffolding overhead, his roots embedding into cracks and crevices, anchoring him to the forge's very skeleton. His branches splayed out, forming a dense canopy of leaves and thorns over his allies.

As the first of Greda's forces rounded the corner, Rootwhisper's vines surged forward. They were swift, thorn-laden whips that struck with precision. The screams of the struck echoed, a grim chorus to the symphony of battle.

Elara and Callan fired from behind the living barricade, each shot precise, their targets illuminated by the eerie glow of Rootwhisper's luminescent pollen that filled the air, sticking to enemy sensors and visors, blinding them amidst the chaos.

Mason, crouched near a pile of rubble, tossed a series of grenades into an advancing cluster of soldiers, the explosions sending shockwaves that Rootwhisper felt ripple through the ground. Each blast was followed by a brief silence—the calm in the eye of the storm.

But the enemy was relentless. A tech specialist managed to deploy a scrambling device, the electronic whir disrupting Sylas's shields momentarily. Rootwhisper reacted instinctively, his entire being pulsating with ancient power as he summoned the forge's latent energies. The ground trembled, metal beams groaned, and from the walls, new growths of hardened wood burst forth, impaling the scrambling devices and their operators.

"Rootwhisper, now!" Kyle shouted, his voice tinged with urgency. The young sapling focused, channeling his essence into a massive surge of growth, vines thicker than a man's arm tearing through the concrete floor and walls, entangling soldiers and crushing the mechanical disruptors they carried.

In the midst of the violent bloom, Rootwhisper's voice echoed, not just in the air, but through the very plant network he commanded, "Back to the earth, from whence you came!" His words were a deep, resonant timbre that shook both ally and foe, a reminder of the ancient pact between flora and fauna.

As Sylas's shields snapped back into place, the remaining enemies were either retreating or neutralized. Nara swiftly moved to secure the perimeter, her movements almost a blur, ensuring no threat remained that could surprise them from the shadows.

Rootwhisper, now covering most of the chamber with his extended form, contracted slowly, pulling back his vines and roots, the thorns dripping with a mixture of sap and darker fluids. The air was heavy with the scent of ozone and plant resin, the undercurrents of gunpowder and blood mingling into a metallic tang.

As the team regrouped, checking their ammunition and wounds, Rootwhisper's foliage rustled softly, his voice carrying a somber note, "We win or we die."

Chapter 19

Chancellor Greda stood at the panoramic window of her command center, overlooking the grid-like layout of Zone R3: The Refuge, a dense cluster of decrepit housing now bustling with the innocent lives about to become pawns in her strategic play. Her fingers tapped an impatient rhythm against the glass, a metered prelude to the chaos she was about to orchestrate.

"The surveillance drones are in position, Chancellor," announced her aide-de-camp, a young officer with a voice that barely concealed his anticipation of the forthcoming action. Greda didn't turn to acknowledge him; her gaze remained fixed on the digital screens displaying live feeds from the drones—her eyes, her ears, her dominion extended.

"Ensure the feeds are live to all units. I want eyes on every exit point. No one leaves, not until I say so," she commanded, her voice firm, carrying the weight of absolute authority. The officer nodded, relaying her orders with swift precision.

Below, the unsuspecting civilians moved through their dilapidated sanctuary, unaware of the tightening noose. Greda watched as mothers clutched their children, elders gathered in quiet groups, all of them shadows flitting through the twilight of their fragile peace. It was necessary, Greda reminded herself, a harsh lesson in the realities of war and survival.

A strategic chime pulled her attention to a secure line blinking on her console. She pressed the receiver to her ear, and the gravelly voice of Riko filled the silence of her office.

"Phase one is ready to initiate on your command. The resistance hasn't made their move yet, but we're expecting them any moment now," the voice reported.

"Initiate the lockdown. Seal the exits. And deploy the second wave of drones for closer surveillance. I want detailed identities on everyone. We may need to leverage more than just their presence," Greda replied, her mind already weaving through the myriad possibilities—hostages, negotiations, direct confrontations.

As the screens flickered to life with new orders, the first cries of alarm rose from the Refuge. Doors slammed, children screamed, the panic raw and palpable even through the digital divide. Greda's face remained impassive, a marble statue carved with the fine lines of necessary cruelty.

"Keep me updated on the resistance's movements. I suspect they won't sit back for long, not when we're threatening their moral high ground," she added, her lips twitching into a cold smile.

The aide returned to her side, a tablet in his hands displaying a schematic of the Refuge. "We have a potential problem. The resistance is quicker than anticipated. Their units are moving into position. It seems they were prepared for this."

Greda finally turned from the window, her eyes reflecting the digital glow of warfare and strategy. "Then let's ensure they understand the cost of their heroism. Prepare for a direct engagement."

Greda narrowed her eyes, focusing on the tactical feeds that streamed live footage from the drones circling over The Refuge. "Increase surveillance resolution on sectors four through six," she commanded sharply. Her fingers drummed against the console, tapping out a rhythm that matched the escalating pulse of her strategic mind.

In the hushed sanctum of her command center, deep within the bowels of the underground network, the urgency of the moment was palpable. Her tech operators worked feverishly, their faces lit by the soft blue glow of monitors displaying maps and troop movements. The air was thick with the electric scent of ozone and anticipation, a storm brewing within the confines of her subterranean fortress.

The screens showed the resistance operatives moving stealthily through The Refuge—a sanctuary turned battleground. This zone, usually a place of healing with its serene ambient sounds and gentle lighting from bioluminescent plants, now echoed with the soft sounds of distant chaos. Greda's lips curled into a sardonic smile. "They think they're clever, using the old tunnels," she mused aloud, her voice a low hum filled with cold amusement. Her hand hovered over the console, ready to unleash her next move.

"Deploy the second squadron of drones. I want eyes deeper in those tunnels. And activate the thermal sensors; let's burn out their shadows," she ordered, her voice devoid of emotion, her mind calculating the trajectories of war as easily as one might ponder a game of chess.

As her commands were executed, the screen flickered momentarily, then sharpened to reveal heat signatures moving rapidly beneath the surface. Greda leaned forward, her gaze piercing the digital display as she analyzed the patterns, her brain synapses firing with predatory precision. "There," she pointed, "focus on that cluster. They're herding the civilians into a bottleneck."

The command room buzzed with low, urgent communications, operators relaying her orders, adjusting satellite feeds, refining drone paths. Every screen danced with data, a symphony of war orchestrated by Greda's unyielding will.

Suddenly, a new feed popped up, showing a group of resistance fighters setting up what looked like rudimentary barriers near the recovery gardens, disrupting the tranquil atmosphere with a desperate blockade—an attempt to slow her forces. Greda scoffed, the sound slicing through the ambient noise of the room. "Prepare the armored units. It's time we crush this little rebellion."

Her gaze didn't waver from the screens, her mind already three moves ahead, predicting, planning, devastating in her efficiency. This was her realm, her rule defined by the uncompromising lines of warfare and survival. Here in the nerve center of her operations, Greda was not just a leader; she was the sovereign architect of fates, the arbiter of life and death.

As the resistance's feeble fortifications appeared onscreen, a tactical overlay of the area materialized, showing her the best points of invasion. "Direct the eastern flank to converge on their position. Use the south corridor for a pincer move," she directed, her commands precise, her strategy lethal.

The room obeyed in orchestrated silence, her will imposed on the chaotic ballet of war outside. The feed from the drones grew more frantic, the images blurring into a whirl of motion as her forces moved in, relentless and unstoppable.

"Zoom in," she commanded, her finger pointing at a particular blip on the screen. The image expanded, bringing into focus a group of resistance members rallying around a young leader.

"Interesting," Greda murmured, her interest piqued. "Mark him for high surveillance. He might be useful."

Greda watched intently, a figure of cold command, as her troops pressed forward. The sudden descent of her forces was a calculated wave, unrelenting and precise, but something flickered in the corner of her eye—a deviation on the drone feed. "Pause there," she instructed, her voice cutting through the hum of the command center.

The room fell silent, operators freezing as they awaited her command. On the screen, one of her surveillance drones—a model designed for predictable, steady reconnaissance—abruptly altered its flight path, veering towards a group of hurriedly moving civilians. It was an anomaly, unexpected and out of protocol.

"Enhance that segment," Greda commanded. The image zoomed in, the drone racing towards the civilians who were clearly part of Callan's evacuation team. Her eyes narrowed in thought, a spark of curiosity beneath her icy demeanor. "What's triggered it?" she mused aloud.

Before anyone could respond, a bright flare burst on the screen. The drone spiraled down, crashing into the debris-strewn streets of The Refuge. The interference was clear—a handheld EMP device, potent enough to disable the drone but risky given the electromagnetic signature it cast.

"Source of the EMP?" she snapped, her mind racing as the implications unfolded. The tactical disadvantage was minor but noticeable; the EMP would alert all nearby drones to the location of its use.

"Tracking now, Chancellor," one of the operators replied, fingers flying over the controls. Within seconds, the screens updated, displaying a surge of movement from her troops, converging on the new threat location.

Greda leaned forward, her gaze fixed on the unfolding chaos. "They've made themselves a target," she said, a hint of admiration in her tone for the boldness of the move. "Deploy additional squads to that sector. Pin them down."

The command center buzzed back to life as her orders were relayed. Screens flickered with new data, drones redirected to flood the area where Callan's team was attempting to hold their ground. The engagement escalated rapidly, each side adapting to the rapid shifts in the battlefield dynamic.

"Show me their positions," Greda demanded, her voice calm but carrying an edge that resonated around the room. The main screen shifted, displaying a heat map of The Refuge. Red dots indicated her forces, while the blue ones—fewer but stubbornly persistent—showed Callan's team, now trapped in a tightening noose of her making.

A new icon blinked into existence on another monitor—a sign of further complications or a tactical advantage? Greda's eyes flicked towards the symbol, deciphering its meaning.

"It appears they've set up barriers, Chancellor," an analyst reported. "Makeshift, but effective in funneling our approach."

"Then we change our approach," Greda concluded, her mind already sorting through possible strategies. "Use the underground passages. Flank them."

As the situation intensified, Greda stood back, arms crossed, a general surveying the battlefield from her digital hilltop. The air around her crackled with the electricity of command, the weight of decisions, and the shadows of impending outcomes. Her face, lit by the glow of the screens, was a mask of focus, the architect of chaos directing the storm of war beneath the streets of The Refuge.

Elara's heart pounded as she surveyed the makeshift barriers her team had erected in the cramped corridors of The Refuge. The echo of distant thuds, the signs of Greda's forces approaching, sent a ripple of urgency through her. She turned to the medical team, her voice steady despite the chaos, "Focus on the critically injured first. Use the regenerative tissue machines judiciously; we can't afford to run out of supplies now."

The air was thick with the sharp scent of antiseptics and the metallic tang of blood. Under the harsh lighting of the medical bay, Elara moved swiftly, her eyes scanning the biometric scanner's readouts. Every beep and whir of the machine translated into a life hanging in the balance, a constant reminder of the weight of her decisions.

Rootwhisper, its branches subtly glowing, murmured soothing tones to a young child with a bandaged head, its presence a calming balm amid the storm of human panic and pain. Elara noted the calming effect the young sapling had on the civilians; its empathetic nature was invaluable here.

Across the room, Sylas was setting up a perimeter defense. His figure was a blur of motion, setting up spore traps and motion sensors that would alert them to any approaching danger. "Elara, we're as secure as we can be without drawing more attention," he shouted over the sound of his tools.

She nodded, turning back to the medical team. "Keep me updated on the supply levels," she instructed a nurse who was frantically sorting through medical kits. The nurse nodded, her face set in a mask of determination. Elara's gaze then shifted to a young man with a deep gash across his torso. The diagnostic tool was blinking red, a bad sign. "Prep him for tissue regeneration, now!" she ordered, her voice cutting through the noise.

The team responded with practiced efficiency, the wounded man quickly sedated and moved to the machine. Elara watched the screen as the device hummed to life, knitting skin and muscle with an eerie precision. It was a race against time, each second stretching infinitely.

Suddenly, a sharp crackle of static erupted from her communicator. "Elara, we've got incoming!" Sylas's voice was tense, a stark contrast to the clinical buzz of the medical bay. Her stomach dropped as she grabbed her biocide launcher, the weight of the weapon both a burden and a reassurance.

She peered through the temporary barricade they had constructed at the entrance. Through the gaps, she could see shadows moving, the distinctive silhouette of Greda's drones scouting ahead of their assault troops. "Everyone, brace yourselves!" she yelled, turning to see the medical staff ushering non-combatants into a fortified back room.

A drone darted past the barrier, its sensors sweeping the area. Elara didn't hesitate; she raised her launcher and fired. The biocide capsule exploded on contact, releasing a cloud of corrosive spores that short-circuited the drone in a shower of sparks. But victory was short-lived; more drones followed, a relentless stream of mechanical predators.

Sylas reappeared at her side, his face grim. "They're pushing hard now. We can't hold them off much longer without heavier firepower."

Callan stood firm, his silhouette cast in stark relief against the flickering lights of The Refuge's medical bay. His gaze swept over the faces of his team and the wounded they protected, a silent vow etched in his expression. "Calm Down," he called out, his voice a calm anchor in the rising storm of panic and fear that threatened to overwhelm them. The walls vibrated with the impact of Greda's forces trying to breach their defenses. Despite the chaos, Callan's demeanor radiated a composed urgency that bolstered the spirits of everyone present.

His hand gripped the Solar Beam Rifle, the weapon's surface cool and reassuring under his touch. He could feel the weight of every decision he had made leading them to this moment. The air was thick with the smell of antiseptics and sweat, a pungent reminder of the high stakes. Each groan of metal, each distant explosion was a heartbeat, counting down the uncertain future they faced.

Turning to Elara, who was coordinating the medical team's efforts, Callan found a silent question in her eyes. He nodded slightly, a silent promise exchanged between them. They had come too far to falter now. Moving toward the center of the room, Callan climbed atop a makeshift platform, drawing the attention of his weary team.

"We knew this path wouldn't be easy," Callan began, his voice cutting through the murmur of anxious whispers. "This war ends tonight!" His words, earnest and resolute, resonated in the cramped space, a beacon of hope in the dim light.

Around him, faces lifted, drawn to his conviction. From the young sapling Rootwhisper, whose gentle glow seemed to pulse in rhythm with Callan's words, to Sylas, whose usual stoic demeanor was replaced with a nod of firm agreement. Callan's gaze then fell on the younger members of their group, their eyes wide with a mixture of fear and admiration, hanging onto his every word.

"The barriers we've built here," he gestured to the fortifications that stood between them and the enemy, "are not just of metal and stone, but of will and resolve. We stand together, united by our cause and by our sacrifices." A murmur of approval rose among the group, the shared resolve knitting them closer together.

As he stepped down, the ground shook—a harsh reminder that the enemy was drawing closer. Callan moved through the crowd, placing a reassuring hand on a young recruit's shoulder, whispering a word of encouragement to a medic struggling to keep her composure.

Then, the real test came. The outer defenses were breached with a deafening crash that sent a shockwave through The Refuge. Callan was at the forefront in an instant, rifle raised, as the first of Greda's drones swooped through the breach. Without hesitation, he fired, the beam of concentrated solar energy searing through the air, striking the drone down in a shower of sparks.

"Get that barrier back up!" Callan's command was swift, the team rallying to his side as they prepared to defend their temporary sanctuary. Beside him, Elara readied her biocide launcher.

Dust swirled around the makeshift barrier and the distant hum of drones grew louder, a sinister chorus in the twilight. Callan steadied his solar beam rifle, peering through the sights at the encroaching shadows cast by Greda's forces. A drone broke through the mist, its metallic body glinting under the weak sunlight filtering through the overcast sky.

"Cover fire!" Callan shouted, his voice firm over the clatter of his team's weapons. Elara, positioned to his left, launched a volley from her biocide launcher, the capsules bursting on impact and sending a shower of corrosive spores into the air. The drone sputtered and crashed, its circuits fried by the potent chemicals.

Sylas, his hands steady on the plasma shield generator, glanced over to Callan. "Barrier's almost up, but it won't hold long against a full assault."

"Keep at it!" Callan replied, reloading his rifle as another drone zipped through the breach. He fired again, the beam slicing through the drone with precision, sending another enemy spiraling to the ground in a flaming wreck. Beside him, the team worked feverishly, stacking debris and metal sheets to fortify their position.

Through the chaos, Callan heard Nara's breathless update in his earpiece. "Thermal scan picked up more than just drones—armed figures approaching from the southeast, potentially hostile."

Callan's eyes narrowed. This was no random patrol; it was a calculated move by Greda. But the figures emerging from the mist didn't charge or shoot. Instead, they moved with a hesitance that was uncharacteristic of Greda's usual assault troops.

"Nara, hold your fire. Let's see what they want," Callan commanded, lowering his rifle slightly but keeping his finger near the trigger. The figures, ragged and worn, halted a few yards out, their weapons lowered.

One stepped forward, a woman with a haunted look in her eyes. "We mean no harm," she called out, her voice hoarse. "We seek asylum."

Suspicion knotted in Callan's stomach. Asylum seekers or not, they were a potential breach in the refuge's security—a risk to the community he vowed to protect. Yet, turning them away could mean missing a vital opportunity to learn Greda's plans.

"Keep them covered," Callan instructed Elara and Sylas, striding forward to meet the defectors at a safe distance. His mind raced through possibilities, each more dangerous than the last. Were they desperate defectors, or a clever ruse by Greda to infiltrate their defenses?

Callan squared his shoulders as the dim dawn light seeped through the mist, silhouetting the ragtag group of Greda's soldiers who had approached The Refuge under a flag of truce—or deception. His solar beam rifle hung heavy over his shoulder, a silent sentinel as he stepped forward into the no-man's land between wary allies and potential foes.

"State your intentions," Callan's voice cut through the morning chill, every syllable sharp with authority. Lena stood to his left, her eyes darting between the soldiers and her tablet, where she received real-time background checks transmitted quietly by Zoe. Zoe, stationed behind a makeshift console set up near the barrier, scanned frequencies for any hint of an ambush or a stray signal that might betray their position.

The soldiers' leader, a grizzled sergeant with scars mapping his exposed arms, stepped forward, his own weapon lowered but ready. "We're deserting," he declared, his voice gruff with exhaustion and edged with an urgency that spoke of recent battles. "Greda's gone too far—her plans, they're…" He trailed off, swallowing hard, his gaze flicking back to his own men, seeking silent permission to continue.

Callan's gaze narrowed, reading the tension in the man's posture, the quick, haunted glances he exchanged with his squad. "What plans?" he pressed, stepping closer. Behind him, Elara adjusted her stance slightly, her biocide launcher at the ready, her presence a quiet promise of violence should it be needed.

The sergeant met Callan's eyes, the weight of his decision etching deeper lines into his weathered face. "An attack, larger than any before. She aims to wipe out half the underground Sectors by sunrise tomorrow." Murmurs stirred among Callan's team at this, a ripple of apprehension threading through them as they processed the gravity of the threat.

Sylas shifted, his hand never straying far from the plasma shield generator's controls. "How do we know this isn't a trap?" he questioned, his voice a low rumble over the sound of the shield humming into life, ready to protect or imprison.

The sergeant sighed, a sound of a man burdened by wars too long fought. "Because we brought proof." From his coat, he produced a small, battered data pad, offering it to Callan. "Coordinates, plans, all of it. We want no part in her massacres anymore."

Callan accepted the device, his fingers brushing against the cold metal, the weight of potential treachery heavy in his grasp. He glanced back at Lena, who nodded slightly, her eyes still on her screen where the truth of the sergeant's words slowly confirmed themselves.

"Fall in line, soldiers," Callan's command echoed with authority as he handed the data pad back to Elara for further analysis. His tone softened slightly, a nod to the shared hardships of war they all bore. "We operate on trust here, earned and given. You're under the Resistance's protection now."

The soldiers, visibly fatigued yet relieved by the acknowledgment, straightened up almost instinctively, a trace of their former discipline surfacing despite the weariness that clung to them like the dirt on their uniforms. "Thank you, sir," the sergeant replied, his voice firm, resonating with a resonance of military respect. "We'll stand by your orders." His squad, catching the subtle shift in atmosphere, exchanged glances of muted hope, rallying behind their sergeant's lead.

Dust danced in the beam of Tibo's headlamp as he crouched, adjusting the last of his homemade sensors along the dank walls of The Catacombs. The makeshift barrier in The Refuge held up just long enough for them to escape to Zone C6. The air was thick with the musty scent of earth and stone, and the eerie quiet was punctuated only by the distant, muffled sounds of the team's cautious movements through the twisting tunnels.

"Alright, little buddy, talk to me," he muttered to the device, tapping it gently. The small screen flickered to life, displaying a series of green blips that began to pulse rhythmically. A grin split Tibo's face under the dim light. "That's what I like to see. You're all set to sing if anything nasty comes this way."

Nara, her figure shadowed against the faint light from her own gear, approached from the tunnel ahead. "All clear up to the next bend," she reported, her voice a whisper in the close confines. "But keep your jokes down, would you? Sound travels weirdly down here."

Tibo chuckled softly, tucking a tool back into his belt. "Right, because it's my jokes that'll give us away, not the clank of Callan's gear." He gave Nara a wink, receiving an eye-roll in return before she turned, her form blending seamlessly back into the shadows.

The tight, winding passageways of Zone C6 were a far cry from the open, tech-filled spaces Tibo preferred, but they were exactly what the team needed: a hidden artery through the city's underbelly, forgotten by all but a few. Callan had brought them here with promises of safety and secrecy, and Tibo's gadgets were set to ensure they kept that promise.

Adjusting his climbing gear, Tibo scanned the rough-hewn walls, his mind racing through calculations of sound waves and motion detection. Every sensor placement had to be perfect; a single misstep could lead them straight into an ambush. "Echo chambers," he mumbled, recalling the briefing. "Gotta love old architecture, perfect for bouncing around both sound and signals."

As he moved to join the others, his boots scuffed quietly against the stone floor. Up ahead, Callan's voice echoed softly, a low rumble of commands as he directed Lena and Kyle in setting up a temporary command post in one of the wider chambers. Tibo slipped his electrostatic disruptor pistol from its holster, checking it reflexively. It was more of a tool than a weapon, ideal for disabling electronics, but down here, who knew what lay in wait.

The Catacombs breathed around them, an ancient giant stirring in its slumber. Tibo felt the weight of centuries above him, a silent reminder of the city's deep scars and deeper secrets. As he approached the chamber where the rest of the team gathered, he overheard Callan's hushed tones.

"We'll hole up here for now," Callan was saying, his figure a dark, steady presence against the flicker of makeshift lighting. "Nara and Tibo have the entry points covered, but stay sharp. We're not out of the woods yet."

"Or rather, out of the stones," Tibo quipped as he stepped into the light, earning a few strained chuckles from the team. His gaze met Callan's, and he nodded, a silent exchange of respect and readiness.

In the dim glow of their temporary refuge, Tibo set up his last sensor, a final guard against the darkness of the tunnels. His hands worked deftly, the familiar motions a comfort amid the uncertainty. As he activated the sensor, its soft beep a whisper in the chamber, he couldn't help but feel a surge of pride.

As Tibo adjusted the focus on his sensor array, a sudden chill coursed through the air, sweeping past the ancient stone walls that bore silent witness to centuries of secrets. The Catacombs were as much a part of the resistance as the fighters themselves. "Okay, you old rocks, keep your secrets," he murmured to himself, the light from his headlamp casting eerie patterns on the walls.

The room they had entered was unlike any other in the winding maze they'd navigated. Here, hidden from the unrelenting gaze of Greda's patrols, the walls were lined with relics of past resistances. Elara and Lena, their figures bent in the dim light, sifted through piles of dusty journals and faded maps, their whispers a ghostly echo in the chamber.

"Look at this, Tibo!" Elara called out, her voice tinged with excitement. She held up a tattered journal, its pages yellowed with age but the writing still legible. Tibo walked over, his eyes scanning the handwritten notes of a resistance leader long gone. "They were planning a revolt right under the city's nose," he said, the weight of history palpable in his tone.

Lena was poring over an ancient map spread out on a makeshift table. "These tunnels," she pointed out, her finger tracing a route that zigzagged across the paper, "they had escapes planned all over the city. Ingenious."

The chamber hummed with a new energy, the discoveries rekindling a fire in the team. Kyle and Mason were on the other side, carefully examining a cache of old weaponry. With each piece they unearthed, the room grew richer in stories and strategy. "Could repurpose some of these," Mason mused, holding up what looked like a rudimentary explosive device. "Old school but might just add the punch we need."

Rootwhisper seemed to absorb the essence of the room, its leaves shimmering slightly in the low light. Tibo watched the plant creature, fascinated by its connection to their cause. "Feels like it's listening, huh?" he joked to Nara, who was adjusting her binoculars.

Nara didn't respond, her focus on a small screen displaying thermal readings from the tunnels they'd left behind. "No patrols so far, but we can't lower our guard," she replied, her voice low and steady.

The emotional weight of the chamber was not lost on Tibo. Here, surrounded by the echoes of past sacrifices, the team felt a profound connection to their cause. "We're walking in the footsteps of giants," Tibo said aloud, not just to break the silence but to acknowledge the magnitude of their journey.

As they prepared to move deeper into the catacombs, Callan's voice brought them back to the present. "We use what we've learned here," he said firmly, gathering the maps and journals. "Every bit of knowledge is a weapon against Greda."

"Hey, Lena, got something here," he called out, waving her over. His fingers danced along the edges, feeling for triggers or traps.

Lena joined him, her eyes narrowing with curiosity. "Careful, Tibo. Could be rigged," she cautioned, her voice barely above a whisper as she watched him work. Tibo nodded, pulling out a small device from his belt, his hands steady despite the adrenaline. A faint click echoed as the panel gave way, revealing a compartment filled with dusty canisters, medical kits, and several stacks of ammunition.

"Jackpot," Tibo grinned, the relief palpable in his voice. He carefully examined one of the canisters, its label faded but just legible.

"Looks like the old resistance wasn't just fighting; they were planning for the long haul," he remarked, handing a canister to Lena.

Meanwhile, Kyle and Mason moved in, their curiosity piqued by the discovery. Mason knelt beside a sealed crate, inspecting it for booby traps. "Old tech, but let's not take chances," he muttered, his hands expertly disarming a hidden explosive device that could have taken them all out. "Good catch," Kyle breathed out, visibly relieved as Mason cracked open the crate to reveal several aged yet still functional devices.

"Let's see if we can integrate these with our current gear," Kyle suggested, already pulling out tools from his bag. Tibo watched, fascinated, as Kyle began tinkering with an old transmitter, his fingers deft and confident.

Sylas, meanwhile, took charge of organizing the newly found supplies. "Food, meds, ammo—this will keep us going for weeks," he noted, efficiently sorting the items into piles for easy access. Tibo chuckled, stepping back to give Sylas room, his gaze sweeping the chamber that suddenly felt less like a tomb and more like a treasure trove.

But the laughter died in his throat as he caught sight of Rootwhisper trembling slightly by the entrance. The plant's deep connection to the place, to the sacrifices made here, was palpable. "Hey, buddy, you alright?" Tibo asked, his tone soft. Rootwhisper's leaves shuddered, a low hum emanating from it.

The emotional weight of the discovery wasn't lost on anyone, especially not on Tibo. He knew the importance of these relics, these resources—they weren't just supplies; they were a legacy, a reminder of those who had fought and fallen in these very catacombs. "We're not just surviving; we're continuing a legacy," he said aloud, more to himself than to the others.

"Let's get these supplies back to the main group," he ordered, but not before pausing to place a hand on Tibo's shoulder, a silent nod to his crucial role in their survival.

Chapter 20

The cool, damp air of Zone V2: The Ventworks whispered around Rootwhisper as the team pressed forward, the faint glow of its bioluminescent leaves casting eerie shadows on the narrow walls. Nara led the way, her movements silent and precise, a figure of concentration with her MSBs guiding their path through the dark labyrinth.

Rootwhisper felt the ancient roots entwined within the structure of the tunnels, whispering tales of the old, of movements unseen and silent wars fought in these very corridors. Each step was a quiet conversation, its roots gently brushing against the stone, feeling for vibrations, for signs of life or threat lurking beyond their sight.

Zoe was a few steps behind, her focus split between the dimly lit tunnel ahead and the screens displaying encrypted communications. She tapped away at her device, ensuring their electronic signatures were masked, a stream of data flowing like a silent river of light in the darkness. The low hum of her equipment mingled with the soft rustling of Rootwhisper's leaves, a duet of technology and nature.

Suddenly, Rootwhisper's tendrils recoiled slightly, the faint tremor of footsteps detected through the network of roots that stretched out like a web in all directions. It sent a silent alert, a pulse of warning that only its plant senses could perceive. Nara halted, her hand raised for a pause, her body tense as she turned her head, listening.

"Patrol ahead, bypassing main shaft," Rootwhisper murmured, its voice barely a whisper, yet clear in the silence of the tunnels. The connection it forged with the mycelial network was pivotal, guiding them through paths less trodden, under the very noses of their pursuers.

With a nod from Nara, the team veered left into an even narrower passage, the walls closing in, the air growing thick with the scent of moist earth and old secrets. Rootwhisper's leaves brushed against the cold stone, each touch a note in the quiet symphony of their stealthy advance.

As they moved, Rootwhisper continued to communicate with the silent sentinels of the underground—the fungi and the moss—that reported back the echoes of footsteps, the distant clank of armor, all the while remaining invisible to electronic eyes and ears.

Zoe, her device now stowed away, followed closely, her eyes scanning the shadows. She whispered back to Rootwhisper, "Signal's clear, they're taking the bait," referencing the false trails they had laid to mislead any followers. Her reliance on Rootwhisper's natural prowess complemented her technical skills, a fusion of old and new warfare crafted in the belly of the earth.

They reached a juncture marked by an ancient engraving, a relic from a bygone resistance. Here, Rootwhisper paused, its glow illuminating the symbol—a reminder of the legacy they carried forward. Nara touched the carving briefly, respect in her gaze, before checking her bearings and nodding to the left tunnel.

As Rootwhisper, Nara, and Zoe advanced deeper into The Ventworks, the young sentient sapling's awareness of its surroundings deepened. Rootwhisper's bioluminescent leaves, usually a soft beacon in the underground's eternal twilight, now dimmed to near invisibility. It was a necessary adaptation, a natural stealth enhancing their silent march through the enemy's domain.

"Stay close," Rootwhisper intoned softly, its voice carrying the hushed, rustling quality of wind-stirred leaves. "The roots speak of disturbances not far ahead."

Zoe, with her eyes never leaving the small screen that displayed their cryptic path, nodded slightly. The tech in her hands was advanced, but here in the ancient corridors, Rootwhisper's primal connections offered unmatched guidance. "Lead on," she whispered back, her voice a shadow in the dark, trusting the plant's unique senses.

Nara moved with ghost-like silence, her eyes scanning the shadows. Her role as scout was pivotal, but in this operation, it was Rootwhisper who illuminated their path—literally and figuratively. The sapling's soft glow revealed an ancient marker, an engraving worn by time yet still clear in its message of resistance. It was a beacon from the past, guiding them forward.

"The old ways guide us," Rootwhisper mused aloud, its tendrils caressing the cold stone. "But they also warn us." At its words, a pulse of subtle energy spread through the network of roots and fungi underfoot, a silent alarm triggered by the presence of something—or someone—unnatural ahead.

The team paused, a silent agreement passing between them as Rootwhisper extended its influence, seeking clarity. "An electronic sentinel lies dormant ahead, cloaked in the guise of the old growth," it explained, its voice barely a murmur. With a deliberate surge of energy, Rootwhisper awakened the dormant fungi around the device, causing it to short-circuit quietly.

"Path's clear," Zoe confirmed after a moment, her gaze lifting from the screen to the corridor ahead. They continued, moving towards the heart of the enemy's operation with Rootwhisper clearing the way, its natural abilities masking their electronic signatures and muffling their movements.

As they reached the target, Rootwhisper's role became more critical. It released spores that carried through the air, a natural anesthetic that settled quietly around the unsuspecting guards. One by one, they slumped, subdued by the potent botanical sedative without ever seeing their assailants.

With the guards neutralized, Nara deftly bypassed the last security measures, and they accessed the core of the Ventworks. Inside, Rootwhisper sensed the vast array of supplies and equipment—ammunition, food, medical kits—all vital to the enemy's efforts but soon to be rendered useless.

"Set the charges," Rootwhisper instructed, as Zoe and Nara prepared the explosives. Their actions were swift, efficient, and synchronized with the timing set to allow a narrow window for escape.

The explosions that followed were thunderous, reverberating through the Ventworks as the team retraced their steps. Rootwhisper led the escape, its glow now a beacon once more, guiding through the quickly shifting terrain as corridors began to collapse.

"Quickly, this way!" Rootwhisper urged, detecting a safe path through the network of its brethren roots and the shifting earth. Behind them, the rumble of destruction was a satisfying confirmation of their success, even as it threatened to bury them in the ruins.

As they emerged from the tunnels, the night air was like a cold slap of reality. They were out, breathing deeply of the free underground air, the mission a success. They had struck deeply, sabotaging a critical node in the enemy's supply chain, unseen and now safely withdrawn into the night, their passage marked only by the quiet whisper of leaves and the faint glow of a sapling's luminescence.

Exhaling a cloud of cold air, Callan surveyed the dimly lit surroundings of The Ventworks. He felt the aftershocks of the distant explosions, a reminder of the outside world's chaos. With a hand signal, he directed his team to the central hub where they'd establish their operations.

"The Ventworks offers us more than shelter," Callan began, his voice carrying through the hum of the underground. He pointed to the layered blueprints displayed on Lena's portable screen. "These tunnels," he traced the routes with his finger, "they give us the strategic depth we need."

"First, the stealth corridors. We can move undetected, shield ourselves right under Greda's nose. This is how we'll keep striking without being cornered," he explained, his eyes scanning the team, making sure every face was with him.

He moved on, "The surveillance nests—Kyle, you've seen their outputs. Top-notch intel without risking boots on the ground. We'll know Greda's moves before they do." Kyle nodded, already mentally tweaking the systems to optimize coverage.

"The rapid transit rails," he continued, "will be our lifeline. Quick insertion and extraction points across the Underworld. This isn't just about surviving; it's about responding fast, hitting hard, and vanishing before they can hit back."

Sylas, standing by a wall, arms crossed, looked over. "And when they come for us?" he asked, the question hanging in the chilled air.

Callan met his gaze, "That's why we fortify. Mason's already working on the entry points. We'll turn this place into a fortress that can withstand any assault."

Elara, her brow furrowed as she tended to a map of potential hazard zones, added, "And the environmental controls—these will let us maintain the zone, keep our people safe from the elements and hidden from thermal scans."

Callan's gaze settled on Rootwhisper, its leaves gently glowing in the dim light. "And we have more than just technology on our side. Rootwhisper, your connection to the plant network around us isn't just about espionage. You'll help us understand this land, turn it from a hiding spot into a home."

The atmosphere in the Ventworks command center was thick with urgency, the static-filled echo of Felix's distress call still resonating through the air. Tibo, standing slightly apart, adjusted his tools with nimble fingers, a slight smirk playing across his face despite the tension. Humor was his shield, his way of coping with the anxiety that such missions invariably brought.

"Location," Callan's voice cut sharply through the buzz of whispered conversations and the soft clatter of keyboards. Zoe was already on it, her fingers flying over the digital map with practiced ease, isolating coordinates deep in enemy territory. Tibo couldn't help but quip under his breath to Kyle nearby, "Bet you five credits she finds him before you finish recalibrating that drone."

Kyle shot him a distracted grin, his attention half on the small drone floating beside him. "You're on, but you're losing this one, Tibo."

Lena leaned into the light of the display, pointing out fortified zones on the map. "Heavy fortifications here, and here," she noted, her tone all business. "There's a thinner line here we might exploit." Tibo leaned closer, his eyes tracing the paths Lena indicated, already thinking about the gadgets in his pack that could come in handy.

As Callan directed Mason to prepare charges for a silent entry and discussed stealth tactics with Kyle, Tibo's mind raced through his inventory of tech. He'd need to ensure all his gadgets were primed for quick deployment. Silently, he admired the way Callan took control, his clear, decisive commands slicing through the uncertainty like a blade.

Sylas, standing like a silent sentinel, received his orders from Callan to guard the rear. The big man simply nodded, his presence reassuring in its solidity. Tibo felt a flicker of relief knowing Sylas would be covering their backs.

Elara joined Callan, her medical gear already strapped on, her expression focused and severe. "I'll lead with you," she said, a statement more than a suggestion. Callan nodded, and Tibo felt a surge of respect for her—she was always ready to throw herself into the heart of danger.

Rootwhisper's role was next on Callan's list. The young sapling, with its bioluminescent glow, seemed almost otherworldly in the dim command center. "Rootwhisper will guide our approach," Callan announced, his voice imbued with a hint of awe for the sapling's unique abilities.

As Callan rallied the teams, Tibo felt the familiar thrill of anticipation mixed with fear. With a final check of his gear, Tibo prepared to follow Callan and the rest into the shadows of the underground. His tools were ready, his mind sharp with adrenaline, and his heart light with the belief that they could face whatever lay ahead. As they moved out, Tibo tossed one last joke over his shoulder to Kyle, the laughter mingling with the sound of their boots on the metal floor, a reminder that even in the darkest times, there was a light to be found.

Elara's breath fogged the inside of her respirator as she followed the team through the damp, narrow passageways beneath the Lumina Citadel. Obsidian walls, cold and unyielding, absorbed the sound of their cautious steps. Every shadow seemed a specter of the unknown, every echo a whisper of threats lurking just out of sight. Ahead, Nara's silhouette flitted between the camera blind spots, her stealth gear rendering her nearly invisible against the dark stone.

"Sylas, status?" Elara whispered into her comms, her voice barely audible.

"Shields holding, but these pulse blasts are getting close," Sylas replied, his tone calm despite the flickering of his plasma shield under the onslaught of stray energy weapons reflecting off the walls.

The corridor ahead branched, leading deeper into the stronghold's heart. Here, the stakes were clear and towering; Felix's rescue was not just about saving a comrade—he was the key to unraveling Chancellor Greda's manipulations that threatened their fragile resistance.

"Elara, we have movement," Callan's voice cut through her thoughts, sharp and urgent. He was ahead, checking the readouts from his scanner, which displayed the outlines of approaching guards. "Two hostiles, converging on your position."

With practiced ease, Elara pivoted on the ball of her foot, raising her biocide launcher. The narrowness of the corridor would work to their advantage, funneling the enemy directly into her line of sight. She steadied her breath, aiming at the spot where the guards would appear. Her finger tensed on the trigger, the launcher's familiar weight a comfort in her hands.

As the first guard rounded the corner, her launcher spat out a series of rounds, the air hissing as the biocidal agents cut through the damp, chilly air. The guard staggered, armor sizzling where the rounds ate through, his scream echoing off the stone before he collapsed, his body crumpling under the unexpected assault.

Rootwhisper manipulated the fungi-laden ground. Vines erupted between the tiles, twisting around the legs of the second guard who hesitated, caught off guard by the sudden ambush. The brief pause was all Sylas needed, his shield slamming forward with the force of a battering ram, pinning the guard against the wall with a brutal crunch.

"Take them down," Callan's command refocused them, his voice a beacon in the dim corridor. They advanced, Elara's boots slipping slightly on the slick floor, her senses heightened to every shadow, every potential threat that could emerge from the darkness.

The network of maintenance shafts was a labyrinth, each turn and dip a potential trap, but Lena's maps promised a route to where they believed Felix was held. Kyle was already ahead, his lighter steps barely audible as he scouted the safest path through the technological fortress they ventured to dismantle.

Their progress was a symphony of whispers, the soft hum of Sylas's shield, and the occasional crackle of disrupted electronics as Tibo jammed the Citadel's surveillance systems, buying them precious minutes. Every nerve in Elara's body was attuned to the murmurs of the underground, her fingers tight around the biocide launcher. Ahead, Nara paused, her hand signaling a halt with a swift, silent gesture.

The maintenance shaft opened into a wider tunnel, casting elongated shadows against the stark obsidian walls. Here, the Citadel's heart pulsed with a more ominous beat, the air thick with the electric anticipation of conflict. Elara scanned the dimly lit expanse, her biometric scanner flickering with data, translating the unseen into stark red warnings on her visor.

"Sylas, shield up," she hissed, her voice a whisper over the comms. Ahead, the silhouette of a security checkpoint emerged, manned by guards in bio-enhanced armor. Their movements were methodical, unnaturally synchronized, a dance of deadly precision.

As they approached, the guards' pulse rifles hummed to life, a sound that sent a shiver down Elara's spine. She watched, heart pounding, as a bolt of energy seared the air, narrowly missing Nara. The smell of singed hair and ozone filled the air, a harsh reminder of the stakes they faced.

"Engage!" Callan's voice broke through the tension, a clear command that unleashed chaos. Rootwhisper reacted first, tendrils creeping through the cracks in the floor, a network of natural sabotage that twisted up and around the unsuspecting guards. The tiles underfoot buckled, sending a shockwave of disarray through the ranks of their adversaries.

Elara did not hesitate. Her launcher thudded, rounds of biocidal agents arcing through the air to meet the disrupted guards. The chemicals met armor with sizzling efficiency, degrading the bio-enhancements with each hit. Screams echoed, a loud boom that mixed with the mechanical buzz of Rootwhisper's assault.

Beside her, Sylas moved, his plasma shield expanding with a roar. He pushed forward, a wall of impenetrable energy that forced the remaining guards back. Their disciplined formation crumbled under his advance.

In the chaos, Tibo's drones whirred to life, small but deadly. They zipped overhead, emitting bursts of high-frequency pulses that added layers of confusion, scrambling what remained of the enemy's communications. The air was rank with the smell of burnt circuits and fear.

Callan advanced, a shadow among shadows, his movements precise and deadly. He reached the first of the fallen guards, retrieving data from the man's wrist console with swift, practiced motions. Every second counted, and their window was closing rapidly.

Elara covered him, her eyes scanning for more threats, her body tense and ready. The corridor ahead promised more danger, more resistance. They were deep in the enemy's den now, every shadow a potential threat, every sound a possible alarm.

Amid this tension, a new element emerged, one that shifted the battlefield in their favor. Rootwhisper, acting on an instinct only it possessed, extended its tendrils into the fissures of the stone flooring. The roots snaked beneath the cold, hard surface, intertwining with the mechanical veins of the Citadel.

With a subtle signal from Rootwhisper, the roots contracted simultaneously, upheaving the floor tiles with violent force. Guards stumbled as the ground beneath them buckled and split, their formations thrown into disarray. Elara seized the moment, her hand steady on the biocide launcher as she fired a volley of grenades into the chaos. The grenades burst on impact, releasing a cloud of fast-acting agent that sapped the vitality of the guards' bio-augmentations, rendering their enhanced abilities null.

The corridor echoed with the sounds of coughing and the clatter of falling gear as the guards struggled to regain their footing. Callan and Sylas didn't give them a chance. Moving with precision honed by countless skirmishes, they charged. Callan, with a grim determination etched onto his face, swung his solar beam rifle like a bludgeon, meeting the helmet of an approaching guard. The impact was met with a crack as the visor shattered, a spray of sparks erupting from the damaged electronics.

Beside him, Sylas was a force of nature. His plasma shield generator thrummed with power, the energy field extending outward to shove another guard against the wall. The guard's armor buckled under the immense force, a grotesque sound of crumpling metal filling the air as he slid down the wall, defeated.

Elara watched for a split second, her instincts urging her to keep moving. The initial surprise of their assault would wear off quickly, and more guards would soon converge on their position. She scanned the corridor, noting the positions of their foes and any further threats that might emerge. Tibo deployed his miniature drones, which buzzed overhead. They emitted sharp, disorienting pulses, scrambling the remaining guards' communication devices, adding to the confusion and hindering their ability to regroup.

The air was thick with the smell of ozone and the metallic tang of blood. Elara knew this was just the beginning. The resistance had breached the walls of the Lumina Citadel, a fortress that had stood unyielded against many who dared challenge it. Now, its halls rang with the sounds of battle.

The resistance had breached the walls of the Lumina Citadel, a fortress that had stood unyielded against many who dared challenge it. Now, its halls rang with the sounds of battle. The crescendo of their mission was approaching, and every move they made was critical.

Kyle dashed ahead, his figure a blur of motion as he navigated the dimly lit corridors. The last known GPS coordinates of Felix blinked on his device, guiding him through the labyrinth of the stronghold. The medical kit bounced against his back with each stride, its contents ready to be deployed. As he reached the cell, his breath came out in heavy puffs, fogging the cold metal air. Inside, Felix and his team lay against the wall. Felix is battered but alive, his eyes blinking open at the sound of rescue. The rest of the team is fine.

Elara stayed back with the rest of the team, her biocide launcher in hand, ready to cover Kyle's intervention. Tibo was beside her, fingers flying over the portable tech workshop, his brow furrowed in concentration. With a swift motion, he activated a series of false alarms throughout the Citadel's security system. The corridors echoed with the sudden wail of sirens, the lights flickering into a strobe of confusion that disoriented the guards.

"Now!" Elara hissed, her voice barely audible over the chaos. Tibo's drones, small and agile, darted through the air, their high-frequency pulses scattering the remaining guards. The drones emitted blinding flashes and deafening noise, creating a sensory shield that allowed Elara to move forward. She launched a biocide grenade into a cluster of stumbling guards, the explosion sending them reeling, their bio-augmentations fizzling out under the chemical assault.

With the guards temporarily incapacitated, Callan and Sylas pressed the advantage. Callan's movements were ruthless, a dance of destruction as he wielded his solar beam rifle with lethal precision. Beside him, Sylas's plasma shield flared to life, a pulsing barrier that knocked back anyone who dared approach.

The team's coordination was impeccable, a symphony of violence orchestrated to rescue one of their own. As they cleared the area around Felix's cell, Sylas took position at the rear, his shield generator creating a formidable barrier against any guards trying to regroup and counterattack.

"We have him," Kyle's voice crackled through their earpieces, a note of relief threading through the tension. "He's hurt, but he'll make it."

Felix's senses, dulled by pain and confinement, sharpened with the words. He lay on the cold, hard floor of his cell, the stench of antiseptic and mildew mingling in the stale air. His eyes struggled to adjust to the dim lighting as shadowy figures moved swiftly towards him. The clatter of their swift, determined steps was a sweet sound after the unending silence of the team's captivity.

First to his side was Kyle, medical kit in hand, his face set in a mask of focused concern. "Hang in there, Felix," Kyle muttered, working quickly to assess his injuries. The familiar faces of Lena, Mason, Zoe, Callan, and Elara appeared from the shadows, forming a protective circle around him. The relief on their faces was welcoming, but there was no time for reunions; the mission was far from over.

Elara knelt beside him, her presence a calming force. Her eyes, always so perceptive, scanned the corridor beyond for any sign of resurgence from their foes. Felix could see the resolve in her stance, the readiness to defend, to fight. This was their element, and despite his pain, Felix felt a surge of pride.

The tunnels echoed with distant thuds and the crumbling of old stone—Mason's work, no doubt. Each explosion was meticulously timed, not just to facilitate their escape but to block pursuit. As debris settled in the background, Sylas's shield flickered at the tunnel's entrance, a shimmering barrier holding back the tide of chaos.

"Stay alert people," Callan's voice commanded, urgency laced with an undercurrent of steel. Supported by Zoe and Lena, Felix was hoisted onto an improvised stretcher. The team moved, a fluid, silent stream slipping through the narrow, bioluminescent-lit passages Lena had mapped out months ago. Their lights danced across the damp walls, casting long shadows as they navigated the labyrinthine underworld of the Lumina Citadel.

The route was treacherous, the air thick with the scent of mold and the sharp tang of ionized particles from the frequent blasts. Felix's mind, though foggy, couldn't help but admire the strategic genius of their escape route, every turn and fork so familiar from the virtual models he'd studied countless times before his capture.

Sounds of pursuit were distant yet ominously persistent. Elara's hand was steady as she held her biocide launcher, her gaze flickering back every few seconds to ensure no follower got too close. Sylas, at the rear, adjusted his shield settings, the energy humming louder with each adjustment, ready to repel whatever came their way.

As they advanced, the structural integrity of the tunnel began to falter, small rocks and dirt clattering down around them. "Watch out!" Mason barked, just as a larger boulder dislodged itself from the ceiling. The team ducked, the boulder crashing down where Felix's stretcher had been seconds before.

Heart pounding, Felix's mind raced—not just with the fear of what lay behind, but with the overwhelming drive to survive, to deliver the information that could cripple Chancellor Greda's reign. This data, secured within his own mind, was the key to dismantling a regime built on deception and control.

Pain throbbed through Felix's side as they moved him with careful haste, his vision blurring at the edges. The smell of damp earth and the ghostly luminescence of fungi painted a surreal picture as they navigated the tight, twisting tunnels. Lena's voice, low and constant, guided them through less stable sections, her familiarity with these paths clear in her confident steps and precise directions.

Over the crackle of their comms, the distant sound of collapsing tunnels and the sharper retorts of Mason's charges punctuated the air. Each explosion was a calculated step closer to freedom, shaking the foundations of the Citadel above and sending vibrations through the ground beneath them. Felix felt each detonation as a shockwave of hope, mixed with the adrenaline that kept his mind sharp despite his injuries.

Ahead, Zoe and Callan moved, scanning for signs of the elite squads that Felix knew were on their tail. The knowledge that Greda's forces were using real-time data to track them added an edge of desperation to the escape. Every second in the tunnels was a second closer to either salvation or recapture.

The echo of drones, those relentless hunters of the Citadel, grew slightly louder, a reminder of the technological net that Chancellor Greda had cast over her domain. Felix could almost picture the neural network's cold, unfeeling calculations as it directed its minions, a stark contrast to the fierce, living spirit of his rescuers.

Suddenly, a sharp, high-pitched whine cut through the low rumble of distant explosions. "Drones!" Elara snapped, her launcher raising in a smooth motion. A series of sharp cracks echoed as she fired, the biocide rounds designed to disrupt the drones' delicate sensors. The whine cut off abruptly, replaced by the clatter of falling metal.

They rounded another bend, the air growing cooler and fresher, a sign that they were nearing an exit. Mason, his face set in concentration, paused to place another charge. "This one needs to count," he murmured, setting the timer with precision. "When this goes off, we'll have a narrow window to get clear before they close in."

Felix's mind worked, even now, at the edge of endurance, analyzing their escape route, predicting enemy movements, calculating odds. The weight of what he knew—the plans, the vulnerabilities of Greda's rule—pressed down on him with the urgency of an unspoken countdown.

As Mason's charge exploded behind them, sealing the path they had just traversed, the shockwave propelled them forward. Ahead, the faint outline of an exit appeared, a mere promise of safety in the shape of daylight. Felix's heart lifted, each labored breath mingling fear with hope. They were almost out, almost safe, but in the world of resistance, safety was just another variable in the complex algorithm of war.

The distant rumble of collapsing sections of the tunnel mingled with the sharper reports of Mason's Blaster Gauntlets working overtime. Rocks and debris created a choking cloud of dust, reducing visibility to a few feet in front of them. Felix could hear Mason's steady voice over the comms, "Charges set, move fast, the architecture won't hold long!"

Felix's stretcher swayed precariously as Lena navigated through the narrowest parts of the tunnel. Her voice was calm but urgent, "Keep your heads down, and watch the ceilings!" The walls around them creaked ominously, the integrity of the ancient tunnel compromised with each explosion meant to slow their pursuers.

Elara's figure loomed beside him, her eyes scanning the unstable tunnel walls through the lenses of her biometric scanner. The device beeped irregularly, a staccato rhythm that matched the increasing intensity of their situation. "Structural weakness ahead, shifting left!" she called out, directing the team away from a particularly dangerous looking fissure that snaked its way down the tunnel wall.

Sylas's shield buzzed to life intermittently, the energy field flickering as it absorbed falling debris that would have otherwise been a fatal shower of sharp rocks and dust. Felix felt a dull thud against his side as a smaller rock bounced off the energy barrier, a reminder of the narrow margin between life and death in their desperate race to freedom.

A loud crash signaled another charge detonating closer than the rest, the impact throwing Felix's stretcher into a harsh tilt. Lena grunted as she corrected the angle, her strength preventing his precarious journey from ending disastrously. "We're almost there, just a bit further," she gasped, her breath labored from the exertion and thick dust.

Raj's voice crackled through, mixed with the static of disrupted communications. "Rear guard holding but they're pressing hard. We need to move faster!" The urgency was palpable, and even through his pain, Felix could sense the escalating danger as Greda's elite forces pushed through the obstacles they had set.

Suddenly, a loud, sharper explosion echoed through the tunnel—a sound different from the controlled demolitions by Mason. "Incoming!" Elara shouted, just as a shockwave hit them. Felix braced himself as the stretcher jolted violently, nearly tossing him to the ground. Sylas's shield expanded, enveloping them in a protective bubble as debris rained down.

Through the haze of dust and adrenaline, the exit finally came into view, no longer just a promise but a tangible gateway to safety. They surged forward, the ground beneath them trembling with the force of another explosion. The tunnel behind them collapsed with a deafening roar, sealing off any possibility of retreat. Felix's heart raced, adrenaline flooding his system as the reality of their narrow escape sunk in.

Mason grunted, a sound of satisfaction and relief mixed with exhaustion, as he glanced back at the pile of rubble. "That should hold them off for a while," he said, wiping the sweat and grime from his brow. The final charge he had set was not just a deterrent; it was a definitive barrier between them and the elite squads dispatched by Chancellor Greda.

As they neared the exit, the sound of their own breathing and the distant collapse filled the air, a stark reminder of the fine line they walked between life and death. The light from the exit grew stronger, casting long shadows behind them. It was a surreal moment for Felix, each step toward the light pulling him further from the dark grasp of the regime that had sought to control his fate.

Emerging into Zone V2: The Ventworks, they were met with the sight of their allies, who had been anxiously awaiting their return. The area was a stark contrast to the dark, oppressive tunnels. Here, the environment was filled with the buzz of activity and the soft hum of machinery, providing a makeshift haven for those who fought against Greda's tyranny.

Zoe was immediately at Felix's side, her device in hand as she activated the communication jammer. "Scrambling the signals now. They won't be able to track us here," she said, her voice firm and assured. The scramble of digital noise over the comms confirmed her success, another layer of security against the pervasive surveillance of the regime.

Medical personnel hurried over, their quick, efficient movements as they attended to Felix reflecting the urgency of their situation. As he was examined and treated for his injuries, Felix shared a look with Callan, who had become a welcome new friend. The exchange was silent but filled with a mutual understanding of what had been accomplished—and what was still at stake.

Felix finally turned to Callan, the weight of the data he carried pressing on him as much as his physical wounds. "It's time," he said, his voice hoarse but resolute. "The information I have... it's going to change everything." Callan nodded, his expression set in a determined line. This was the moment they had risked so much for, the chance to turn the tide in their struggle against Greda.

As they prepared to move out, the ground shook once more—a distant but powerful reminder of the chaos they had left behind. The final collapse orchestrated by Mason had not only sealed their pursuers out but also marked the beginning of a new phase in their rebellion. It was a cataclysmic shift, both literally and metaphorically.

The tremors of the collapsing tunnel reverberated through the Ventworks, a resounding echo of their actions. Debris settled in the background, dust particles catching in the beams of light that filtered through the ventilation shafts. It was a cinematic end to a perilous journey, the impact of their escape resonating deeply with each member of the team.

Their rescue mission had succeeded.

Chapter 21

Gathered around the central strategy table, Callan's eyes met Felix's with a mix of relief and urgency. The dusty, cavernous room of The Ventworks hummed with the low chatter of allies, but here at the table, a focused silence prevailed as Felix shared the crux of their findings.

"Project Lumina's backbone is its DNA compatibility system," Felix began, his voice steady despite the fatigue etching his face. He nodded towards Ava, who laid out digital schematics of Lumina's interface across the table's surface. The holograms flickered with intricate codes and genetic markers. "By introducing chaotic data into their system, we can corrupt the experiences, making them... unlivable."

Milo, tapping away at a portable device, chimed in. "I can engineer a virus that targets the genetic database. Once we inject it into their system, it will start rewriting data randomly, which should lead to system errors and malfunctions."

Ava pointed to the schematics, highlighting key entry points for the attack. "These are the system's most vulnerable access points. If we synchronize our attack here and here, the feedback loop will amplify the virus's effects."

Callan, absorbing every word, finally spoke. "What's our window of opportunity?"

"Narrow," Felix replied, scanning the projections. "Once they detect the anomaly, they'll move quickly to isolate and purge the corrupted data. We'll need to be fast and precise."

Tara leaned forward, her eyes scanning the room's shadowed corners. "And while the tech team does their part, we'll need a diversion. Something big enough to draw their security forces away from the main servers."

"That's where I come in," Raj added, his voice booming slightly over the hum. He unrolled plans for a series of controlled explosions that could serve as the needed distraction. "Strategically placed charges here, here, and here along the outer sectors will create a believable threat to their physical infrastructure."

Milo's voice broke through the stillness, his words carrying a tremor of doubt that seemed to resonate with the flickering lights above. "Wait, if we corrupt the DNA data while people are logged in, isn't there a risk to the users? Their real bodies might react negatively to the sudden dissonance in their virtual experiences."

Felix absorbed the question, his mind racing through the implications. He nodded, slowly, the depth of the issue sinking in. "Milo's right. The DNA link isn't just digital—it's biological. Disrupting it could have... lethal consequences for everyone connected to Lumina."

A chill seemed to sweep through the room as Ava, usually the epitome of calm, looked up sharply, her analytical mind processing the potential disaster they were on the brink of unleashing. "So, we're talking about potential casualties in the billions? Innocent people who think they're just escaping reality for a while?"

The stark realization hit them all like a physical blow. Callan, fists clenched, his voice rough with frustration, slammed a hand down on the table. The impact echoed, mirroring the severity of their predicament. "We can't risk that. We're fighting to save these people, not condemn them."

It was Tara always thinking three steps ahead, who found the sliver of hope they needed. "What if we find a way to disconnect the users safely before we launch the attack? We need a medical solution to sever the DNA link without harm."

Felix's gaze snapped to Tara, a spark igniting in his eyes. Callan, stepping forward, his voice carrying the weight of command, made the final call. "Felix, you and your team will stay here to develop the medical protocol. The rest of us will head to the surface. It's a split operation—medical safety here, direct confrontation in the Citadel and The Surface. We strike on two fronts; we can't let Greda fortify her position any further."

Callan's words were shattered by the harsh crackle of the comms unit. The sudden noise caused a few heads to turn sharply towards Ava, who moved to answer the call. The voice that came through was frantic, urgent, a clear distress signal that cut through the residual hum of their planning.

"We've got another situation—coordinates coming through now," the voice said, urgency tainted with static, the words barely rising above the noise.

Trapped but not defeated, Jax Thorn sat with his back against the cold, unyielding wall of a high-security cell within the Citadel's deepest layer. Hidden beneath layers of surveillance, his only connection to the outside world was the subvocal microphone clasped tight against his throat, a lifeline to his team. As Callan's voice came through, a mixture of determination and urgency, Jax assessed his bleak surroundings with a critical eye.

"Jax, we're moving in. Felix's team is staying back to handle the medical sabotage plan to take down Project Lumina once and for all," Callan's voice resonated in the confined space, both stern and strained.

From the shadows of his cell, Jax activated the holographic display on his wrist, barely visible under the dim light. His fingers glided over the floating images, pulling up schematics of the Citadel's security layout. Despite his confinement, his presence remained commanding, a spectral force within the fortress's veins.

"The risk is too high for a frontal assault, Callan," Jax whispered, the subvocal mic catching every syllable. "I'm setting up guidance for your entry point from here. Remember, the civilian count is high today—collateral must be minimized."

His android allies, disguised as maintenance units, stood in silence around him, but outside of his high tech prison, blending seamlessly with the Citadel's mechanical bustle yet alert to their leader's plight. Each one was a cog in a larger plan set in motion, ready to spring into action on Jax's command.

As Lena's distractions began outside, the Citadel's outer sectors started to churn with orchestrated chaos, drawing guards and automated defenses away from the core where Jax was held. In the background, Kyle's tech enhancements operated silently, disrupting Greda's surveillance network just enough to keep their movements hidden.

Nara's voice then cut through the tension, "Infiltration routes are clear, Jax. We've bypassed the main checkpoints, but be wary of secondary scans."

"Deploy the decoys," Jax commanded, his voice resolute as he traced potential exit routes on his map. "And Raj, make sure those charges are non-lethal. We're here to save lives, not end them."

The Citadel was more than just steel and wire; it was a living entity of control and suppression. Jax, at its heart, felt the pulse of both the danger and the opportunity it presented. Here in the shadows, he was not just a captive but a central node in the network of resistance.

Zoe's voice through the encrypted comms was the next cue in their carefully orchestrated plan. "All teams are green. Distraction in T-minus 30 seconds. Good luck, Jax."

Confined within the high-security cell of the Lumina Citadel, Jax Thorn felt the distant vibrations from explosions and combat. The sounds of conflict were muffled, filtered through thick walls and layers of security, yet each tremor was a signal, a coded message of hope that Callan and the team were close.

The small room was stark, lit only by the dim glow of a security light that cast long shadows across the cold floor. Despite the minimalist surroundings, Jax was far from idle. He sat cross-legged, a tangle of wires and a makeshift interface spread out before him—a jury-rigged connection to the Citadel's surveillance network he had managed to establish using scraps of discarded maintenance tech.

Each vibration brought a flicker on the makeshift screen, a blur of movement, an echo of the battle raging towards him. He had no visuals, no sound, but the data pulses he intercepted provided a narrative he understood all too well—the determined advance of his rescuers.

The sharp, sudden increase in network static told him more guards were being deployed, their digital signatures a storm of activity that signaled desperate defense measures. Jax tapped into the feed, his fingers moving with practiced ease as he sent tiny disruptions back along the line, subtle but enough to slow the enemy's coordination, to blur their communications just when clarity was crucial.

He could almost picture Callan at the front, leading with that genuine, magnetic way that he does. The thought brought a grim smile to Jax's face, his heart beating in sync with the imagined pulse of solar beam rifles and the hum of energy shields.

A sudden, more intense tremor jolted the cell, closer this time. The light flickered overhead, and Jax braced himself against the wall, his eyes narrowing as he processed the implications. Not part of the planned assault—a rogue element, or perhaps a trap set by Greda's forces anticipating their route.

His interface buzzed, a surge of data flooding in as security protocols near his location went on high alert. "They're almost here," Jax murmured to himself, his voice a whisper lost in the confines of his cell. He re-routed what little power he had, boosting the signal of his improvised device, pushing it to send one last piece of guidance to his friends.

"Left corridor, third junction, panel fourteen," he subvocally transmitted, hoping the message would reach Callan or any of his team. It was the fastest, safest path now, one that would bypass the bulk of the newly deployed defenses.

He reset the interface to monitor only, conserving energy, withdrawing into the shadows of his cell to wait. Every sense was heightened as the sounds of battle grew louder, the metallic taste of adrenaline sharp on his tongue.

Jax concentrated on the data streaming across his makeshift interface. He traced every pulse of digital noise that sketched a map of conflict beyond the confines of his cell. The vibrations through the Citadel's framework were more frequent now, a rhythmic pounding that matched the rapid beat of his heart.

The faint glow from his wrist display illuminated his determined face as he monitored the progress of Callan and the others. They were moving deeper into the heart of danger, and with each passing moment, the stakes climbed higher, not just for him, but for the entire resistance.

Suddenly, the interface flickered, a surge of static signaling an increase in network activity. Jax's fingers flew over the controls, adjusting frequencies to maintain clarity. He caught a brief transmission from Kyle, barely a whisper of sound, but enough to know that the next phase of their plan was in motion. Hacked drones, a swarm of electronic eyes and ears, were now creating blind spots in the Citadel's iron-clad surveillance system.

Jax felt a surge of hope. Kyle's technical wizardry was peeling open the fortress's digital defenses layer by layer, allowing Callan and the team to press forward with less risk of detection. Yet, every second brought new challenges. The defenses were adapting, evolving in response to their tactics. The Citadel was alive, its technological heart beating in a sinister rhythm of anticipation and preparation.

From his position, Jax could do more than just watch; he could interfere, disrupt, and guide. His hands moved with precision, tapping into the Citadel's security loops, injecting coded anomalies that would take precious time to untangle. "Hold the line," he whispered into the subvocal mic, a mantra for both himself and his distant comrades.

The tremor of an explosion rolled through the cell, closer now, the sound muffled but unmistakable. Jax's eyes widened as he processed the information—a planned distraction by Lena and Mason, or something unexpected? He scanned the data, his brain racing to adapt their strategy in real-time.

"New hostiles deploying from the eastern sector," Jax subvocally transmitted, warning of the sudden spike in security detail mobilization. His voice was calm, a contrast to the storm of data and danger surrounding them. "Reroute to corridor B7. I've disabled the surveillance nodes there."

As he sent out the new route, Jax felt the isolation of his cell more acutely. The physical barriers between him and his team were impenetrable, yet digitally, he was there, moving amongst them, a ghost in the network, guiding, protecting.

The screen showed a sudden flurry of movement—a convergence of security forces toward the area his team had been heading. "Too close," he muttered, adjusting his interference, spreading digital chaff to confuse and delay their pursuers.

Just as the corridor seemed to stretch endlessly ahead of them, a sudden burst of static erupted through Jax's improvised network. His pulse quickened as he decoded the frantic signals—it wasn't just the routine patrols they were up against but a deployment of elite guards. The very air felt charged with a new, dangerous energy, escalating the peril. "They're stepping up their game," he murmured, his voice barely a vibration against the subvocal mic.

As Jax monitored the incoming data, his mind raced with possibilities. Each flicker on his screen was a potential disaster or a narrow escape. The tension was palpable, not just in the tightening of his muscles but echoed through the digital whispers of the network. Callan and Sylas, leading the charge, were now directly in the path of these highly trained adversaries. The stakes were high, and failure loomed ominously close, threatening not just the mission but the future of their resistance.

Then, amidst the chaos, a strategic pivot from Mason and Lena reshaped the battlefield. Remote explosions, calculated and precise, erupted far from their current location, orchestrated to draw these elite forces away. The screens flickered with the shift in guard movements, a tactical dance of shadow and fire. Jax's fingers flew over the controls, redirecting the flow of information to aid this new strategy.

This diversion created a vital opening, a sliver of opportunity in the otherwise impenetrable defense of the Citadel. Callan and Sylas, seizing the moment, pushed forward with renewed vigor. Jax could almost see it—the determination set in Callan's jaw, the unwavering focus in Sylas's eyes as they exploited the thinned enemy lines.

The corridor ahead, once a daunting stretch of uncertainty, now represented a clear path towards Jax. His heart raced as he adjusted the surveillance feeds, hacking into the Citadel's confused network to clear the way for his friends. Every adjustment he made was a step closer to his own liberation, each command a defiance of the grim fate Greda had intended for him.

Amidst the digital chaos, Jax remained a calm nexus of control, his mind sharply focused on the evolving tactical landscape. He redirected drones, hacked security protocols, and manipulated data streams with a deft touch, all while keeping his team invisibly tethered to his guidance.

The walls of his cell seemed to close in, the shadows darker and more menacing as the sounds of battle drew nearer. The metallic taste of adrenaline was ever-present, sharpening his senses as he prepared for the moment of his team's arrival. He was ready, every line of code he sent a beacon guiding them through the labyrinth of steel and secrets.

As he sent another flurry of commands through the network, a low rumble echoed through the cell. It was different from the vibrations of conflict—it was the sound of hope, the resonance of approaching liberation. Jax leaned back against the cold wall, a slight smile playing on his lips as he envisioned the door to his cell finally swinging open, the faces of his team breaking through the oppressive darkness.

With each passing second, the anticipation built, a crescendo of digital and emotional energy converging on this single, critical point. Jax was more than ready. He was a warrior in his own right, fighting with bits and bytes instead of bullets and blades, his mind a weapon tailored perfectly to the battlefield of the future. The final showdown was imminent, and Jax Thorn was at the heart of it, the architect of their victory or the harbinger of their defeat.

From his cell, Jax could feel the shift in the air as his team made their critical advance. Nara, with her unparalleled stealth and sharp instincts, led the final push towards the high-security section. He watched her progress through the network's eyes, her movements a series of ghostly blips on his screen, each one closer to his confinement.

Jax's surveillance screen pulsed with fresh data, a visual echo of the adrenaline coursing through his veins. His fingers hovered over the interface, each movement calculated and precise, like a conductor leading an unseen orchestra through a crescendo of digital warfare.

"Left corridor, third junction, panel fourteen," he had directed earlier, his voice subvocal but firm. Now, he watched as that route proved its worth, allowing Nara and the team to bypass layers of newly deployed defenses. Their approach was nearly silent, a testament to their skill and his planning.

The intensity of the mission reached its peak as they neared the outer barriers of Jax's cell. He adjusted the interface to its maximum capacity, pulling every ounce of power from the makeshift setup. The walls of his cell seemed to pulse with the rhythm of his heartbeat, the dim light flickering in time with the distant echoes of their approach.

On his screen, he saw the convergence of their paths, a digital dance of coordination and fate. Each team member was fully engaged, their roles defined by months of preparation and hardened by the fires of their shared cause. Kyle's drones provided a live feed of the corridors leading to Jax, creating a patchwork of safe passages through the digital fog of war.

Lena's voice crackled through the comm, her tone imbued with the weight of their shared history and the battles they'd endured. "For Jax, for us, for freedom," she affirmed, her words not just a signal to move but a vow etched into the very air of the Citadel.

Jax's hand paused above the console, his eyes not on the screen but on the solid door of his cell. The physical barrier that had kept him from his comrades was about to come down. His mind raced through the last checks of the network, ensuring their approach was covered, their back guarded against any last-minute surprises from Greda's forces.

As the team prepared to breach the final doors, Jax felt a surge of conflicting emotions. Pride in his team's capabilities, fear for their safety, and an overwhelming urge to be there, beyond the digital shadows, fighting alongside them. But he knew his role was here, in the nerve center of their operation, until the very end.

Jax concentrated on the data streaming across his makeshift interface. He traced every pulse of digital noise that sketched a map of conflict beyond the confines of his cell. The vibrations through the Citadel's framework were more frequent now, a rhythmic pounding that matched the rapid beat of his heart.

The faint glow from his wrist display illuminated his determined face as he monitored the progress of Callan and the others. They were moving deeper into the heart of danger, and with each passing moment, the stakes climbed higher, not just for him, but for the entire resistance.

Suddenly, the interface flickered, a surge of static signaling an increase in network activity. Jax's fingers flew over the controls, adjusting frequencies to maintain clarity. He caught a brief transmission from Kyle, barely a whisper of sound, but enough to know that the next phase of their plan was in motion. Hacked drones, a swarm of electronic eyes and ears, were now creating blind spots in the Citadel's iron-clad surveillance system.

Jax felt a surge of hope. Kyle's technical wizardry was peeling open the fortress's digital defenses layer by layer, allowing Callan and the team to press forward with less risk of detection. Yet, every second brought new challenges. The defenses were adapting, evolving in response to their tactics. The Citadel was alive, its technological heart beating in a sinister rhythm of anticipation and preparation.

From his position, Jax could do more than just watch; he could interfere, disrupt, and guide. His hands moved with precision, tapping into the Citadel's security loops, injecting coded anomalies that would take precious time to untangle. "Hold the line," he whispered into the subvocal mic, a mantra for both himself and his distant comrades.

The tremor of an explosion rolled through the cell, closer now, the sound muffled but unmistakable. Jax's eyes widened as he processed the information—a planned distraction by Lena and Mason, or something unexpected? He scanned the data, his brain racing to adapt their strategy in real-time.

"New hostiles deploying from the eastern sector," Jax subvocally transmitted, warning of the sudden spike in security detail mobilization. His voice was calm, a contrast to the storm of data and danger surrounding them. "Reroute to corridor B7. I've disabled the surveillance nodes there."

As he sent out the new route, Jax felt the isolation of his cell more acutely. The physical barriers between him and his team were impenetrable, yet digitally, he was there, moving amongst them, a ghost in the network, guiding, protecting.

The screen showed a sudden flurry of movement—a convergence of security forces toward the area his team had been heading. "Too close," he muttered, adjusting his interference, spreading digital chaff to confuse and delay their pursuers.

Just as the corridor seemed to stretch endlessly ahead of them, a sudden burst of static erupted through Jax's improvised network. His pulse quickened as he decoded the frantic signals—it wasn't just the routine patrols they were up against but a deployment of elite guards. The very air felt charged with a new, dangerous energy, escalating the peril. "They're stepping up their game," he murmured, his voice barely a vibration against the subvocal mic.

As Jax monitored the incoming data, his mind raced with possibilities. Each flicker on his screen was a potential disaster or a narrow escape. The tension was palpable, not just in the tightening of his muscles but echoed through the digital whispers of the network. Callan and Sylas, leading the charge, were now directly in the path of these highly trained adversaries. The stakes were high, and failure loomed ominously close, threatening not just the mission but the future of their resistance.

Jax's interface suddenly washed over with a stark, white noise as alarms blared throughout the Citadel. It was an unexpected reboot; his eyes widened as the realization hit—Tibo's jamming had been bypassed. "Compromised!" he subvocalized, the urgency clear even in his subdued tone. The security systems were reengaging, doors began locking down section by section, sealing the team inside an ever-tightening trap.

From the isolation of his cell, Jax watched in horror as the schematics updated in real-time, corridors blinking red one after another. The team was suddenly at a significant disadvantage, their progress halted. He could hear the distant march of reinforcements through the interface, an ominous drumbeat growing louder. "Callan, Elara, fallback positions now!" Jax commanded, the digital network his battlefield as he desperately rerouted their paths to temporary safety.

As the elite guards converged, Jax's fingers danced frantically over the holographic display, each tap a hope to delay the inevitable. His mind raced, calculations and strategies forming and dissipating in the span of heartbeats. The room felt colder, the shadows deeper as the weight of the situation settled upon his shoulders.

Then, amidst the chaos, a spark of hope—Kyle's ingenuity shone through. The young engineer, under the harrowing scream of alarms and the echo of closing steel doors, managed to assemble a makeshift decryptor from components in his portable tech workshop. His hands were steady, even as the air around him crackled with the tension of impending capture.

"Working on the override, Jax," Kyle's voice crackled through the subvocal receiver, a lifeline thrown in the digital darkness. Seconds felt like hours as Jax observed Kyle's progress through the network, the young engineer's avatar moving through the layers of security protocols with a deftness that belied the high stakes.

With a final, decisive click, the locks on Jax's cell disengaged, the door swinging open with a heavy thud that resonated like victory. Jax stepped out, his legs weak but his mind sharp. The cell had confined him physically, but mentally, he had never been more free. He immediately began to relay crucial intel to his team, his voice a commanding echo in their ears, "North corridor, I've unlocked it. Move!"

Reinvigorated by Jax's release and the invaluable data he provided. Nara and Callan exchanged determined glances, their movements synchronized with the precision of seasoned warriors. The chaos of the battlefield shifted, becoming a dance of defiance against the overwhelming odds.

Rootwhisper's influence was subtle yet profound, the mycelial network beneath the Citadel responding to its ally's call. Roots and fungi coalesced into barriers, their growth accelerated, twisting through the cracks of the facility to block the advancing guards.

The chaotic environment Rootwhisper intensified now played in their favor. As the roots and fungi barricaded the path of the advancing guards, Nara took the lead, her steps silent and swift as she navigated through the tangled corridors. Elara, checking her launcher one last time, whispered with resolute determination, "It's now or never. Let's make this count."

Jax, though physically weakened from his confinement, kept his focus on the array of screens and data feeds that he continued to manipulate with a deft touch. His hands moved with practiced ease, each adjustment a critical countermeasure against Greda's relentless forces. The freshly unlocked pathways and the obfuscations caused by the smoke bombs provided a brief tactical advantage that the team exploited with precision.

The corridors of the Citadel, now a labyrinth of smoke and shadow, turned into a battleground where each member of the team moved with deliberate intent. Kyle's makeshift decryptor had not only freed Jax but also instilled a renewed vigor within the team, each member energized by the tangible result of their combined efforts.

As they reached the sewers, Nara's expertise came to the forefront. Her knowledge of the layout, previously scouted and memorized, allowed them to evade patrols and navigate through less monitored routes. The sewers, dank and echoing with the distant sounds of the Citadel above, offered a stark contrast to the high-tech oppression they had just escaped.

The extraction was methodical, each member covering angles and potential threats as they moved. Sylas, with his shield generator, took up the rear guard, ensuring that any pursuit was effectively stalled. The strategic retreat, though forced and fraught with danger, showcased their ability to adapt and overcome under pressure.

Upon reaching The Zone V2: The Ventworks, the team debriefed in the safety of their makeshift command center. The walls, lined with screens and equipment, cast a soft glow over their tired but triumphant faces. Jax, now among his comrades, shared the critical intelligence he had gathered about Greda's upcoming operations.

Gathered in the makeshift command center within the depths of The Ventworks, Callan, Felix, and their team huddled around Jax as he prepared to share the critical intelligence gleaned from his recent harrowing experience inside the Citadel.

"Thanks to a deep dive into their most protected files, I've uncovered something called 'Project Exodus'," Jax began, his voice steady despite the fatigue etched in his features. Felix, always keen on data, leaned in, his eyes sharp. "It's a sub-program of Lumina, focused on advanced genetic manipulation—specifically designed for real-time DNA adaptation in virtual environments."

Callan, grasping the gravity of the revelation, saw a flicker of hope. This was the breakthrough they needed to address the DNA compatibility issue that had plagued Project Lumina and threatened countless lives.

"Essentially," Jax continued, "Exodus includes technology that can dynamically adjust and stabilize DNA sequences. It was intended to enhance the adaptability and user experience within Lumina."

Felix's mind raced, already syncing this new information with their strategic objectives. "So, we could use this to implement what you're calling a 'Safe Mode'?" he asked, piecing together the tactical implications.

"Exactly," Jax affirmed. "This Safe Mode would temporarily decouple the DNA link between the user's physical body and the virtual interface during any system disruptions, effectively preventing harmful biological feedback."

Ava chimed in with a critical operational query. "And we can deploy this remotely?"

"With a specialized virus targeting the Exodus sub-program," Jax explained, "modifying it to activate this Safe Mode automatically at the first sign of data corruption detected within Lumina."

Milo looked intrigued. "That means even if chaotic data breaches the system, it won't rewrite or corrupt the user DNA but will trigger a protective protocol, safeguarding their biological integrity."

Callan nodded, seeing the broader picture align. "This ties directly into what Felix's team has been gearing up for. You can target your efforts on integrating this Safe Mode into Lumina's framework using the access points Jax identified."

Tara, who had been silently assessing the escape routes and entry points, now saw her role expand to ensuring these plans were executed seamlessly on the ground.

Raj added, "And the algorithms Jax found can predict potential stress points in Lumina's DNA interface, allowing for preemptive adjustments. This reduces the risk of catastrophic system failures."

Felix stood, a look of intense focus on his face as he spoke. "This isn't just a tactical advantage—it may be both a taking down and repurposing of Project Lumina."

As the team nodded in agreement, Callan felt a spark of hope ignite within him. The intelligence Jax had brought back was more than a strategic asset; it was a critical piece that aligned perfectly with their mission to protect lives and counter Greda's oppressive regime.

"Let's prepare for implementation," Callan declared, his voice confident. "The underworld has suffered long enough."

Chapter 22

Jax's affirmation reverberated in the sterile confines of his cell, the final word lingering like an echo, a promise of a breakthrough that could shift the tides in their prolonged struggle. He leaned back against the cool metal wall, allowing himself a fleeting moment of relief.

Almost instantly, a sharp pain stabbed through his temples, a piercing intrusion that gripped his skull with an increasing ferocity. Jax grimaced, pressing a hand to his forehead as if he could physically hold the pain at bay. His vision blurred, and the stark white walls of his cell seemed to pulse with a rhythm synced to the throbbing in his head.

He tried to stand, to pace away the agony, but his legs buckled, sending him crashing to the cold floor. The impact sent another wave of pain through his head, and he curled into a fetal position, his body instinctively trying to protect itself from the invisible assault. The room spun, a carousel of flashing lights and distorted shadows, each blink a snapshot of his deteriorating condition.

"Something's wrong," he managed to gasp into the subvocal mic, his voice a strained whisper, barely audible over the ringing in his ears. The static crackle of his team's voices broke through intermittently, their words tinged with confusion and growing alarm. "Jax, what's happening? Report!" Callan's voice cut through the chaos, sharp and commanding.

"I don't—," Jax started, but the sentence fractured, lost in a crescendo of internal screeching that drowned out all other sounds. It was as if a high-frequency alarm had been triggered inside his skull, its sole purpose to destabilize and debilitate.

His hands clutched at his head, fingers digging into his hair as he tried to claw away the noise, the unrelenting pressure building with each heartbeat. The pain was uncharted, a relentless tide that threatened to sweep away his consciousness.

Through the haze of his torment, Jax's thoughts scrambled for a foothold, a strand of logic in the onslaught of pain. With a Herculean effort, Jax activated the holographic display on his wrist, the familiar glow a beacon in the storm of his suffering. His vision doubled, then tripled, the simple act of focusing on the screen a battle against the waves of pain that crashed over him.

He tapped into the surveillance feed, his fingers trembling, each movement an exercise in sheer willpower. He needed to warn them, to tell Callan and the others about his suspicion before it was too late. But the words stuck in his throat, a silent scream as the pain crescendoed, obliterating all other sensations.

The room tilted, reality warping into a nightmare of light and shadow. Jax's breaths came in ragged gasps, each inhale a knife to his chest, each exhale a surrender he was loath to give. The walls closed in, the ceiling pressing down as if to crush him under the weight of his own dread.

And then, amidst the cacophony of his own destruction, a voice broke through, a single thread of clarity in the storm. "Jax, hold on! We're trying to—" But the voice faded, a dying echo as the pain surged to an unbearable peak.

The world inside Jax's skull screamed. Blood thundered in his ears, each pulse a hammer strike against the walls of his consciousness. He tried to focus, to claw back some semblance of control as he fought against the waves of pain that threatened to pull him under.

His vision narrowed, the edges of his cell blurring into a gray haze. The stark white lights overhead seemed to pulse with a sinister intensity, each flicker a mocking reminder of his helplessness. The metallic tang of fear mingled with the sterile air, a bitter taste that clung to the back of his throat.

"S-something's not right," he choked out, his voice a strained whisper that barely made it through the subvocal mic. The team's responses were a distant murmur, distorted and warped by the overwhelming noise that filled his head.

The pain intensified, a sharp, stabbing agony that centered behind his eyes, pushing him to the brink of consciousness. His hands fumbled at the communicator, desperate to send a final message, a warning. But his fingers slipped, numbed by fear and pain, useless against the slick surface of the device.

Without warning, the sound within his head crescendoed into an unbearable high-pitched scream, a sound meant for him alone. It was as if the very wiring of his brain had become a live circuit, overloaded and screeching with too much power. The agony was blinding, all-consuming, erasing thought and reason and replacing them with primal terror.

His knees buckled, and he hit the floor hard, the impact sending another jolt of pain through his skull. He curled into himself, arms wrapped around his head as if he could physically hold his crumbling world together. His breaths were short, ragged gasps, each one a fight against the darkness that edged his vision.

Jax's thoughts fractured, splintered shards of rationality that drifted just out of reach. He was vaguely aware of his own voice, a hoarse, ragged scream that tore from his throat unbidden. It was a sound of pure, unadulterated fear, the kind that chilled the blood and haunted dreams.

And then, in a horrific crescendo of pain and noise, the world exploded. The sensation was grotesque, as if his head had become too small to contain the force inside it. There was a moment of excruciating pressure, a feeling of being inwardly crushed and expanded all at once.

Then, nothing.

The control room went deathly silent. Felix, eyes wide and locked on the screen, could barely process what he had just witnessed. The aftermath of Jax's death, the gruesome spectacle of flesh and machinery intertwined in ruin, was broadcast in unforgiving clarity on the monitors that lined the walls of their underground headquarters.

His heart pounded against his ribs, an erratic drumbeat that seemed to echo the chaos he had just seen. He could still hear Jax's last, strained words crackling through the comms, a desperate warning cut brutally short by the explosion. The image of Jax's face, contorted in agony before being obliterated, was seared into his mind, replaying over and over like a nightmarish loop.

Around him, the room was frozen in a tableau of horror. Team members stood motionless, faces pale, some with hands over mouths, others with fists clenched at their sides. The air was thick with the metallic scent of fear and electronic burn, a stinging reminder of the reality they faced.

Felix's breaths came in sharp, shallow gasps as he tried to marshal his thoughts. His role as a leader demanded action, a response, but all he could feel was a gut-wrenching emptiness. Jax had not only been a cornerstone of their resistance, his friend, but the best chance they had of dismantling Greda's oppressive regime. And now, he was gone—obliterated in an instant by something so insidious, so personal, that it mocked their every precaution.

The silence was abruptly broken by Ava, her voice shaky but urgent as she addressed the room. "We need to check everyone—now!" she declared, pulling them out of their shock. "We don't know what is happening but whatever it was, it was in his head."

Felix nodded, the strategic part of his mind kicking into gear despite the turmoil within. He stepped forward, his movements automatic as he assisted in coordinating a rapid, thorough scan of all team members for any similar implants. The tension as each person was scanned was palpable, each beep of the scanner a spike of collective anxiety.

As the team worked, Felix's eyes kept drifting back to the screen where Jax's last moments had played out. The logical, tactical side of his mind raced through possible countermeasures, adjustments to their security protocols, new strategies to protect against such intimate and devastating attacks. But underneath that, a deep, cold rage was building. Greda had crossed a line not just strategically but personally.

The scans turned up clean, a small relief in the sea of dread, but it did nothing to quell the fear that had taken root. Felix knew that their safety was only temporary; Greda's reach and resources seemed limitless. The horror of Jax's death was not just the loss of a friend and ally; it was a stark reminder of their vulnerability, of how close each of them was to the same fate.

Felix barely had a moment to internalize the gravity of Jax's gruesome end before a sharp pang shot through his own skull. It was a searing, penetrating agony that gripped him suddenly, clenching like a vice around his temples. His hand instinctively went to his head, fingers pressing into his forehead as if he could physically hold the pain at bay.

The buzzing started low, a sinister whisper that quickly escalated into a shrill scream inside his head. It drowned out the sounds of the control room, the urgent movements of his team, and the strategic plans they had just begun to form. All Felix could hear was the overwhelming noise that seemed to come from nowhere yet filled every recess of his mind.

His vision blurred, the screens and faces around him melting into indistinct shapes and colors. He staggered, one hand bracing against the cold metal table to keep from falling. His breathing became labored, each inhale sharp and each exhale a struggle against the growing pressure in his head.

"F-felix, are you alright?" Callan's voice reached him through the storm, distant and distorted.

"I—I don't..." Felix tried to respond, but his words were cut off by the intensity of the noise, now a loud boom that seemed to echo the chaotic rhythm of his rapid heartbeat.

The pain intensified, and Felix felt something shift inside his head, a sensation so alien and terrifying that it froze him to his core. It was as if something within him, some integral part of his being, was about to rupture.

His knees buckled, sending him crashing to the floor. His tactical visor clattered away, skittering across the concrete under the harsh overhead lights. The room spun violently, a whirlpool of faces and colors that spiraled into darkness.

Felix's team rushed towards him, their voices raised in alarm, but their words were muffled, as if he were underwater. He could see the fear in their eyes, a mirror of the horror he had seen in Jax's final moments. The realization that the same fate awaited him was paralyzing.

He tried to warn them, to tell them to stay back, but his voice was a mere whisper, lost beneath the internal screaming that filled his skull. His hands clawed at the floor, fingernails scraping against the concrete as he struggled against the inevitable.

The last thing Felix saw was Callan's face, distorted by a mix of fear and determination, reaching out to him as if he could somehow halt the horror. Then, with a force that seemed to split the very fabric of his reality, Felix felt the explosion from within.

There was a moment of excruciating pressure, an intense compression that gripped his entire head, and then a release so violent it obliterated all sensation. His vision filled with a blinding light, and then darkness swelled, consuming everything.

As the echoes of his existence faded, so too did the scream in his head, replaced by a silence as deep and vast as the void that now claimed him.

Chancellor Greda watched the scene unfold from her command center, her eyes reflecting the cold blue of the monitors that displayed the grim tableau. The chaos within the rebels' strategy room was palpable even through the sterile digital feed, their shock and horror a tangible wave that rippled across every screen in her network. Her fingers danced lightly over the glass interface, bringing up multiple views of the devastation her plan had wrought.

"Activate all channels," she commanded crisply, her voice devoid of emotion but filled with the power of absolute authority. Around her, operatives moved to obey, their actions swift and efficient, a mirror of the ruthless precision Greda demanded of all her subordinates.

Within moments, every screen in the underground society flickered to life, a captive audience of billions now tuned to the frequency of her choosing. From the vast digital billboards that lined the city's central arteries to the smallest handheld devices, every pixel painted the picture she orchestrated.

"This is the fate of those who oppose us," Greda's voice echoed through every speaker, her tone even, her delivery impeccable. The feeds switched between the lifeless bodies of Felix and Jax, their ends marked by the brutal efficiency of her strategy. "Let this be a lesson to all," she continued, her eyes scanning the data streams that flowed in response to her broadcast. "Rebellion against Project Lumina is futile."

The technology that enabled such control was born of Greda's vision—a network of nano-detonators, so small they could be carried in the molecules of air. Once inhaled, these devices lodged themselves within the brain, undetectable and deadly, waiting for her signal. It was a masterpiece of manipulation and fear, a tool forged in the fires of her ambition to maintain order at any cost.

Back in the strategy room, Callan's face filled one of the screens, his expression one of dawning horror as he realized the extent of Greda's reach. It was not just a battle of arms and strategy, but a war waged in the very air they breathed, in the sanctuary they had believed impregnable.

"See how easily we can reach you," Greda whispered, more to herself than to the audience that hung on her every word. Her finger hovered over another command, the power to unleash more havoc a mere touch away.

The screens briefly showed her operatives in motion, their movements clinical as they prepared for further instructions. This was no mere demonstration of power—it was a message etched in the very essence of terror.

As she watched the rebels scramble, their attempts to regroup almost pitiful in their futility, Greda felt a surge of dark satisfaction. This was not just about crushing a rebellion; it was about cementing a legacy of control so absolute that even the thought of dissent would be a risk too great to contemplate.

Her gaze returned to the main screen, where Callan stood looking at where he thought Greda's hidden camera's were. He did not budge. His anger was evident. "Secure all ventilation," he said. His tone cold, never taking his eyes from where he thought the cameras were.

Greda smiled thinly, knowing the futility of his actions. The seeds of fear were already sown, growing in the dark, watered by the blood of his closest allies. The Verdant Overlord had his network of spores, Greda had her network of nano-detonators— and no one but Riko was the wiser. Until now.

And as she turned away from the monitors, the screens still flickering with the images of chaos she had authored, the silence of her command center was a stark contrast to the turmoil she had unleashed. It was the calm at the center of a storm, a storm that Greda herself had become.

Greda paused, her gaze returning to the screens as if a new idea sparked. Her lips curled into a sly smile, the idea taking form, manifesting into an announcement that would twist the knife further into the wounded heart of the resistance.

"My dear citizens," Greda began, her tone mockingly gentle, "it seems I owe a debt of gratitude to Felix's team."

She paced slightly, her eyes alight with malicious pleasure. "You see, it was their ingenuity that taught us how to protect ourselves against breaches the very essence of Lumina's defenses. And it also taught me," she continued, her voice dripping with feigned regret, "how to broadcast to billions of people just like they did."

Her smile widened as she let the implication hang in the air, the silence punctuating her next words with terrifying clarity. "So, thank you, Felix, wherever you are," she said, her gaze piercing through the camera as if she could see right into the eyes of every viewer, her tone turning cold and hard. "Your contributions have been... invaluable, dead man."

Turning her back to the camera, Greda gestured to her technicians. "Now, let us ensure everyone understands the price of disobedience." At her command, the screens shifted from her image to live feeds from various sectors of the underground society.

Thousands of terrified underworld civilians, collars locked around their necks, filled the screens. Their eyes wide with fear, they stood immobilized by the squads of Greda's enforcers. "These collars," Greda's voice returned, now booming over the images of despair, "contain explosives. A small demonstration of our control."

Without another word, she pressed a button on her console. The result was immediate and horrifying. A thousand collars activated, the explosions succinct, brutal. Heads vanished in clouds of gore, bodies slumping lifelessly to the ground as screams echoed through the feeds.

"As you can see, disobedience will not be tolerated," Greda's voice continued, each word enunciated clearly to maximize its chilling effect. "Every citizen is now part of our new order. Step out of line, and you share their fate."

The screens flickered back to her, standing confidently, the architect of a new era of terror. "This is the reality of our world," she declared, her eyes sweeping across the countless faces now frozen on her screens, her voice a harbinger of the new rule. "Compliance is your only salvation."

Her words lingered in the air, heavy with the weight of iron and blood, as Greda turned back to her command console. The holographic displays lit up her face, a ghostly reflection of power in the dimly lit room. Her finger hovered over a single, ominous button marked with a stark, red symbol. It was time to keep her promise.

"Activate the final measure," Greda commanded, her voice steady, devoid of emotion. The room was silent except for the soft clicks of compliance from her tech operators. Screens flickered as data streamed in real-time, a digital heartbeat syncing with the pulse of the underground world she ruled with an iron fist.

With a precise push, the world shifted beneath her command. Across the underground, alarms blared, the sounds of chaos erupting like a well-orchestrated symphony. The screens showed images of people—men, women, children—suddenly halted in their tracks, their faces turning to their nearest screens, which flickered to life with Greda's imposing image.

"Let this be a lesson," her voice boomed across every speaker, every device connected to Lumina and beyond. "Disobedience carries a price—a price that will be paid by all."

Her gaze fixed on the live feeds, her expression impassive as the sequence initiated. Sector by sector, the designated targets—a calculated number to match the hours of Felix's defiance—were extinguished. Drones, like harbingers of death, delivered precise, lethal strikes. Explosions erupted in synchronized bursts, the underground lit by the fires of retribution. From living sectors to marketplaces, no area was spared the wrath of her decree.

Each explosion was a punctuation, a stark period at the end of her sentence. In mere moments, 1,036,000 lives were snuffed out—a number not random but meticulously calculated. Each life represented a unit of defiance from Felix, and each life was a message in itself.

Greda stood, watching the destruction unfold, each feed another testament to her unyielding control. The screams, the pleas, the chaos—they were all just background noise to the silence she felt inside. This was the order of things; this was necessary.

"Broadcast it all," she whispered, more to herself than to anyone else. "Let them see the cost of their heroism, the price of their resistance."

As the final echoes of destruction reverberated through the underground, Greda's face remained on every screen, her eyes cold and unyielding. "Remember this day," she continued, her voice a calm amidst the storm of terror she had unleashed. "Remember what happens when you defy the order of our world."

She turned off the broadcast, the screens going dark one by one, leaving the population in a deafening silence broken only by the distant cries of grief and despair. Greda's eyes did not waver; her heart did not feel an ounce of remorse. This was the burden of leadership, the necessity of power.

In the solitude of her command center, the screens now dark, Greda allowed herself a slight nod of satisfaction. The message was clear, the lesson taught. The rebellion would think twice; the people would remember fear. This was her world, her order, her rule.

As she stepped away from the console, the faintest echo of her own words lingered in the air, a ghostly reminder of the power she wielded and the promises she always kept. She warned Felix to turn himself in, and now the world knew her warnings did not go without global punishment.

I hope *Vegetation Wars: Roots of Rebellion* has left you both thrilled and chilled, as we went deeper into how I think the world will look in the year 3173. The dark and desperate struggles of Callan and his allies are recorded in this second book of the *Vegetation Wars* trilogy. This installment amplifies the tension and terror as our heroes navigate a world where the lines between man, machine, and nature blur into deadly conflicts. Chancellor Greda's ruthless grip tightens, pushing Callan to the limits of his humanity and beyond, challenging his ideals with every harrowing turn. As alliances shift and secrets unravel, the saga escalates into a breathtaking narrative that tests the bonds of trust and the essence of humanity. Thank you for joining me in this relentless journey through a post-apocalyptic wilderness where survival is just the beginning. Brace yourself for the final chapter of this trilogy, where futures will be forged in fire and the battle for the soul of this new Earth will reach its epic conclusion in *Vegetation Wars: The Dawn of the Overlord.*

Afterword for *Vegetation Wars: Roots of Rebellion*

Dear Reader,

As the final page of *Vegetation Wars: Roots of Rebellion* turns, I find myself pausing, reflecting not only on the journey of Callan and his comrades but also on the paths we ourselves traverse in our lives. This book, the second in the *Vegetation Wars* trilogy, is a narrative spun from the threads of countless hours of writing, dreaming, and relentless dedication. It's a deadly mixture of conflict, hope, and the relentless pursuit of survival in a world that both challenges and changes those who dare to navigate its depths.

Writing this sequel has been an adventure in itself, one marked by late nights and early mornings, by the exhilaration of breakthroughs and the perseverance through inevitable challenges. Each character's development, each twist in their story, has been guided by a commitment to exploring the profound themes of resilience, betrayal, and the indomitable human spirit that strives against all odds.

In *Roots of Rebellion*, we go deeper into the dystopian world where the boundaries between humanity and nature blur, crafting a narrative that is as much about internal landscapes as it is about external struggles. The sentient vegetation, which once served as mere backdrop, now emerges with potent force, intertwining with human destinies to reshape the future of an Earth scarred by past follies.

This book was born from a blend of personal experiences, extensive research, and an unyielding passion for storytelling. My military background, particularly in Military Intelligence, has infused the narrative with a realism that I hope resonates with you. The tactical engagements, the espionage, and the strategic survival are elements inspired by real-world scenarios, honed through training and service.

Your support as readers is invaluable. It is your engagement and feedback that fuel late-night writing sessions and invigorate the narrative paths I choose to explore. This journey would be hollow without your companionship. Many of you have reached out with words of encouragement, insightful questions, and poignant reflections, all of which have been a source of motivation and a reminder of why I write.

To the team that has stood by me through this process—editors, beta readers, and publishing professionals—your expertise and patience have been the backbone of this book's journey from a flicker of an idea to the fully formed saga that lies inked on these pages. Thank you for your commitment to maintaining the integrity and quality of this work.

As we look ahead to the final installment of the *Vegetation Wars*, the stakes are higher, and the battles grow ever more fierce. The lines between friend and foe will blur further, and the warriors of this ravaged Earth will face choices that might alter the course of their world forever. The narrative threads we have followed will converge in ways unexpected, yet inevitable—a culmination of the saga that I promise will be both satisfying and thought-provoking.

Thank you for allowing me to share this world with you. For every word read, every emotion felt, and every moment you chose to spend in the company of my characters, I am profoundly grateful. Here's to the battles fought, the alliances forged, and the tales yet to be told. May we meet again in the pages of our final journey together.

With deepest appreciation and anticipation for the adventures that await,

—Antonio T Smith Jr.

www.ingramcontent.com/pod-product-compliance
Lightning Source LLC
Chambersburg PA
CBHW080600300726
48975CB00010B/2743